ARCHANGEL

Also by J.E. Ribbey

The Last Patriots Series
American post-apocalyptic thrillers
Archangel
For You, My Dove
Rise of the Eagle
Operation Gray Owl

Young American Adventures
Middle grade historical fiction
The Innocent Rebel
Defiant Retreat
Under the Wing of the Storm
Deceptive Victory

ARCHANGEL

THE LAST PATRIOTS

J.E. RIBBEY

SORAYA JUBILEE PRESS
An imprint of The Jubilee Homestead LLC,
Stanchfield, Minnesota

Copyright © 2021, 2023 Joel and Esther Ribbey

Printed in the United States of America

Library of Congress Control Number: 2023911005

Print ISBN: 979-8-9875823-6-7
eBook ISBN: 979-8-9875823-7-4

Editing and Cover Design by Esther Ribbey

To our four incredible children, whose hearts are woven into
every page of this story.

We would never wish such a journey on you, but if events such
as these ever came knocking on our door, we know your faith,
hope, and love would never be defeated.

We love you.

Acknowledgements

We would like to thank our family and friends, who helped make this book a reality through editing, encouragement, and publishing support.

Most of all, we thank our Savior, Jesus Christ, who put this story in our hearts to share with the world and gave us the ability to put it on paper.

We pray the ripples of this story will move into eternity.

Preface

Life is a constant battle: a battle for the heart, a battle for the mind, a battle in the flesh. From a young man drowning in addiction, to the point of suicide; to a soldier on the front lines in Afghanistan; to a father and husband battling the challenges of today, while being hounded by the demons of the past; my life knows no end of combat. Yet, in the midst of all the battles, both won and lost, there has always been one constant light, an unwavering ray of hope: the love of Jesus. He is my anchor, my shepherd, my Savior. His righteousness is my only stand.

Through all this conflict, an eye for the enemy's divisive and destructive strategies has been honed. Whether he is using sin to divide us from our Father or hate to divide us as a nation, his tactics are always the same and, today, are on full display. As Abraham Lincoln once said, "At what point then is the approach of danger to be expected? I answer, if it ever reach us, it must spring up among us. It cannot come from abroad. If destruction be our lot, we must ourselves be its author and finisher. As a nation of freemen, we must live through all time, or die by suicide."

This book is written from a father's heart, should such a terrible day ever come. As much as it is meant to be an exciting story, it is also a warning: freedom is fragile and dangerous. The freedom to rise is yoked to the freedom to fall, the freedom to succeed with the freedom to fail, and the freedom to try with the freedom to do nothing. Yet, if it dies, all that remains is slavery.

Prologue

Back when it all started, the United States had grown so divided that neighbor no longer trusted neighbor. The government, corrupt, had failed. The media fueled division at every turn, and Americans began to kill one another based on hearsay, color, religion, and pure frustration. Too many people were reaping where they had not sown, too many laws trampled people's freedom.

A second civil war broke out after three years: Left vs. Right, communism vs. capitalism, brother against brother. No side was willing to consider the views of the opposition and were even less willing to admit their own failures. The government was toppled in an overnight coup and, the following morning it was all-out war.

In truth, there were four sides to the war: the liberal Left and the conservative Right, those without a cause who took the opportunity to loot, steal, and murder any and all who stood in their way, and those who tried to avoid the whole thing entirely. The Reddings were such a family.

Unbeknownst to America, busy with herself, on the other side of the world, Russia had begun to retake the territories of the old USSR, China had taken Taiwan, and North Korea had gone to war with South Korea. The Middle East had broken out in mass war between Sunnis and Shia, with the other factions taking part here and there. Israel was immediately under siege from all sides but was holding her own.

America's unrest lasted four years. Millions lost their lives, once proud cities were nothing but ruins. The country was on the brink of self-extinction when an even more horrifying surprise led to an uneasy truce among the Americans who remained. Russia and China invaded.

With the USSR reformed, Russia and China made a pact. Neither country wanted to see the United States recover and become a world power once again, and neither wanted to go to war with the other. So, with the United States distracted, they decided to make their move. Their agreement divided the country in two: the Chinese taking from the east coast to the Mississippi River, the Russians taking all territory west of the Mississippi River.

The remaining Americans were unaware of their plan until ships landed on the coasts. The war had knocked out all mass communication, so there was no warning as the two armies advanced, unchecked, across the country. Within a month, all major cities had been taken with little resistance.

Chapter 1

Smoke drifted through the air. The sky, gray with clouds, hung heavy over the ashes of a life which had once been but would never be again.

He was only seventeen, yet the scene in front of him wasn't an unfamiliar one. In fact, he had all but forgotten the life he'd had before all of this. Ignoring the heat that rolled off the charred remains of his family's home, he poured the last shovel full of earth on his father's grave. There was no time for words. None were needed anyway. As he looked into the eyes of his two brothers, his sister, and his mother, he knew they felt the same.

Swallowing the lump in his throat, he announced, "We have to go. Now."

"Go where, Aaron?!"

"Away, Mom! Dad would want us to get out of here."

It wasn't that Sara was in denial. She had let herself believe her husband was somehow invincible and that, no matter what happened, he had planned for it and everything would be ok. Now, the cold, hard reality was being pounded into her heart with every clang of a shovel driving in a crude wooden cross. Her husband was gone.

"Ok," she agreed as she watched fourteen-year-old Seth finish setting the homemade monument. Wiping a tear that traced its way down her cheek, Sara closed her eyes, inhaled deeply, held it for a moment, and let it out. It was her first real breath without him. She gently touched the blunted top of the cross and, turning, walked away.

One after another, the family turned from the fresh mound to get their things. Last to leave was eleven-year-old Caleb, the youngest Redding.

"Do you believe we'll see Dad again?" he asked, blinking back the tears burning at the corners of his innocent brown eyes.

Slipping an arm around his little brother's shoulders, Aaron pulled him close, "I sure do, buddy. I sure do."

Together, they walked back into the woods where a carefully buried container held everything they had left in the world. Climbing in through the hatch, Aaron started handing supplies up to the others. Five minutes later, the pile of gear almost reached their knees.

Picking up a pint-sized rucksack their father had packed for Caleb, Aaron helped his brother shrug into it and buckled the chest strap. He was grateful that his father had seen this day coming and prepared them for it. Now, it was only too obvious he had waited one day too many to bug out. After handing Caleb his .22 rifle, Aaron picked up a camouflage ball cap and put it on his little brother's head with a reassuring nod.

Next, Aaron moved to Seth, whose pack was bigger. Seth needed no encouragement. He was a rock. Even though his pack was heavy on his young frame, he would never show it. Aaron knew Seth would do his part and then some. He was the kind of kid who would never give up, never show his pain—loyal to the bitter end, Mama's right-hand man. She'd be able to count on him now more than ever.

Sixteen-year-old Leah, tall and thin, stood next to Seth. Her rucksack was about the same size as Caleb's but heavier. She carried her mother's .22 pistol. It was small and light and, out to about twenty-five yards, Leah was deadly accurate with it. Aaron lifted her chin gently with his hand. Her brown eyes, red from tears, met his.

"We *will* be alright," he said.

Leah gave him a wobbly smile and holstered her .22.

Aaron turned to his mother. Sara's pack was as large as his and, like the others, was filled with survival essentials and ammo. It was bulky but not too heavy, and she managed it quite well. Aaron passed her her rifle and gave her a nod.

Finally, reaching for his own pack, Aaron hesitated. Beside it, lay the heaviest bag of all. A man's pack: his father's. Without a second thought, he passed over his own bag and grabbed the heavier one, adding only a few extra items from his own. Taking up his father's AK-47, he paused to take stock of the five of them. His mother was returning from the container of supplies with a bottle of water for each of them, along with their winter coats with their hats and gloves stuffed in the sleeves.

"It might be autumn now but, if we survive long enough, we'll be dealing with winter as well," she explained, passing them out. They helped each other strap the coats to their packs. There was nothing else left. It was time.

"Aaron," Sara quickly said. "I want you to lead us. It has to be you."

Aaron looked long into his mother's eyes. The mixture of pain, determination, and confidence he saw there was humbling. Slowly, he nodded.

Aaron had never envisioned himself the leader of anything, but he shared his father's gift for strategy and detail, and he had more of a grasp on the complexity of their current circumstances than anyone else in the family. He had a way of looking at situations beyond what the average person could see, and then predict, with surprising accuracy, the most likely outcome. This ability allowed him to compartmentalize his emotions and feelings so he could reach his goal. Emotions at a time like this could not be afforded. So, he put them away.

"We'll head into the river valley and lay low until morning. I'll try to have a plan by then," Aaron said, looking from one person to another.

Nodding their agreement, the five of them fell into a tactical column with Aaron taking point. Next came Sara, followed by Caleb and Leah, with Seth at the rear. As they passed through the yard, Aaron turned for one last look. *I'll keep them safe, Dad, I promise.* Taking a deep breath and squaring his shoulders, he faced forward again and walked away from the fresh mound of earth time would soon level, marked only by the simple wooden cross with two words scratched deeply into the grain: John Redding.

Keeping off the main roads made for slow going, but it helped deter pursuit. Years of neglect meant nature had reclaimed some, if not most, of their route. Aaron knew the Chinese hadn't been in the area long, and their numbers did not allow them to cover the majority of unpopulated areas. As the five of them plodded along, Aaron fought to wrap his mind around their situation.

How had things come to this: his family on the run, America lost, his father gone? His father, John Redding, seeing the signs, had acquired their AK-47, Mosin-Nagant, and other firearms years earlier. He had replaced the wooden stocks with composite, added optics, gathered ammo, and trained them all to use them. They had prepared survival gear and practiced roughing it, while calling it vacation. Most of their neighbors had thought they were more than a little strange at the time. John wanted them to be ready if America ever were to fall.

When it all began, they were, for the most part, left alone. They lived out in the middle of nowhere and had good relationships with their neighbors. Their gardens, chickens, and milk cow had provided them with the essentials, and anything they lacked could be obtained through bartering with the folks that lived near enough.

Aaron would never forget the day his family had seen a Chinese convoy rolling up the interstate. Never in his wildest dreams did he ever imagine seeing Chinese troops in podunk Minnesota. With no media to speak of, there was no way of knowing about the invasion except through word of mouth, and there were fewer and fewer mouths around every day. At first, the Chinese had simply moved in and set up checkpoints on the main roads. They seemed satisfied to contain, manage, and use the people still living in the area. Then, they built outposts and more soldiers and equipment arrived. They searched every home and confiscated every firearm and munitions they found.

Some of the Americans had resisted, and small skirmishes broke out. The fighting usually concluded with the Chinese losing a handful of soldiers and the Americans either killed or captured, and then publicly executed.

The Reddings had done their best to avoid any contact with the Chinese until six months ago, when John had caught two of them attempting to rape Leah as she walked home from the nearest neighbors, a couple of miles down the road. In the blink of an eye, her father had broken one soldier's neck with his bare hands and shot the other with the man's own rifle. He had taken the long way home with her through the woods, and the Chinese had never figured out what happened.

From that point on, John determined they had to do something. He and Aaron began conducting night missions, strategically planned with the utmost care. They would watch the road checkpoints at night. Once they knew the soldiers and their schedule by heart, they would hit the outgoing night watch just after they were relieved. Usually, there were only three or four soldiers, sometimes as few as two. In the dark, the tired soldiers were easily surprised; they would stumble groggily down the road with their rifles over their shoulders and, in a matter of seconds, they were all dead.

Aaron's father had developed a sort of crossbow that would launch a quarter inch thick steel rod with a razor sharp, one-inch-wide tip right through a man's skull at close range. They weren't exactly accurate at a distance, but from five feet away they were perfect. The tricky part was dealing with a third or fourth guy while keeping the whole thing quiet. The easiest method was to shoot the two groggy soldiers in the rear of the formation, then, when the others heard the attack and turned around, jump them.

Aaron thought back to their first ambush. He had never contemplated killing anyone before the Chinese had shown up. Even after the incident with his sister, though the thought would enter his mind from time to time, nothing could have prepared him for the emotions of that night. He had never been more afraid in his whole life. They went over the plan again and again, practiced knifing each other and shooting the crossbows. Going out night after night on the road, they watched the soldiers march by from their hiding place.

Then, the time had come. They loaded the crossbows, dressed in black, rubbed soot on their faces, necks, and hands, went over the plan one more time, and prayed for God's protection. It was a cool night in March. The winter snow had almost all melted away, and fog hung heavily in the air. Everything was dark. Wet. Cold. Wisps of steam swirled in the air with every breath. Arriving at their hiding place an hour before the changing of the guard, they checked their weapons. His father gave him a reassuring squeeze on the shoulder and spoke with regret that things had come to this.

Time crawled for an hour until, finally, they heard the distant sound of marching soldiers: the checkpoint's replacements. As they marched closer, Aaron's pulse pounded in his ears so loudly he was sure his enemy would hear it, but the soldiers just kept marching.

The checkpoint was a quarter mile up the road, a half mile from the outpost. Aaron and his father set up midway between the two in the hopes that the noise of their ambush would not be heard from either, giving them plenty of time to make their escape. That was the plan. . . .

Aaron could still remember all the questions that ravaged his mind in those brief moments. What if something went wrong? What if the soldiers were more alert than usual and spotted them before they were ready? What if he missed with his crossbow? What if his father was wounded or killed? What if . . .?

His mind transported him there now, hunkered in that ditch, the sound of approaching soldiers echoing in his ears. . . .

"Aaron!" his father whispered. "They're heading back. Get ready, son. We go on my mark."

As the soldiers approached, Aaron could see they were marching, well, staggering really, groggy as usual. His heart pounded, fish swam in his stomach, sweat ran off his forehead and moistened his palms. He gripped his crossbow, closed his eyes, and tried to steady his nerves. *Were they really about to kill these men?*

"Aaron!" his father's sharp whisper pulled him from his questions once again. "Here they come. Let them pass. You take the fourth one in line; I'll take the third."

Seeing them now, only twenty yards off, Aaron quietly unbuckled the safety strap on the hunting knife that hung on his belt. He pulled upward slightly. The blade slid easily, and he returned it to its place. Ten yards. His heart racing, he gripped the crossbow tightly and felt for the trigger. Five yards. He gave his father one last glance. John was holding his crossbow close, his eyes wide in the darkness, following the soldiers as they approached. He looked so calm, but Aaron knew otherwise. Now the soldiers were directly in front of them. Aaron could see their shadowy forms in the moonlight. Four more steps, three, two, one . . .

"Now!"

Aaron moved quickly, more on impulse than thought. The soldiers were only two steps away when they burst from the ditch. He heard the other crossbow go off just as he reached the fourth soldier. Putting his own crossbow on the man's head, he pulled the trigger.

Like a flash of lightning, that sound, that feeling, that scene was seared into his memory forever. His arrow slammed through the man's head just in front of his left ear. The soldier crumpled to the ground before he could utter a sound. Aaron followed his father's lead and drew his knife, lunging for the second soldier as the man wearily turned to see what the commotion was. Like a crazed animal, Aaron leaped on the man, throwing his left hand over his mouth and his knife into his chest, just as he and his father had drilled over and over again before this night.

The man fell with his back to the ground. Aaron spun and landed on top of him, his hand still holding his knife that stuck out of the man, the man who now writhed beneath him struggling for his life, a life that was already lost.

Aaron felt the soldier's warm blood pouring out of the wound, covering the hand that held the knife with a vice-like grip. At last, the soldier lay still, no more muffled cries, no more panicked thrashing, no more life. Nothing. Aaron lay on the man, huffing wildly, a monster, a madman, someone he had never known.

"Aaron," his father's panting voice broke through his madness as he pulled Aaron to his feet, "We have to go."

Four bodies lay contorted where four men once stood. He didn't know what to feel. Blankly, he watched his father walk over to the bodies of the third and fourth soldiers and retrieve the bolts.

"We'll need these again," he explained.

Aaron trudged back to his crossbow laying where he had dropped it next to the fourth soldier. He would never look at it the same again. Before tonight, it had only been a tool, a theory, something that could kill. Now, it was a fact, a weapon, an instrument of death, and he had killed with it.

"Let's go," his father said again, and the two of them headed off into the woods.

It was the first of many such nights.

At first, the killing troubled Aaron. He hated himself, but he had come to agree with his father that the Chinese could not be ignored. The outpost had grown strong. The PLA no longer simply existed among them with random outbursts of violence; now they treated the Americans who lived under their jurisdiction like serfs. They were expected to work the land and give all the increase to the outpost, who then delivered it to the PLA district headquarters where they used it to feed their army. The Americans were left with next to nothing to live on.

Aaron and his family worked their farm with everything they had, secretly keeping back some of the food in the buried container in the woods behind their home. Aaron and his father had continued their ambushes on a purposefully random timetable, hitting different checkpoints each time, sometimes traveling up to a day's distance and using the rivers and creeks as trails, just to keep the Chinese guessing.

After a couple of months, the PLA grew tired of the ambushes and began going house to house through the whole district dragging out families, searching for weapons again. If they found any, they executed the men in front of their families. No one knew who was conducting the ambushes and people were terrified.

Eventually, the PLA efforts began to work; Aaron and his father stopped their nighttime excursions. They could no longer bear the suffering of their neighbors. Their home had been searched, but nothing was ever found. Aaron could hardly bring himself to make eye contact with neighbors who had lost loved ones because of him.

At least, that is how he had seen it before today. Now, all he understood was that the PLA would continue to kill, steal, and destroy with or without reason.

It had all started last night while they were sitting down to dinner. The table was lit by a single candle. The electrical grid had gone down during the civil war, and fuel had long run out for generators. Father had been about to say grace when there was a knock on the door. . . .

"Is that the river?!"

Aaron looked up, shaken from his thoughts. The road in front of him dropped down into a vast valley blanketed with trees and, in the distance, the St. Croix river sparkled in the late afternoon sun.

"Yeah, Caleb, that's the river," Aaron replied.

"Finally! If I had to walk much further, I think my legs would fall off," Caleb confessed.

Aaron led the beleaguered band into the valley and up a small tributary a short distance before halting in a scant clearing under some pines.

"We'll camp here tonight. I'll try to have a plan figured out by morning."

Dropping their packs, everyone collapsed, too exhausted emotionally and physically to think. Pulling out their mosquito nets and wool blankets, they went to sleep. All except Aaron, who took the first watch.

Chapter 2

Leaning back against his pack, Aaron took a deep breath and closed his eyes. His family was safe for now, so he let his mind wander back to their kitchen and that fateful knock on the door.

Everyone had looked around the table in surprise. It was very uncommon to have visitors, and even less common for someone to come calling at night. The PLA had issued a curfew after their first couple of ambushes. No Americans out after dark; anyone caught out after dark was shot on sight.

His father got up from the table and walked toward the door. There was a second knock. He turned the handle and cracked the door enough to see out. A woman's voice spoke. Aaron could hear quiet sobs. His father opened the door and motioned the visitor in. Aaron recognized her in the candlelight. It was Hanna, who worked a farm almost a mile south of their own, the closest neighbor the Reddings had.

"Come and sit down, Hanna," his father invited. "Tell us what happened."

Aaron could see a dark stain on her blouse and what looked like handprints on her jeans.

"It's my husband," Hanna cried as she collapsed into a chair. "They've killed him and my Jonathan!" Her face distorted as her sobs ended in a wail of anguish.

John put his hand on her shoulder, and his mother went to hug her.

"Oh, Hanna, I'm so sorry!" she said.

"They just showed up at our house this afternoon claiming they were doing another weapons search. Mike said we had nothing to worry about 'cause we don't have any weapons left. They came out with a pistol they claimed they found under our bed and, before I knew it, an officer pulled out his gun and shot Mike and then Jonathan!" She began to cry again, and then suddenly shouted, "They planted that gun. My husband wouldn't lie to me about that!"

"Why? Why would they frame Mike?" Sara asked.

"Does it matter?" Aaron's father muttered.

"Nothing has happened lately to provoke them," Sara continued, shaking her head, her brow furrowed.

Aaron's father pulled his hand from Hanna's shoulder. Ducking his head a little to look into her eyes, he promised, "I'll make this right, Hanna. I'll make this right. Did you recognize any of them?"

"Yes, a few of them do the night guard at the checkpoint on Pheasant Road."

"That doesn't give us much time. You'll stay with us tonight, Hanna, and tomorrow we'll help you bury them," John said.

"No, I—I'd rather stay at my place. Mike and Jonathan are there. I know how to get home without being seen. I made it here, didn't I? Thanks for your compassion. I didn't know where else to go." Without another word, she disappeared out the door into the night.

Aaron watched his father trot out the back door. He returned a few moments later with the two crossbows and hunting knives. Several wet spots speckled his back, the beginnings of an evening shower. Aaron's mother tried to talk him out of going. She reasoned that the mission needed careful planning like all the others, but John insisted this was different. This mission was a statement that, from now on, the invaders were going to have to answer for their crimes against Americans. And they were going to answer for this crime tonight.

There was a clap of thunder, followed by the familiar drumming of heavy rain on the steel roof.

"Go to bed, Aaron," John said, looking toward the sky with contempt. "We can't do anything in this weather. If it clears in time, I'll get you."

Shortly after midnight, the storm broke. Aaron was awakened by his father's insistent shaking.

"We're on!" he whispered excitedly.

By the time the two of them had navigated through soggy forest trails in the pitch dark and arrived at the checkpoint, it was six thirty in the morning. They had half an hour until the night shift would be relieved. Aaron saw two soldiers leaning up against the outside of the guard shack: a small square building with a window on three sides and a door facing the road, fighting to keep their eyes open. Their heads bobbed with the weight of a long night. Through the window, lit by a single bulb, he could just make out a third soldier asleep in a chair. The sun was beginning to cast its glow on the eastern horizon, and a cool September breeze blew right through Aaron's wet clothes, sending a shiver up his spine.

"Looks like there are only three of them tonight," his father whispered. "We'll take the two leaning against the shack and then hit the last one inside together."

Aaron nodded, a nagging feeling in the back of his mind. They had never hit an illuminated guard post before. They had never conducted an ambush this close to sunrise, with so little preparation and no intelligence. . . .

"On my mark, Aaron. You take the one on the left. I'll take the one on the right," his father whispered, never taking his eyes off the target. "Go!"

Aaron rushed out of the ditch and closed the distance to the soldier in four quick strides. Before the man could even get his wits about him, Aaron sent his bolt smashing through them, pinning the man to the wall. His father had done the same. They turned the corner of the shack in stride and were about to rush in when Aaron's father pulled up short, frozen in his tracks. Skidding to a stop, Aaron followed his father's gaze. There, in the ditch on the other side of the road, were twenty soldiers, rifles leveled.

"Run!" John yelled.

They dove behind the guard shack as all hell broke loose. Rifle rounds exploded through the small structure in a continuous volley. Aaron and his father scrambled to the ditch in a panic and rolled in.

"This way!" his father shouted over the sound of gunfire.

They crawled on their bellies for a few more feet before an abrupt silence froze them in place, waiting and straining to hear what the soldiers were doing. They heard a Chinese command, followed by the crunch of trotting boots on the gravel road.

"We have to move," his father whispered, panting. "Now!"

Leaping from the ditch, they ran into the thicket bordering the road. The soldiers opened up again. Bullets shrieked all around them. They flew like wild animals with dogs on their heels. Leaves and branches exploding off the trees around them, they staggered and stumbled for two hundred yards before pulling up, gasping for air. The shooting had stopped, but they could hear shouting soldiers and barking dogs closing in.

"We need to get home," his father gasped.

"Home? They'll follow us!"

"They knew we were coming."

"How?"

"Hanna. It had to be," John shook his head, perplexed.

"Why would she . . .?"

"It doesn't matter now. We have to get home and get everyone to the woods. The soldiers will be there soon." His father was already running for home as he finished his sentence, Aaron on his heels.

Less than an hour later, they staggered onto their property, exhausted. Sara was in the yard feeding the chickens. She took one look at them, chests heaving, covered in mud and sweat, and knew something had gone terribly wrong. She had heard the shots echoing in the distance and prayed that it was for some other reason but, when she saw her husband and son, she knew everything had changed.

"They knew we were coming," John's voice cracked, his throat burning from the escape. "They'll be here soon; we have to go."

Sara yelled for Seth, and he appeared in the barn doorway.

"The soldiers are coming, get your sister and grab the packs!"

"Coming here?!"

"Yes, now move!" she snapped.

Seth tore off for the buried container, stopping only to fetch his sister from the garden on the way.

Caleb, hearing all the commotion, came running from the house.

"What's going on, Dad?" he said, his voice trembling with worry at the sight of his father and brother.

"The soldiers are coming," John said as calmly as he could. "I'm sorry, son. I shouldn't have gone last night."

Aaron could hear the regret in his father's voice. It was the same regret he had expressed the night of their first ambush.

"I'll go get the weapons," Aaron said, his throat so dry the words escaped as a whisper. On his way to the woods, he passed Seth and Leah, wide-eyed with fear, returning with the packs.

Aaron hopped down through the small opening in the container and grabbed his mother's Mosin-Nagant and his father's AK-47. Turning around, he saw his father's arm reaching down through the opening.

"I'll take them, son."

Aaron handed the rifles to his father, along with a satchel of bullets, and three loaded magazines. Next, he grabbed Caleb's .22, a pistol for Leah, and a box of ammo and handed them up. Lastly, he grabbed two 12-gauge shotguns: his and Seth's. He handed them up to his father, then looked around. The container was still half full of supplies, but there was no time. They needed to leave now.

By the time he surfaced from the hole, John had loaded all the weapons and ammo into a wagon and was headed to the house at a brisk walk. Aaron couldn't believe his father could move that fast after what they had been through. He pulled himself out of the hole and onto his feet. After closing the container, he trotted to catch up.

Arriving at the house, Aaron could see that Seth and Leah were already wearing their packs, and his mother was busy adding some food and water she had just brought from the house. His father had begun to distribute the weapons and ammo when the first soldiers showed up at the end of their long driveway.

"We're out of time," his father said in disgust.

"We'll never outrun them," Sara groaned.

"Then we'll have to fight them." Frustration turned to resolution and, without missing a beat, John laid out the plan.

"Sara, take the compost mound next to the chicken coop. Seth, you're behind the coop. Cover her rear. Caleb, I'm sorry, son, but I'm going to need you to fight today."

John had done his best to spare young Caleb from the horror of the past several years but, today, it had found him. Caleb nodded his head as John ruffled his hair.

"I need you in the window well on the southeast corner of the house. Leah, you take the one on the northeast and cover his rear. Aaron, you're with me; we'll head up the woods by the driveway and hit them from the old brush pile."

His father, an army combat vet, was a soldier through and through. He could read a battlefield better than most folks could read a GPS. No one questioned him, they just moved. Seth and Leah stashed the packs and scattered to their positions.

Aaron's heart pounded in his chest, in his head, in his hands. Today was different. They had always been fighting for family and country, but today they were fighting from home. Today, it wasn't only their lives on the line; it was all on the line. On this day, everything they were, everything they loved, everything they believed hung in the balance. . . .

From her spot atop the compost pile, Sara fed rounds into her Mosin-Nagant. Her husband had practiced with her for years, preparing for this day if it ever came. Today it had. The windage and elevation knobs on her scope were worn from use. The marks John had made for the various ranges, from fifty yards all the way out to five hundred yards, were almost gone, but it didn't matter. She knew them all by feel.

From her perch, she could see clearly all the way down the driveway: three hundred and fifty yards. Catching a glimpse of Aaron and John slipping through the woods, she knew they could use a distraction. Slowly, she chambered a round, switched off the safety, and touched her finger to the trigger. This was for her family; this was for freedom.

She leveled the scope on the first soldier and twisted the knob to three hundred yards. The crosshairs hung just below the soldier's right eye. She breathed out through her nose, held her breath, and . . .

The rifle went off with a loud CRACK! Through the scope, she watched the soldier crumple, his comrades running for the ditch on either side of their driveway. She retracted the bolt, ejected the shell, and then slammed it forward, loading another. She stared through the scope; the soldiers were inching their way up the driveway using the ditches on either side. She put her cross hairs on the nose of the first soldier in line, just to lead him a bit. Again, she held her breath and pulled the trigger.

The soldier rolled over in the ditch.

Now, the remaining soldiers, nearly twenty, split up. Ten went up through the pasture toward the house, and the rest continued up the ditch in an apparent attempt to flank them.

From the pasture, a machine gun opened up on the house. Glass shattered as rounds ripped through their home. Sara prayed Caleb and Leah were laying low in their makeshift fox holes as a second machine gun opened up from the ditch, sending rounds into the compost pile and shredding the chicken coop.

Seth hit the dirt as Sara rolled off the pile and scooted around behind the coop to join him. The compost pile acted as a berm, providing some protection from the lead storm raging around them.

Aaron and his father checked the road to make sure reinforcements weren't waiting in hiding. The empty troop truck and clear road was proof enough. They were now behind the only advancing soldiers.

Ducking behind the brush pile in the woods, John motioned toward the machine gun blazing from the driveway. Aaron gave him a thumbs up and they moved up the ditches. John took the west ditch and Aaron the east. Approaching the soldiers, Aaron leveled his shotgun on the back of the man bringing up the rear and pulled the trigger. The man's back exploded as the lead balls from the shell ripped through his uniform. He rolled forward, his face sinking in the mud.

Aaron heard his father's AK-47 open up from the other side of the ditch. Round after round, after round, it fired until the enemy machine gun fell silent.

Aaron lost track of his father as his own position grew intense. The next soldier on his side of the ditch turned around just as Aaron reached him. Aaron pulled the trigger at point blank range, and the man slumped forward at his feet. He pumped the shotgun again. As the last soldier was turning around to face him, he slammed the pump forward, but it stopped short. He slammed it forward again and again. In a moment of horror, everything seemed to move in slow motion; his weapon had jammed.

The soldier's rifle swung wildly toward Aaron's chest, his face stricken with fear, teeth clenched in panic. Aaron slammed the pump back in a futile attempt to clear the jam. The soldier pulled the trigger just as something, a blur, flew between them knocking the soldier to the ground.

Aaron clinched his eyes shut, heart pounding in his ringing ears, his mind unwilling to comprehend what his eyes had just witnessed. His father's back faced him, a gaping hole oozing blood just beneath his right shoulder blade. John held the soldier down in the mud, his right hand delivering fatal wounds with his hunting knife. Aaron slumped to his knees, his lungs heaving and his mind spinning as his father finally rolled off the soldier to face him. They stared at each other, knees to knees, then his father coughed and spit blood in the mud. He reached out his hand and put it on Aaron's shoulder, drawing his breaths shorter and shorter.

"It's ok, son, y—you'll be ok," his murmured words slurring together, his eyes full of love. "You're a st—strong young man, Aaron."

Aaron couldn't take his eyes off the blood that was beginning to run down the corner of his father's mouth.

"I need you t—to keep them safe for me, Aaron. N—never quit, son. Never quit on them." He took a deep breath, wincing from the pain. "I love you, boy." Then he slumped forward, his head resting on Aaron's shoulder.

Tears burned in Aaron's eyes as he began trembling. He brought his hand up to his father's head and, running his fingers into his hair, he lost control.

"No, no, no, no, Dad . . . no, Dad!" Tears streamed down his face, mixing with his snot and his father's hair, as he pulled his head tight to his shoulder, kissing him over and over. "I love you, Dad. Dad, I love you, I love you!" He rocked back and forth, holding his father in his arms. "I love you, Dad!"

Nothing mattered now. Aaron forgot about the Chinese, about his siblings, about his mother. His hero, his friend, his father lay dead in his arms.

From her position behind the chicken coop, Sara heard the machine gun on the driveway go quiet. Turning to Seth, she said, "I'm going to take a look."

Seth nodded.

Hearing the familiar sound of Caleb's .22 firing near the house, Sara leaned around the corner of the coop in time to see two soldiers moving behind the house toward Leah. Another was pinned down in the yard behind the septic mound near Caleb. Sara motioned to Seth to help his siblings. Gathering himself, he bolted to the house just as the machine gun in the pasture opened up again.

Sara crawled back up the compost pile and peeked over the edge. Swinging her rifle toward the driveway, she hurriedly searched with her scope. There was Aaron, hunched over but moving. She couldn't make out her husband, but she could see the soldiers on the driveway had been dispatched. Satisfied, Sara swung her rifle defiantly toward the rattling sound of the machine gun. Steadying her sights on the gunner's helmet, she held her breath and pulled the trigger. The machine gun fell silent. To her left, the QBZ-95 fire of a Chinese soldier was followed by the boom of Seth's 12-gauge. She rolled toward the house just in time to see Caleb wing the last soldier with his .22. Instantly, she raised her rifle and dropped the soldier before he could recover. Moments later, Seth rounded the corner of the house with Leah and gave Sara a thumbs up. They were ok.

Sara glanced up at her house. Black clouds billowed out a second story window. She cringed at the sight of her home in flames, but there was no time to mourn its loss. It was just a house.

John and Aaron. Where were they? Standing atop the compost pile, she scanned the pasture looking for any signs of life. Convinced they were all clear, she took off at a trot down the driveway.

As she neared Aaron's position, she knew something was wrong—horribly wrong. Aaron knelt, hunched over a body with his head on the man's chest, shaking with sobs. Her stomach heaved, pain seemed to explode in her chest, and she knew. He was gone.

In their eighteen years of marriage, she had never doubted her husband would come through for them. Even during the civil war, as everything they had known flew apart and she realized their dreams would only ever be just that—dreams, she wasn't afraid because he was there. As sure as the dawn, he would see them through. She had come to know many men in her life, and he was the best of them. He was her love, and now he was gone. Sinking to the ground next to Aaron, she took her husband's body in her arms, stroked his face, and wept.

Within moments, Seth arrived with Caleb. Caleb collapsed against her and she put an arm around him, watching as his eleven-year-old mind did its best to comprehend the ugliness of the truth in front of him.

Seth's eyes fell on his father's face, pale and empty, blood still staining the corners of his mouth. All his life, he had lived to make his father proud and, though he was Mama's boy, he was a man's man. Today, the sight before him overwhelmed him. Despair filled his face, and he let the tears fall.

Seth heard his sister jogging toward them and moved to intercept her.

"Leah, wait!"

"What happened?" she asked in growing panic. She leaned around Seth to see into the huddle on the driveway, and soon her mind put together the pieces.

"Daddy!" she shrieked. "No! Not my daddy! Please, God. Not my daddy!"

Seth caught her as she crumpled. Leah was Daddy's little girl, the twinkle in his eye. She never felt more loved and secure than when they were together. She leaned into Seth, sobbing, longing only to be held by her father's strong arms while he told her everything would be ok. But Daddy wouldn't save her from this nightmare. Daddy would never be there to save her again.

***

How much time passed as they mourned their father, Aaron couldn't be sure. Why did time always seem to stand still during the traumatic things in life? It's those events one wants to forget, but instead, tragically, things slow down and every horrible detail is inscribed in your deepest memory forever. At last, Aaron raised his head, his father's last words still rang in his ears: *Keep them safe.*

"I'm sorry, Mom, but we have to leave. We can't stay here." For a moment, no one moved. Aaron stood up and moved to his mother, placing his hands on her shoulders. "Mom?"

Sara carefully laid John's body on the ground and slowly rose to her feet, still trembling from shock. Caleb stood with her, slipping his arms around her waist and burying his face in her shoulder.

Wiping away his own tears, Aaron looked over to Seth, still standing with Leah. "Seth, would you help me carry him?"

Seth nodded, and together they walked around to their father's head. They each slipped one of John's arms around their neck, lifting him by the leg on the same side, so he was in a semi-sitting position. Together, they walked up the driveway toward the house, now fully engulfed in flames.

They laid him near the barn in the shade of his favorite oak tree. The sun was high in the sky by the time Aaron and Seth completed digging their father's grave. Had they lived further south, they would have run out of time and had to leave him but, as it was, they lived in a very remote district housing only minimal soldiers with limited equipment. Sara had killed their radio operator on her second shot, and no one had stayed behind in the truck to radio out.

Even the smoke from the house gave little need for concern since the PLA were known for burning the houses of resistors. It might even buy them time if the Chinese assumed it meant the attack had been successful.

They were fifteen miles from the district outpost, and a third of its soldiers were now lying dead on their property. It would take the outpost some time to raise concern over their absence, send someone to survey the scene, and report back. It would be even longer for them to organize troops and equipment for a second assault. The fact of the matter was, these Chinese had never been in a serious conflict before and had no reason to suspect today would be any different. They were unprepared for the defeat they had just suffered.

Aaron and the rest of the family gathered around the grave. Leah grabbed their father's Bible from his pack and placed it under his hands. Aaron and Seth wrapped him in a quilt and lowered him to the bottom of the hole. There was no time to make him a proper box. They all stood staring into the hole, somehow hoping their father would sit up, or move, or . . . something.

At last, Aaron took a shovel and filled it with earth.

"Goodbye, Dad. Until we meet again." He poured the dirt into the hole.

Seth followed his lead and, together, they buried their father.

Chapter 3

"Aaron . . . Aaron!"

Heart racing, Aaron bolted upright, recoiling as daylight flooded his eyes. Searching for clarity, he remembered where they were and why. He wanted to close his eyes and never open them again. His body ached everywhere, and he didn't know if he could bring himself to face the day.

His mother knelt next to him, holding out a tin cup full of spruce needle tea. She had come across the idea in a survival guide after the coffee had run out a couple of months into the war. Made only of boiled stream water and a small bunch of spruce needles, he had to admit it did have a refreshing effect.

Aaron took a sip as he watched her busily pack up their sleeping gear. The warm liquid felt good on his dry throat. Glancing around their simple camp, he noticed Caleb and Leah were up huddled together quietly eating some bread Sara had grabbed the day before. *This was it; this was life now.*

"Where's Seth?" Aaron asked.

"He went to the stream to try fishing, but I think he just needed time alone to process . . . everything," Sara said.

Aaron understood. Seth was as tough as nails, and he seemed to process things better alone. "I'm so sorry, Mom."

"I know, Aaron. I'll be fine, just don't . . ." she took a deep breath and held up her hand to stop him. "I'll be fine."

She didn't look fine. Nobody was fine, but he knew she would never let it show if she could help it.

"So, what do we do now?" she asked briskly, changing the subject.

"We'll follow the river north, like Dad always talked about."

"Do you think we can still make it?"

He paused at the question. He knew what she meant: *without Dad.* "Yes," he answered at last. "It won't be easy, but I believe I can get us there."

She handed him a piece of bread, "Ok, Aaron. Like I said before, we'll follow you."

Seth reappeared just as Aaron was finishing his last bite.

"Catch any fish, Seth?" Aaron asked encouragingly.

"No," he said, his eyes on the ground.

"Have you had anything to eat?"

Seth nodded.

"Well, let's get ready to move out then. We have a lot of walking to do." Aaron tried to sound motivating, like his father always did, but that was hard to do when he didn't want to move either.

Slowly, the family got up, loaded their packs, filled their water bottles, and started off, following the game trails that paralleled the river northward. In between ducking under branches and stepping over fallen logs, Aaron began to construct a plan. They had spent time in the Boundary Waters when he was a child. All he could really remember were the trees: so thick a person could hardly walk through them, and the ponds, lakes, and streams seemed limitless. He was sure, if they survived the trip, they would be safe there.

The trek was nearly two hundred miles. They had a lot of gear, and Caleb was still quite young. Aaron figured they could make around eight miles a day. At that pace, the trip would take them about twenty-five days, with the occasional day to rest. Besides the natural dangers, there was the PLA to watch out for: patrols, checkpoints, outposts, and even Chinese settlers who had recently been showing up by the hundreds. They really had waited too long.

After a couple of uneventful hours on the trail, they came across a small group of houses on the edge of the river valley.

Gesturing to Sara, Aaron asked, "Think we should stop and take a look?"

"Could be treasures in there," she said optimistically.

Pausing at the crest of the valley, the Reddings peered out of the brush to survey the layout of the buildings. The events of yesterday had them all on edge, and they couldn't afford any surprises, emotionally or physically. There were three houses at the end of a remote gravel road, yards overgrown, one roof caving in. Once proud structures, full of life and memories, they represented a time all but forgotten. Now, they lay rotting like corpses of colossal beasts, waiting for scavengers to come along and pick off their last remaining valuables.

"Coast looks clear," whispered Seth.

The words had hardly escaped his mouth when the distant sound of a military truck echoed up the road.

"Crap!" Seth exclaimed, ducking lower in the brush.

In a few moments, a Chinese troop truck pulled into the clearing and stopped. Four soldiers jumped out and ran into the house furthest from the Reddings. They could hear yelling and a woman scream, then the soldiers emerged with two Americans: a man and a woman somewhere in their fifties.

Two soldiers threw the man to the ground, then jerked him to his knees, while a third put a rifle to the back of his head. The woman was tied to the truck, facing him. The muffled words of the interpreter were too difficult to make out, but it was clear they wanted something, and the only things they ever came looking for were weapons, food, or information.

"Let's go," hissed Aaron, starting back down the valley.

CRACK!

He whirled around just in time to see the soldier standing behind the man hit the ground.

Within another second, the driver of the truck slumped forward, his face on the wheel.

The third shot left a pink mist in the air where a soldier had been peeking up over the hood of the truck and, with a fourth ear-splitting crack, a soldier low crawling under the truck ceased crawling.

Aaron turned in disbelief as his mother slid the bolt forward on her rifle, chambering her last round. A lone soldier emerged hastily from ransacking the house and froze at the sight of his fallen comrades. It was the last thing he ever saw.

Sara's last bullet sent the soldier crumpling to the ground. Everything was still. Still and quiet. The man and woman were frozen in place. The only sound was Sara reaching into her satchel, grabbing new rounds, and feeding them into the magazine, all by feel. She never took her eyes off the clearing. Finally, she slid the bolt forward loading the first round.

Aaron, anger now replacing his shock, grit his teeth. "You cover us from here, Mom. Seth and I will go check it out." By his tone everyone knew this was not the time to argue. Seth got up and followed him.

Working their way around the clearing, using the houses for cover, they cautiously moved toward the troop truck. Reaching the tailgate, they could hear the woman speaking.

"It's as if the Archangel of God smote them with his mighty hand."

Aaron looked into the back of the truck. Empty. There was some chatter on the radio, but nothing and no one else. The woman continued to praise the Almighty as Seth and Aaron moved around to the side of the truck she was bound to.

"It wasn't the Archangel, God, or Santa Claus. It was my crazy mother," Aaron cut into her exaltations angrily.

The woman whirled around, startled. She looked relieved to see Americans and, as Seth cut her free with his hunting knife, she said, "Oh child, God uses whoever is handy at the time."

Aaron looked at Seth and rolled his eyes. It wasn't that he didn't believe in God; his family was quite spiritual. He just couldn't get over the fact his mother had put them all in danger for a couple of people they didn't know, who probably weren't going to make it anyway.

The woman hugged them both and, before each could escape, sandwiched their faces between surprisingly strong hands and kissed them soundly on the forehead. Her husband wrapped her in a quick hug, and they brushed the dust off the worn clothes covering their thin frames.

Smoothing down her dirty blond hair, she said, "My name is Kathy, and this is my husband, Tom."

Turning toward the wood line they had come from, Seth gave the all clear thumbs up. Sara and the others emerged from the woods and made their way toward the house.

"I'm Aaron, this is Seth, and there's your Archangel." He pointed to his mother as she crossed the clearing.

The woman squinted in the direction Aaron was pointing, then exclaimed in an awestruck whisper, "She's an angel indeed. I prayed God would save us from the hands of our enemies and save us he did." Tears ran down her face.

When Sara, Leah, and Caleb reached the others, Kathy threw her arms around Sara, kissed her on the cheek, and thanked her over and over again. The man also thanked her and, ruffling Caleb's hair, said, "Your mother is my hero, son."

Aaron broke into the lauding, "Those soldiers will be missed soon enough; we need to go."

"Can we come with you?" Tom asked. "We obviously can't stay here."

"No!" Aaron's sharp answer came a little too quickly, even to his own ears, and he tried to explain himself.

"It's better if we all stay separate. Large groups are easier to spot and harder to take care of." After what Hanna had done, he doubted he would ever trust another outsider again.

"Then where do we go?" Kathy asked.

"Go north," Aaron offered. "Get lost in the woods up there. Who knows, maybe the Canadians will take us in. We can help you get packed, then we part ways." His tone was firm but kind.

The man nodded and headed into the house to look for some packs.

"How did they know you were here?" Sara asked.

"They've known about us for a while, just never paid us any mind. Something must have happened for them to come after us that way," Kathy answered.

"What did they ask you?" Aaron continued.

"Mostly about our whereabouts yesterday and if we had any weapons," she replied.

Aaron glanced nervously at Sara.

Just then, Tom returned with a couple of old backpacks.

"These will have to do," he said apologetically.

Sara, Seth, Leah, and Caleb followed Tom and Kathy into the house to help them pack. Aaron elected to remain outside on guard. He was still upset with his mother and wasn't quite ready to be sociable. Sara had set him as the leader and then ignored his call and got them into this mess.

It worked out this time, but what if it hadn't? We could be burying another family member right now. Keeping us safe was the last thing Dad said to anyone, and he said it to me!

The group returned from the house fifteen minutes later with Tom and Kathy. "Well, they're all ready to go, except for grabbing some supplies off the soldiers here," Sara reported.

Aaron gestured his approval while avoiding his mother's eyes.

Kathy gave everyone one last hug while Tom shook their hands.

"Good luck! And thank you," Tom said.

As the Redding family headed back into the St. Croix River Valley, Sara noticed the stoic expression on the face of her eldest and tried to break the stony silence.

"They gave us a couple of cans of kidney beans they'd been saving as a thank you. I think I'll cook them up for supper. They'll help us keep up our strength."

Aaron made no acknowledgement of her comment, but she heard his muttered, "No doubt they're to die for."

Sara knew he hated confrontation, especially with her. The knowledge that, in his mind, she had let him down was a hard pill to swallow.

That afternoon, they forded the Snake River. A couple miles later, they waded up a small creek before picking out a secluded alcove under a group of evergreens, a stone's throw north of the water. It was a good spot to camp for the night. The wind was out of the south which would allow them to build a small fire to cook the beans on and, by crossing the river and walking in the creek, there wouldn't be a scent trail for dogs to follow if there was any pursuit, not that they expected one. The further north they went, the fewer and fewer outposts and soldiers they should run into. That is, if they could stay out of trouble.

"Ummm, Aaron?" Sara spoke up, elbows deep in her pack. "Where are my saucepans?"

Looking up from the sticks he was collecting, he paused. Suddenly, he smacked his hand to his forehead. "They're in my pack . . . back at the house. I'm sorry, Mom. I didn't even think about that when I left it behind."

"Well, obviously I didn't either," she forgave him with a smile. "At least we have the bean cans!"

Aaron helped his siblings get their mosquito nets and blankets set up. Seth helped their mother get a fire going, and Caleb and Leah fetched water from the stream with the water jugs from their mother's pack. The smell of cooked beans soon had everyone's stomachs rumbling. Each of them took turns with the sporks their father had put in their packs, eating the beans right out of the can. Though they didn't taste like much, they did do something to relieve the pains growing in everyone's bellies.

"Thanks for supper, Mama," Leah said. The others echoed their agreement.

Sara felt tears burning the corners of her eyes. *Supper* . . . how had it come to seeing a couple cans of beans as *supper?* She wished she could give them more, wished things could go back to the way they were before all this. She didn't want to go to bed alone again. She didn't want to wake up in the morning and do this all over again. The pain and loneliness burned in her chest but she wouldn't allow them to see it. They needed her strong; they needed her to believe there was still hope.

She picked up the empty bean cans and walked to the creek. *Just keep breathing, Sara. . . .*

Sara had been gone for a solid half hour, and Aaron was beginning to worry, when she finally reappeared. "Everyone is already tucked in for the night; it's been a long day," he said, rising as she approached.

"I'll take first watch tonight, Aaron. You get some sleep," Sara spoke softly.

"Nah, I'm not tired yet," Aaron lied. They were all tired, but he couldn't bring himself to sleep just yet. He had too much on his mind.

Sara sighed, "I know you're upset with me about today, but I didn't have a choice. Those people were Americans, Aaron."

"Americans!" Aaron exploded in a harsh whisper. "Mom, America is dead. We're all just people now. People just trying to stay alive!"

"Oh, son." Sara looked at him sympathetically. "America isn't dead. Do you really believe all this country amounts to is a government, some infrastructure, and an army? America is a belief, the dream, the vision we live by, and the fire that burns in our hearts. Without America we're simply the 'not so United States.'

"That's what happened during the civil war, before the Chinese invaded—we forgot who we were. We lost sight of the vision that made this country great! We forgot how to work hard together, about liberty, about the millions of lives lost in defense of the American spirit!

"America isn't the land, the lakes, the rivers. It's the seed planted in each one of us: that men and women were born to be free, were born to do great things. No matter where people come from, the shade of their skin, or the accent of their English, America is the hope of a better tomorrow. She cannot be killed, son. No, not as long as there are Americans who still carry her in their hearts." She lightly jabbed her finger in his chest. "That's what your father believed. That *is* what I believe."

"Well, Dad is dead," he retorted, eyes glistening.

"And would he have wanted America to die with him?" she gently returned.

Aaron had no response. Pushing himself to his feet, he walked over to his mosquito net and slumped into his bed for the night.

Sara stayed up for several more hours feeding bits of wood into the small fire.

"I miss you, John. I wish you were here to hold me. I don't know what to do. I don't know how to take care of them like this. We need you . . . I need you. Why did you leave me, John? My Love . . ."

And she let herself cry, hard, for the first time since holding his lifeless body in that damp, cruel ditch.

"Jesus help me . . ."

Chapter 4

In the morning, Seth reported there was nothing to report. He had taken the second watch, and the night had been quiet. As Aaron had suspected, the PLA did not seem to have sufficient resources to mount any kind of serious search this far north. But how long would that last? In the last two days, they had killed around twenty-five soldiers. A number, Aaron guessed, the Chinese had not lost since they first started showing up this far north. Sooner or later, they were bound to attract more attention, which is why they needed to stay low and keep moving.

"I hurt all over," whined Caleb. "And I'm so hungry my stomach hurts."

"Mine too," agreed Leah as she put her arm around her brother, giving him an encouraging squeeze.

As much as Aaron wanted to keep moving, he knew they had to make it together. At this pace, they would all be dead in a week.

He smiled. "I think we'd better rest today. After all, it's Sunday. Dad would want us to take the day off."

Sara took a couple of freeze-dried meals from her pack and mixed them with water in the bean cans she had saved. She cracked a smile at the irony of the label on the food packages: "Feed My Starving Children." She and John had volunteered to pack meals at Feed My Starving Children years ago, back when America was the charity capital of the world. She had never imagined then that some of those meals would feed her own starving children while they still lived in the very country which had packed them.

"Dear Jesus, what happened to us? When did we forget who we are?" she said under her breath as she looked at her children: dirty, cold, and hungry.

She was sure there were those in the world who believed that America deserved this fate for her pride, for always standing in their way, for always assuming she was right. Sara could only imagine what the world looked like now and, if she was right, the world was realizing that, with all her shortcomings, America had been doing all right.

It wasn't China who had brought down America. It was Americans who had forgotten who they were—humans—people who make mistakes, even while doing their best. People who had forgotten living here was a privilege and replaced the selfless, thankful culture of America with one of entitlement. Unity was replaced with every man for himself and, as the old coins used to say, "United We Stand," well, divided, the country had fallen.

"Looks like it's going to start to sprinkle here in a bit, Mom." Aaron's voice shook her from her thoughts. "I'll set up the tarp."

"Thank you, Aaron." She studied him for a moment. "You really are doing a great job of looking after us. Dad would be proud."

Aaron's eyes met his mother's, but he quickly looked away. It surprised him how deeply the compliment affected him. He had no greater desire than to be like his father and know that he made him proud. He was doing his best in an awful situation . . . he just hoped it was enough.

He set up the tarp with Seth's help. They strung a line of paracord between two trees, laid the tarp over top, and tied down the four corners to other nearby trees, forming an A-frame roof. By the time they were done, the soup was ready and the family sat down with their sporks once again.

"Aaron, would you mind saying grace?" Sara asked gently.

"Sure," he agreed with reservation. He hadn't prayed since the day his father died. "Thank you, Heavenly Father, for this day of rest and for this food. Thank you for our family and keeping us safe." He paused for a moment, recalling the death of his father. "And Lord, if you could tell Dad we miss him we'd really appreciate it. Amen."

"Amen," Sara echoed.

They took turns eating spoonsful of warm, delicious soup from the two tin cans. The taste and warmth on this drizzly day worked wonders to boost their spirits. After breakfast, Sara dug in her pack and found the deck of cards. Forming a circle, they huddled under their blankets and played King's Corner. It was the first time they laughed and played together since leaving their home.

Sara looked out through the open end of the tarp. All three boys were out in the drizzle collecting enough firewood to get through the day before it was soaked too thoroughly to burn. She was thankful for the rare moment alone with her daughter.

"How are you holding up, Leah?" Sara asked tenderly.

"Well, I'm tired, and I miss Daddy. I miss my warm bed in our warm house. I miss the chickens; I even miss my chores. I miss my life, Mama. I'm not like Aaron or Seth, or even Caleb. I've never really wanted adventure. I just want home. No more surprises, no more running for my life, no more death . . . I don't belong out here." Tears filled her eyes.

Leah was stronger than she looked, and she kept herself from coming apart. Life had been hard for all of them for a long time and complaining had never done a thing to change that. The whole family had risen to the challenges, and Sara was so proud of them for it.

"Leah, you're such a precious girl, and your brothers need you more than you know. You have always been like a second mother to Caleb and a big help to me, and I need you. You're my right-hand woman. You may not belong out here in the woods, but you do belong in this family. This team would be in trouble without you." Sara gently lifted her chin, "I'm proud of you, girl."

Leah had been holding her own, but her mother's touch seemed to break through her guard, and she flung herself into her arms and sobbed. Sara held her awhile. Then, she sat up, wiped her tears with her sleeve, and said, "Ok, Mama, I'll do my best."

Sara pulled Leah close, looking deep into her eyes, "It will take all of our best if we're going to make it." She lifted her face and kissed her daughter on the forehead.

Just then, the boys arrived bearing armloads of wood.

"This should get us through today and tonight," Aaron reported proudly.

Even Caleb had carried an impressive load and strutted in front of the girls before laying it down.

Sara smiled, "Whoa, boy! Now that's a load."

Caleb beamed.

"Seth and I were thinking we would try our hand at fishing this afternoon. Anyone else want to come?" Aaron asked.

The rain had stopped and the sun had begun to break through the clouds. It was turning out to be a warm September day after all.

"I'd like to go," Leah said, looking at her mother.

"Well, go on then, just don't go far."

The three siblings headed off toward the river with their fishing lines while Caleb and Sara kept an eye on the fire and played a few more games of cards.

They were fortunate to be on the fringe of the Chinese invasion. Further south, helicopters, drones, and armored vehicles were much more commonplace. Even a small fire could have given their position away but, as it was, they were safe for today.

Aaron, Seth, and Leah returned after a couple of hours, laughing and teasing quietly. The sound of their merriment brought a smile to Sara's face.

"So, how'd it go?" she asked.

Aaron held up a stringer of seven fish: two good size bass and five panfish larger than a man's hand.

"I destroyed the boys," Leah announced proudly.

"She's right," admitted Aaron, "Seth and I only caught one apiece. Leah brought in the rest."

"Well done, honey! Looks like we'll be having fish tonight!" Sara said joyfully.

"I'll get them cleaned for you, Mom," Seth offered. "Caleb, come give me a hand."

Caleb nodded and followed his older brother over to a fallen log: a perfect makeshift table. Leah got out the fry pan, the only pan they now had, and the salt from her pack. It was all they had for seasoning, but it was better than nothing. Soon, Sara had the fish frying.

"This has been a good day hasn't it, Mama?" Caleb asked with a smile.

"Yes, it has," Sara replied thoughtfully. *I have so much to be grateful for.*

It was midafternoon when the five of them sat down to a meal of fried fish. Fish wasn't anyone's favorite and, with only salt to add to it, there was much to be desired in the flavor department. Even so, when they were all finished, Aaron admitted it felt good to be nearly full for a change. After dinner, they all lay back on their packs to rest.

"I can't remember the last time I felt so satisfied," Sara said, with a relaxing sigh. "Thank you all for today."

"Well, we'd better enjoy it. Tomorrow's going to be another long day on the trail," Aaron murmured, with his head back and his eyes closed.

"Why do we have to go so far?" Caleb whined.

Aaron sat up and patiently explained, "Because, buddy, if we don't, we won't make it to the boreal forest in time to prepare for winter, and that would mean bad things for us all."

"How will we know when we're there?" asked Caleb.

"Remember when we went to Grand Marais for vacation when you were little?"

"Yeah."

"Do you remember the trees?"

"Kinda."

"There's a beautiful forest of nothing but evergreens so thick the sunlight doesn't even reach the ground in some places. Moss hangs from the branches of trees, creeping across the ground, covering everything. The air is so still and silent it feels like anything more than a whisper would be irreverent, almost like it was sacred. I've never forgotten the sights, the smells, and the sounds of it. That's where we'll be free, and I'll know it when I'm there." With that, he settled back and closed his eyes again.

Sara smiled to herself, there was more to this boy than she had ever realized. *Perhaps he was born for a time such as this.*

She sent her family to bed early that night and, again, took the first watch. It was nearing midnight when a muffled whimper caught her ear. Crawling over to where her children all slept, she heard sniffling from under Caleb's blanket. Gently, she placed her hand on his head and slid the hair away from his wet eyes.

"Caleb," she whispered, "come here, honey."

With a sob, he climbed out of his blankets and snuggled into his mother's lap the best he could, wrapping his arms tightly around her neck.

"I miss Daddy!" he cried into her neck.

"Oh baby, I know you do," she rocked back and forth gently, holding her son. "I do too. Shhh. It'll be ok, honey. We'll figure it out."

By sunup, the Redding family was already on the trail. Aaron hoped to make good time after a day's rest. Sara and Aaron had looked over the old map of Minnesota from his father's pack and guessed they were about nine miles from where the Kettle River tributary flowed into the St. Croix River. That would be their goal: to make the Kettle River before dark.

The forest trails were thickly grown over in parts and almost impassable in others. For hours, the Reddings hacked, climbed, and stumbled their way ahead. Reaching a small creek, Aaron halted.

"Let's rest here and get some water." He leaned his AK against a tree and slipped off his pack. Everyone followed suit.

Sweat soaked straps left silhouettes on their shirts and their feet swam in their boots. Sara handed out the iodine tablets and they filled their bottles in the creek. The water was cool, clear, and refreshing.

"How's everyone doing?" Aaron asked, sipping on his water bottle.

He got a thumbs up from Seth, a nod from Sara, an "ok" from Leah, who had made it her goal not to complain, and an, "If I take another step I'm going to die," from Caleb.

"You'll make it, buddy, we all will," Seth reassured him.

Aaron was really coming to appreciate Seth. He was rising to the occasion. He may have only been fourteen, but he was a warrior, fearless, loyal, and strong. Aaron had come to count on that strength.

After a good rest and several more hours on the trail, the Reddings happened upon an abandoned cabin sitting at the end of a long gravel driveway. The cabin was huge: two stories, made of real logs. A regular wooden castle. The steel roof appeared to have protected the structure well.

Aaron checked the map. *Only half a mile to the Kettle River.* "Well, I think Seth and I will check it out. If it's clear, we'll spend the night. Mom, you cover us from here. Leah, help her spot, and Caleb, you watch her back." Taking one more long look at the house, he moved his safety lever from safe to fire, and nodded at the others.

"Let's go, Seth," he whispered, leaping from the bushes in a trot toward the house.

The boys cut across the back lawn, leapfrogging each other from cover to cover, always looking back at Sara to make sure the coast was clear. At last, they reached the back door. Seth tried the handle. It was locked. Surprisingly, this house had not yet been looted. It had probably been some rich folks' vacation home and, when things hit the fan, they had forgotten all about it along with everyone else.

Taking one final glance at Sara, Aaron gestured to Seth's shotgun. "Smash it."

A look of pure glee spread across Seth's face. Raising his shotgun, he sent it through a glass panel in the door with gusto. Reaching in, he turned the deadbolt.

"After you, my good man," he said in his best English accent.

Shaking his head, Aaron swung the door open, rifle at the ready. Empty.

The boys made quick work of clearing the rooms. No one had been there for years, and the only occupants were a few mice and a red squirrel. Aaron jogged down the stairs to the back door and gave the all clear.

***

"What a Godsend," Sara said as she went through a closet of women's clothes close enough to her size to wear. Leah, too, had found a new outfit and the boys were busy raiding the men's clothes. The house had five bedrooms, three bathrooms, and a monster kitchen opening into an enormous great room.

"I wish we could stay here forever," Caleb smiled wistfully, sporting his new blue jeans, shirt, and hoodie. A little on the big side, maybe, but not cumbersome.

Everyone changed clothes, which was a morale boost in itself. Days of dirty clothes had a way of dampening one's spirits.

"Check these out!" Seth exclaimed, holding up a pair of binoculars. "You could probably see the Boundary Waters from here with these things."

Aaron laughed, "Probably. Hang on to those; we can use them."

Sara rummaged in the kitchen and came up with several cans of stew, corn, peas, beans, and even a large can of fruit cocktail. She replaced the empty cans in her pack with a new, small copper pot for cooking and boiling water.

Leah found an almost full box of stick matches, some candlesticks, and a pair of scissors. Seth had tackled the den and came up with a couple animal snares, a few pieces of fishing tackle, a filleting knife, and a couple of canteens. Caleb discovered enough wool socks for them all. He took all the bars of soap from the three bathrooms and discovered the hand pump sand point well in the front yard.

From the second story balcony, Aaron surveyed the area. Satisfied they were safe and that the balcony would serve well as a night watch post, he turned to go back downstairs when something caught his eye. A propane tank, nearly completely covered by wild grapevines, protruded from the abandoned lawn. *If the house had been forgotten, perhaps the propane had been also.*

Instead of joining the others, Aaron went out the back door and over to the tank. After peeling away the vines, he flipped open the cover to check the gauge. Just under thirty percent. A smile spread across his face. Filling the pail hanging by the pump, Aaron brought water into the kitchen where Sara was still busy scavenging.

"What's that for?" Sara asked when she saw him with the water.

Aaron walked over to the stove. Taking a match from the box Leah had found, he turned on a burner and lit it. Sara nearly fell over when she saw the blue flames dance.

"You mind cooking tonight?" he said, winking.

"Not at all," she smiled in delight, "I would love to cook tonight."

"Also, I was thinking we could all use a bath," Aaron went on. "We can heat water on the stove and fill the tub. May take a little effort but Seth could really use it." He gave his brother a shove. Seth grinned, shrugging his shoulders.

After a hot dinner of stew and vegetables in real bowls, followed by hot baths and clean clothes, the family decided it would be best if they stayed together in the master bedroom, close to the night watch. They wrestled in an extra mattress for Seth and Aaron to take turns on and the rest fit on the king-sized bed with room to spare.

"This feels like heaven!" Leah sighed dramatically as she and Caleb climbed under the goose down comforter.

Sara decided to join Aaron on the night watch for a bit before heading to bed. They sat out on the balcony together. The night was cool and crisp without a single cloud in the sky. A sliver of a moon hung in the east, and a billion stars twinkled overhead.

"There's just one thing I can't make any sense of, Mom . . ." Aaron started, "Hanna was an American, and a friend. . . ."

Sara studied him for a moment then, looking back into the night, sighed. "You mean how could Hanna have sold us out?" Without waiting for an answer, she continued.

"I've wrestled with that myself but, in my heart, I know that harboring anger or hatred toward Hanna won't change anything. We don't know the whole story, son. Maybe they had her family and she had no choice, or maybe she just lost her way. That's what will happen if we forget who we are. We'll forget the hope, the good fight, and we'll act like animals, only trying to save ourselves. We must remember that we're all one, with one enemy: the darkness, in whatever form it takes. America is who we are. . . ."

Aaron pondered his mother's words. He really wasn't so different from Hanna when she put it that way. He would have passed Kathy and her husband by without taking any thought for their lives if he had had his way.

"Well, I'm going to bed. Don't forget to wake Seth in a couple of hours for his shift." She kissed him on the head and crawled into the king bed with the others.

Aaron looked up, admiring the stars. He and his father used to lay out on the small hill in their front yard in the springtime and watch the stars at night. A deep sigh escaped him. In the coolness of the night, his breath swirled in the air like a cloud before being carried off by the breeze.

His reflections were interrupted by the distant wailing of a siren. Grabbing Seth's binoculars, he focused them up the road. From his perch on the balcony, he could see the glow of lights silhouetting the trees to the west. Now, there was someone shouting something on a megaphone. *What was it?*

The glow appeared to be nearly three miles or so west, down the gravel road, and a bit to the north. He decided to wake his mother. He felt bad; she had only been sleeping for half an hour, but he wanted her to see this.

When Sara arrived on the balcony, Aaron handed her the binoculars.

"It started five minutes ago. What do you think?" he whispered.

"It's definitely the Chinese, though I can't make out what they're saying. It sounds like broken English."

"Think they have any Americans down there?"

"I don't know. Why else would they be using English?"

"What do you think we should do?"

"Well, how about I run over there and find out what I can and, when I get back, we can decide. I promise not to jump into anything. We're a team." She gave him a reassuring nod.

"I should be the one to go. I'm faster."

"Yes, but I think everyone one else needs you here. If anything happens, you would be better able to protect them. I just have to be sneaky."

Aaron paused a moment, and then sighed. "Ok, but take Seth with you for backup, just in case."

Sara woke Seth and filled him in on the details. Seth was more than happy to go. He loved the adventure they were on, and danger was just his game. Within five minutes, he was ready to go.

"Seth," Aaron said, looking him dead in the eye. "You be careful and keep her safe. You guys get back here in one piece. Do your loon whistle when you get close. I don't want to shoot you by mistake."

Seth rolled his eyes, and then gave Aaron a smile. "We'll be ok, big brother."

Time lagged while Aaron waited for them to return. He was exhausted from the day's hike, but anxiety kept him wide awake. Maybe he should have gone instead of Seth. No, Seth was fine. He would take care of her. Besides, if anything had happened to them, he would have heard shooting. There was no way Seth would be taken without a fight.

He checked on Caleb and Leah, sleeping soundly. Aaron smiled. He checked his watch: 5:30 a.m. The sun would be coming up in another hour. *Where were they?*

As six o'clock rolled around, Aaron heard a familiar whistle. Seth was quite convincing; sometimes the loons at a lake would even call back to him. Aaron trotted down the stairs to the back door to greet them.

"Well, what did you see?" Aaron asked, hugging them both in relief.

"Looks like the Chinese are constructing another outpost," Seth answered. "Not sure what all the noise was about, but we did see some Americans under guard filling sandbags."

"How many?"

"Americans or Chinese?"

"Both."

"Well, I'd say I could count maybe seven or eight Americans and twenty Chinese," offered Sara.

"That's a lot of soldiers," Aaron said, biting his lower lip.

"That's a lot of Americans, Aaron," Sara interjected.

Aaron shot her a steely glare. *Not again.*

"What if that were Leah, or Caleb, in there?" she continued.

"I think we could take 'em if we got the jump on them, Aaron," Seth interrupted.

"We don't need this trouble," Aaron pleaded.

"What about their troubles? We could free them, Aaron."

"And if we fail, we'll be in there with them!"

Sighing, Sara looked down the road. "Ok." Turning, she walked to the door.

"ARGHH! Wait, Mom . . ." Aaron caught her by the arm. "Maybe we can put together a plan. If it seems feasible, we'll give it a go. But if anything looks wrong, we are calling the whole thing off and getting out of here."

"Thank you," she smiled.

"Ok," Aaron sighed. "What did they have for equipment?"

"A couple of troop trucks, a skid steer, no helicopters," Seth replied.

"Could you draw what you saw, Mom?" Aaron asked.

"I can try."

They all moved into the kitchen. Dawn was breaking and the windows in the kitchen and great room would afford them the most light.

"It was maybe a hundred yards square with a small guard tower in each corner," Sara said as she drew a square on a napkin, putting a smaller square in each corner.

"Where were those vehicles, Seth?"

Seth took the pen from his mother. "The two troop trucks were in a small area just west of the gate. The gate is here in the center of the south side," he said, drawing two short lines perpendicular from the south wall representing the gate.

"Is that the only gate?" Aaron asked.

"Yes."

"Are there any buildings?"

Seth drew three small rectangles in the northwest corner of the square and a fourth larger rectangle almost dead center. "These three shipping containers are probably being used as barracks. This one has all the radio antennae and a satellite dish on the roof," he said, pointing to the container closest to the center of the north wall. "This rectangle in the middle is a canvas tent with some tables under it. Some of the guards were hanging out there. I'm not sure where they kept the Americans. They were all working nonstop the entire time we were there."

"What about cover? Is there a good position for you to set up, Mom?"

She took back the pen and drew a small oval an inch off the northeast corner. "This is a mound of brush, dirt, tree roots, and other rubble cleared to make room for the compound. It's probably around twenty feet high and would put me on a level plane with the guard towers and give a clear line of sight over the whole compound."

"There's a fairly deep ditch on both sides of the road leading into the compound. The ditch makes right angles about eight feet before the gate, and then stops after about ten feet." Seth volunteered as he drew a bold "L" shape on either side of the gate indicating the ditch.

"Seth, if the world hadn't gone to hell, you'd have made general someday," Aaron said, giving him a brotherly shove. "Where's the generator? If we're going to pull this off, we're going to need to take out their communications before they can call for help," Aaron said, looking at each one of them.

"It's here," Seth offered, drawing a small square just east of the headquarters container right next to the north wall.

"What are these walls made out of?"

Seth shrugged, "Not much yet. A few strands of barbed wire with some sort of coiled wire on top, but the Americans are filling sandbags fast and the south wall is about three feet high already."

"What are you guys doing?" asked a groggy Caleb.

Startled, the three turned toward him.

"Just talking honey," Sara reassured him. "Would you like some breakfast?"

Sara grabbed the can of fruit cocktail and the opener and peeled off the lid. Handing it to Caleb, she said, "Save some for everyone else."

"Can I have some?" Leah said, coming down the stairs.

"Sure sweetie, help yourself."

Leah slid into a chair at the table, "That was the best sleep I've had in ages."

"Sleep?" Aaron said, realizing how tired he was. "I think we'd better get some rest today, looks like we're going to have another busy night."

The rest of the day was spent sleeping in shifts, planning, cleaning weapons, and praying that they wouldn't all get killed.

Finally, evening arrived. They went over the plan one more time, making sure everyone knew their role.

"Do you understand your job, Caleb?" asked Aaron.

"I make sure no one sneaks up on Mom, and then leave with her when we're finished," he replied confidently.

"Good. Leah?"

"I spot for Mom and help her keep an eye on you guys with the binoculars."

"Perfect. Seth?"

"I wait in the brush as close as I can get to the generator. When Mom starts shooting, I take it out and then engage any soldiers coming out of the containers. Always keeping my head down of course," he added with a wink.

"Mom?"

"I get into position on the rubble mound with Leah, wait until I see you and Seth in position, then I take out the guard towers starting with the northwest tower near Seth. Once the towers are clear, I provide cover fire for you boys. When I get the all clear from you, I head back to the cabin with Leah and Caleb and wait for you."

"All right, and I'll be waiting in the ditch by the gate. When the guard towers are clear, I'll head through the gate and engage as many soldiers as I can. When the compound is clear, Seth and I will make sure the Americans get out and then meet you all back here."

Aaron put his arms around all of them. "I love you guys. Lord, please keep us safe. Amen. Let's go!"

They left the cabin at a trot, disappearing into the dusk.

Chapter 5

Sara was grateful for the sound of the generator as she and Leah climbed into position atop the rubble pile. She had left Caleb tucked between a couple of logs at the bottom where he would have adequate concealment while watching their backs. The mud on the pile was damp with dew and, by the time they had slipped and stumbled their way to the top, both girls were wet to the skin. Sara shivered as she slid her rifle into position. Leah, shivering beside her, pulled out the binoculars and scoured the area for the boys by the light of the guard towers.

"I see Seth; he's nearly there, Mama," Leah whispered.

Swinging her scope over to the northwest corner of the compound, Sara looked intently into the brush near the generator. A bush shook slightly, and she caught a glimpse of Seth's gray hoodie. *So far so good.*

"Aaron made the corner. He just gave a thumbs up," Leah reported next.

Sara let out a sigh of relief. Now it was all up to her.

The searchlights may have been a problem for the boys had they not currently been employed as work lights. Aaron was the only one in real danger of being seen due to the work being done on the front wall and the eyes of five Chinese guards, including the tower guard, watching the prisoners work.

"Mama, I think they're ready," Leah said, shivering.

"Are you?"

"I don't know," Leah said honestly.

"I know," Sara said, heart already drumming in her chest. "Watch the guard tower by Seth. We'll take that one first, then the one in Aaron's corner, after that the other two. You must keep an eye on everything as best you can. If the boys get into trouble you have to let me know. It's not going to be easy, but they're counting on us. The only way we're all getting out of this is if we all do our jobs and God has mercy." Taking a deep breath, she moved the safety to fire.

Seth hunkered in the bushes. The generator, only twenty feet away, vibrated the ground beneath his feet. All he could hear was the loud hum of the diesel engine, but he was sure his heartbeat was in there somewhere.

Aaron had decided taking out the generator was counterproductive. Without the lights, they would be blind too. Instead, Seth was to shoot up the power panel feeding the headquarters container. This would effectively knock out communications without taking out the lights their mother would need to cover them.

From his position, Seth could see the power panel on the back of the headquarters container: a gray box, twelve inches across and eighteen inches tall, with a thick cable running into the bottom. He checked his shotgun, a shell was in the chamber, the safety off.

"Come on, Mom, you can do it," he murmured under his breath.

Almost as if by command, he heard the shot ring out over the hum of the engine. He glanced up at the tower in time to see the guard crumple. Exploding from the bushes, Seth covered ten feet in a couple strides and pumped two shells into the box.

`Dropping to a knee, smoke rolling out of the box, Seth put the bead of his gun on the chest of the first soldier to emerge from the container only fifteen feet away.

With a loud BOOM, a wad of shot peppered the man's chest and face as Seth pumped another shell into the chamber and steeled himself for the next one.

As the tower guard in Aaron's corner dropped, Aaron shot out of the ditch, charging the gate. He dropped two soldiers, distracted by Seth's antics, before blasting the chain that held the gate shut. Once inside, he took cover behind one of the troop trucks and took stock of the situation. The Americans who had been working on the wall were all lying on the ground taking cover. As he looked on, one of the remaining prisoner guards slumped over the wall, blood soaking the back of his uniform.

With a thud, something slammed into Aaron's back. Whirling around Aaron found himself eye to eye with one very surprised guard. In a terrified fury, Aaron pulled up his rifle and fired three times as the soldier was attempting to do the same. The guard fell forward, grabbing Aaron's arm as he slid toward the ground. Sinking to his knees, the dying man looked up at Aaron, eyes full of fear, blood beginning to form in the corners of his mouth, then he slumped to the ground.

Aaron fought to catch his breath, adrenaline coursing through his veins, his head spinning.

Seth had crawled between the strands of barbed wire and was now hiding behind the headquarters container reloading his shotgun. The panel box, smoking beside him, was still spitting sparks. He could hear troops running about on the front side of the containers, sporadic gunfire echoed off the walls.

As he shoved the third shell into the tube, pain ripped through his thigh. Instinctively rolling behind the generator, he pumped a shell into the chamber. Heart pounding, he put his hand on the pain and brought it up to his face. Bright red blood glistened on his palm. He heard two cracks of distant rifle fire, followed by the now familiar sound of a body hitting the ground. Blood flowed from under the generator. Seth knew he had to get to Aaron on the opposite end

of the compound.

Quickly, he loaded the last three shells into his shotgun and peered around the generator.

"Mom!" Leah shrieked. "Seth's hurt! Seth's hurt! They shot him, Mom! I saw it!"

Sara jammed the last bullet into her magazine and slammed the bolt, chambering the round. Her pulse quickened as she searched for him, as she searched for her son.

"Where is he, Leah?" she yelled, all stealth forgotten.

"By that engine thing!"

Sara spotted Seth sitting behind the generator. There was no time to assess his condition. A PLA soldier was almost on him. She leveled her scope on the man's head. Squeezing the trigger, she felt something stumble into her.

"You missed, Mom!" Leah shrieked.

"What happened to Seth, Mom! What's going on!" Caleb yelled fearfully from behind her shoulder.

"Get off me, Caleb!" Sara yelled in panic as she rolled over, ejecting the empty shell.

The soldier was creeping his way around the front of the generator now. Sara held the cross hairs on the end of his nose giving him a slight lead and pulled the trigger again.

"You got him!"

Sara quickly chambered another round and scanned the area surrounding Seth. Another soldier ran out of a barracks container. Sara dropped him in his tracks. Shooting instinctively now—those were her boys down there—she dropped another and another as they ran about in a frenzied panic. Her ears rang and sweat ran down her face as she pivoted her rifle back and forth.

"Seth is heading toward the gate, Mama. It looks like he's limping," Leah said.

Sara found him in her scope. He was indeed limping, but she was relieved to see him moving so well.

"They need our help," she said, turning to Leah and Caleb.

When she saw the tears in Caleb's eyes, her gaze softened.

"Caleb, I'm sorry, honey. Seth was in trouble and I had to act quickly. I think he's alright, but they still need our help. Your brothers need you. Are you with me?"

Caleb nodded, swallowing both tears and panic. The three of them slid their way down the rubble pile and headed for the eastern wall.

"Aaron! Aaron! Are you there?"

A familiar voice shook Aaron from his shock. It was Seth.

"Yeah, I'm over here!" he yelled above the chaotic gunfire of the last few soldiers.

Peering around the corner of the truck, he saw Seth hunkered down behind the nearest corner of the tent. Seth lifted his shotgun when he saw Aaron's face, then lowered it as recognition dawned. Motioning for Seth to join him, Aaron opened fire in the direction of the remaining soldiers. Seth hobbled as quickly as he could across the opening and dove behind the truck, bullets whizzing past them both as he did.

Aaron spun back behind the truck, catching a glance of the blood staining Seth's pants. "Are you alright?"

"I'll be alright, haven't had time to look at it, but I think they just grazed me. Hurts like fire though," Seth sat up, wincing.

"Only a few of them left. They were running for the containers as you came across. You'd better stay here; I'll find a way to deal with them." Aaron slapped him on the shoulder and started moving again.

Working his way along the east side of the tent, Aaron poked his head around the corner looking toward the containers.

The booming of Chinese guns filled his ears, and bullets whizzed by his face. He dropped to his belly as rounds perforated the tent.

The crack of a rifle sounded to the east, followed by another.

Aaron looked in the direction the sound was coming from. There was Sara, kneeling with her rifle resting on the top wire of the eastern fence. Aaron could hardly believe his eyes when he saw Caleb hit the fence beside her, jaw set, his little .22 blazing.

Peeking back around the edge of the tent, Aaron saw the last two soldiers ducking behind a half-finished pile of sandbags. He knew what he needed to do. Jumping to his feet, he sprinted around the tent to the west wall of the compound, then turned north at a dead run. The distracted soldiers never saw him coming.

He jumped over the sandbags, emptying his magazine into the remaining guards.

In the stillness that followed, the humming generator was the only sound to be heard. The Redding family stood frozen in their places. Aaron pulled a loaded magazine out of the pouch on his belt and slammed it into his magazine well. It was over. Turning at the sound of his brother's voice, Aaron saw Seth helping one of the Americans to their feet.

"It's alright, you're safe now."

He had completely forgotten about the prisoners. Leah appeared at Seth's side and, together, they got all the prisoners up out of the mud.

"Please! You have to help my brother!"

Aaron turned around to face the voice. A young woman, with caramel colored skin and loosely curled black hair held back in a makeshift headband, stared at him—into him. Her eyes were dark, almond shaped. Her face was round but chiseled and had dried mud caked to it in places. She was of medium build and not quite a head shorter than Aaron. Her tattered gray-green hoodie was covered in dirt and mud. Her blue jeans, a couple of sizes too big, were held around her waist with a length of twine. At the sight of her, Aaron did a double take. She was beautiful.

"Uh, where is he?" he said, swallowing hard, trying to remember her question.

"They took him into one of the containers last night. I don't know what they did to him. One of the soldiers grabbed me so Ty hit him, then they took him in there. I could hear him screaming . . ." Her voice broke and tears mingled with the mud on her cheeks, leaving streaks running down her chin.

Aaron looked at his brother, "Seth? We'll need to clear those containers."

Sara was busy tending Seth's wound. Looking up at Seth, she said, "Let me get a bandage on this first."

"I saw some medical equipment in the tent. I'll go and get a bandage," Leah offered.

"Caleb, please go with her," Aaron said, "Just in case."

Aaron looked at the remaining American prisoners who were standing awkwardly around, not sure what to do. "You'd better clear out of here. The PLA will learn of this soon enough and they'll not be kind to anyone they find."

"Where? How?" one of the prisoners asked.

"Grab some gear, only what you need, only what you can carry, and head north. There's lots of forest up there. Get deep enough and it won't be worth the trouble to find you."

"What will you do?" the man asked.

"We'll do the same, but we're going to be slowed up by Seth's leg. Don't worry about us; we can take care of ourselves. Now, get going," Aaron urged firmly.

The prisoners scattered, grabbing gear and weapons as quickly as they could.

"I'm all set," Seth said, wincing as he stepped toward his brother.

"Not yet you're not," Aaron countered, handing him a Chinese QBZ-95 and a couple of extra magazines. Then he pointed at the shotgun. "That thing nearly got you killed." *That thing got dad killed . . .*

The two boys headed toward the containers with their mother, the young woman, Leah, and Caleb in tow. When they reached the headquarters, Seth leaned against the wall near the door, his hand on the handle. Aaron positioned himself behind some crates so that he would have a clear line of sight into the container once the door was opened.

"Please be careful," whispered the woman, "My brother could be in there."

Seth held up three fingers, then two, then one; he jerked the door open.

Aaron tensed, ready to pull the trigger, scanning the room from end to end in a split second.

"Clear!"

The boys moved to the second container and repeated the process.

"Clear!"

They came to the last container. Seth held up his fingers again as everyone looked on, involuntarily holding their breath. Three, two, one . . . As he flung the door open, Aaron scanned the room.

"Clear," he panted as he began breathing again. "He's here."

The woman burst into the container, "Ty?! Ty, can you hear me?"

"Soraya . . ." came a labored whisper.

Aaron stepped into the container, followed by Seth and Sara.

"Seth, help me get him down."

They walked over to the man who was tied hand and foot to the four corners at the far end of the container. His shirt had been torn off, his face bloodied, his ribs purple with hemorrhaging. Seth and Aaron cut his feet loose, and then carefully cut his hands free, lowering him onto a cot along the wall. The woman hugged him gently and kissed him on the forehead.

"Water . . ."

Aaron grabbed a canteen off the wall and handed it to the woman. She held it to her brother's lips and tilted it. The man took a drink, coughing, then wincing from the pain.

Seth pulled Aaron outside. "He's in real bad shape, they won't make it without us, and we won't be able to move fast with them."

"I know, but we can't leave them. The Chinese will kill them."

"The Chinese will kill us all if they catch us!" he whispered fiercely.

"If we can get them across the Kettle River tonight, maybe a mile or two more, and find a place for them to hide, we should be safe for a couple of days."

"*If* we can get him across the river," Seth muttered.

Sara walked out of the container and headed for the medical supplies in the tent. "Boys, help me look for a gurney!" she called over her shoulder.

"Looks like we're taking him with us," Aaron said, glancing at Seth.

"Perfect," Seth huffed.

Sara grabbed an armful of medical supplies, bandages, painkillers, antiseptic, and an instant ice pack. Aaron found a gurney in the back of one of the trucks, and they all headed back to the container where everyone else waited.

Sara patched up Ty with Soraya's help and, by 3 a.m., they were ready to go.

"Wh—who are you guys?" asked Ty as they gingerly helped him onto the gurney.

"I'm Aaron, this is Seth, Caleb, and Leah, and the Archangel who watches over us all is my mom, Sara," he said, putting an arm on his mother's shoulder. Aaron felt her shiver as he withdrew his arm.

"Hang on a sec."

Aaron ran over to one of the trucks. Pulling out his hunting knife, he climbed up on the tailgate and cut a large square swath out of the canvas bed cover. When he returned, he threw the tarp around his mother's shoulders, running a cord through two grommets to hold the cloak in place and give it a sort of hood. Sara gave him a smile.

"Ok, let's get going," he said as he and Soraya lifted Ty off the ground.

The group made it back to the cabin to grab their gear as the glow of dawn appeared on the horizon. Aaron looked at the weary and wounded troop, staggering and limping into the small yard, and wished he had something better to offer them than more running.

"Ok guys, we have to make this as quick as possible. The Chinese probably already know something's up, so let's get cleaned up, grab what we can, and get out of here."

Seth groaned as he gingerly lowered himself on the large wrap-around porch, "I wish we could stay here for a week."

Sara knew everyone agreed with Seth, but nobody said so. They all knew staying would be suicide.

"Caleb, we need some water," Sara spoke up, getting everyone into motion again. "Leah, please help Soraya get washed up and maybe find some new clothes. Aaron, help me take care of these boys, would you?"

Seth's bandage was already soaked through with blood. With pursed lips, Sara cleaned his wound better with the cold water, and then replaced the bandage.

"You are *not* walking on this leg anymore, Seth. You'll bleed to death."

Seth raised an eyebrow, "Do you have another suggestion?"

"Yes. Aaron, please go make some crutches. Leah and I will take turns helping with the gurney, and we should probably take some of the weight out of your pack as well. I have some extra room in my bag—"

"Mom!" Seth broke in with an exaggerated eye roll. "I'm fine! I'll use your crutches, but I can still carry all my stuff. My back is fine!"

Sara gazed at her son through narrowed eyes. She could see she wouldn't win this fight. Seth wasn't about to let go of a single bit of the manhood which had been put upon him at such an early age. He would die first. It was up to her to make sure that didn't happen. Not an easy job with this one.

"Alright," she nodded as she stood up to move on to her next patient.

There was no point in telling him to let her know if it got to be too much for him. He would never admit to such weakness.

Ty was a little more complicated. His wounds may not have been as deep, but there were far more of them. The young man hadn't uttered a word since leaving the outpost, but Sara knew he must be in severe pain. She saw a mixture of bitterness, distrust, and resignation in his eyes as she knelt beside him.

"You're a very brave young man," she said softly, washing the blood and dirt away.

Ty just grunted and looked away, wincing at the cold water.

"I believe you have an amazing story. Someday, I'd like to hear it." Sara did her best to clean and bandage all his cuts and gashes, knowing infection would be his greatest enemy.

Aaron returned from the trees with some makeshift crutches just as the girls came out of the house. In a matter of ten minutes, they had gathered all the gear they could carry. Seth strapped his gun to his pack and let Caleb help him to his feet. Aaron took stock of his little band, standing with determination, looking to him for the word, and then bent to help his mother lift the gurney.

"Hey, bro." Aaron winked at Caleb. "How about you take point?"

Caleb's eyes widened, and a small smile tugged at the corners of his mouth. "Yes, sir!" he answered as he scampered to the front of the line.

As the rag tag line disappeared into the trees, the distant rumble of approaching helicopters reached the clearing.

Chapter 6

Aaron stood up slowly from the perch where he had spent the last watch of the night overlooking a fork in the St. Croix River. It's not that he expected trouble from that direction, it just beat staring into the leaves and branches only a few feet behind him. He was cold and stiff. There had been no fire to sit by during the chilly night. Even though they had crossed the Kettle River yesterday and had walked two more miles up the riverbank of another small fork, having a fire would be risky.

They had been careful to erase any sign of their presence back at the cabin. Even if a searching patrol came across it, there would be no link with the attacked base. There was no one left to tell the story and taking the time to decipher whether it had been a prisoner revolt, or an outside attack would not likely rank high on the priority list.

Dawn had arrived, but there was no point waking the others; there would be no traveling today. Seth's leg would need time to mend, and Ty couldn't even walk yet. Ty. Aaron couldn't quite figure that guy out. He was obviously brave and loved his sister, or he wouldn't have gotten pulverized trying to protect her, but he didn't seem thankful for their help at all: bitter was more like it. His sister, though, had been grateful enough for both of them. Soraya had taken her turn carrying her brother's gurney, helped set up camp, even offered to take one of the night watches.

She made him curious. He had never expected to find such a flower in the middle of the shadows of death and suffering. He remembered, with some embarrassment, how his jaw had almost dropped at the sight of her walking toward him back at the outpost. He turned and looked at her sleeping peacefully beside her brother.

"You don't belong here," he whispered.

A few blankets down, Sara began to stir. Sitting up, she began rummaging in her pack. Everyone else remained motionless under their blankets. Aaron watched his mother find what she was looking for and stiffly stand up. Apparently, she was also feeling the strain of the gurney from the night before. He smiled as she walked up to him with her Bible now in hand, blanket pulled tightly around her shoulders.

"Good morning, Mom," he whispered, giving her a smile.

"Hey, Aaron," she smiled back. "How are you feeling this morning?"

"Pretty stiff, I guess."

"Me too. I think I'm going to go sit and read by the river for a little bit," she said as she walked past him. "Don't worry, I'll stay out of sight," she called back over her shoulder.

Aaron didn't really know what to do while he waited for the others to wake up. There was no fire to tend and, therefore, no water to heat or wood to collect. *Oh well*, he thought, *people still have to drink*, so he grabbed a couple water bottles and walked to the little river. He was careful not to go the direction his mother had gone, knowing she would appreciate a little privacy. Still, he caught a glimpse of her through the trees; she sat with her arms wrapped tightly around her legs, her head resting on her knees. At first, he thought she was praying but, when she raised her head to wipe away a tear, he knew it was more than that.

She was the most amazing woman he knew. Not that he had known many since the war had started. Despite losing her husband suddenly and being forced to run, she hadn't let it change her. She still loved, taught, and cared for her children with everything she had. She even fought for people she'd never met, just because they were American. Sometimes, Aaron realized, he forgot she was only human. Seeing her sorrow and vulnerability reminded him she had not only lost her provider and protector; she had lost her best friend.

The camp was beginning to stir when Aaron returned. Seth was limping back from the trees *without* his crutches; their mother would have something to say about that. Soraya was helping Ty sit up and get comfortable. Leah was climbing out of her blankets.

"Where's Mama?" The inquiry came from a little face under a tousled mop of hair peeking out of the top of Caleb's blanket.

"She's down by the water having some alone time."

Aaron set the water bottles down and walked over to him with a sly smile. "You need a little morning snuggle, do you?"

"NO!" Caleb squealed as Aaron scooped him up, blanket and all, and sat down, tying him up in a tight squeeze.

Everyone looking on smiled in amusement as the wrestling match began. Seth called out encouragement as Caleb tried to squirm, kick, and punch his way out of his brother's hold. After a couple minutes, he finally escaped from Aaron's grasp and everyone cheered the indignant victor.

"Nice moves, kid," Aaron laughed, standing up and dusting himself off.

"Who's ready for some breakfast?" Leah interjected, holding up a ready-to-eat meal taken from the outpost.

"I am!" Caleb volunteered.

Everyone found a seat to enjoy their odd assortment of semi-edible substances someone, somewhere, had labeled as food and sold to the military to keep their soldiers alive. While they were eating, Sara returned from the river and rejoined the group. She had a smile on her face, but Aaron could see the traces of tears water had failed to wash away. Leah must have seen them too, because she quickly got up and brought her mother some breakfast with extra care.

"Thank you, honey," Sara smiled reassuringly at her daughter's clearly concerned look. "Well, team," she turned to face everybody, "how is everyone this morning?"

"Wonderful!" exclaimed Soraya, "It's amazing how a little freedom can raise the spirits."

"And how taking it away can dampen them," Seth interrupted sourly, kicking a crutch away with his good leg.

"Speaking of which . . ." Aaron piped up, "Seth, tell Mom how helpful you found your crutches already this morning while you were up and about."

The blood quickly rose in Seth's face as his eyes shot daggers at his brother. Sara, putting two and two together, quickly turned to her son.

"Seth Redding! Do I have to keep my eyes on you every minute? Whose team are you on? We need that leg to heal!"

Seth hung his head, a frustrated sigh escaping him. "You're right, Mom. I'm sorry."

Sara turned back to her breakfast and Seth grabbed the crutch he could still reach. Glaring at Aaron, he tossed it at his older brother's feet and declared in a low voice, "By the way, these crutches suck!"

"Feel free to make your own!" Aaron threw back.

"Maybe I will!"

"Boys!" Sara stopped them. "This isn't helping. Aaron, let's talk about the plan."

"Ok . . . Mom and I decided while we were walking yesterday that we need to hole up here for a couple days and take it easy. We're in a good spot, close to water but not the main river, and there isn't much chance we'll be looked for this far away from the base. We still need to be careful about fires, but we should be fine here. After a couple days to recover, hopefully Seth and Ty will be good to go again and we'll get moving."

Everyone either murmured or nodded their agreement, and then the ladies offered to clean up breakfast. Seth and Caleb wandered off into the woods determined to "make the greatest crutches the world had ever seen."

Early that afternoon, Leah found herself leaning against a tree staring at nothing while her hands mindlessly fiddled with a broken twig. Suddenly, something nudged her foot. Looking up, Soraya's grinning face met her surprised expression.

"Hey, you, I'm tired of sitting. There must be some blackberries or raspberries around here somewhere the birds haven't found yet. Wanna come with me to look for some?"

Soraya's adventuresome smile was irresistible, and Leah jumped up to accept the invitation. She hadn't had a friend nearby since she was six and, once the war began five years ago, she had never again had the chance to see the ones who were far away. To say she was starved for female friendship would be an understatement. Her brothers were nice and her mother was understanding, but none of them could fill her desire for a true friend.

The girls started off, exploring the woods to the north of their camp. The dense undergrowth hampered their quest as they hopped from one game trail to another, looking for places where the sunlight reached far enough through the trees to ripen some berries.

"So, how long have you guys been on the run?" Soraya ventured, holding up a thin branch for Leah to duck under.

"I don't know. We left on . . . let's see, I guess it was Friday. So, that would make it only five days ago. Wow, it feels like so much longer than that since Daddy was killed."

"Oh, I'm so sorry!" Soraya said gently, "I didn't intend to bring up bad memories; I didn't know."

"No, it's ok. I guess we just haven't talked about it much."
Leah looked away, trying to blink back tears which had risen
involuntarily.

"He must have been an amazing man to have a family like
yours. To figure all this out and survive, and then take on an entire
outpost just to save a few strangers. I wish I could have met him."

"Our neighbor set us up and the Chinese came for him and
Aaron. We killed them all, but not before . . ."

Leah suddenly surged forward through the trees, overcome by
the images floating through her head she had tried so hard to bury.
Running wouldn't make them disappear. She knew that. But if she
didn't do something, she would break. Finally, her tears dried, and
her heart quieted enough for her to slow down to a walk once
more. Able to notice her surroundings again, she saw she had run
right up to the edge of a berry thicket.

Remembering Soraya, she felt guilty and looked back to see
her companion had been keeping up with her at a distance. She
smiled at her new friend gratefully and motioned to the thicket.

"Look! Berries!"

The girls had found an area where several raspberry plants held
a healthy crop of juicy, dark fruit. It was so nice to eat something
fresh for a change that each of them had consumed a large handful
before remembering the others at camp.

"You don't suppose we should bring any of these back for the
gang, do you?" Soraya asked mischievously, popping another juicy
morsel into her mouth.

"Well, at this rate there won't be any to bring back anyway!"
Leah giggled, then sighed. It felt so good to laugh. It felt even
better to have a friend.

"I guess we better bring *some* back or they'll never forgive us."

The girls began filling the wide mouthed water jug Leah had
brought along.

"So, what about you, Soraya? What's your story?"

Soraya looked at Leah thoughtfully, as if considering what to say. Leah met the look and saw such a deep mixture of sorrow, love, and even compassion flowing out of Soraya's very soul; she almost felt like weeping without having heard a single word.

"Well, we lost our parents at the beginning of the war. Ty kept us hidden, and we learned how to survive in a big city torn apart by fear and hate. Then, one day Russians appeared out of nowhere. We escaped across the river only to fall into the hands of the Chinese."

Leah was beginning to think Soraya was sparing her too many details until she heard the word *Russians*. "Russians? We've never heard about any Russians!"

"Really? Well, we never saw any again."

"So, you've been a prisoner all this time? Since the Chinese first came?"

"Pretty much, yes."

"That's awful! How did you . . . I mean, did they . . .?"

"They never hurt me. They worked me plenty hard but, I don't know, maybe it was all my mama's prayers since I was little. My faithful Father kept me safe. And then He sent us you!" She finished with a huge smile. "It's so good to be free!"

It seemed like a short time later their jug was half full and they decided they had better return to camp before anyone began to worry.

That evening, Aaron decided to risk a fire. He had never understood how something as simple as a campfire could change the entire atmosphere, but he knew he'd never deny its power. The flames seemed to invite peace and reflection. People relaxed in its warmth and it took the awkwardness out of silence. Hot food, even if it did come straight from a can, was a feast.

They shared their tin cups, sipping some of the tea they had found in the cabin. The song of nearby frogs filled the air as the sun slipped behind the horizon. The scent of autumn surrounded them, warm enough to give a false sense of security to unwary travelers, crisp enough to light the embers of the slowly changing maple leaves.

The day of rest had been good for all of them. Ty was moving around a little better, Seth's leg had stopped bleeding, and he and Caleb had diligently labored over designing a comfortable and durable pair of crutches. Everyone's spirits were high.

After darkness fell, one by one, everyone slowly retired to their blankets and dreams until only Ty and Aaron were left, sitting in the flickering glow of the flames.

"So, why did you guys risk your lives to rescue us?" Ty asked, staring into the fire.

"We heard the sirens go off in the distance," Aaron began, "so we decided to investigate and, when we did, we saw Americans being held captive. We worked out a plan, decided it was possible and worth it, and, well, we did it," Aaron answered matter-of-factly.

"Americans," Ty scoffed. "America is dead."

Aaron snorted.

"What?"

"I used to think the same thing," Aaron replied.

There was a minute of awkward silence. Then, lost in bitter memories, Ty spoke. "Our daddy was African American, a Baptist preacher in St. Paul. He went on a missions trip to South Korea fresh out of seminary. While he was there, he fell in love with a beautiful Korean woman, a pastor's daughter. The trip was only a month long, but during the last week he asked the Korean pastor if he could marry his daughter. He knew it was a long shot, but he loved her. The pastor was so impressed with my father he actually said yes. They were married the day before he had to leave.

"Together, they built a mission in St. Paul and raised my sister and me. Their last project was a mission to reach out to the incoming Somali refugees with love and care, helping them get settled and such.

"When the civil war broke out a bunch of white folks showed up at our door. My father hid Soraya and me in a closet. Then, he and my mom went to confront the mob. I could hear people yelling at my dad, calling him a Muslim, trash, telling him to go back where he came from . . . I guess they didn't know he was born in Detroit. There were gunshots. I heard my mom screaming, 'Oh, my God, Jesus, no!' in her Korean accent."

Ty paused and only the bullfrogs dared break the silence. After a minute passed, he took a deep breath and continued.

"After the gunshots stopped, I could hear the mob move off down the street. I waited a few minutes and crept out of the closet to the front door. I told Soraya to wait in the closet, but she didn't listen. She beat me to the door and opened it.

"I can still hear her wailing as she collapsed next to my parents." His voice grew harder. "I can still remember the sight of my father's chest riddled with holes and half of my mother's face missing. They shot her in the back of the head." Ty finished through clenched teeth, bitter tears burning down his ebony cheeks. "America is dead. It died with my mother. It died with my father."

For a moment, both young men sat staring into the flames, both a million miles away, to a place, a time, before this night—lost in pain time could not wash away.

Ty finally broke the silence. "My parents were good people, and I have hated whites since that day," he quietly declared, staring into Aaron's own tear-filled eyes.

Aaron cleared his throat. Swallowing hard, he spoke, "When I watched my father take his last breath, his life pouring out of a hole in his back as I held him in my arms, I thought my life was over. He was my world, my hero, my friend. He was my America.

Our neighbor, someone we trusted, sold us out to the Chinese, and my father was now dead. That was all the proof I needed that America was dead. Then, my mom reminded me of what my dad had taught us, what he believed, and how he lived. He used to say apples come in many colors but, at the core, they're all apples. He would say individual apples can have bad spots, but it doesn't make them a bad apple. But if an apple is rotten at the core, it's a rotten apple. You wouldn't throw out an entire apple tree because it had a pail of bad apples. That would be foolish. When you look at it that way, the type of apple tree doesn't matter at all really, only the individual apples. He said it was the same way with Americans; at the core, we're simply Americans. It's the condition of each core which determines a bad American from a good one. We may have different skin tones, but America is a color of the heart.

"My dad believed people make up America, not the land or the government. The people. People who believe in the freedom of all mankind, who believe by working together anything is possible, who are proud to work hard, and overcome challenges in the hope of a better tomorrow. Those people are rare; they're Americans, and they're worth dying for. That's what my father believed. It's what I'm trying to believe too."

Aaron met Ty's gaze. "If we keep our parents' America alive in our hearts, then they didn't die for nothing. The real reason we fought for you is because my father lived and died showing us how. As long as we're alive, Ty, then America is too."

The two of them sat in silence, the flames of the fire a blur. They were orphans. Orphans without the strength left to look at one another, lost in space and in time, lost in pain. Lost.

Ty struggled to his feet, blinking away tears he had not allowed to fall, he walked stiffly to his place next to Soraya and buried his pain in his makeshift pillow.

Looking to the star-laden sky, Aaron said, "I'm doing my best, Dad, I don't know what else to do."

The next day passed much like the previous one, except Ty seemed to avoid conversation as much as possible. No one thought much about it since it made sense he would have a lot on his mind. Only Aaron knew the heavy nature of what that was.

Ty and Seth were mending nicely and, though they wouldn't be able to travel fast, it was time to start plotting the next leg of the journey. Late that night, Sara and her two oldest sons sat alone by the fire. A question had been tugging at the back of Aaron's mind all day, but he hadn't had a chance to bring it up until now.

"We haven't decided if Ty and Soraya will be staying with us or striking off on their own."

Looking up in surprise, Sara replied. "Of course, they'll be staying with us. Ty isn't capable of taking care of them yet." The idea of her family separating from the brother and sister had never occurred to Sara; she found herself scrambling to wrap her mind around the disagreeable line of thought.

"He's stronger than you give him credit for, Mom. Besides, if they don't go looking for trouble, like we seem to be doing, they won't need to defend themselves. The woods are plenty thick enough for two people to remain invisible. I like the idea of them staying with us too, but that's two more mouths to feed, two more people to hide and take care of in emergencies. It's more risk. I just don't know. What do you think, Seth?"

"No, wait," Sara interrupted, eyes flashing. "You can't just send them away. They need us! We're the only family they have! Besides, they'd be an asset to our team!"

"Mom," Seth stepped in, "Everyone else we've saved also needed us, but we never brought them along, and for good reason. If we say yes to one person, where do we draw the line? We can't feed and protect a big group of people. Ty is gonna slow us down even more than my leg will. What if something bad happens? One weak link is enough. We can't afford two."

Sara's eyes darted back and forth between her sons in growing despair. Her mind couldn't argue with their logic, but her mother's heart searched for an alternative. "There has got to be a way to make it work," she reasoned in frustration.

"I've already been wracking my brain, and I can't think of a solution. Every possible scenario brings more difficulties, more risk. I tried, Mom. It just doesn't seem smart to stay together." Aaron threw his hands in the air.

A voice spoke from the shadows. "We'll be leaving in the morning, so you don't need to worry about it." Ty stepped into the light of the small fire.

"Ty, that's not necessary, we're just trying to figure things out," Sara said quickly, looking at the others to back her up. Seth's eyes never left the fire. Aaron said nothing.

"No, it's fine. We can take care of ourselves," Ty replied resentfully, then trudged back into the shadows.

"Perfect, boys! That was just perfect!" Sara exploded.

"Seth's right, Mom. We can't continue with two invalids and hope to make it with any time to spare to prepare for winter. And I, for one, don't plan on leaving Seth behind," Aaron spoke in their defense.

"How do you know, Aaron? How do you know we wouldn't make it in time?" Sara said, exasperated.

"I don't know for sure, but today is October 1st. By mid-November we'll be freezing to death and, in case you haven't noticed, we aren't moving very fast! What point is there in rescuing these two if we all end up dead in the end? If we get caught one of these days, I can help Seth make a run for it. I can't carry two, Mom! I'm not trying to screw anyone here—I just want us to live; I want us all to live!" Aaron's eyes filled with tears as he realized he was standing and all but shouting at his mother.

Sitting back down, he said, "I—I'm sorry, Mom, I'm doing the best I can . . ." His words trailed off.

"I know, Aaron," Sara said softly. "I'm sorry, too." She inhaled deeply and let it out. "Let's just go to bed. We're all tired. We can figure it out in the morning."

They nodded their agreement, and Aaron volunteered to take first watch. Neither Sara nor Seth argued with him.

"I love you," Sara said fondly, giving Aaron a half hug.

"I know, Mom."

Frustration and sorrow hung over everyone. They were angry but not with each other; they were angry with the situation, with what had become of people, of America. It wasn't right to make friends and then have to run them off.

The world wasn't right.

Chapter 7

Ty and Soraya left at first light, just as Ty had promised. Seth had the last watch of the night and saw them off. Leah had helped Soraya put together a pack for the two of them before they left the cabin, so they had adequate supplies, including a couple Chinese QBZ-95's with extra magazines, more medical dressings for Ty, some field rations swiped from the outpost, and a few essential tools they would need.

Seth gave Ty a compass he found in the cabin. "Head north," he told them, "Maybe we'll see each other again someday."

Soraya told him to thank their mother for all her help and to tell Leah goodbye.

It was another hour before Seth got the rest of the family up and moving; he wanted to give Ty some time to put distance between them. It would be easier that way.

"Where's Ty?!" Sara asked him the moment she climbed out of her blankets, hands on her hips.

"He and Soraya left at first light and, before you say anything, there was no changing his mind," Seth answered defensively.

"Ty knows what he's doing, Mom. They'll be alright." Aaron backed up his brother.

"They've lasted this long, and that's saying something," Seth tried to reassure her.

Sara nodded her acknowledgment, but she didn't like it. "I'm going to get some water." She grabbed an empty water jug and headed to the river.

"I already got us some," Seth called after her, but it didn't matter.

"Let her go, bro, she just needs to think it through, that's all, she'll be ok," Aaron said, helping himself to the water jug Seth was holding, and taking a swallow. He handed the jug back, "Let's get ready to move out."

By the time Sara returned with more water, the camp was all but packed up. The older boys helped Caleb get his pack back in order while Leah and Sara cooked up a little freeze-dried breakfast for everyone.

"How's the leg, Seth?" Sara asked.

"Stiff, sore, and ready to go."

"I still want you using those crutches."

"That's why I'm holding them," he replied sarcastically.

"Holding them isn't the same as using them."

Aaron cleared his throat, "I think we'll shoot for six miles today. The map shows an obscure little road, looks like there might have been a couple of houses on it. Maybe we can scrounge up a few supplies and, if the area looks clear, sleep on a bed again. I think we should take it easy on that leg for a few more days; we have a long way to go yet."

"I could make it ten miles," muttered Seth under his breath.

After breakfast, the band got their gear together and hit the trail. Aaron insisted Caleb take point, knowing his little legs would keep the pace more manageable for Seth, but he didn't say as much.

The six-mile trek took nearly the whole day. Sara insisted they take a long lunch break to give Seth some time to rest. It was four in the afternoon by the time the five of them sat hunched in the brush at the edge of what had once been the yard of a small hobby farm. Seth took out the binoculars and glassed the area, while the rest of them listened intently for any signs of human life.

"Are those . . . chickens?" whispered Leah.

"I hear it too," Caleb said.

Seth swung his gaze toward the barn just as three hens strutted into the barnyard. "They're chickens alright," he said.

"That could mean people," Aaron reasoned.

Sara pulled up her rifle, resting it on a branch, she scanned the house. "Looks deserted. The roof is caving in on the one side and some of the glass is broken in the lower story windows. Still, I think you and I should go check it out. Seth can cover us with my rifle."

"Yeah, I think so too," Aaron agreed. "Let's head up behind the propane tank and then hit the front door."

Sara handed Seth her rifle and unslung the Chinese QBZ-95 from his shoulder. "You good, Seth?" she had noticed him leaning heavily on his crutches for the last mile.

"Yeah." He winced as he assumed a kneeling position. "I got your back."

Aaron and Sara cleared the house in a matter of minutes; the only occupants were a couple of stray cats. They gave the all clear and Caleb and Leah approached the house with Seth hobbling along beside them.

Leah and Caleb spent the remaining daylight trying to catch one of the feral chickens while Seth laid on the only mattress in the house that had not been completely ruined by rodents. Aaron was busy leaning over the map on the porch charting their progress and figuring out the next step, while Sara cooked up a couple cans of stew from the cabin.

"It's hard to believe chickens have survived out here all this time," she commented in Aaron's direction.

"Uh huh. Pretty crazy," Aaron absently replied, without looking up from his map.

Seeing her first attempt at conversation had fallen flat, she tried again, "So, how are we doing?"

"Well, at our current pace, if we only stop and rest every few days, and there are no more surprises, we should get there in about twenty to twenty-five days. That's cutting it pretty close, Mom, I don't know if we'll have enough time before the cold hits."

She walked over to the deck and sat down next to him. "What about hopping a train?"

Aaron's gaze followed his mother's finger as she pointed to a set of tracks on the map. He hadn't even considered a train.

"It could save us a lot of time, and effort, for that matter," she added.

He considered the possibility for a moment. "I think it might be possible if we boarded the train here as it left Hinckley. It would have to slow down near the turn, and we could jump on one of the cars. We would have to jump off while it was rolling somewhere before Duluth. I assume Duluth is where the trains are heading, with the port there. Unfortunately, that means there's bound to be a crap ton of soldiers. *But* it could save us a week and a half of walking," he said, raising his eyebrows. "Maybe more."

"Do you think it's actually possible?"

"Won't know till we get there and scope it out. If it's possible, it'll be dangerous."

"What isn't dangerous anymore?" Sara sighed.

"Mom, look! We caught one!" Leah exclaimed, running up to them clutching a red hen in her arms, her little brother close behind.

"Wow!" smiled Sara, "I had no doubt you guys would get one sooner or later."

"Let's eat it," Aaron suggested with a wink.

"NO! Arrrggg, Aaron! We're going to *keep* it!" Leah retorted, stomping her foot down.

"Leah, how on earth are we going to keep it? We're on the move all the time. It'll just run away the first time you put it down," Sara stated sympathetically.

"Oh, let her keep it."

Everyone turned to see Seth leaning in the doorway.

"Look, you won't let me do anything anyway. Let me make her a leash for it, and I'll scrounge up something for her to carry it in. Who knows, maybe it'll lay eggs."

"Oh please, Mama, please let me keep her. I already gave her a name—Daisy. I'll take good care of her," Leah pleaded.

Sara looked at Aaron, who just shrugged his shoulders. "Well," she finally sighed, "I guess since you've already named it . . ."

"Thank you, Mama, thank you, thank you," Leah gushed, throwing one arm around her mother's neck, squeezing the hen between them.

"You're her new hero," Sara said dryly, looking at Seth.

"Awe, it's just proof we haven't lost our humanity," Seth replied as he and Leah headed off to the barn in search of a leash.

"Thanks for the backup, Aaron."

"Hey, she's not my kid," Aaron chuckled.

The rest of the evening went on without incident, everyone grateful for the hot stew. Watching Leah's chicken try to figure out her new leash provided some much-needed comedy. After the stew, they played a few hands of cards and then settled in for the night. As Aaron closed his eyes, he thought to himself, *A couple more days of walking and a train ride, and we could be halfway there.*

In the morning, Sara rebandaged Seth's leg, which was healing remarkably well considering the walking they had done. Leah stuffed Daisy in an old bowling ball bag Seth had found in one of the house's closets. Everyone pitched in and got their gear packed up, and they hit the trail again. Aaron was happy to leave Caleb at point. He seemed to enjoy it up there, and the pace agreed with Seth's leg.

"Looks like there will be a few houses near the end of today's trek; maybe we'll be able to rest indoors again tonight," Aaron said as they moved out.

They headed up the Kettle River valley toward the town of Hinckley. The valley wasn't nearly as broad, nor as densely wooded, as the St. Croix River valley, and Aaron couldn't help but feel like his little band was more exposed than ever. He hated the thought of going anywhere near "civilization," but the possibility of knocking seventy or eighty miles off their trip was too good to pass up. They desperately needed the time it would buy them. Winter would be a foe with its own fury, and it would take time to prepare for it.

As they plodded along, Aaron found himself captivated by the mosaic of foliage that danced in the breeze all around them. Beautiful blazing maples, golden poplars, crimson oaks, and amber tamarack mixed with a splash of evergreen here and there. The sight was breathtaking and, like Soraya, it seemed out of place in the world Aaron knew.

A smile crept across his face, *Soraya* . . .

By the time they stopped for lunch, Aaron was starting to wish he had given his mother the backup she was looking for yesterday afternoon. That crazy chicken was going to get them all killed. As far as he was concerned, Leah might as well be carrying a siren that said, "Stupid Americans hiding over here!" The hen simply would not shut up. There were a couple times on the trail he was sure Seth was going to blow the hen off the face of the earth.

"Leah, your chicken is driving me crazy," Seth complained as he sat down to rest.

Leah pulled the hen out of the bag and tied its leash to a small tree. Almost immediately, the chicken quieted down and began to rummage through the leaves looking for things to eat. She gently filled a small cupped leaf with water and gave it to Daisy.

"She's quiet now," Leah pointed out.

Slapping his forehead with his palm, Seth shot Aaron a look of exasperation.

Aaron just shrugged. "'Proof we haven't lost our humanity,'" he mimicked Seth.

Leah stuck out her tongue in Seth's direction and began talking to her pet. She tossed the chicken some crumbs from her lunch.

Looking on, Aaron wished more than ever he could give her a normal life. He envied her innocence. After all they had witnessed, after all they had done, she was still his sweet little sister. *Would there be anything of her left by the time they made it, if they made it?*

"Are we really going to ride a train, Aaron?" asked Caleb eagerly.

"If it seems safe enough, yes."

"I've always wanted to ride a train!"

"We have to get there first. Speaking of which, we better get moving again. A couple more hours, guys, and we'll call it a day."

Leah packed up Daisy, and they were back on the trail again. The next couple of hours passed quickly. Caleb set a brisk pace out of excitement over the possibility of riding a train. Daisy had resigned herself to the bag and was much more civil on this leg of the journey. Seth's mind was occupied with the pain in his leg at this pace and how best not to show it. Sara let her mind wander to days she had spent with John, walking in the woods on days like today.

Aaron could think only of the train. Would it work? What could go wrong? Where should they get off? By the time he had worked through all the possibilities of failure, he was about to call the whole thing off. But the nagging in his heart, brought on by a chill in the air, told him they had to try.

As the Reddings neared the end of the day, they heard the distressed sounds of a man's voice drifting through the trees, just off the river valley. Aaron moved to the front of their little column and signaled Sara to join him. Creeping to the edge of the woods, they peered out.

In front of them stood a farmhouse, in remarkable condition considering the times. It was two stories, dirty yellow with what used to be white trim. The shingles on the roof were old but still holding their own, and the windows were intact. Sara nodded toward a small patch of tilled earth containing tomato plants, a few stalks of corn, and what appeared to be some type of squash.

There was the voice again: pleading. This time, it was more distinct and seemed to be coming from the front yard.

"Why would you turn on your own?" the voice pleaded. "Please, just let me be. I won't be trouble to no one."

There was the sound of a fist striking flesh, and then the muttering of two other voices.

"I can't see, Mom, we have to move."

"It's a shorter distance to the back of the silo, next to the barn, I think we should be able to see from there."

"Better have that thing ready, this could be fast," Aaron warned, motioning to Sara's rifle as he switched off the safety on his AK-47.

The duo raced through the weed filled yard to the silo and dropped behind it. Aaron slipped between the two buildings and glassed the front yard. Two men, who appeared to be American, were hauling another man toward the road, his hands bound behind his back. A small truck waited at the end of the driveway, some sort of Chinese symbol on its door.

"Mom," he whispered. "You'd better come take a look."

Sara joined him at the opening, pulling up her rifle as the men came into view. "I think they're all American. But why . . .?" Sara asked.

"Keep your rifle on them, I'm going to try and talk to them. Something isn't right."

"Aaron!" Sara whispered loudly, but it was too late; he was already walking toward the men, his rifle at the ready.

"Excuse me!" Aaron said loudly.

The man closest to Aaron wheeled around, leveling his pistol in Aaron's direction.

A familiar *CRACK!* split the air and, before the man had even finished raising his arm, he was flung to the ground, blood oozing from a hole in his chest. Aaron lifted his gaze from the dead body to look at the other man just as the second shot went off.

The man's head jerked backward, and he crumpled to the ground. There it was again, that eerie silence, the silence of death. The bound man had fallen to his side on the ground, trembling.

A stunned, "Umm, are you alright?" was all Aaron could think of to say.

"Who are you?" the man asked, his voice quaking.

"I'm Aaron, and your Archangel over there is my mother, Sara." Aaron went over and helped the man back to his knees.

The man looked toward the silo where Sara now stood, her makeshift cloak waving in the wind, scanning their surroundings. She walked toward them tucking a loose strand from her ponytail back behind her ear.

"What did those men want with you?" she asked, not waiting for introductions.

"They were bounty hunters. Apparently, they don't have to live in the camps, or do any forced labor, if they hunt rogue Americans."

Aaron knelt behind the man and cut him free.

"Thank you," he returned, a little unsure. "My name's Mark. My wife and daughter are hiding in the house."

"I'll go get the others," Sara said, slinging her rifle over her shoulder.

"You and your family need to get out of here. Soon," Aaron told him firmly.

"This is my family's farm, has been for four generations, and I intend to hand it down to the fifth."

"You're kidding, right?"

"No, we've lasted this long. We intend to weather the storm." Aaron shook his head at the man's foolishness. "This isn't a storm! They're going to kill you and your family. This is their land now."

"Where would we go? The Chinese are everywhere; this is as good a place as any."

"Go north to the boreal forest. It would be a waste of resources to search the entire forest for a handful of American stragglers. Your odds of survival are much better there."

"We'd never survive the winter up there, and the trip would be the death of my wife and daughter!" Mark argued back.

"Americans hunting Americans; could it get any worse?" Seth asked as he approached.

"Mark, this is my brother, Seth, my sister, Leah, and this is Caleb."

"Nice to meet you all. Do you have a place to stay the night?"

"Well, we had considered staying here, but now we need to keep moving," Aaron spoke with determination. "The Chinese will miss those guys soon."

"No, they won't. The Chinese send them out, and I don't think they want them back until they have someone to turn in. Those two aren't the first bounty hunters to die here; they just got the jump on me this time. My wife and I would be honored to have you as our guests tonight."

Aaron looked around at the others. Everyone looked like they could use another night up off the ground.

"You're sure about the bounty hunters?"

The man nodded.

"Alright, we'll stay here for the night."

"Yessss!" cheered Caleb.

Mark went to the front door of the house and called inside, "Sue, Abbie, come out here. It's alright. I want you to meet some heroes."

In a few moments, a young woman appeared in the doorway. Around five feet tall, she had shoulder length red hair and flashing green eyes. She wore blue jeans and a gray sweater, which was beginning to separate at the left shoulder. By her side stood a girl who couldn't have been more than nine. She had her mother's hair and eyes, though her eyes were not quite as bright. She was barefoot, wearing a pink skirt and a purple hoodie.

"Oh, Mark, I heard the shots, and I was sure they had killed you," Sue clung to her husband, concern etched in her face.

"That was these kind folks here; they saved me. This lady here is a crack shot with that rifle." He patted his wife reassuringly and put his arm around his daughter. Holding out his hand to the Reddings, he began the introductions. "Everyone, this is my wife, Sue, and my princess, Abbie. Sue, Abbie, this is uhh . . ."

"I'm Sara, this is my eldest, Aaron, that's Seth, Leah, and this strapping young man is Caleb," Sara finished, putting her hand on Caleb's shoulder.

"They're gonna stay here for tonight," Mark said.

"Oh, that would be wonderful," Sue offered with a smile. "We haven't had guests since the second year of the war, well, welcome guests that is. I'm afraid I don't have much to cook up, just some venison Mark killed the other day with homemade tomato sauce."

"That would be absolutely heavenly!" Sara reassured the woman with a smile. "We haven't had fresh meat in over a week."

Everyone followed their hosts into the dim interior of the farmhouse. Little Abbie brought some water for her father and the Reddings to wash up with, and Sue got busy with dinner preparations.

As the adults began to settle around the big farm table in the kitchen, Abbie shyly walked up to Caleb and, tipping her little red head to the side, asked, "Would you like to play a game with me?"

"Uh, sure," he agreed, and followed her through the doorway into the next room.

It was only a matter of minutes before the sound of giggling drew Leah, bored with adult conversation, from her seat to join them.

Sara pulled the cleaning kit out of the butt stock of her rifle and quickly tore a small strip of cloth from the frayed edge of her canvas cloak to ram through the barrel as Mark was sharing the story of the last pair of bounty hunters who'd come by.

Aaron and Seth exchanged several looks as it became clearer by the moment the survival of Mark and his family, up until this point, had been through no fault of their own. Sue kept stealing curious glances at Sara's progress, obviously new to the concept of a gun savvy woman. Sara viewed her rifle as the most important possession she owned, and cleaning it was an art not to be rushed.

"You know, things are about to get really bad around here." Aaron felt obligated to educate this poor farmer on reality. "The Chinese are constantly expanding and, once winter hits, it will be next to impossible to hide. You'll eventually run out of ammo. If you leave now, you can get far enough north to be out of danger of discovery and can build a shelter in peace. Sure, it may be tough for a little while figuring it all out, but at least your wife and daughter won't be in danger from bounty hunters. I'm sure we could help you pull together some supplies and help you get on your way."

"I appreciate your concern, I really do. You already went out of your way to save me and mine, and I won't quickly forget that. This place has survived this long, and we have everything we need right here. We ain't about to walk away and start all over just 'cause of some trespassers."

It required all of Aaron's strength not to let his jaw drop in amazement. *What was this guy thinking?* He threw a quick look to Seth to make sure he was keeping his mouth shut. They were generous and gracious hosts, and a smart comment would be poor gratitude. Despite the man's apparent ignorance, Aaron respected the loyalty and determination on Mark's part.

"Well, we could at least lend you a hand with burying those bodies before we go."

"Wouldn't hear of it! You have plenty of walking ahead of you, no sense in breakin' your backs over those fellas. I'll just add 'em to the rest out back."

Sue then announced dinner was ready, and the Reddings enjoyed the best meal they had had in weeks. Shortly thereafter, they settled into two spare rooms: Sara and Leah in one, with the boys sharing the other. Mark offered to take watch so the travelers could get some real rest. Aaron didn't know if it was a good idea to accept the offer or not, but weariness won the argument and he retired with his brothers.

Chapter 8

In the morning, the Reddings gathered their gear and met on the front lawn. A south wind blew a warm breeze through the yard, and the sun seemed to shine with a warmer glow. They had eaten well, slept well, and enjoyed great company. Today, they would arrive in Hinckley where, if their luck held out, they could catch a train nearly all the way to Duluth.

"I wish you would reconsider and join us, Mark," Aaron offered once more, sticking out his hand.

"No, no, I have my mind made up. We're going to stay," Mark answered firmly, shaking his hand.

"Well, best of luck to you then. Might want to work on some fortifications, or maybe some sort of alarm system. I would hate for them to get the drop on you again."

"I just might do that. Thanks for saving my hide, Aaron."

"Thanks for allowing us to spend the night."

The two men parted ways. Leah gave Abbie a hug, and Abbie said goodbye to Daisy. Caleb waited his turn and handed Abbie an agate he had found on the trail.

"Something to remember me by," he said shyly.

Seth shook Mark's hand and followed Aaron while Sara gave Sue a hug.

"I hope to see you again someday, Sue," Sara said with a smile. "I'd love to get that venison recipe from you."

Sue smiled and nodded, wiping away tears. "God bless you all. Be safe."

With the goodbyes concluded, they fell into a column and disappeared into the forest.

Fifteen minutes down the trail, Caleb piped up. "How many miles are we walking today, Aaron?"

"According to the map, about six. But it's hard to tell for sure with the bends in the river."

"I miss Abbie," Caleb confessed in childish innocence.

"Liked her, did ya?" Aaron asked with a chuckle.

"She was really nice, and her hair was pretty, just like the leaves."

"Yeah, she was sweet. Maybe we'll see her again someday," he said it, though he highly doubted it.

Seth snorted sarcastically, which earned him a sharp glance from his mother.

"I hope so," Caleb said, sighing.

The warmer weather, combined with high spirits, aided the Reddings in making good time. They arrived at Grindstone River, a tributary of the Kettle which flows just north of Hinckley, at around three in the afternoon. Another half hour of walking and they were a quarter mile from the train tracks.

"The woods are pretty thick here. I think if we skip the fire tonight, we should be able to camp out here and gather a little intel. Leah, you must keep that chicken quiet or it's not going to make it. Feed it, talk to it, whatever you have to do. Mom, find a high spot where you can see the trains coming into town and where they begin to pick up speed on this side again. We need to know how much time we've got.

"Seth, I know you want to get back into the fight, but I need you. And that means your leg has to be one hundred percent. Stay here with Caleb and Leah, and keep your eyes peeled for Chinese troops or more of those bounty hunters. I'm going to get a little closer and glass the town from up in one of these trees, count troops, and see if I can figure out their patterns. If we all do our jobs, we just might get that train ride." Like a football quarterback calling a play, Aaron gave everyone their orders, then the huddle broke.

Sara liked Aaron's tree idea and found one for herself which gave her both cover and a clear line of sight to the town and also to the north of it where the tracks crossed the river. Aaron slipped into a tree thirty yards to her south and began his survey of the town with Seth's binoculars.

"Can't believe I'm stuck here babysitting," Seth moped.

"Who are you calling a baby!" Leah sassed. "I can do stuff. You guys just won't let me. I'm not a baby."

"Wow, sorry. Sheesh. I guess you just seem to, you know, be more like a kid."

"Well, I'm not. I'm older than you, Seth Redding! I just don't think all this planning, and shooting, and camping is all there is to life."

"It is right now."

"Maybe for you! I like to stop and see everything else going on in these woods that isn't us—isn't this stupid, broken world. Most of the time it just seems so hopeless. I hate thinking about it. I want to remember what it's like to be a normal human being, not just a soldier wondering if I'm even going to make it through the day."

"Girls!" Seth muttered.

"Grrr! Seth, you're so frustrating!"

"Frustrated is more like it."

Leah rolled her eyes, "I'm done talking to you. Caleb, let's just play some cards."

It was midnight before Aaron and Sara returned to camp. They had watched two trains come and go, moving around what seemed to be troops, supplies, and coal.

There was a small depot guarded by only a handful of troops, but the small number of guards didn't really help because the barracks building, holding plenty of backup, was within fifty feet of the lone guard tower. The depot was well lit at night; they would need to be sure not to board the train until it was beyond the lighted area.

The good news was that both trains had many flatbed cars they could easily jump on, and the trains took a good long while before getting up any real speed after leaving the depot.

"So, what do you think?" Aaron asked Sara as they walked back to camp.

"I think we should scout it out for another day but, if tomorrow is anything like tonight, it seems doable."

"The guards in town seem pretty complacent. If we wait until the train cleared the lights and boarded it in the pitch dark, the engineers would have no way of knowing we were on board. We just may catch a break here."

"Does it look possible?" Seth asked, rising as they approached.

"We're going to give it another day but, from what we could see, it looks fairly easy to pull off," Sara replied confidently.

"Tomorrow maybe we should all go. You know, so we can get a feel for it," Seth offered.

"It's not a horrible idea. It takes a lot of patience, though. What do you think, Aaron?" Sara said, looking at Aaron.

"You all would have to keep quiet; we don't want to blow this," Aaron warned. "Now, let's get some sleep. It's late."

Aaron had taken the last watch and, although the sun was already up, he decided to let everyone sleep in. It would be a long night, but one he hoped would lead to a train ride north sometime in the next few days. He took the time alone to reflect on how far they had come.

"Thank you, Lord, for getting us this far," he prayed, studying the map.

Inhaling deeply, the familiar smell of autumn leaves filled his nostrils. Chipmunks scrapped over nuts a few feet away. The Grindstone River flowed by, carrying fallen leaves on its swift, crystal currents. The poplars surrounding their little camp swayed in the morning breeze. It was a beautiful morning. In another life they may have stopped here on vacation. He sighed. *In another life* . . .

"We *have* gotten pretty far, haven't we?"

"Mom!" Aaron spun around at the voice behind him. "When did you . . .?"

"Well, let's see, sometime after your eyes closed and before they opened again." She smiled, "Don't worry, son, I had your back. This has been a long and heavy journey for you; many an older man would have quit by now. You're doing well, Aaron."

He looked down at the map still in his lap to hide his embarrassment. Her confidence meant the world to him.

"By the way, I've been meaning to ask you, why do you keep introducing me as an archangel?"

He glanced up, a little surprised by the question. Chuckling, he started his explanation. "Well, you remember Tom and Kathy? So, when we went down there, after you had blown those PLA to kingdom come, Kathy kept going on and on about being saved by an archangel of God or something. At the time, I thought it was ridiculous, a joke. At first, it was just kind of humorous to introduce you that way. Then, the more I thought about it, the more I realized you've always *been* that person, even before all this started—watching over us, keeping us safe. I always knew, no matter what kind of trouble Seth and I got into, you would get us home. Knowing you're out there, well, it helps me do my part. . . .

So, I guess that makes you our archangel," he finished, shrugging his shoulders.

"You really think all that about me? Wow," Sara said in surprise. "Well, I am honored to be your archangel, Aaron. I pray I can be that person for you always." She walked up to where her son still sat and, leaning over, planted a kiss on the top of his head before walking back to her place next to Caleb.

The Reddings spent most of the day in preparation for that night. Sara and Aaron decided everyone might as well take all their gear with them on the scouting mission; there wouldn't be anyone in camp to watch it and, if something went wrong, they might need to bug out in a hurry. For Caleb, night couldn't come soon enough. He had been waiting to take a train ride all his life and, if everything went well, he would get his chance very soon.

Finally, the sun had set and, as the last light of dusk began to fade, the Redding family positioned themselves on the north side of Hinckley, a hundred yards from the tracks.

"The first train came in last night at around 7:00 p.m. That's in about half an hour. I guess we'll see if they're on any sort of a schedule," Aaron whispered.

At 6:50 p.m. the sound of a train heading up the tracks percolated through the trees.

"It's a train!" Caleb whispered, a big grin on his face.

"Right on time," Leah added.

The train was fifty cars long, most of them a rusty orange, some still bore faint graffiti from before the war. About half of the cars were full of coal; the other half were flatbeds with various materials and supplies strapped down by thick tie downs. The train creaked and clattered as it slowed down near the depot. Apparently, this train was just passing through. It never stopped, but still took a while to pick up speed on the north side of town.

"We could make that jump easily," Seth whispered.

"There's probably going to be a second train tonight. We already have all our gear . . . maybe we should just go tonight," Sara reasoned.

"Oh yes, Aaron, please!" begged Caleb.

"I don't know. It seems like we should have no problem, but what if we haven't thought of everything yet? What if something terrible happens because we didn't slow down and think?" Aaron countered.

"There's no way to plan for everything, son. If there was, your father would be here," Sara gently replied.

"I wish he was here," Aaron sighed. "Alright, if the train arrives on time, and everything seems clear, we'll go tonight."

"Yay!" Caleb excitedly whispered.

Aaron couldn't help but be a bit excited himself; he was tired of walking, and just a few hours on the train would cut their trip by a week and a half.

As the time neared eleven o'clock, the Reddings moved into position under the edge of the train bridge. Aaron was positioned roughly twenty yards from the bridge between two stacks of old railroad ties. He had a clear line of sight down the tracks and would be able to signal the others when it was time to make their move.

The faint rattling of a train quickened Aaron's pulse. He looked over toward the others, their silhouettes barely visible in the moonlight. He couldn't see them, but he knew that from their haunt under the bridge, they had to know the train was coming.

The train groaned as it slowed down near the depot. Aaron watched a few soldiers get off and a few of the soldiers from the depot board one of the first few cars. Then, she was moving again, ever so slowly. Hunkering down in his hiding spot, Aaron held his breath as the engine and first few cars lumbered by. He slipped his head around the corner of the pile, watching the cars. The first twenty cars or so were full of coal; the next several were flatbeds of supplies. By the time the last coal car had rumbled by, the train was moving briskly. Aaron trotted over to the bridge.

"Get ready," he hissed loudly.

The first few flatbeds were nearly empty, with only a few items tied down under tarps. Then came the car Aaron had been waiting for. It was loaded with stacks of crates at various heights with a somewhat open area near the center.

"This one!"

Aaron grabbed Caleb and threw him on board, gear and all. Seth and Sara managed by themselves. Then, together, they helped a timid Leah safely on board. Lastly, Aaron jumped on. Taking one last look back at the depot, he smiled. No one had noticed them.

"Are we all good? Is everybody good?" Aaron asked into the near darkness.

"Yep," Sara answered back. "Caleb, come over here by me; here's a spot we can lay down. Leah, do you have enough room there?"

"Yeah, I think so."

"Wow," Seth gave a half laugh, "was it really that easy? We should've done this at the beginning!"

"I know," Aaron agreed. "It's nice for something to be simple for a change. We won't be on here long though. Let's get a little sleep if we can. We're gonna have to jump in two to three hours. Seth, would you mind taking watch? I'm running on empty."

"Uh, sure, I can do that."

"Ok, just keep your eyes forward. We have no idea what's up ahead. If nothing comes up before, watch for signs that we're approaching Duluth. Wake us up, and we'll jump as soon as the train slows down for a hill or curve."

"Ok," Seth said, slight hesitation in his voice.

The rest of the family adjusted themselves as best they could in the dark and fell asleep. Away from the lights of Hinckley, the night was dark. Clouds hid most of the stars, and the glimmer of the slight moon was too faint to reach between the crates of the flat car carrying the Redding family north.

Seth grunted softly as he shifted his weight away from his sore leg. He had never admitted it, but the pain of his wound had been taking its toll on him. Most nights, the constant discomfort had kept him from sleeping well. It was getting better though. Yesterday had been the most pain free he'd felt yet. Even so, all he wanted to do was sleep . . . instead, he was on watch. He didn't mind. Aaron needed the rest too. After all, Aaron did far more watches than anyone else; he deserved the break.

He tipped his head to the right to see further down the tracks. The soft glow from the massive headlights illuminated the way ahead, but otherwise the world was blanketed in blackness. Leaning his head against a large crate, Seth could feel his weariness overtake him and the vibrating motion of the deceptive iron serpent lulled him to sleep.

Chapter 9

Someone was shaking him vigorously.

"Seth! Seth! Wake up! We have to jump—now!"

Cracking his eyes, the world was still dark, and the train seemed to be slowing. *The train was slowing!* Seth bolted up, wide awake.

"Seth, we have to jump now!" Aaron shouted, pulling him to his feet.

Seth steadied himself, his mind reeling. Aaron handed him his pack. Down the tracks, he saw a light—and soldiers, the engine already beyond them. Someone took his hand.

"Alright! On three. One, two, three!"

Together, they jumped from the train, rolling to the bottom of the soggy ditch.

Shouting and rifle fire broke out from the direction of the lights. The Chinese had seen them.

"Mom! Mama, don't leave me!"

In horror, Sara looked up from the ditch to see Caleb clutching tightly to a crate, still standing on the edge of the flatbed, the Chinese almost upon him. "NO!" she cried, chambering a round and swinging up her rifle simultaneously.

"No, Mom!" Aaron whispered, urgently pulling her barrel toward the ground. "There are too many! If we start shooting, we're all dead: Caleb, too!"

Sara wrenched her gun back and Aaron had to wrap his arms around her to keep her from shooting. "He's my son, he's my son!" she groaned through clenched teeth as she fought against him.

"Mom!" Aaron held her face in his hands looking straight into her panic-stricken eyes. He repeated, "If you want to save him, we have to survive this!"

The cry from the flat bed had drawn the attention of the Chinese from Aaron and the others, and several soldiers were swarming toward the little boy. The rest of the Reddings used the unfortunate diversion to move from the ditch to thicker cover, watching helplessly as the PLA snatched a terrified Caleb from the train. He thrashed wildly, but the two men who reached him first had little trouble throwing him from the train into the waiting arms of a dozen soldiers. For a few moments, they only shouted at him in Mandarin. Then, binding his hands, they put him back on the train along with several soldiers.

As the train pulled away, Caleb disappeared with it into the darkness. Sara fought the urge to run after him. She looked on, unable to comprehend what had just happened, but there wasn't time for processing. With Caleb securely on the train, the PLA had fanned out in search of the rest of the stowaways.

"We gotta go, we're the only hope he has," Aaron whispered urgently. "Seth, grab Mom, don't let her go. Move now!" They headed off, quickly and quietly, into the darkness.

The swamp they had landed in was thick with young poplars and dogwood brush. It didn't take them long to circumnavigate the small depot and the pursuing soldiers; they had done this many times in the swamps back home. After putting plenty of distance between themselves and the PLA, Aaron thought it best to hole up for the rest of the night. The reality of what had just happened was finally breaking through, and they needed to get their bearings. They needed a plan. Dropping their packs on the ground, the four of them sank to their knees in physical and emotional exhaustion.

"It's all my fault, Mom! I fell asleep. I should have told you I was so tired, but I didn't want to let everyone down. I'm so sorry," Seth whispered, tears running down his face, his head in his hands.

"No, it's my fault, Seth, we should never have gotten on that train. I knew it would be dangerous. I just couldn't see past the time it would save us," Aaron protested, putting his hand on his brother's shoulder.

He looked toward their mother. She remained where she had dropped, panting from their escape. What bothered him was she wasn't moving. Her face was like a stone, her eyes staring blankly.

"Mom?" Aaron whispered. She made no response. "Mom!"

Her head snapped up at the sharp sound, her eyes bearing the agony of her soul. Then, she crumbled. "We have to get him, Aaron. He's alone! What if they're hurting him? What if they send him to China or kill him? He's just a boy. Did you see his face when they grabbed him? He was screaming for me, and I did nothing!" She began to rock back and forth in the dark, hugging her knees, trying to keep herself together. "My baby . . ." she murmured.

Leah had begun to cry softly. Caleb may have been her little brother, but he was more like her son. She had helped her mother care for him since his birth, watched him, played with him, and taught him. All she could envision now was the Chinese torturing her terrified little brother.

Aaron could not afford such thoughts. Once again, a world of responsibility had been thrust upon him, and there was no hiding from it. Again, he was forced to stow his emotions in order to keep his ship afloat. Was he terrified for his brother? Absolutely. But the others would never know it. As long he kept himself occupied with "The Mission," he knew he could hold himself together.

"We'll get him, Mom. We'll find a way, and we *will* get him," Aaron vowed.

The cool night seemed to resist the dawn as the remaining hours of darkness lagged on. Finally, a sliver of gray took hold in the east, and Aaron breathed a sigh of relief; the dawn had not deserted him. He grabbed Seth, and they started back toward the tracks to get their bearings.

Caleb stood trembling before an angry PLA officer. He had arrived in Duluth an hour after his capture and had immediately been thrown into an empty shipping container until morning. Caleb was not so grateful for the dawn, with it had come more shouting soldiers, and now this guy.

The man muttered something in Mandarin and an interpreter translated it for Caleb.

"I am Captain Li, the Chief Security Officer of this district and commander of this post. What is your name?"

"Caleb."

"Do you know why you are here?"

"No."

"You are here because your family has abandoned you."

"That's not true!"

The officer raised his hand holding a bamboo cane. Caleb cringed and the officer lowered his arm.

"My soldiers tell me you were not the only one riding our train. The rest jumped off and left you there. Do you know where they were going?"

"No."

The officer raised his hand again.

"I don't, I promise. I'm just a kid."

The officer's cane slammed into Caleb's cheek, nearly knocking him to the ground.

"Where were they going?!" the translator asked again.

Tears filled Caleb's eyes as his mind raced to find something acceptable to say. When nothing came, he began crying helplessly. The officer, convinced he would get nothing more out of him at the moment, waved his hand, and the soldiers drug Caleb back to his container and threw him inside.

In the daylight, Caleb noticed a small tear in the container near the top of the back right corner. It was only three inches wide and eighteen inches high. He probably had a crane operator's mistake to thank for that. The narrow shaft of light revealed a roomy container, nearly twenty feet long, eight feet high, and eight feet wide.

So far, he was the sole occupant. A pile of folded cardboard lay near the back, otherwise it was empty. Caleb trudged to the back of the container and squatted down in the cardboard rubbing his cheek, trying to still the growing fear that threatened to overwhelm him.

Where is my mom? Where is Aaron?

Seth and Aaron returned to Sara and Leah. The brothers had only been gone an hour and, though Aaron would have liked to have gathered more information, he dared not leave his mother alone for very long.

"We're near the tiny township of Boylston, which is where Caleb was captured," Aaron said. Still panting, he pulled out his map to show her.

Sara leaned in close, anxious for anything that would get them on the move.

"We're here in this swamp. The tracks are here, and this must be some sort of turntable at Boylston. That's why there were troops here," Aaron explained.

"And Caleb?" Sara probed.

"These tracks only lead to Duluth; they must've taken him there. It makes sense; Duluth is an easy way to ship troops and supplies around the Great Lakes area and to the coast. It's going to be big and well-fortified; he'll be there."

"How do you know that?"

"They'll need prisoners to work the docks I imagine."

"You hope," Sara clarified, searching his eyes.

"It's all I've got, Mom," Aaron apologized, feeling her anxiety. "We know the tracks end in Duluth. It's enough to get us moving. We can make it there by tonight if we're careful. Seth, Leah, grab your gear, we're moving."

The Reddings tramped north through the swamp as quickly as the terrain would allow. Branches and briers tore at their hands, faces, and clothes, but it didn't matter. Caleb mattered.

By nightfall, they had arrived in the woods southwest of Superior, Wisconsin. Exhausted, they crawled into an abandoned lake house; not even Sara had the strength to do any scouting tonight. Together, they polished off the remainder of their drinking water and went to sleep wondering what they would find in the morning.

Chapter 10

Squinting into the sunrise the next morning, Caleb was back in front of Captain Li. He hadn't noticed yesterday, but the man was hardly taller than he was. He wore a greenish gray uniform with a few decorations on the chest and a scowl on his face.

"This is the last time I am going to ask you. Where are the others going?" demanded the interpreter.

"I don't know! Honest. Just away from you guys," Caleb insisted.

The two soldiers holding Caleb swung him around and lifted his shirt. Panicking, he squirmed in vain against the tight grip of the soldiers.

"Are you certain you don't want to tell me?"

Caleb remained silent. He didn't know what to say. What was going to happen to him?

Before the sound of the bamboo cane splitting through the air even reached his ears, unbelievable pain shot up Caleb's spine, exploding in his brain. His cry of surprise and pain reached across the compound. He didn't have long to process the shock of the first strike before it was followed by a second and a third. Caleb thrashed wildly trying to escape the rain of blows. The soldiers released him, and he fell to his face in the mud, sobbing.

`A boot rolled him over. Caleb looked up to see the smug face of Captain Li sneering down at him. He muttered something in

Mandarin, and the soldiers hauled Caleb away. This time, they didn't stop at his container, instead, they tossed him into a smaller ten-foot container. As the door slammed behind him, he began to cry again. His back throbbed with the pain of each stripe. *Why were they hurting him?*

"Stop crying," grumbled a man's gruff voice from the darkness. "That's what he wants. To see you cry. Now, pull yourself together. They'll be getting us for work soon."

The voice wasn't wrong. Caleb was still consumed with his pain, and the fact there was a man somewhere in there with him, when the door to the container opened. Light flooded the box, nearly blinding Caleb. Shouting soldiers waved violently at him, and he was pushed out the door from behind. Someone had him by the arm and was dragging him along. *Dragging him where?* As Caleb's eyes adjusted to the light, he saw massive ships, soldiers, Americans, seagulls, a blue sky, and the grizzly old man who was dragging him along.

After walking nearly a quarter mile, they stopped in front of a large ship. One of the soldiers, pointing at the ship, barked out, "You work here today."

The old man grabbed Caleb and hauled him up the narrow gangway onto the ship's deck. Then, he spoke in a gravelly voice, "This is our job. We clean all the ship's quarters until it's ready to return to sea. If we fail the inspection, they cane us; if we take too long, they cane us; if we do everything right, they still cane us."

Caleb stared blankly at the man, overwhelmed. The figure before him was easily old enough to be his grandfather. His long, unkempt gray hair hung down into his long, unkempt gray beard. His face looked as weathered as the boards they were walking on. Hard eyes stared back at Caleb, eyes full of a strange mixture of anger and pride. But mostly anger.

"My name is Samuel, but call me Sam. I'll show you the ropes, but you've got to keep up."

Caleb nodded and followed the man.

As morning dawned, Sara, Aaron, Seth, and Leah found
themselves on a wooded ridge glassing the cities of Superior and
Duluth for any indication of what had happened to Caleb. Most
of the once proud cities resembled something out of a post-
apocalyptic movie, all except for a small stretch of Duluth which
still seemed to be in operation.

"I can't tell for sure, but those could be Americans working
over there," Aaron pointed to the docks.

Sara's scope wasn't as powerful as Seth's binoculars, but it told
her enough. That was the only part of either city with any activity.
He must be there, she thought, daring to hope there still might be a
way to save him.

"We have to get closer," she pleaded.

"There are a lot of Chinese down there. I see a small war ship
in the harbor, a few smaller military vessels, and that compound
looks super built up. This place is crawling with soldiers, a lot of
soldiers. . . . How are we going to pull this off?" Seth asked, trying
not to despair.

"One step at a time," Aaron stated firmly. Rolling to his feet,
he marched down the ridge, the others close behind.

There was only one bridge to their south crossing the river
between Superior and Duluth. As they surveyed it from the safety
of the woods, Aaron was glad simply to see the bridge intact.
Now, they had to find a way to cross it. Night, of course, would
be the best option, but Aaron knew his mother wasn't going to
put up with any delays on this endeavor. They would be crossing
in daylight.

At first, the bridge wasn't getting much traffic, which wasn't
surprising considering the location of the Duluth's compound and
the fact there weren't many Americans left to use it. Then, they

heard the familiar rumble of a troop truck coming down the road. It crossed the bridge and drove toward the compound. Seth checked his watch: 10:05 a.m.

"Must be a checkpoint change out; it's ten o'clock," Seth whispered to the others.

"Well, that should give us plenty of time to cross before the next one. The town over there looks completely deserted. I can see some rail cars and a couple sets of tracks; they may be using those lines yet," Aaron said, handing the binoculars to Seth. "What do you see, Mom?" he asked her, not so much because he thought he might have missed something, but to keep her mind engaged. His mother had hardly said a word all morning.

"I don't like the idea of being in town for very long, feels wrong. I heard some sort of aircraft last night; it would leave us mighty exposed," Sara answered, not taking her eye from the scope.

"Yeah, I thought I heard it too," Leah added.

"Let's hope they aren't using thermals, or we're really sunk," said Aaron.

The beleaguered band made their way to the bridge. The coast looked clear, and they crossed it at a trot. Once in the small suburb of Duluth, they navigated the narrow streets lined with tattered buildings and burned-out cars. They found the wreckage of the streets almost more difficult to navigate than the narrow game trails of the woods. It was nearly two o'clock by the time they reached the town's northwestern corner. The sound of a troop truck sent them ducking inside one of the few remaining houses as it rumbled across the bridge.

"Do we have any water? I'm so thirsty, and my head is killing me," Leah moaned, her face scrunched in pain.

The boys did a quick check and came up empty. Aaron looked over at Sara who was positioned by the door, rifle in hand, waiting for the danger to pass.

"Mom?"

"What?" came an absent response.

"We need water."

"We can't stop, we have to keep going."

"Mom!"

"What?!" Sara whirled toward Aaron, irritation clearly displayed on her face.

"We have to find water. Without it we won't make it."

Sara lowered her rifle to one hand. Stepping toward Aaron, she furiously pointed north with her other hand.

"Did you see that place? Caleb is out there! Every minute we spend here is a minute closer to never seeing him again. Do you understand that?! Finding water isn't going to bring Caleb back!"

"No, but it will keep the rest of your family alive long enough to help you find him!" Aaron flung out his own arm, but his finger was pointing to Leah, who had slunk to the floor holding her pounding head in her hands. Seth remained frozen against the wall, trying to blend into the torn wallpaper.

Sara finally looked down and saw her daughter in a heap of her own agony. The frustration clouding her vision was swept away. She dropped down beside Leah, wrapped her arms around her and started crying.

"I'm so sorry, honey. I'm sorry I let this happen to you!"

"Mom, it's not your fault," Aaron spoke up again, "it's just . . . we have to look at this realistically. We aren't gonna get Caleb out tonight. This is a big deal; it's gonna take time and planning. I'm sorry, but we have to keep living and stay strong somehow. And that means finding water."

Sara slowly settled back on the floor with her arms across her raised knees, her head buried. Aaron could only guess how she was taking what he was saying. He waited patiently for her to break the silence.

Finally, lifting red eyes to her son, she said, "Ok, let's find water."

Caleb looked down at his hands, red and throbbing. Blisters had formed on his palms; some had already broken open. He had been mopping all day, starting with the ship's cabins, then the mess room, the captain's cabin, the head, and was now finishing the bridge. He ran his fingers across the blisters and winced in pain, his eyes filling with tears. *Where was his family? Why hadn't they rescued him yet?*

"You've got to stop all that crying, boy. You need to get hard, real hard," Sam instructed, while scrubbing the bridge windows. "Do you have a name?"

"Caleb," he answered, without looking up from his hands.

"You crying is what Captain Li lives for. He hates us. He believes *we* believe we're better than he is, and we have got to prove to him that what he believes we believe, is true."

Caleb looked up at the old man, trying to make sense of what he had just said. The bushy gray brow was furrowed, and the look in his eye told Caleb he was serious.

"That's right, kid. Every time he breaks one of us, he gets a sick satisfaction. To him, we're getting what we deserve for being proud, for putting our nose in everyone's business, for trying to control the world. We're dogs to him, dogs needing a lesson, and he aims to see we get it. He hates us because we have had the one thing he can never have: freedom. It's arrogant to them for a man to see himself as an individual, to have his own dreams, and the liberty to pursue them. All he knows is what he's told. All he does is what he's told to do. Freedom is as foreign to him as we are, and we must prove we're the better. He's a slave as much as we are, and he knows it. Get hard, Caleb, get real hard. Never let him see you break."

Sam stared intently out the bridge window watching Captain
Li strut down the wharf. Sam's voice was almost trembling with
hatred, "We'll see who breaks who. . . ."

Caleb grabbed the mop handle and, though the pain felt like
fire, he started in on the bridge floor with a new intensity. He
wasn't entirely sure he understood everything Sam had said but he
understood enough to be inspired to rise above the pain.

As the workday ended, the ship was inspected by Captain Li,
who claimed they had missed a spot in the head and caned them
both twice for the infraction. Caleb did his best not to show the
pain, but the stripes from his morning caning had not yet healed
and as the second blow blasted across his back, he let out a
whimper, and a hot tear rolled down his cheek. They were each
handed a military ration and a liter of water and marched back to
their container. Once the door was shut, there was no visible light
to speak of, except for a hairline crack between the joints of the
hinges.

"Sam?" Caleb called out.

There was a scratching noise, and then a light flickered. It hung
in the air for a moment before coming to rest atop an emergency
candle.

"Where did you . . .?"

"I stole it from the ship; a lot of things go unnoticed on a ship
that size," Sam said, his self-satisfied smile barely visible in the
glow.

"Won't we get in trouble?" Caleb asked.

"I've been here for six months, and they've never come to call
after work hours. Besides, with those boots, you can hear them
coming from a mile away."

Caleb was glad for the light; he had never liked the dark and,
without his mother there, the darkness made him feel lonelier than
ever.

"I'm sorry I cried, Sam. I tried to be hard like you said, but it
hurt so bad," Caleb apologized as he fought to open his dinner.

Sam reached over and took the meal out of Caleb's raw and swollen fingers and tore it open. "Here you go, kid."

The two of them ate their meals in silence. Once Sam had finished eating, he poured some of his water into his meal bag, tore open his salt packet with his teeth, and emptied it into the water.

"Come here, kid."

Caleb walked over to the man, not entirely sure he should.

"Put your hands in the water," Sam commanded in his normal gravelly tone.

Caleb eyed him suspiciously.

"Put your hands in the water," he repeated roughly, "we have to keep them from getting infected."

Caleb lifted his hands and lowered them slowly toward the bag.

"This is going to hurt like hell, but you gotta leave them in there. Get hard, son. You turn the pain into anger, curse, do whatever you have to do, but you leave your hands in the water for a good long while. If you get an infection, they'll shoot you like a dog."

Caleb finally thrust his hands into the water.

Pain, indescribable pain, fired through the nerve endings all over his hands, traveled up his spine, and exploded in his mind— pain like he had never felt before, burning, stinging, gnawing pain. He tried to jerk his hands out of the water, but Sam caught them in one huge, gnarly fist and plunged them back in again.

Sam looked him dead in the eye, their faces inches apart, his teeth grit, as Caleb fought to get away. "Give it a minute, dig in boy, you can do it! Use your mind to fight the pain!"

Caleb stopped struggling. He had never encountered a more ferocious man in all his life.

"You feel that? You're getting used to it," Sam said, letting go. "All pain is that way. Once you learn how to get past the initial burn, it gets easier. The real battle is in your mind." The old man dumped out the water and sat down on a stack of cardboard.

Leaning against the wall, he stared into the blackness beyond the candlelight.

"How did you get here, kid?" he asked after a moment.

"My family was heading north to escape the Chinese when we decided taking a train would be easier. It was a good idea until we had to jump off. It was dark, and the train was moving, and there were Chinese soldiers up ahead. I got scared when the others jumped, and I just held onto a crate. The next thing I knew, the soldiers started shooting, and I couldn't see my family. Then, a bunch of soldiers grabbed me, tied me up, and put me back on the train. I got here yesterday. They kept asking me where my family was headed, and I told them I didn't know; so they beat me and brought me here."

"Why didn't you just tell them your family was headed north?" Sam asked.

"I couldn't do that. My family is a team, and that would be like helping the other team win!" Caleb protested.

"So, you do have a little grit," Sam said in surprise.

"My family is going to rescue me, though; they've rescued people before."

"I wouldn't get my hopes up, kid. This place is a fortress, and Captain Li has soldiers on guard around the clock. I've seen a few folks try to escape, but they've all been recaptured and shot," Sam responded dryly.

Caleb contemplated Sam's words, but he disagreed. He knew his family was out there, coming for him. Maybe even tonight.

The Redding's had discovered a small pond formed in the abscess created by a gravel mining operation some time before the war. The water was only a hundred yards from the house they had ducked into earlier that afternoon. Unfortunately, it was a hundred yards of wide-open gravel. There were a couple of buildings to the north of the pond, but the daylight made everything a risk. Reluctantly, they had decided to wait until dusk, and the cover of darkness, before heading out to recover some water. Leah's migraine was manageable for the moment thanks to some pain pills Sara had picked up when Seth had been wounded.

As the sun set, the boys prepared themselves for the quick jog to the pond. Each of them carried one of the water jugs and their rifles. Sara would cover them from the doorway of the house.

"Ready, Seth?" Aaron asked as they stacked by the door.

"Ready as I'm going to be."

"Let's go."

The boys trotted across the open gravel, grateful for the moon lighting their way. As they reached the pond, each boy plunged his container into the water.

"This reminds me of when we used to head out to the pond behind our place on summer nights with our pellet guns and flashlights hunting bullfrogs," Seth whispered with a smile.

"Yeah, I remember the first time Mom cooked up some of those frog legs. I thought she was crazy, but Dad tried one, so I had to too. They really weren't too bad. I'd give my left leg for some frog legs right now, I'm so hung—"

A large hand clasped around Aaron's mouth, and a strong arm grabbed him around the shoulders. He jerked his head up to see Seth also being attacked from behind. Seth thrashed wildly and drilled his assailant right in the nose, knocking them both back.

"Calm down, calm down! It's me!" hissed a man's voice from behind Aaron.

Seth was already reaching for his rifle.

"It's me! Ty!" repeated the voice, "Don't shoot!"

Aaron pulled the man's hand off his mouth, "Ty?"

He spun around to see Ty's smiling teeth glowing in the moonlight.

Seth cringed, recognizing the young woman lying on the ground moaning. "Ohhh, crap," he whispered. He reached for

Soraya, but she pushed him away. "I'm *sorry!* I didn't know it was you."

"I think you broke my nose," Soraya's voice was muffled by her hand.

"We'd better get her back to Mom," Aaron said.

While Aaron and Seth finished filling the jugs, Ty went for the things he and his sister had stashed in one of the gravel pit buildings. When he returned, they all hurried back across the gravel yard to the house.

Aaron took point and called out in a loud whisper as they approached the house, "It's us, Mom, don't shoot. Everything's ok. We have Ty and Soraya."

Sara lowered her rifle as they filtered in through the front door. "Boy, is it good to see friendly faces," she exclaimed.

Ty hesitated for a second, then smiled, "Yeah, friends." He held out his hand to shake hers, but it was pushed away as he got wrapped up in a hug instead.

Seth cleared his throat, "Umm, Soraya might need a little help. There was an, umm, accident."

Sara looked at Soraya's bleeding nose in the faint light. "Let's go to the basement. I need to look at this by candlelight."

Aaron handed a jug of water to Leah, and the group moved down the stairs. Sara dug in her pack and found a candle and some survival matches and set Soraya up near an old end table. She had Seth bring her a shirt from the closet for a rag and poured water on it.

"Tilt your head back, Soraya, let me have a look at it." She felt around as she dabbed away the blood. "Well, it isn't broken, probably will be tender for a few days, though. What happened?"

"Seth hit me."

Sara spun toward Seth in shock.

"That was after she jumped me!" he fired in defense.

"Really, it's Ty's fault," Soraya said. "He said we should sneak up on you so we wouldn't get shot, then he said Seth would be the more manageable of the two. He was wrong on both counts."

This brought a smile to Seth's face, and he winked at Aaron, who rolled his eyes.

"She's right, you should have just called out to us. We wouldn't shoot Americans without provocation."

"Well, to be fair, we're here and no one was shot, so I guess the plan worked," Ty said with a grin.

"Humph," grunted Soraya.

"So, what *are* you guys doing here?" asked Aaron.

"Heading north, just like you said. We were about to leave when we saw you guys going for water. The only way to get around Duluth is going to be at night," Ty replied.

As Ty looked around the room, even in the dim candlelight, he could tell something was terribly wrong.

"What's going on?" he asked.

Aaron's eyes met his through the shadows, "We won't be going around Duluth."

Chapter 11

S o, what's the plan?" Ty asked soberly, after Aaron completed the tale of Caleb's capture.

"We're going to Duluth and, if he's there, we're going to find a way to save him," Aaron answered hopefully.

"We'll go with you," Soraya volunteered, putting her arm around Sara.

Ty nodded in agreement. His eyes met Aaron's. "Caleb is a good apple."

Aaron looked at the two of them, then at Seth, Leah, and his mother. He wanted to be noble and tell them it wasn't their fight, but the truth was they needed them. If they were to stand any chance of success, they would need all the help they could get. He hated asking for help, always had, but this was for Caleb.

"Thanks," he said humbly.

Without a word, Aaron ran upstairs and grabbed his map. Returning, he spread it open on the floor for everyone to see.

"We're here, just north of this little town," he explained, pointing. "We need to get up here somewhere west of Duluth so we can get eyes on this active part of the port. If Caleb is in Duluth, he's there."

"If we pushed, we could probably make it by morning," Ty reasoned.

"The traffic seems pretty minimal, other than the rail lines. This road to the south of the compound has a troop truck that runs a circuit every four hours, relieving a checkpoint guard over in Superior," Aaron added.

"Then let's get moving," Sara pressed.

"Right," Aaron said, searching the eyes of each one of them one last time. Seeing only determination, he gave a short nod, "Let's go."

The night air was cool and refreshing. The dew on the leaves made for quiet hiking, and the only sound to be heard was the high-pitched chirping of wood frogs. Aaron set a brisk pace using the glowing hands of his compass to guide the little band north. As they closed in on the port city, level ground gave way to ridges and ravines. The wet leaves, no longer an ally, caused them to slip and stumble along the path. Together, they conquered ridge after ridge, not one of them accepting defeat until, at last, they reached the old Interstate 35 that ran into Duluth. They paused in the ditch on the south side of the road catching their breath.

"How much further?" puffed Leah, wiping mud from her hands onto her jeans.

"About another mile up the other side of this road, maybe a mile and a half, and we should be able to see the port," Aaron panted. "Everyone ok?"

Aaron couldn't make out most of the responses to his question, more like grunts really, but he knew the mettle of his team. They would make it tonight.

"Let's go."

Up and over the road they went. Following the ditch for another mile, they paused at a small gravel road turning to the north of the interstate, cutting through the woods blanketing the steep incline.

"Probably some houses up there," commented Seth.

Aaron could see the first light of dawn breaking on the eastern horizon; they were out of time. "It's as good a place as any. Mom, what do you think?"

"Will we be able to see the compound from there?" Sara gasped.

"It's going to have some serious elevation up there, I would hope so," Aaron answered.

Sara studied the eastern horizon for a moment. Aaron knew she wanted to race in and rescue Caleb, but she wasn't stupid. They would need a place to hide, and soon.

"Sounds good to me."

They made their way up the steep road, through overgrown weeds, and over fallen trees, until they arrived at a large two-story cabin.

"Sam? You said Captain Li is a slave just like us. He doesn't look like a prisoner to me," Caleb stated, as he swirled a brush around the stainless steel toilet bowl he was cleaning.

"In his heart he is," Sam replied, without looking up from his faucet.

"In his heart? What does that mean?" Caleb queried.

The old man sighed and looked over at the curious youngster, "He just is. Now, finish up that toilet. We have a lot of ship left to clean."

Caleb went back to scrubbing the toilet. "If he's a prisoner, why doesn't he just escape?"

Sam eyed him. "Before everything hit the fan did you ever visit a dairy farm?"

"No."

The old man grumbled under his breath and sighed again. "Well, on a dairy farm all the cows are treated exactly the same. Sure, the farmer provides them with everything they need: food, water, shelter, protection, even their health needs are met. They live in the same conditions as all the other cows do and get fed the same. When the farmer wants something from them, he takes it. That's kinda the way the country Li comes from works: everyone shares everything. Their government provides everything for them, and when it wants something . . . it takes it."

"Doesn't sound so bad," Caleb commented innocently.

The old man ran his hand down his face in disbelief and tried again. "Have you ever been to a zoo?" he said in frustration.

"Yeah, I think so. When I was little."

"Well, it's the same in a zoo. All the creatures have their needs met: food, water, shelter. They should be happy, right? But if you look into a caged lion's eyes and stare into his soul, you can see the light once burning there has long since gone out. He might be breathing, but he isn't living. He's just a shell, nothing more—something to be gawked at for the profit he brings the zoo. Captain Li is like that lion. I have never seen a wild lion, but I have stumbled upon a moose once."

Sam's eyes stared off into another world; his face softened.

"I was out hunting, working my way through the woods north of here—woods so thick the sunlight didn't even reach the ground in some places." His voice was a soft whisper now. "I came to a clearing with a small pond. As I swept the last cedar bough out of my way, I saw him: an enormous creature of majestic design. He was knee deep in the pond, but still taller than me at the shoulders. His coat was a rich coffee brown and, on his head, he wore a crown of the most massive antlers I have ever seen anywhere. The sight took my breath away. I laid down my rifle and, as I did, he looked at me, looked right through me to my soul, and I beheld his. There was a wild freedom in his eyes blazing as though he was the sacred guardian of all that's wild and free. I knew no man could ever tame such a fire, only a fool would even dare. He didn't need all his needs met by some human force; he would have scoffed at the notion. His world is one of danger: wolves, bears, mountain lions, the cold, harsh winters of the far north. Food is scarce, and there's no shelter except what the woods afford. But he would trade all the comforts man could offer him for the ability to live free in that wild place. Good or bad, his fate is his own to decide. He's the guardian of his own life and, by his choices, he will live or die. But he'll do so on the wings of freedom," Sam finished, his voice trembling.

He looked at Caleb, who had completely forgotten all about scrubbing the toilet.

"That's what it is to be free, boy," Sam said. "Many in this country wanted to live like them." He motioned to a Chinese flag on the wall. "I've never seen a wild animal fight its way into a cage the way this country did . . . fools! We mistook having all the comforts of life met for living and sold our soul for a loaf of bread. Freedom is dangerous. The freedom to succeed is married to the freedom to fail. The freedom to rise from the ashes, with the freedom to go up in flames. But real life is an adventure, and we can't live that from a cage. To be American is to live dangerously, dangerously and free." His gravelly voice trailed off. Then, snapping himself back to reality, he threw Caleb the mop and said, "Now, enough questions for today. When you finish here, I'll be on the bridge. Bring the mop."

"I can't see anything through these trees!" Sara complained as she looked out the second story window of the cabin.

"We had to stop somewhere. The sun was coming up," Aaron said in frustration.

"I'm going to find somewhere I can see. I have to know if he's down there, Aaron."

"Wait! I'll go with you," he offered, following her.

"No, Aaron, I'll go," Soraya broke in, meeting them at the bottom of the stairs.

Aaron looked at her in surprise, but her eyes told him she understood what she was offering.

"They'll be alright," Ty assured him. "Come on, let's work on figuring out the next step."

The next step . . . what is the next step? Aaron thought to himself. He walked into the old living room where a large glass coffee table sat, surrounded by what was left of a brown leather couch and loveseat. Pulling out his map, he laid it open on the table.

"This map is no help at all. Duluth is just a large black dot. We're going to have to come up with a map of the city itself somehow. Maybe if we search an old gas station or tourist shop after dark, we can come up with something."

"Doesn't sound too difficult," Ty remarked.

"We're going to need a lot more information about this compound. I don't know how to tell my mother, but this is going to take a lot of planning; planning takes time."

"She seems pretty smart, your mom, and she trusts you. I think if you just tell her, she'll understand."

"The truth is, I'm finding it hard myself not to run down there, guns blazing, and get him back. I just know it would get us all killed."

"Yeah," Ty sighed and put his hand on Aaron's shoulder, offering whatever sympathy he could.

"It's my fault, I . . ." Aaron began.

"What's this?" Leah asked, pointing to Soraya's pack.

The two young men looked up from the table.

"Oh, that's just some bow and arrow thing Soraya picked up at a house we scavenged a couple days back. It's too small for me and, honestly, neither of us have any clue how to use one. I told her to leave it, but she insisted it might be useful sometime down the road. She's as stubborn as our mama was, and I learned from Dad sometimes it's simpler just to let women have their way," Ty finished with a teasing grin.

Leah rolled her eyes at the comment. "Do you think Soraya would mind if I looked at it?"

"Leah used to have one like that. She was really good with it but, after everything hit the fan, she wore the string out, and there was no way to replace it." Aaron explained, a touch of pride in his voice.

"I don't think she would mind, like I said, she can't even shoot it," Ty answered.

Unstrapping the bow from Soraya's pack, Leah inspected it closely. It was a beautiful black compound bow with turquoise flower embellishments on the limbs. She ran her finger down the black and turquoise striped string. The feeling stirred up memories of better times. The bow was in mint condition. The quiver held six arrows: four with hunting broadheads and two with field points. There were four additional field tipped arrows still attached to Soraya's pack. A matching black and turquoise release hung fastened around the riser.

She took it off and buckled it around her wrist. Clipping the release to the string, she took a deep breath and pulled the bow back. The draw was solid, she guessed around forty-five pounds, similar to her old bow. The draw length was slightly shorter than she would have liked, but a little extra bend in the elbow took care of that.

Ty watched her in amazement. "Is that what that thingy is for?" he said, pointing to the release. "We had no idea why it was hanging on there."

Leah blushed when she realized he was watching her, but her curiosity drove her to ask the question, "Do you think it would be ok if I shot it?"

"Go right ahead, I'd like to see how it works myself."

Leah selected one of the black carbon arrows from the quiver and walked up the stairs to the loft overlooking the living room. Drawing the bow back, she set the sights on one of the buttons still visible on the back rest of the love seat. Touching her finger

125

to the release, the arrow slammed into the cushion in the blink of an eye. The arrow, sunk up to the fletching, was four inches to the left of the button. Leah quickly adjusted the sight, nocked another arrow, and sent it flying. The arrow slammed into the button, driving it through the back of the couch.

"Holy crap!" Ty exclaimed.

"Told you she was good," Aaron said, eyebrows raised.

Leah, still blushing, walked down the stairs and retrieved the arrows. "It's a beautiful bow," she said simply, laying it back down on Soraya's pack.

Just then, Seth walked in rubbing his eyes. "What's all the racket? Can't a guy get some sleep?"

"It's nothing. Sorry, Seth," Leah said.

"Nothing?! She just shot that itty-bitty button, from up there, with a bow!" Ty exclaimed.

"That's not that amazing. Where'd you get a bow?" asked Seth, still a little irritated.

"It's Soraya's," Leah said, annoyed by her brother's lack of appreciation for her skills.

"Ah," was all Seth said as he walked back into one of the bedrooms.

"You know Seth; nothing impresses Seth but Seth," Aaron said, shaking his head.

The rest of the morning was spent resting. The long nights and high emotions were taking their toll on everyone. Aaron couldn't ignore the uncomfortable feeling in his gut that he should have gone with his mother. He had no idea where they were or how long they intended to be gone, and Soraya wasn't exactly G.I. Jane. He laid down on the couch and closed his eyes trying to relax, he was wiped out. Eventually, exhaustion overtook his racing mind, and he sank into a deep sleep.

Sara and Soraya climbed up the ridge behind the house, moving north as they went. The trees were still too dense to see through. So, they kept on, hoping to find a clear point overlooking the city. After roughly forty-five minutes of climbing and hiking, they finally found what they were looking for: an area had been blasted away from the side of the ridge, leaving a wide, open unobscured view of Duluth.

Sara handed the binoculars to Soraya and crouched with her rifle's scope trained on the Chinese compound, which they could now see clearly only a half mile away.

"He has to be down there somewhere," she whispered, "Oh Jesus, please let him be down there."

After a few minutes of silence, Soraya spoke up. "It looks like most of the activity is in the north half of the compound. I see soldiers drilling in that open area . . . I can't see any prisoners yet. . . ."

"Yeah, it just gets so much further away up there; it's hard to see."

Soraya held out the binoculars, "Here, use these. They're not too bad."

"Thanks."

Sara laid down her rifle and scanned again with the binoculars. "I see some ships docked, but they're too far away to see individual people. They're definitely loading up whatever is coming in on those trains onto the boats though."

Sara found herself frustrated with their lack of success. But what did she expect? To hike up here, hold up the binoculars, and see Caleb standing out in the open waving his arms at the cliffside? As ridiculous as it sounded, that was exactly what she realized she had hoped for. With a sigh, she lowered the binoculars and turned to Soraya who was waiting patiently.

"I'm not leaving until I either see Caleb, or it gets dark."

"I know." Soraya held her gaze.

"This might take all day."

"I know."

Satisfied and grateful, Sara went back to her surveillance.

"I'm guessing, by the activity near those ships, that unless the prisoners are all inside somewhere, they're probably working in the shipyard. Who knows when or if they'll come out in the open close enough for me to recognize him?"

"We can take turns scanning the whole area until that happens. Let me know when your eyes are tired and I can watch for a bit."

"Ok," Sara agreed, without looking away from the compound.

Soraya moved back from the edge a little and made herself comfortable.

Sara tried to convince herself she could handle the wait, but the truth was impossible to hide as she continued to frantically search every corner of the compound she could see. Eventually, all the images blurred together before her exhausted eyes, and she had to surrender the binoculars to Soraya.

They soon fell into a pattern of trading places, one searching for Caleb, while the other rested their eyes. The hours dragged on. Soraya had dozed off a few times while Sara was watching for Caleb, but Sara had not been able to relax enough to even pretend to fall asleep. It was finally drawing toward evening. The sun was sliding down the back side of the ridge they were on, but its brilliant colors danced across the water in front of them, creating an amazing display of colorful light.

It was Soraya's turn with the binoculars. Little had changed in the compound since they had begun their watch. Suddenly, without looking away from their target, Soraya broke the silence.

"How are you doing, Sara? I mean about Caleb and all this."

Surprised at the question, Sara had to think for a minute. She hadn't had the luxury of friends in an awfully long time and, since she lost her husband, there had been no one to share her deepest feelings with. She had quickly learned to bury them. Now, here was a girl, no, a woman, one who had earned her respect and even love, asking to be let inside. It *would* be nice to have someone to talk to again . . . maybe. With great difficulty, she attempted to put into words the pain and fears which had ravaged her heart since the night she had seen her baby standing alone on a train car.

"I feel . . ." she began slowly, "I feel scared. My baby was stolen from me, and I don't know if I can get him back. I feel like if I take time for any purpose other than finding him, that the window of opportunity to save him closes that much more, and I get that much closer to losing him forever."

She paused and Soraya remained quiet, still searching the compound for the small familiar face, giving Sara time to process what she was feeling.

"I don't think I've been very easy on the other kids. I don't think I even stopped for a breath until we were in the house where you met up with us. I finally saw what I was doing to poor Leah . . . I think the last time I really, *really* looked at her was the day I let her keep that silly chicken." Sara's short laugh turned to a surprised little gasp, "Her chicken! It's gone! She must have lost it somewhere since we got on that accursed train." She flung an arm out in disgust, "See? I'm horrible! Poor Leah, she loved that little creature, and here I am: acting like nobody else matters except Caleb."

Soraya could see this was going nowhere. Sara was caught in an endless cycle of worrying about one child, then the others, and back again. Putting down the binoculars for a moment, she turned to face Sara.

"You know, every single one of your children supports you one hundred percent in all your efforts to get Caleb back. No one is complaining about a lack of attention. I've never been a mother, so I can only imagine the pain you're going through. We all have your back, Sara, don't worry about us."

It didn't go unnoticed by Sara that Soraya had lumped herself in with her children. It gave her even more fire to bring her family together again. She smiled back at Soraya, her eyes glistening.

"Thank you," she managed, "that means a lot." She looked out over what she could see of the compound from her secluded seat back in the brush. There was a resigned frustration in her voice when she spoke again.

"I'm realizing more and more each day what a monumental task this will be. I just want to run in there and grab him, and hold him, and never let him go again. But I can't. I know I can't. I don't like it but, after staring at this place for hours, I can now see this is going to take a long time. I pray he doesn't give up on us," she ended in almost a whisper.

Soraya had returned to her constant scanning. She knew nothing she said could ease any of Sara's pain. She also knew, even from her young years of experience, sometimes just talking out loud can lighten the burden one carries, even a little. If she could be a listening ear for Sara, this amazing woman of God she had come to love dearly, she would feel blessed.

The peak of the sunset was over. They knew their time was running out. Soraya's eyes were starting to burn again when she noticed some increased activity near the shipyard.

"I think something is happening," she reported to an anxious Sara. "There are suddenly way more people over by the ships. I think they're Americans! Oh, they're starting to head this way . . . I can kinda make out some faces. . . . There are a few men . . . there's two more . . . I see an old guy. . . . A kid!" she gasped, "I see a kid! Quick, quick, look!"

Sara snatched the binoculars out of Soraya's hands and quickly focused on the near side of the shipyard. "Where? Where? I don't see . . . It's Caleb!" It was Sara's turn to gasp. "It's Caleb!"

Chapter 12

It was dark by the time Sara and Soraya made it back to the house where the others waited. They had practically run all the way. Soraya's face bore a welt where a branch had snapped back as Sara had blown by it. The slight stinging was nothing compared to the importance of the news they carried, and she gave it little thought. Breathless, they burst through the door and were met by Ty, who was on guard duty, watching for their return.

"We saw him!" Sara blurted, eyes alight with excitement. "Where is everybody?"

"Aaron is in there, sleeping on the couch," Ty answered, "the rest are down in the basement. What did you see? Is he ok? I'll go get Aaron."

"No, wait." Sara stopped him. "Let him sleep. I don't mind repeating everything when he wakes up. He hasn't had good rest in a while. Let's go downstairs and we'll tell you all about it."

After her chat with Soraya up on the hill, Sara had resolved to never again sacrifice the well-being of her other children in her quest to rescue Caleb. Right now, that meant letting Aaron sleep.

When Aaron awoke, less than an hour later, he opened his eyes to darkness. *I can't believe I slept this long,* was his first thought. His second thought had him jumping to his feet in alarm. *Why aren't Mom and Soraya back yet?*

He quickly made his way through the darkness and ran down the stairs. Pulling up short in surprise, he saw Sara and Soraya, along with everybody else, huddled around a table with a single candle burning in the center.

They all looked up at the racket descending the stairs and, as he reached the last step, Sara jumped up and ran to him. Flinging her arms around him, she cried, "We saw him, Aaron! We saw Caleb!"

Such profound relief washed over Aaron it brought tears to his eyes. The intensity of his reaction surprised him, and he realized he had been ignoring a nagging fear that all this was for nothing and they would never see his brother again. With new hope, he joined the rest of his family at the table and, for the next hour, they discussed every detail the women had gathered from their vigil above the compound.

As the moon rose in the night sky over Duluth, the mission was clear. Caleb was alive; he was close, and they were going to find a way to rescue him.

First of all, they needed to find a better location from which to plan the daunting feat. From the bluff the girls had spent the day on, about a mile north of the cabin, they had seen another two-story home just below them. The only catch was, it was a mere twenty yards off the rail line. Aaron and Ty had volunteered to scout out the house while Sara and Soraya got some rest. Seth had pleaded to come along, but the thought of leaving Leah as the only sentry while the others slept hadn't seemed like a good idea.

About halfway between the cabin and the bluff ran a small creek, forming the western border of a moderately sized cemetery. The glare of moonlight on granite monuments gave the boys pause as they reached the creek.

"Do you think we should go around?" asked Ty in a whisper.

"Go around?"

"Yeah, you know . . ."

"These folks are dead, Ty. It's the ones down there I'm worried about," Aaron answered, motioning with his head toward the glowing lights of the compound.

The entrance of the cemetery afforded them a bridge across the creek. The water was sure to be cold on a night like tonight. The cemetery had not been well-kept in years, but the rocky soil and mature trees had slowed the growth of underbrush. The boys had little trouble making their way to the far side. From there, they jogged the last quarter mile up the railroad tracks to the house. Just as Sara had said, it was the only house in northwest Duluth on the west side of the tracks.

The house was large with a brick-red shingled roof. The front door had been kicked in some time ago, and some of the windows on the first story had rocks thrown through them. The second story, on the other hand, seemed to have weathered the intrusions with little damage. On the northeast corner of the second story, a sliding glass door led out to a balcony facing the lake.

"I think it's worth a look around. If we can see the compound from up there, this might be the place," Aaron said optimistically.

"Pretty close to the tracks. We'd have to keep our heads down during the day, and the basement windows would need to be blacked out like the cabin to have any light at night."

"Yeah . . ." Aaron answered, considering the risks. "Well, let's get moving; we need to get back before Seth kills Leah."

"Or the other way around," Ty said.

The young men entered cautiously through the front door, grateful for the moonlight. Once inside, they found themselves standing in a large, openly laid out living room that adjoined the dining room. The tell-tale signs of looters were present everywhere. The walls were bare, vacancies gaped where appliances once stood, and all the easily movable furniture was missing.

Crunching on broken glass, they made their way across the living room to a flight of stairs which lead to the second story. There was no mistaking the acrid odor of mildew mixed with rodent urine as they headed up the stairs. The aroma didn't give them pause, however; in fact, it was familiar, almost every house either of them had scavenged smelled similar. The pungent odor was almost reassuring; if people were still using the house, it was likely they would have found a way to deal with the rats.

Reaching the top of the stairs, they walked down the hall toward the master bedroom. On the way, they stopped at a bedroom. Ty opened the door and took a step inside.

"SCREECH!"

Jumping in the air, Ty swung his rifle off his shoulder as a rat darted out from under his foot. Losing his balance, he fell, landing on his back.

"AHH!" he shouted at the rat. Aiming his rifle down the hallway, he fought to catch his breath.

Aaron helped him back to his feet. "A little jumpy, are we?" he said, chuckling.

"I hate those things," Ty replied, his hand on his heart. "Rat almost gave me a heart attack."

"By the sound of it, the feeling was mutual," Aaron returned, still grinning as he continued down the hall.

The master bedroom was better lit than the rest of the house, and Aaron gave Ty a smile as they neared the sliding glass door leading to the balcony. From their vantage point, the entire compound lay visible, lit up like a Christmas tree in the dark.

"Ty?"

"Yeah."

"I think this is the place," Aaron said in awe.

"Yeah, I think so too."

Even without binoculars, the boys could make out all ten guard towers, the shipyard, the rail yard, and a large building near the shipyard with a whole conglomerate of antennas on the roof. Other than the guards at their posts, there was little activity elsewhere inside the wire.

"I've seen enough. Time to get the others," Aaron whispered.

They were forced to wait for a coal train to pass before leaving the house. As the engine rolled by, the engineer had no idea he was being watched by the two clandestine youths.

Back at the cabin, Seth paced impatiently in the candlelit basement waiting for Aaron and Ty to return from their scouting mission. Leah sat with her back against the wall trying to keep her mind occupied with positive things.

"Seth, you wanna play cards?" she asked gently.

"I don't know," he replied. "I can hardly think anymore. I can't sleep. It's my fault he's gone," he confessed in a moment of surprising honesty. "If I hadn't fallen asleep, he would be here."

Even in the dim light, she could see his soft brown eyes filled with regret and, for the first time in a while, Leah saw him for what he was: a fourteen-year-old boy.

"Seth, what you have done up to this point is the stuff I used to read about in my books. You're just a boy. You were tired. Your body is a wreck; accidents happen. The fault for what happened to Caleb belongs to all of us. We're a team. But I believe we're going to get him back."

He looked at her with tears in his eyes. "I'm worried about him, Leah. We have no idea what they're doing to him. I wish it were me," he said under his breath.

"I know you do, Seth, and that's why I believe we're going to get him back. We all would trade places with him. That's love, Seth. Love doesn't fail."

"How do you know?" he asked, wiping a tear from the corner of his eye.

"Because it's in the Bible. Daddy wrote it on the inside cover of the one he gave me when I turned ten. I've never forgotten it," she gave him a sympathetic smile.

Seth stared into the tiny flame flickering on the floor next to Leah, contemplating her words. He did love Caleb, always had, and one thing he decided right then and there—he would never fail him again.

Straightening up, he looked at her with a gentle smile, "Yeah." Shrugging his shoulders, he said, "Sure, I'll play cards."

They were on their sixth round of King's Corner when Ty and Aaron showed up with news about the house. Leah went and woke up her mother and Soraya, who had made it clear they wanted to be present when the boys returned with their decision on the house.

"Well?" Sara asked, entering the basement.

"We think it's going to work. You can see the entire compound from the second story balcony door. The house seems to be in good enough shape to work as a base of operations. The basement was too dark to see anything, but I think if we block out the windows, like Ty suggested, we should be able to work by candlelight without attracting any attention," Aaron concluded confidently.

"What about the trains?" Soraya asked.

"The house is far enough up and off the tracks to keep it from drawing more than a passing glance from the engineers. Actually had a train go by while we were there and, as far as I could tell, he never even looked our way," Ty said, looking to Aaron to back him up.

Aaron nodded, "I think you ladies did a good job. Seth, Leah, thanks for watching over them. We have plenty of night left to get to the new house and get some sort of headquarters set up before dawn if everyone is up to it."

"For Caleb!" Seth called out, shouldering his pack.

For Caleb . . .

As the morning light rose over the vast lake, Sam and Caleb were marched to a new vessel awaiting them at the wharf. This ship was small compared to the previous ships Caleb had cleaned, but its gray color, flags, and deck-mounted guns drew his attention. He had always been fascinated by tales of historic naval battles, and to get the chance to board a real military vessel, well, under less captive circumstances, would have been a dream come true.

When they reached the bottom of the gangway, they were met by Captain Li and his dedicated interpreter. Captain Li rattled off something stern and unintelligible, pointing at the ship with his bamboo cane. Then, he pointed the cane at the two prisoners and squinted his already squinty eyes. This action was followed by sterner words and finished with a jab to both their chests. The interpreter began with equally stern words.

"This warship belongs to the People's Republic of China! The captain of this ship is a friend of Captain Li! Any failure to perform your duties on this ship will be met with extreme discipline! You serve the People's Republic of China, and you are expected to act like it!" the interpreter concluded with conviction. Then, the two men turned sharply and marched away.

As Sam and Caleb climbed the gangway, Sam leaned over to the boy and muttered, "You better get hard fast, boy. Today is going to hurt."

Sam's words hung like a cloud over Caleb as he worked the mop through the ship's galley. Oddly enough, the combat vessel was the cleanest ship Caleb had worked on thus far. The discipline of the sailors on the vessel had the ship looking in tip top shape before Caleb even started.

"This is going to be easy," Caleb said, catching up to Sam who was on his hands and knees cleaning one of the berthing compartments.

"Nothing is easy with Captain Li. That smug little dock rat would flog us even if he could see his reflection in the damn toilet seats!" the old man snarled. "Don't give him an excuse; get back down to that galley and make it shine!"

Caleb ran back down the stairs to the galley. Sam was more cantankerous than usual, and he decided not to test him. His hands were still sore, but calluses had begun to form and, as Sam had prophesied, the pain was getting easier to bear.

He scrubbed the ovens with every tool in his arsenal, even climbing inside on his hands and knees. He polished the stove tops and worked the griddles until he had ground his nails down to a nub. He scrubbed stains that were immovable, he scrubbed stains that didn't exist, he scrubbed until his hands ached. He washed the tables, changed out his water, and then washed them again. When he was done, the entire place gleamed. Sam came in and inspected Caleb's work. With a satisfied expression, the old man said, "Good, now help me in the head."

The fugitive band arrived at the house a couple of hours after midnight. Sara and Leah blacked out the basement windows with some blankets they found in a bedroom closet. Ty, Seth, and Aaron moved the large dining room table to the basement and rounded up a few chewed-up mattresses for them to sleep on. Soraya pulled together the last of the food any of them had so they could at least have one meal.

When they were all finished, they sat around the dining room table and ate a hodgepodge of ready to eat meals with canned corn and peas. They were all tired, but a new feeling of optimism had somewhat lifted the cloud which had fallen when Caleb was captured. He was alive and, at this point, it was all any of them could ask for.

As the sun came up, the entire crew found themselves staring out the second story balcony window. Seth held his binoculars to his eyes as the compound sprang to life below them.

"There!" he said, pointing to two figures who had emerged from a block of shipping containers.

"Can I see?" asked Leah.

Seth reluctantly handed her the binoculars. She took them and focused the lenses where Seth was pointing.

"Oh, Caleb!" she exclaimed. "It's really him, Mama."

As she handed the field glasses to her mother, Leah began to cry, overcome by a wave of emotions. Tears of joy and hope mingled with those of fear and dread, but she was glad to see her little brother alive.

They watched from their perch as Caleb was led, along with an old man, to a Navy vessel docked in the harbor. A short man in an impressive uniform poked them both with a stick, and then they went on board and out of sight.

"Well, it looks like Caleb has gone to work, so should we," Aaron suggested.

"Right," Sara said, reluctantly putting down the binoculars.

"We have to come up with a list of supplies and intel we need to gather before we can even create a plan," Aaron said, looking at each one of them.

The rest of the day they spent putting their heads together to figure out what they knew and what they needed to know, what they had, and what they would need. The lofty vantage point of the house afforded them enough basic intel on the compound to lay the initial groundwork of their plan.

Caleb couldn't remember a time in his life when he had been so exhausted. As the workday drew to a close, he ached from his head to his toes. But he stood with pride as Captain Li boarded the ship for his inspection. Surely, not even he could find something they had missed on this ship.

The prisoners followed behind the captain and his interpreter as he inspected every part of the ship. As Caleb had suspected, the captain inspected thoroughly but came up empty. Lastly, they arrived at the galley, and he inspected the ovens, the griddles, the tables, the floor. As he finished, he walked over to Sam and Caleb who were waiting for the final word next to one of the serving counters. The captain addressed them harshly and waited for his interpreter to translate.

"You will receive six stripes for disobeying my orders to have this ship spotless by leaving a mess here on the floor."

"What mess?!" Caleb burst out.

With a sneer, the captain set down the cup of tea he had been holding, and with his bamboo cane he knocked it off the counter onto the floor. The porcelain cup shattered as soon as it made contact with the unforgiving planks, sending a spray of tea three feet in all directions. In an instant, he grabbed Caleb by the back of the neck and threw him to the floor, facedown, where the cup had landed. Lifting the cane, he delivered six blows to the boy's back; then it was Sam's turn. The old man glared at him with contempt, but slowly he turned around. When Captain Li finished with Sam, he yelled something and slammed his cane down on the counter before turning around and marching out of the room.

"Clean it up!" the interpreter yelled and then hurried after the captain.

Sam turned around and looked at Caleb who was still on his hands and knees where the captain had left him. Caleb was breathing hard but, when Sam looked in his eyes, it wasn't tears he saw, it was anger.

"I'll get a mop," Sam simply said and headed out the door.

Caleb turned his head to stare at the tea and broken bits of porcelain on the floor. He clenched his jaw, unable to understand what had just happened. It didn't make any sense. *I did my best job, did it well and, in the end, it didn't matter. What did I do to deserve this?*

Sam returned with the mop, helped Caleb to his feet, and cleaned up the whole mess himself. After finishing, he walked Caleb down the gangway, grabbed their rations, and they were escorted back to their container for the night. The old man couldn't help but feel sorry for the boy. He had tried to warn him, but there are some things which must be experienced in order to understand.

Chapter 13

Y ou'd better eat, kid." Sam's gravelly voice broke the silence of their humble container.

"I'm not hungry," Caleb muttered.

In the faint light the pain and confusion on the boy's face was pitiful.

"If you don't eat, he wins," the old man prodded.

"He wins anyway."

"Kid, you're taking it too personally. He hates all of us. Do you really think he treats any of the other prisoners any better? We're dogs to him, dogs to be broken so we learn our place, and he aims to see we do."

"But why does he hate us?" Caleb said in exasperation. "We did everything he told us to!"

"It isn't about what we did or didn't do today, Caleb. It's about who we are." The old man sighed. "Where Captain Li comes from, everyone's the same, like ants in an ant hill. Everyone works for the good of the State. No one is independent of the State; everyone is a product of the State and, therefore, everything they have is the State's," he explained. "This is the only type of thinking he's been allowed to know. Captain Li believes because we're independent, have individual rights, and can pursue individual happiness, we're inherently selfish, arrogant, and rebellious. Now, China considers this their land. As far as they're concerned, we need to be put in our place and become part of the ant hive so to speak."

"Is he right?" the boy asked, hanging his head.

"Of course not!" Sam sputtered. "A man's life is a gift from his Creator. What he does with it is up to him. It's not for another man, or government for that matter, to tell him how to live his life. It's his gift to live. Freedom is a difficult thing to understand when you've never experienced it. To a bird raised in captivity all its life, flying might seem terrifying, having to find its own food, or make its own shelter. But to a free bird, captivity can clearly be seen as captivity. It's the free bird which has the ability to live to its full potential, to raise its young where they belong, to take on the challenges inherent with freedom in its own way."

"Sam? What did you do before the war?" Caleb asked, looking at the old man.

Sam snorted, "I was a Biology Professor at the U of M. Feels like a lifetime ago."

"Is that why you always talk about animals and stuff?"

"I suppose it is . . ." he managed a crooked grin.

"Did you have a family?"

At this, the old man's face turned grim. "Eat your ration, boy," he grunted and laid down on his side with his back to Caleb.

"It's killing me, Aaron, not knowing how he's doing, what he's going through. Tonight, when I watched him walk back to the containers, he didn't seem the same, he walked stiffly, with his head hung. Ugh!" Sara groaned, holding her head in her hands. *All I want to do is hold him in my arms, brush away his bangs, and tell him everything is going to be alright.* She fought to keep her emotions in check.

"We'll get him back, Mom, one step at a time." Aaron gave her shoulder an encouraging squeeze.

The last bit of sunlight had all but disappeared behind the ridge when the group gathered in the basement to plan the night's events. The list they had compiled during the day would require a lot of work and a great deal of stealth to achieve. Soraya had asserted it would be more efficient to divide and conquer the list. The others agreed and, eventually, decided to split the group into three pairs. Sara was paired with Seth, Ty with Leah, and Aaron with Soraya.

They also set up a twenty-four-hour schedule with each group rotating through sleeping, guarding the house, and working on their assignments. Each morning and evening they would all gather for three hours to compare notes, work on the plan, eat, and hang out. Aaron and Soraya had volunteered to be the first team out every evening. Tonight, their mission was simple: find a coffee can or two.

As Aaron and Soraya vanished into the dark, Leah and Ty, who would be going out next, waited on guard. Their mission would be to gather as many dry twigs and sticks as they could carry and pile them in the corner of the basement. Sara and Seth's mission would be to lay Seth's snares in the cemetery, fill the water jugs, and try their hand at fishing in the creek. If everyone did well, they should finally have something to eat for breakfast. They had agreed at the meeting that if they did not take care of themselves first, there could be no rescue at all.

"Are you nervous?" Leah asked. "About going out tonight?"

"Not really," Ty shrugged. "Soraya and I've been livin' on our own since the war started. I've been out at night in cities like this many times."

"I haven't. This is the first time I've gone anywhere without somebody from my family since . . ." her voice trailed off.

"Since what?"

"Earlier this year a couple of soldiers grabbed me while I was walking home and tried to . . ." she paused, looking at the floor.

"Wow, I'm sorry. . . ." he said.

"My dad saw them and came running, before either of them knew what was happening, he had killed them both. I had never seen him look more terrified than when he turned and looked at me. He held me tightly and told me he was so sorry he had let that happen to me. From that day on, we were no longer peaceful people."

Ty studied her.

"I know I'm not your father, Leah," he said, looking her in the eyes, "but I'll have your back tonight," he said, giving her a reassuring smile.

She returned his smile shyly and walked over to the balcony door. "I wish Caleb knew we were close. He must be so afraid," she said softly.

As the night wore on, the teams came and went, each doing their best by the light of the moon to cross as many items as they could off the list. Leah and Ty collected several armloads of branches and piled them neatly in the basement. Aaron and Soraya had a rougher time coming up with a suitable can and, eventually, had to settle for a gallon steel pail.

Sara and Seth had the most exciting night of all. The cemetery, with its large oak trees and patches of thick weeds, had proven to be excellent trapping grounds. Rabbit and squirrel trails were everywhere. The oak trees presented their quarry with an irresistible food source and the brush was the perfect cover to allow for a substantial population of the rodents to thrive.

This was the stuff Seth lived for. It would only be a matter of time before something found its way into their traps. At the creek, they had rolled over a few logs and found a handful of nightcrawlers. Within moments of his first toss, Seth had hooked and landed a large fish.

"Mom, I'm sorry about Caleb," Seth ventured, sliding the fish onto the stringer. "Leah says we're all at fault, and maybe she's right, but I'm sorry for falling asleep."

She looked at him fondly, "Leah's right, we all had our part to play in what happened. Looking back isn't a good way to move forward. We'll stumble for sure. Caleb is alive. I thank God for that, and when I saw him out there today, somehow, I just knew I'll have him back again."

"Yeah, Leah said it's love," he said simply.

"Yeah," Sara returned, treasuring his words in her heart.

By the time they needed to return to the house, eight trout were on the stringer.

Aaron spent the last shift of the night working on his steel pail idea. With Soraya's help, he removed one of the downspouts from the house and took out one of the rear basement windows. By the time everyone arrived for the morning meeting, Aaron was ready to present his creation.

"Ta da," he announced, grinning.

"Aaron, that's amazing!" Sara exclaimed.

"What is it?" Leah asked.

"Why, it's a stove, of course," Aaron said, a little deflated. "Here, I'll show you. I basically copied the hobo stove out of Mom's survival guide but altered it enough so we can cook indoors."

He stuffed a handful of twigs through a cut out near the open end of the upside-down pail, which sat on the concrete basement floor.

"You feed the fire like this. The bottom of the pail will act as the cook surface, and the gutter coming in the back here will funnel all the vapors from the fire out the window," he explained as he followed the downspout all the way to the window where Soraya had stacked rocks around the gutter so it was positioned in the center of the opening. "If I've done everything correctly and the wood is really dry, there shouldn't be any smoke at all."

Bending over, he lit the twigs and the fire roared to life. Then, he led the group out the back door to observe the makeshift chimney.

"See," he said triumphantly, "No smoke." He was positively beaming with pride.

"Where do you people come up with this stuff?" Ty asked in amazement.

"Our dad was a bit of a survival nut," Leah said apologetically.

"Well, care to test it out, Mom?" Aaron asked hopefully.

"You bet!"

Sara went to work preparing the fish they had caught, lamenting not having anything to bread them with. Sighing, she pulled out their only seasoning: salt, and sprinkled it on the fish. When the fish were finished, she brought them over to the table where they were all seated discussing the successes of the night and figuring out their assignments for today.

"Thank you, Mom," Aaron said, as she placed one of the fish in front of him.

"Don't thank me, thank Seth. Those fish didn't know what hit them," Sara said humbly.

"Pays to be good at something, eh, Seth?" Aaron jested with a wink.

Sara said grace, and the group dug in. When breakfast was finished, everyone sat back, thankful to have something in their stomachs once again.

Chapter 14

It had been eight days since Caleb had entered Sam's world. The old man had resisted getting close to anyone, mostly because, in his heart, he knew he wasn't worth getting close to. Today started like all the others before it; they were led to a ship, given their supplies, and assured punishment if they failed to perform. The two prisoners were working together in the ship's head as they had done many times before.

"I thought my family would have rescued me by now," Caleb muttered, scrubbing yet another stainless steel toilet.

"You have to accept that they may not be out there to save you, son," Sam said sympathetically. "Or maybe they believe you're dead and have moved on. At any rate, this place is a fortress, guarded by an army. It would take an army to save any of us. Keep your chin up, it gets easier."

"Why? You don't."

Sam was taken aback. He hadn't really given it any thought; it was just something you say to people who are down.

"Sam? Why don't you ever smile?" Caleb asked, looking up at him from the toilet.

The old man knew Caleb was right; he had given up on himself long ago. He hesitated, wanting to pass the question by. But as the boy sat there staring into his decimated heart, his childish innocence, like a can opener, opened him up involuntarily. With his head hung low, he began his tale.

"Every man, who is a man, carries in his soul a fire, a fire which guides all he does, gives him the fuel he'll need to win life's battles. This fire he joins with his wife's, if he's blessed enough to have one, and passes to his children. Without this fire, a man simply cannot live."

He paused, his mind traveling far away from the present. "His fire is made of three flames: faith, hope, and love. It's more important for a man to pass on this fire than his DNA, more important than the blood which flows in his veins or the air in his lungs. The fire is his legacy, and a good legacy in this life is kin to immortality. You can kill the man but, if he's a good one, his legacy may never die." He looked into Caleb's eyes with tears glistening in his own. "I had a chance to be that man."

Somehow, in a single moment, the man had aged a hundred years. Even his angry fire was gone; his blue-gray eyes seemed empty except for regret. Sam drew a deep breath and continued.

"I did have a family once. A beautiful wife and three amazing children. I had always dreamed of earning my doctorate in biology and teaching at a major university. I wanted to publish papers with my name on them. I wanted to be recognized for my accomplishments. I worked and worked teaching high school biology during the day and pursuing my doctorate at night.

I never realized the burden I placed on my wife. When she asked me to take a break from it all and be part of the family, I accused her of standing in my way, of not appreciating all my hard work. She endured my antics for as long as she could, then, one day I came home from work and . . . they were gone."

He gazed into the mirror in front of him. "At the divorce trial I was so disgusted with her I didn't even fight for custody of my kids. I thought my life would be better off without them," he scoffed at himself. "A year later, I earned my doctorate and, shortly thereafter, a teaching position at the U of M. I came home night after night to an empty apartment where I drank myself to sleep. I had achieved my dream, only to find it an empty one. By the time the war started, I realized my mistake. I tried to find her. I followed every lead I could, but I never found them," he finished, pounding his fist on the mirror in despair.

"I'm sorry, Sam . . ."

"I'm beyond sorry . . . I'm lost."

"Maybe, somehow, we'll get out of this and you can find them."

"There's no getting out of this for me. It's what I deserve."

Caleb and Sam finished the ship without further conversation. When Captain Li arrived to inspect their work, he paused when he reached Sam. For the first time since his arrival, the proud old man made no attempt to look the captain in the eyes. The conversation with Caleb had done all the breaking he would need for the day. Without saying a word, the captain turned smugly and walked back down the gangway, assuming he had finally won.

Caleb and Sam walked back to the containers in silence. This time, it was Caleb who carried the old man's ration and led him back to his place in the container. It was the first time Sam had spoken of the demons of his past, and the confrontation had exposed a mortal wound he had concealed long ago.

Only a sliver of a moon hung in the night sky over the house as Aaron and Soraya prepared for their second outing of the night. Soraya sat at the table, committing a few new items on the list to memory, while Aaron smeared ash from the makeshift stove on his nose and cheeks.

"Huh," Aaron chuckled.

"What?"

"I just realized—yesterday was my eighteenth birthday."

"Happy birthday, Aaron."

"Thank you."

"I guess that makes you a man now," she jested.

"Yeah . . ." Aaron scoffed. "My dad would say it isn't age which makes a man, but maturity. He used to tell us he had served with eighteen-year-old men and worked with thirty-year-old boys."

"I think your dad would see a man when he looked at you," she said with confidence.

Aaron was grateful for the ash as he felt his cheeks flush. "I hope so."

He walked over to the table and took a seat, Soraya's eyes following him. Even with soot on his face he looked handsome, like a ruddy warrior heading off to battle. She had come to admire him very much. He seemed wise beyond his years and carried himself with humble poise.

"Aaron? Do you have dreams for after all . . .?" Her query was cut short by the distant echo of rifle fire.

Aaron leaped to his feet, the blood draining from his face. "LEAH!" he breathed in panic.

Ty and Leah raced to the doorway of the small shop they were scavenging. Chinese rifle fire rang out in the direction of the compound gate. Ty peered around the corner of the building just in time to see the flash of a figure dart through the gate light and into the lower city pursued by several troops armed with rifles and flashlights.

The column of bobbing lights moved up the hill heading west through the town, firing off rounds as it went.

"I think a prisoner is escaping!" Ty exclaimed in a loud whisper.

"Caleb?" Leah asked excitedly.

"I don't think so, I only caught a glimpse, but I think it was a man."

Ty suddenly turned and grabbed Leah by the shoulders, half scaring her to death.

"Leah! If we can get that guy, he might be able to help us free Caleb! Let's go!"

Without waiting for her reply, Ty quickly maneuvered down the street to intercept the figure pursued by the column of lights.

Leah raced after him, her eyes hardly able to make him out even though he was only a few feet in front of her.

"Ty! Ty, slow down, I can't see a thing," she hissed after him, but it was no use. She trotted along in the pitch dark in the direction Ty ran. Clouds had moved in, completely blocking out the moon's faint light. Terrified, she slowed to a walk, straining in vain to make out her surroundings.

"Sam!"

"I heard it too, son."

Caleb had been jerked out of a sound sleep when the first shot rang out. He was now sitting bolt upright in the blackness of their container, heart pounding a mile a minute. The muffled sounds of frenzied shouting and the pounding of a hundred boots filled the air. He heard Sam get to his feet and feel his way to the door.

"What's happening out there?"

"Shhh! I'm trying to listen!"

"It's my family! They're here! They came to get me!" Caleb sprang to his feet.

Just then, the base's siren started its wail.

"A prisoner must be trying to escape," Sam called through the darkness. "They're gonna catch him, whoever he is. Poor guy." With that, he shuffled back to his cardboard bed.

"It could still be my family, Sam. It has to be my family."

"It's not your family, kid."

"Why not?"

"For starters, there would be a lot more shooting. I've heard prisoners try to escape before. This is exactly what it sounds like. Trust me."

Caleb dropped back down to his own pile of cardboard. What could he do anyway? He couldn't even see his hand in front of his own face in this can, let alone find out if his family were out there looking for him. Sam was probably right, he usually was.

"What will they do if they catch him?"

"You'll get to see tomorrow. They'll make an example of him," he said with a growl. "It won't be pretty."

"What if they *don't* catch him?"

"They always catch them."

"But what if they don't?"

"They will! Now, go to sleep. We won't know what happened until morning anyway."

At last, Caleb laid back down. His pounding heart didn't let him sleep, though. Sam's doubts about his family were a little discouraging. *Are they here? Will they ever come?*

Aaron took the stairs up to the master bedroom two at a time, AK in hand, Soraya right behind him.

"Mom, wake up!" he shouted, bursting into the room.

Sara always slept in that room. She liked to be close to the big windows looking out over the city and the compound. She jumped up, instantly wide awake.

"There were gunshots!" He was already opening the doors to the balcony.

"What's going on?" asked Seth's worried voice from behind them.

"There was shooting out there," Soraya turned, her voice strained.

"Oh no!"

Suddenly, the shrill wail of a siren split the night, and immediately searchlights swung crazily toward the city. All four of them were now leaning over the railing, trying to find answers through the thick darkness.

"Come on, Ty. Come on," Soraya kept murmuring under her breath.

"They're chasing someone," Aaron said, tersely. "Look, there's flashlights over by the gate. I'm going out there."

He handed the binoculars over to his mother and started back to the stairs.

"If Ty and Leah are in trouble we have to know. Cover me the best you can, Mom. I'm not gonna just sit here and wait!"

"I'm coming, too!" Soraya ran after him.

"Be careful!" Sara called to their retreating forms.

A hand reached out from the darkness and grabbed her.

"Leah!" Ty whispered, pulling her to the ground beside him.

Leah, filled with rage, her heart pounding, spat out, "You left me!"

"Shhh! Listen!" Ty hissed, cupping his hand over her mouth.

In the darkness, Leah could barely make out the sound of footsteps over the siren, picking their way toward them clumsily through rubble.

"Cover me," Ty said, shoving his rifle into her trembling hands as the footsteps grew close. Leah felt Ty's body lunge away from her and then there was a thud, muffled grunting, and then Ty whispering again.

"Shut up! We're Americans, we're here to help you." He pulled the man to the ground next to Leah, his hand over his mouth.

"Stick with us and don't make a sound, we've got to get clear of here and wait until the drama stops, then we can get you to safety."

Ty stumbled along through the dark, dragging the man by the arm, Leah at his heels, until he was satisfied they were clear of the soldiers. The man grunted as Ty accidently bounced him off an old light pole.

"There isn't a chance in hell of those guys finding you on a night this dark. They run around like a pack of wild dogs barking in the dark hoping to catch a cat . . . stupid," Ty muttered under his breath.

"Perfect! It's even starting to rain! How on earth are we going to find our way back in this crazy dark!" Leah hissed.

"Easy, we moved north to grab this guy, all we have to do now is head west until we hit the tracks, then work our way south to the house," Ty said confidently.

Aaron knew the tracks would be the quickest avenue to maneuver themselves closer to the action. They started out at a quick pace, only to find the trees shrouding the rail line blocked any visual of the pursuing soldiers, and the echo of the siren off the nearby buildings made it impossible to make out their proximity to the situation. In frustration, Aaron stopped altogether after a few hundred yards, his ears straining to hear gunfire, a soldier's shout, anything to give him a sign as to what was going on. Soraya pulled up next to him in the dark. Reaching out, she found his hand and took it.

"Where are they, Aaron?" she whispered over the siren.

"I don't know."

As abruptly as it had begun, the siren went quiet. An eerie silence fell over the city. Aaron strained to hear in the dark, his ears nearly deafened by the siren. There was the sound of soft raindrops and then, through the black, he heard a fiery whisper.

"I can't believe you left me in the dark like that!" Leah's voice hissed. "Then, you scare the crap out of me by grabbing me and throwing me to the ground! And then you have the audacity to cram this stupid gun into my hands. What am I supposed to do with this thing?! I don't know how to shoot one of these!"

"What?! Are you serious? Give me that thing!"

"OW! Fine, here take it!"

"It's them!" Soraya whispered excitedly.

"Ty!" Aaron whispered loudly. "It's Aaron, you guys ok?"

In a moment, the two teams were face to face.

"Thank God!" Leah exclaimed.

"Amen to that," Aaron said, trying to contain himself. "What happened out there?"

"We got a prisoner," Ty announced triumphantly.

"Are you crazy? We don't take prisoners!" Aaron blasted.

"No, not one of them, an American."

"Really?! An American? You got an American? How? Who is he? Does he know Caleb?" Aaron asked in a frenzy.

"I don't know, he hasn't said anything . . . maybe they cut out his tongue or something."

"Well, we better get him back to the house," Soraya interjected, "Sara is worried sick about you guys and we're getting wet."

When they reached the house, Sara and Seth met them at the door.

"Leah!" Sara grabbed her daughter as she moved inside. "Are you ok? What happened out there?"

"We got a prisoner!" Ty again announced proudly.

"Guys! Can we move this downstairs?" Aaron got everyone's attention. "I can't see anything up here."

As the troop reached the basement, the candle's soft glow fell on the face of the unknown prisoner. Ty cursed as a new revelation dawned, "He's a Chinc!"

Chapter 15

Ty slammed the wide-eyed soldier up against the wall, pinning him with his arm.

Seth swung his rifle from his shoulder and leveled it inches from the soldier's forehead. His eyes blazing with fury, he growled, "I'll kill him!"

Aaron grabbed Seth's rifle barrel and pushed it to the side, glaring. "You pull that trigger and we're all in for it. Now, put that thing away!"

Lowering his rifle, Seth returned his older brother's glare. "This could be one of the scum who took Caleb!" he snarled.

The soldier shook his head side to side wildly as if to disagree with Seth.

"There are more ways to deal with him than shooting him," Ty offered, eyeing the man with disgust.

"And what would that prove?" Leah interjected. "That we're no different than they are. To kill him for being Chinese is as horrible as them killing us simply for being American."

Again, the soldier vigorously nodded, this time, in agreement with Leah.

"This isn't some wild animal you can turn into a pet, Leah, it's a Chinese soldier!" Seth railed.

"No one is killing him!" Sara cut in. "Leah's right, we're better than this."

Everyone froze for a moment, staring at her. She walked over to the prisoner who stood terrified at the base of the stairs, Ty's forearm still pinning him to the wall.

"He may be a soldier but, when I look at him, I see a terrified boy. Maybe as terrified as my boy and, at this moment, he's alone in hostile hands. Have we fallen so far we no longer see the man in the uniform?" She shook her head, "I don't know what we're going to do with him, but we will *not* be his executioners."

The room fell silent as she searched their eyes. After a moment, Soraya spoke up.

"What are you even doing here?" she asked rhetorically, eyeing the man.

"I don't know," he answered in almost perfect English. His captors straightened when he spoke, they hadn't expected him to sound so much like, well . . . like them.

He continued. "I was running from the soldiers into the dark, then I was grabbed and thrown to the ground with my mouth covered and a voice told me to "shut up!" So I did. Then, I was dragged down the street, thrown into a pole, and then we met all of you on the tracks."

Soraya half smirked as he finished. *Not exactly the kind of answer I was looking for. Of course, he's here because of us.*

"How old are you?" Sara asked.

"Eighteen."

Aaron sighed and shook his head. *We're the same age, just living in two different worlds.*

"Do you think Ty can let him go, Aaron?" Sara asked.

"I don't know. I'd feel a lot better if he was restrained in some way."

"Seth, go get the paracord," Sara said. "Ty, bring him over to the chair here."

Ty led the still wide-eyed soldier to a folding chair near the table, where the light shone brighter.

Seth returned with the paracord. Sara gently tied the man's hands to the folding joints of the chair. "There, now you have a little room to breathe." She said, giving him a gentle smile.

"Why were you running from the soldiers?" Aaron asked, arms crossed.

The young man considered a moment, as though trying to figure out where to start. Then, he began . . .

"When I was in China, I studied to be a linguist. I was particularly good, the top of my class. Then, my country decided to invade your country. Apparently, they ran short of interpreters because, before I was scheduled to start my enlistment, they came to my house and informed me I was to report for duty. After training to be an interpreter, they stuck me on a ship. I arrived here only a couple of months ago." He took a deep breath and continued.

"I was placed under Captain Li's command. He assigned me to prisoner interrogations and, at first, I simply interpreted for the interrogating officer. Then, during one interrogation, Captain Li showed up and didn't believe the prisoner was telling all she knew. So, he beat her, and beat her, until the woman quit breathing. When he saw my distaste, Captain Li told me I would be conducting the next interrogation, and he expected me to get the same result. I knew I could never torture another human being so, when a train arrived with new prisoners earlier today, I decided to run away. I planned to leave around midnight when most of the guards are very tired. But when I left my room, I bumped into Captain Li. I panicked and bolted past him, managing to make the gate before he could warn the soldiers. The rest you already know."

You could have heard a pin drop when he finished. No one knew what to think. What was he? A friend or foe? They all sat staring, confounded by the boy in front of them. He spoke their language, ran from their enemies and, if his story was true, had refused to harm their countrymen.

"I never wanted to be here . . ." The boy said, staring at the floor. "And now, I can never go home."

"What's your name?" Sara asked kindly.

"Wu . . . Long Wu," he said, without lifting his eyes from the floor.

"Well, Wu, what are we to do with you?" Sara sighed, leaning back in her chair.

"Give me some water, please?" the young man asked shyly.

Sara's chuckle broke some of the tension. "Yes, yes I think that's a fair request. Let's all get a little water and take a deep breath. Then, we can take this up again with clear heads."

Sara climbed the stairs to grab a water jug and their tin cups. When she returned to the top of the stairs, Aaron was waiting for her.

"We shouldn't be having this conversation in front of him," he said firmly.

"And what do you suggest we do? Leave him alone with one of the girls while we have our little meeting? The basement is the only room in the house we can safely use light. You just want to shove our guest in a dark closet while we decide his fate?"

"It's just awkward with him there. Besides, we don't know if we can trust him."

Sara thought for a moment. "Wu's right, Aaron, we brought him here. I don't believe he was sent here to spy us out. If they knew we were here, they would have just come up here and killed us all. Something in my heart tells me he's telling the truth and, right now, we're all the hope he has."

"He's Chinese, Mom!" Aaron whispered harshly.

"He's a human being, Aaron! And if we're going to decide his fate we may as well have the guts to do it in front of him." She turned and started down the stairs.

As Sara returned to the group, she eyed them all, knowing they had heard their conversation. She had as much reason as anyone to hate the Chinese but, when she looked at Wu, she didn't see a soldier, all she saw was a boy. She poured him a cup of water and held it to his mouth. He drank it quickly and thanked her. Then, she turned and served the rest of them.

Aaron reluctantly joined the semicircle they formed around Wu. He respected his mom above anyone else and hated being at odds with her. But his job was to keep them safe, and here she was again—making it difficult.

"The truth is, we can't afford to take prisoners." He cleared his throat. "We aren't animals. We're Americans. And, in this country, a man has the right to stand trial and defend himself. We don't condemn people based on their appearance, or nationality, or what their fellow countrymen have done. That being said, I'll be the first to admit, I'm not comfortable with simply trusting Wu based on his story alone."

"Well, we can't just let him go. What if he returns to the base and rats us out?" Ty pointed out.

"That's the problem. We can't kill him. We can't let him go, and we can't just trust him," Aaron finished, eyeing his mother.

"We already have a guard scheduled around the clock; why can't we just guard him till we know better?" Leah suggested.

"Prisoners have to eat. We hardly have enough food as it is; now you want us to feed one of them?" Seth rolled his eyes in disgust.

"You're right, Seth. We'll just starve him to death," Leah returned sarcastically. "Barbarian."

Wu couldn't understand why the young lady was on his side, but he appreciated her compassion and made a note, if he survived this meeting, to avoid the angry young man called Seth.

"We're wasting time," Soraya said. "The truth is we already know what we're going to do with him."

Everyone stared at her in surprise waiting for her to finish.

"We aren't going to let him go, we aren't going to starve him to death, and we aren't going to trust him right away. As unideal as it is, he's our prisoner and, until we rescue Caleb, that's just the way it's going to be."

Wu's ears perked up at the word "rescue." Somewhere in the back of his mind the name Caleb was familiar, but what was it? He racked his brain, and then he saw it. *Caleb was one of the names on the prisoner duty roster. . . . Where was he assigned? Oh yes, he worked with the old man cleaning ships' living quarters.*

"The young lady is right," Wu spoke up.

Everyone, surprised again, turned to look at their prisoner.

"I did not expect such treatment from Americans. You could have killed me," he said, looking at Seth. "But you didn't. I am an enemy in your land. I understand you cannot trust me. I appreciate your struggle over this matter." He acknowledged each one of them. "I think maybe I can help you with Caleb."

The sound of her son's name stirred Sara's heart. "You know my son?"

The door screeched open and gray light filtered into the small container. Two soldiers met Sam and Caleb as they emerged from their cardboard quarters. A stiff breeze sent a chill up Caleb's spine. This was no ordinary morning. Instead of marching the prisoners to work, the soldiers marched them toward the headquarters building.

As they approached, Caleb noticed formations of soldiers standing in perfect ranks on the puddle-spotted wharf. Low hanging clouds swirled in the sky above them, the last remnants of the storm the night before. Waves, still hammering the jetty, sent a spray that misted the resolute blocks of soldiers as they awaited Captain Li's appearance.

Caleb and Sam were marched to a small formation of wavering prisoners in the center of the military array. Even the stringent smell of the wharf could not suppress the odor of neglected humanity, which now assaulted Caleb's senses. He decided to risk a glance down the row of teetering prisoners. He was aware of other prisoners on the wharf. He had seen them from the bridge of the ships they cleaned or at the containers at the end of the day. He had no idea there were so many. There must have been thirty of them, all in varying degrees of malnutrition and neglect, not a one so healthy looking as he.

"Keep your eyes front, kid, here he comes. Prepare yourself for something terrible," Sam muttered under his breath.

As if on cue, a breeze danced across the puddles and lifted the Chinese flag standing behind the podium on the small platform. Captain Li ascended the stairs in full military dress, his chest embellished with ribbons from his exploits, a yellow cord formed a loop on the left shoulder of his forest green uniform. Caleb had to admit, the man looked impressive as he navigated the platform in three sharp strides.

Once he reached the podium, the officers in charge of the platoons called out a series of commands which were obeyed by the attending soldiers in perfect unison. The thunder of two hundred stomping boots echoed over the wharf as the soldiers performed their spectacle. Then, with his army locked in position, he began his oration.

It was time for the morning gathering, and the dark basement had been abandoned in favor of the brighter master bedroom upstairs. Brighter was a bit of an overstatement. Last night's storm had left its dreary, damp shadow as far as the eye could see. Still, it was much better than huddling around candlelight.

Ty and Leah had yet to make an appearance. Last night's events kept them up longer than normal and there was no reason to wake them just yet. There had been no more missions attempted, partly due to the storm, but mostly because of their new "guest." Last night's conversation had been exhausting, with spiraling cycles of anger, fear, desperation, and just enough hope to keep it complicated. The result was less than satisfactory, but as much as either side of the matter could expect. Wu would remain their prisoner. In exchange for his life and care, he would supply them with all the knowledge of the compound he could to aid in the rescue of Caleb. Afterward . . . well, they would have to cross that bridge later.

Aaron sat on the floor pouring over his ever-present map spread out on a low wooden coffee table, carried up from the living room for this purpose. It was only for appearances, though; his mind couldn't seem to move on from the trouble which had entered their lives last night and was currently slumped down in a corner with his hands still tied together.

It was going to complicate life dramatically to have a person in camp they couldn't trust. Wu had done his best to explain he would have no motive for turning them in, since doing so would mean condemning himself. Still, all he would have to do is whack whoever was left on guard at the house, and he would have all the survival gear he could run off with.

Soraya and Seth entered the room and distributed the breakfast they had prepared downstairs. It was fish. Again. The trapping success had diminished as of late and, though Sara and Seth occasionally found berries on their trips, they never lasted long. After handing Sara her share, Seth stayed by her side at the big windows. She almost never left those windows during daylight hours. Seeing him safe and alive every day was the only reason she could stay with the plan and keep herself from charging in after him.

This morning the plan was to get Wu's description and explanation of everything in the compound they could see. If he could tell them how it was run and how the layout worked, they would have a lot more to go on in creating a plan.

"Something different is happening over there," Sara announced to the room, eyes still focused on the compound. Everyone looked up from their breakfast. Aaron jumped up, peering over her shoulder.

"They're all forming up in rows. Wow, there are a lot of soldiers down there."

Wu got himself to his feet and came over to look, careful to keep a respectful distance from the family.

"They're even bringing out the prisoners now. Where's Caleb, where's Caleb? They're so huddled up in the middle I can't find him. . . . What on earth is going on over there?" Sara asked. Turning to Wu, who was now standing against the wall at the end of the windows, Sara repeated her question. "Wu? Do you know what's happening over there?"

"It's for me." His eyes were locked on the formation, but they seemed to be looking through it rather than at it.

The sadness in his answer caught every listener by surprise.

"What you are seeing is to make sure what I did last night never happens again. Next, I suppose they will send bulletins to every outpost with my picture. If anyone finds me, I am a dead man." Finally, he looked away from the compound, "I no longer have a country."

Seth grunted sarcastically and walked away from the window. "Join the club!" he quipped over his shoulder.

Wu looked up, Seth's words sinking in. He really *saw* them now, as they stared out the window. *A people without a country.*

Caleb puzzled over the morning's events while sweeping out the captain's quarters on a large cargo barge. Everything Captain Li had said seemed oddly directed at the soldiers of the compound.

The captain had gone on and on about the privilege of serving in the People's Liberation Army. Of the great honor bestowed on them to conquer China's enemies. That every one of them had a duty to the People's Republic of China. Then he had sternly warned everyone present that a failure to perform one's duties, or worse, to reject one's duties, would be met with the most severe punishment he could devise.

During the last part, it became very apparent to everyone he was quite mad. For a moment, he had lost his composure and was literally spitting as he waved his arms in fury. Then, he tidied his uniform, performed an about-face, and marched off the stage.

"Sam?" Caleb asked. "That formation didn't seem so terrible." He looked over at the old man who was hardly paying attention to the chest of drawers he was dusting.

"Sam? Are you alright?"

Flinching, Sam returned to reality, knocking over a small clock.

"Did you notice?" Sam asked, a strange energy dancing in his eyes.

"Notice what?"

Sam grabbed him by the shoulders. "There was no example made. . . . I've seen it four or five times, whenever a prisoner attempts to escape, they catch him and, in the morning, he's caned and then shot in front of everyone as an example. . . ."

Caleb eyed the man, clearly at a loss.

"Whoever caused all the fuss last night made it," he said in wonder.

"Made what?"

"Are you kidding . . .?! Argh, he escaped, boy! He had to have, or we would have witnessed his final moments this morning!" Sam whispered excitedly.

"Ok . . ." Caleb said, stepping back from the eccentric old man.

"Do you know what this means? If he can do it, so could we!"

Caleb cracked a smile, watching the man practically dance with excitement. He liked excited Sam far more than moody Sam.

"I thought you said you didn't want to escape?" Caleb challenged.

Sam grew serious. "I wouldn't be doing it for me, son, but you deserve a better life than this. If there's even a slim chance of getting you out of this dump, I'm willing to take it."

The two captives cleaned the vessel in record time, Sam humming as they went. For the first time since his divorce, the old man had something to live for. Tonight, they would not pass the time in idle conversation. No, tonight they would conceive a plan, a plan to escape.

Chapter 16

Two days had passed since the prisoner escaped. Sam racked his brain all that night and the following day, trying to come up with any way they could possibly escape without getting killed.

Breaking out of their container was impossible. The door was double bolted, and they had never been permitted to see how the compound operated at night. On the way to and from work, they were escorted by guards. But once on board the ships they were left to themselves with a guard posted at the bottom of the gangway. There was no reason to follow them around the ship. The only place to go would be the freezing waters of the lake, and a failure to perform their duties would only mean severe punishment.

"If we're going to escape, it will have to be during work," Sam concluded.

"How? There are soldiers everywhere. We can't even get off the ship!"

Sam looked out the massive bridge windows of the barge. "I haven't figured that out yet; keep mopping."

"I'm sick of mopping."

"All the more reason to let me think."

"We could steal a ship," Caleb suggested.

"Kid," Sam sighed, slapping his palm to his own forehead. "Let me do the thinking. Please."

"Two days ago, you didn't even want to escape," Caleb grumbled.

The old man glared at him but decided to let the comment go. *How to get off a ship, out of sight, and then through the gate? During the day, impossible; at night, more impossible!* Sam felt his hope beginning to fade. *There has to be a way . . .*

"Sam, you're not cleaning. What good is planning an escape if we're beaten to death before we get the chance."

The old man let out a humph and went back to washing the windows.

The day seemed to drag as Sam reasoned through, and then rejected every idea that came to him.

Caleb gave up trying to help and set his mind to ensure they didn't earn a sound beating for Sam's distracted behavior. Then, as they were finishing in the galley, it hit him.

"What if we used a lifeboat, Sam?" Caleb said, handing him a half empty jar of peanut butter.

The old man pondered this idea for a moment, taking a fingerful of peanut butter from the jar. They had made it their practice to "empty" any opened containers of food and discard them as a part of their "thorough" cleaning of any vessel.

"They would catch us trying to lower it or notice it missing and come looking for us. We would never make it out of the harbor. Nice try though, kid," he sighed, crawling back inside the stove he was working on. Then, all at once, he burst back out, staring at Caleb wide-eyed. "Wait! Not a lifeboat, a life *raft!* Many of these ships don't carry enough lifeboats for the entire crew, so to make up for it, ships have several inflatable life rafts. They're usually stored out of sight and wouldn't be missed like a lifeboat would, we could launch it off the back corner of the ship which can't be seen from the dock."

"How would we get out of the harbor?" Caleb asked, taking the last bit of peanut butter from the jar, then throwing the empty container into his garbage bag.

"Well, I haven't gotten that far yet, but I think the idea is worth considering," Sam said with a half-smile.

"Can you finish considering it when we're done?" Caleb asked nervously.

Sam took a deep breath and let it out.

"Sure, kid."

On their way back to the containers that night, Sam took notice of everything. He had made this trek hundreds of times since coming to the wharf but had never cared enough to take notice of his surroundings. Tonight, he was a whole different Sam, mentally logging everything as they went.

The guards on the docks come with the prisoners, leaving the docks deserted. The only light after dark will be the safety lights lining the railing and a larger light at the base of the dock tower. There's only one guard tower at the base of the docks. The rest line the wall of the compound, one tower every hundred and fifty yards or so. The gate closest to the containers, the main gate, always has two soldiers on duty and is controlled from inside the small gate shack.

Unfortunately, that was all the intelligence the old man could conclude before they arrived at their humble "home" and were locked in for the night.

"I miss my mama . . ." Caleb mourned as he lit the nightly candle.

Sam had almost forgotten the kid had recently been separated from his family.

"I'm sure you do," he managed compassionately. "If all the stories you've told me about your family are true, I think it's safe to say they did their best to find you. I'm sorry I never got the chance to meet them, Caleb."

"I don't want to believe it, but they must be dead. . . ." Caleb's voice choked. "They would've come for me otherwise."

Sam didn't have an answer for Caleb's broken heart. The kid was probably right. He pulled out another candle he had lifted from the ship and lit it. Tonight was a two-candle night. Then, with a grin, he produced a deck of cards he had found under a sailor's mattress.

"Do you play cards?"

Smiling, Caleb moved to the light.

"We'll get through this, kid. I promise. I'll find a way," Sam assured him, shuffling the cards.

"Well, there's no way to candy coat this; with or without Wu, we're going to run out of food soon," Sara reported at the beginning of the evening's gathering. "Seth and I have been fishing like crazy every night, and the fish just aren't biting like they used to. The snares are coming up empty more often than not. I don't know what we're going to do if we can't come up with another source of food, and soon."

Aaron agreed. "Based on Wu's description of the compound I have worked up a plan which I think has a possibility of success. It's not complete by any means, but it will give us a better foundation to work from. There are many moving parts and, therefore, supplies, to pull together for this plan to work, which means we're going to be here for a while. Besides, we really need to have at least a small amount of food set aside for our retreat after the rescue. We may not be able to stop for a while."

The master bedroom was quiet as everyone mulled over the situation.

"We could eat Wu," Seth teased.

Wu's head shot up from his corner at the suggestion.

"He's joking," Sara reassured him.

"What about the compound? I'll bet they have loads of food in there," Ty ventured.

"Wu? Is there any way to get food from the compound?" Aaron asked.

Wu thought hard for a moment. There certainly wouldn't be a way to get food from inside the compound, but maybe they could acquire some of it another way.

"I don't think it would be wise to try and take any food from inside the base, but the trains leaving from there are always carrying boxes of military rations in crates. Some flat cars are entirely rations. Those cars go all the way to the troops in Minneapolis. Today is Saturday; the train for Minneapolis heads out tonight."

"Wouldn't the first outpost the train rolls by notice the missing boxes and realize they had been taken from somewhere between Duluth and the outpost?" Soraya asked. "That could mean trouble."

Again, Wu pondered her question.

"The way they're stacked in the crates is like this." He drew them a diagram of the boxes inside the crates. It was less than perfect, since his hands were still always tied together, but the idea was clear.

"If you only took these two boxes from the middle of each crate, no one would know they were missing until they were unloaded. There's a lot of distance between here and Minneapolis and more than a few scattered Americans, I'm sure."

"Well, it's a better idea than any I've thought up. How will we know which crates are rations?" Aaron asked.

"They will be marked like this," Wu said, drawing a Chinese character.

Sara gave Wu an approving nod. He had a good heart and a quick mind; she hoped the rest would recognize it soon.

By the time the gathering was over, they had formulated a plan. Wu had given them the information they needed to make the night a success. Now, they just needed to pull it off. Two groups would go out, one would board the train as it made the turn down the tracks that passed the house. As soon as the first group could manage it, they would begin throwing the boxes of rations off the train. The second group would then carry the boxes back to the house, making as many trips as necessary. Lastly, the first group would jump off the train, before it got up to speed a couple of hundred yards past the house, and then help the second group get all the boxes back. The third group would have to wait up with Wu while the others were out.

"If this works, I think we can take the rest of the night off. Lord knows we could use it," Aaron added.

Sara and Seth would stay behind with Wu while the others headed off once more into the dark. Aaron and Soraya would be the boarding party while Ty and Leah managed the boxes back to the house.

Like clockwork, the eight o'clock train departed the wharf. As the gate closed behind it, the raiding party reached their positions and hunched quietly in the dark.

Aaron's pulse quickened as the engine rounded the corner. One by one, the cars rolled by. The first carried a handful of soldiers, followed by a couple flat cars; one bore a military helicopter. The helicopter was followed by a dozen fuel cars, then came flat cars stacked front to back with crates. As the second car of crates pulled past them slowly, Aaron recognized the symbol for rations.

"This one!" he whispered loudly and jumped from the ditch, Soraya by his side.

Together, they climbed to the top of the stack where Aaron produced a small pry bar he had found in a garage. Stapled to each lid was a single white piece of paper. Aaron thought it best not to leave any obvious signs of their tampering, so they took pains to avoid the note. Together, they pried the lid off one of the crates, laid it to the side, and pulled out the first box. Aaron shook it just to be sure and, satisfied, he threw it off the train into the ditch.

They repeated this process all the way down the car, always careful to nail the lid back on the crate before moving on.

The night air felt refreshing as they worked feverishly, trying to score every possible meal, as the train slowly began to pick up speed.

"Only two more crates to go, Aaron."

"No, leave them; we need to get off this thing."

"We need them!"

Knowing arguing was only going to waste time, Aaron finished nailing down the lid and moved onto the next crate. They wrenched open the lid, each of them grabbing a case and tossing it in one motion. Aaron nailed the lid on and moved to the last crate, the train was really picking up speed now. He tore the cover loose but lost it to the wind off the side of the train, it was no use worrying about that now. They pulled out the last two cases and launched them from the train.

"Be careful," Aaron warned as Soraya slipped her leg over the side of the stack. As she went to swing her other leg over the side, the train hit a bump in the track shaking the car. She lost her footing and fell over the side, her scream pierced through the train's rattling as she hung on with only one hand.

Without taking the time to think, Aaron threw himself over the side, raced down the car, and jumped. Hitting the ground, he did a tuck and roll and was back on his feet, running beside the car.

"Let go, Soraya, I'll catch you!"

Looking over her shoulder she was barely able to make him out in the darkness. "Aaron! I'm scared!"

"You have to let go!" he yelled, running out of breath as he jogged to keep up.

Closing her eyes, she let go. Backward, away from the train car, she let herself fall.

Aaron raced to intercept her, throwing his arms around her just in time to break her fall, sending the two of them tumbling into the ditch.

"Trains!" Aaron grumbled, laying on his back at the bottom of the ditch.

"Ok, you were right, we should have left the last two," Soraya admitted climbing off him. "I'm sorry," she said, reaching out her hand to pull him up. "Thanks for saving me, Aaron."

Aaron felt his cheeks redden. "I didn't really save you, I mean, well I guess I sorta did," he said, stumbling over his words.

Soraya chuckled at his struggle and decided to help him out. "We better get moving. The others will be waiting on us."

"Yeah." he managed to choke out. *What is wrong with me?*

They decided to recover the crate top Aaron had lost off the train since any evidence of their heist could be their undoing. Besides, it worked great as a litter to stack boxes on. A little battered, the pair limped their way back toward the house, loading boxes onto the lid as they went.

"You guys ok?" Leah asked, noticing the mud all over Aaron from his fall.

"Yeah, we'll be alright," Aaron said, rubbing his backside.

"Well, these are the last of the boxes," Ty said, carrying two under each arm.

The four of them arrived at the house laughing and joking in hushed tones as they entered. Everyone was glad something had worked out for a change.

As Ty stacked the last four boxes on the pile, Sara reported. "That's twenty-four cases!"

Smiles appeared on every face while warm candlelight danced on the pile of loot.

"Hey, Wu . . . is this you?" Seth asked, pointing to the slip of paper fixed to the crate lid.

Everyone drew close, inspecting the mud-stained figure. The image certainly bore resemblance to their captive, although the boy in the picture was clean and in perfect military attire.

"Wu, what is this?" Aaron asked.

Wu stood in mournful silence as he read the warrant to himself.

"What does it say?" Sara asked, moving to stand beside him.

"It says I'm a deserter. It says if anyone finds me, they're to turn me in and, if I resist, to shoot me. One way or another, I am a dead man."

Aaron looked long into Wu's face as he stood staring down at the paper. He watched as several emotions chased each other across the young man's features, features so different from his own, and yet every emotion he saw there he himself had intimately known. Aaron turned abruptly from the group and went upstairs.

Sara watched him leave in surprise. Glancing back at Wu, she got an inkling of what was going on and followed. She found him out on the balcony looking into the night sky. There were enough lights shining in the compound to see if anything was going on, but Aaron wasn't looking at the compound. His gaze went out over the lake, beyond the lake. The battle waging inside him was so palpable she could feel it as she stepped to his side. He stood with white knuckled hands, gripping the iron railing. His body was stiff as a board, his face like stone.

Silently, they breathed the cool night air, Sara waiting for the right words to come. After a moment, they did. "You saw Wu's heart down there, didn't you?"

Aaron didn't respond.

She waited.

"He isn't going to hurt us . . . is he, Mom?" It was more of a statement, really.

"What does your heart tell you?"

"That we're the only thing standing between him and death. That he's lost everything he's ever cared about. He has nothing left." He took a deep breath and finally looked into his mother's eyes. "But he wants to live. I saw it in his face." His voice grew in intensity. "I don't know what to do! My job isn't to take care of him, it's to take care of you, of Caleb, our family! What if letting him become one of us isn't safe? What if he betrays us?"

"When is love safe, Aaron? Love is never 'safe.' But it's love which makes life worth living. It's love which gives us a reason to be here. We aren't here because it's 'safe,' we're here because we love. And one day, when we walk out of here with Caleb by our side, it won't be because it was the 'safe' thing to do. It will be because we loved enough."

She paused and smiled slightly at the torn expression on Aaron's young face. Lovingly, she lifted her hand to it and smoothed his furrowed brows with her thumb. "Hey, God isn't the author of confusion. Ask Him what's in Wu's heart. He won't hide it from you."

"Yeah," Aaron breathed, starting to relax just a little.

After another quiet moment, she asked, "What do you see when you look at Wu?"

He gave a low chuckle. "Actually, he almost reminds me of Leah."

"Really . . .?"

"Yeah, it's like he doesn't even belong in this mess. He belongs in a world of peace, with regular tea times, walks in the park, and his books! I don't think he wanted to have to choose sides, but now he has and going back isn't an option. I honestly think he just wants to belong somewhere. He's smart. He knows he doesn't stand a chance out there on his own. If the Chinese don't kill him, any random American he runs into sure will. Besides, I don't think he wants to be alone. In reality, he has absolutely zero motives for hurting us in any way."

"I think I agree with you," she smiled. "So, what does this mean for us now?"

"Well, I guess we go ask him what he wants."

Ty, Soraya, Leah, and Seth sat on chairs around the table
tearing into rations from the night's haul. Wu had sunk down to
the floor in the corner opposite the stairs, his head on his knees,
an untouched ration next to him. When Sara and Aaron
reappeared in the basement, Leah offered each of them a ration.

"There are twelve in each box!" she said excitedly.

Aaron motioned that he would pass and cleared his throat.
Everyone at the table paused and looked up.

"Here's the deal. This piece of paper proves Wu is telling the
truth," Aaron said, holding up the warrant from the crate. "He's
a stranger in a strange country; any of his people who find him
will either turn him in or kill him. Any American who finds him
will do the same. On his own, he's as good as dead." Pausing,
Aaron let his words sink in. "Now, tonight wouldn't have
happened if it weren't for Wu's intel. On top of that, he's cut off
God only knows how many days of recon on the compound." He
paused again.

"Mom and I have discussed it, and we believe Wu should be
given the option to join us. We're a team, and it would be wrong
for us to make this decision without your consent, so I'd like to
put it to a vote. Before we vote, does anyone have anything they
would like to add?" He looked around the room.

Wu was now sitting upright, watching this curious spectacle.
These Americans were not at all what he had expected. He, for
his part, had not yet considered the option of "joining" them. He
wasn't even sure what they were, how they lived or expected to
survive. Before tonight, they were literally living fishing trip to
fishing trip. On the other hand, without them, he probably
wouldn't be living at all.

"Alright, since no one has voiced their opinion, I guess it's
time to vote. All those in favor of giving Wu the option to join us
raise your hand."

Wu's heart raced as Aaron gave the word. He watched as each
hand went up. First Aaron, Sara, Leah, and Soraya, after a

moment's hesitation, Ty, and lastly, Seth, not wanting to be the odd man out, raised his hand. The vote was unanimous. A strange emotion washed over him, hope mixed with gratitude and something else, something deeper.

"Well, what'll it be?" Aaron asked, staring down at him curiously.

Wu searched their faces trying to discern if this is what they really wanted or if they just felt like it was their only option.

"Are you sure this is what you want?"

"Well, the paper says you're a deserter, so we won't set our expectations too high," Aaron jested.

For the first time since his capture, Wu cracked a smile. "Alright, I'll join you," he said, rising to his feet. "Thank you all very much." Wu bowed to them in humble gratitude.

Aaron pulled out his hunting knife and cut Wu free.

Sara walked over and threw her arms around him in a welcoming hug. Wu glanced at Aaron, his arms pinned by her embrace, not exactly sure what to do.

"For better or worse, you're one of us now," Aaron chuckled.

"Maybe now you can tell me what I'm eating," added Soraya.

The band of vagabonds spent the rest of the evening in storytelling, games, and laughter, even Seth managed to bury his resentment and join the fray.

Chapter 17

Captain Li was no fool. He knew the prisoners couldn't escape the containers at night; the doors were double bolted from the outside and any attempt to cut through the walls would make such a racket the guards would be sure to hear it.

Then, there was the fact that all the prisoners were separated, kept in pairs so there would be no opportunity to collaborate with their fellow prisoners and put together a joint escape. Keeping them in total darkness at night meant there was no way for them to communicate ideas other than by mouth, making it difficult to draw up a plan.

Lastly, they were under guard all day. All the other workers had direct supervision while they worked the docks from dawn to dusk.

Sam and Caleb had their ages to thank for their lack of supervision. Captain Li assumed the old man and little boy hadn't the strength or energy to be dangerous, and so they were left unsupervised aboard their floating prison while they worked. The only guard was posted at the bottom of the gangway. There was no other way off the ship.

Yup, as much as Sam hated the man, he had to admit that Captain Li knew how to maintain prisoners with minimal effort. *Or does he?* Sam grinned at the thought of making a fool out of

Captain Li. He'd show that overgrown Chinese puppet what good ol' Americans could do!

He was in the process of cleaning the bridge windows which, much to Caleb's dismay, was about the only part of the ship he cleaned anymore. He pulled a rectangular piece of cardboard and a pen out of his waistband and took notes on the changing of the dock guards at noon. Today's task was to note everything he could on the compound guard schedule, their placement, field of view, and attentiveness. So far, things were going well.

"Sam, the head is a disaster. There's no way we're finishing this ship on time if you won't help me," Caleb complained from the doorway of the bridge.

"I am helping you, boy! Helping you get out of here," the old man grunted.

Caleb just stood, staring at him.

"Ok, ok, I'm coming!" Sam muttered, sliding the cardboard back into his waistband.

His plan was beginning to take shape. They would drop a life raft off the stern of one of the smaller cargo ships, then climb down the mooring line and drop into the raft. Next, they would have to quietly paddle the raft under the end of the massive dock. On a calm day, there was roughly four feet between the bottom of the dock and the lake. On a rough day, they would drown for sure.

For the plan to work, they would have to wait under the dock all day. Once it was night, they would be free to paddle their way north of the compound, make land, hide the raft, and make a run for it. Sam just needed to find a way to pull it off without the guards on the dock noticing two prisoners rowing about the harbor in a bright yellow raft in broad daylight.

"So, what are we gonna eat when we escape?" Caleb asked.

"I suppose we'll have to hit the galley first and grab things like peanut butter and canned goods, not a lot, just enough to get us a few days away from here. We're going to need some tools too, a couple of knives maybe, some rope, and something to carry it all in."

"Where are we gonna go?"

"I think we'll head north, like your family. I believe they had the right idea. It's thick up there, and I don't think the Chinese have much interest in places where there isn't any civilization. I'm not the best woodsman, but I think I could figure it out." He said the last part more in hope than belief.

Caleb smiled at the thought of Sam agreeing with his father's plan. He missed his family and thought about them often. But as Sam had said on their first day, the pain didn't hurt as bad. For the moment, he was glad simply to have Sam. Caleb swirled the mop in his bucket, wrung it out, and slapped it back on the floor. *Maybe everything will be ok.*

The day ended like every other day: an inspection, followed by a disappointed Captain Li and a couple lashes. Caleb had reached the point where he hardly winced at the pain. The lashes were as normal a part of his day as dinner.

Leah shivered as a drop of rain rolled down her collar. It was going to be another cold, wet night in the city. She nervously fiddled with a small lighter in her pocket. It was from a box Sara and Seth had scored while scavenging an abandoned gas station. It was a handy source of light on nights like this one. Tonight, it was up to Ty and her to find a map of Duluth so Aaron could work out the details of the plan. The plan . . .

Aaron had spent most of the evening laying out the plan he and Sara had concocted based on Wu's intelligence. The rescue would take place on a clear night with the wind blowing from the southwest. There would be two teams: a diversionary team and a rescue team. The diversionary team would infiltrate the compound through a hole cut in the perimeter fence on the southwest side. They would take out the lone guard and the two dogs guarding the coal cars awaiting dispersal. Next, one of them would make their way across the compound to the headquarters building, climb the fire escape, and sever the communication cables going to the dishes and antennae.

As soon as communications were down, a couple of the coal cars would be set on fire and, riding the southwest wind, the smoke would create thick camouflage for the rescue team to conceal themselves in. Once the cars were lit, Sara would snipe as many of the guard tower lights as she could hit from the south side of the compound. Hopefully, the soldiers would race across the compound to the southwest corner to engage the "hostiles," leaving the rescue team with minimal resistance as they worked, hidden in the smoke, to find Caleb.

There was the probability they would release other prisoners in their search. Leaving them to be punished wasn't an option, so they had to be ready to take them along. For the sake of survival, they hoped it wouldn't be many. Once they had Caleb, the rescue team would head out through the main gate and through the city to the north, meeting up with the diversionary party at a rendezvous point.

Not all the details were ironed out yet, and assignments hadn't been made, but that was the plan in its incomplete form for now.

The immensity of the compound did little to give Leah hope that any plan could succeed. But Caleb was in there, which was why she was here. She kicked around some fallen pamphlets, most of them had long since been illegible, and moved on. This was their third gas station tonight and, so far, they had come up empty.

"We have to keep looking. Maybe we can find a gift shop or something, but I think most of those are going to be closer to the lake," Ty whispered, his breath forming small clouds.

The two of them worked their way through the debris-laden street toward the lights of the compound looking for any sign of another gas station, bait shop, or gift store. It was slow going. The steep, wet streets filled with rubble, in the pitch dark, were impossible. Leah slipped and nearly fell, but Ty caught her by the arm and helped her regain her footing. Once she had her feet under her, she jerked her arm out of his hand.

"Whoa, what was that for? I was only trying to help."

"Now you want to help me, after leaving me in the dark the other night!"

"You're still sore about that? Leah, I thought you were right behind me. I didn't know you hadn't followed me."

"And then you cram that stupid gun in my hands and jump on Wu, like I was really going to be able to defend you . . . or myself for that matter!"

"I'm sorry about all that, I really am. I just thought you knew how to take care of yourself. Your family seems to, and you shot that bow so well. I just figured you could do the same with a gun."

"Well, I am not my family. I have never shot anything except my mom's tiny pistol, and that was at a lifeless tin can. You promised you would look after me out there, Ty, I trusted you."

"You're right, Leah. I messed up, and I'm sorry. I *will* take care of you out here and, this time, I won't assume anything."

"You'd better."

"Ah, there we go, just like my old man used to say, tell a woman she's right, and she'll let it go."

"TY!"

"I'm just kidding, just kidding," he chuckled.

They arrived at a small strip of stores about six blocks from the compound containing a bait shop, an all things camping store, and a couple of shops missing their signs completely.

"Wanna take a look?"

"Are you going to take care of me?" Leah returned, half in jest.

They entered the bait shop where a few reels of line and other tackle still hung on their hooks. Ty pocketed the line, along with some hooks, and a few other odds and ends from the fishing section. Looking over the maps, Leah grabbed one labeled

Boundary Waters Canoe Area, and then the dim light of her lighter glinted off a laminated map labeled Duluth.

"I got it!" she nearly yelled in excitement.

"SHHHHH! You want to get us killed?" Ty warned as he crossed the small shop, his feet crunching on bits of broken glass.

"Yeah, I think this is what he's looking for. Nice work." He gave her a playful nudge. "Let's go ahead and check the rest of these shops. We might find some useful stuff, then we won't have to check them again."

Her steps were lighter as they continued through the other shops. Every successful mission was one step closer to getting Caleb out of that awful place. In all honesty, she couldn't wait to be clear of Duluth. The soldiers unnerved her. She would be thrilled if she never had to look at another man in uniform again.

By the time they were finished, they had a fairly good haul: some basic fishing gear, a couple bottles of lantern oil, a few pairs of hiking boots of different sizes, and a jug to carry water.

Leaving the shops, Leah looked back over her shoulder at the compound. This was as close as she had ever been to the prison-like fortress, its high fences topped with razor wire, guard towers complete with armed guards and large halogen lights. It was a menacing sight, sending chills up her spine. *God help us . . .*

Back at the house, Aaron beamed as he looked over the map Leah had delivered.

"It's perfect!" he said, giving his little sister a hug. "Now, besides finishing our plan, we can mark where we've been so we don't waste time looking for stuff where other groups have already looked. When each group gets back from a mission, we'll mark it down as best we can."

Ty laid out their other treasures on the table. Then, it was time for his team to hit the sack. Within moments, Sara and Seth emerged from their beds upstairs and came down to take their first shift on guard. Aaron and Soraya were busy studying the new map in preparation for the night's mission when Sara joined them.

"Ah, I see the night has already met with success," she said, glad to see another item crossed off the list.

"Yeah, it's going to be a big help," Aaron said. "If everyone marks where they've been, we should save significant time scavenging. And, come time to pull off this rescue, we'll have a pretty elaborate plan drawn out on this thing."

"It must be nice to have a new map to hover over," she teased him, winking at Soraya. "What are you guys going after tonight?"

"Intel. I need to draw up the compound on this map and start fine tuning the final plan. We're going to spend most of our shift out on the balcony filling in details. I think I'll have Wu sit up with us if he's willing," Aaron answered, ignoring his mother's previous comment.

"I'd be glad to help," Wu said from behind them.

"Crap! Wu, how do you do that?" Aaron spun around. "You scared me to death!"

"Sorry, I am light on my feet."

"You guys go on up and get started. I'll be up in a sec," Aaron said.

After Soraya and Wu were out of sight, Aaron turned to Sara, frustration now revealed on his face.

"Mom, we're desperately out of time. The nights are already too frigid for anyone to safely survive out there."

"But we aren't out there, Aaron, we have this house, and we're doing ok."

"Until we get Caleb! Then what? We have to have time to get north, build a shelter strong enough to last the winter, collect wood to keep us warm, and enough food to get us through. And our iodine tablets aren't going to last forever!" He flung out an arm in exasperation. "Why didn't Dad leave this summer? We wouldn't be in this mess," he muttered.

"Aaron, he was planning to leave in the spring, and we would've had all summer to prepare something. But then Hanna happened, and here we are. Please don't blame him. You know he would never have wished this on any of us."

"What am I supposed to do, Mom? Everyone expects me to have everything all figured out, and I don't. I don't know what to do. I don't know if this will work. We might all end up dead, and it will all be on me!" he said, holding his head in his hands.

"I know, Aaron, and I'm grateful for everything you're doing. No one is better at this type of strategy than you. I'm sorry, but that's just the way it is. You're the best shot we have and, no matter what happens, we're a team. We *have* to try."

"What are we going to do when we get up north? It's going to be mid-November at this rate."

"We'll do our best and leave the rest up to God."

"I was afraid you were going to say that. That's not a plan, Mom."

"Aaron, you have to focus on the problem in front of us now. The sooner we overcome it, the sooner we can tackle the next one. It's no use worrying about a hill we may never climb," she said calmly.

Aaron sighed. "That's exactly the part I'm worried about."

"I know . . ." she said, touching her hand to his face.

Aaron went up the stairs to join the others. Although he didn't feel encouraged by their conversation, it felt good to be reminded he wasn't the only one who understood the gravity of their circumstances.

Sitting on the balcony, looking out over what was left of Duluth and the compound, Aaron, Soraya, and Wu went to work on the map sketching in the borders of the base, the gate, guard towers, prisoner containers, and the headquarters building. Wu showed them the barracks, the mess hall, and the generators.

"Wu, I'm glad you're with us," Aaron said.

Wu nodded.

"I'm sorry for what happened to you; we know what it's like to not have a home."

"But you have your family. I have no one." Sighing, Wu looked out over the lake. "My mother has probably already been told of my treachery. I have disgraced my family. Even if I could go home, they wouldn't have me."

"If we succeed in rescuing my brother, you'll be a hero. At least in our eyes."

The sound of incoming helicopters put an abrupt end to their conversation, sending them scrambling into the bedroom. The trio watched out the patio door as two military helicopters flew over the city and landed in an opening near the southern end of the compound. After fifteen minutes, the helicopters lifted off and flew back the way they had come.

"What are we going to do about those things?" asked Soraya.

"We'll have to keep trying to pattern them and, if that's not possible, just hope we get lucky."

"You're all very brave," Wu commented.

"You're pretty brave yourself, Wu," Soraya replied.

"Well, I am supposed to be. My name means Dragon Courage."

"No kidding?" Aaron asked in surprise. "I hope some of that rubs off on me."

"On me too," laughed Wu.

Chapter 18

Time. It mocked Aaron at every turn. Days had already turned into weeks as the Redding band worked to accomplish the tasks necessary to pull off the rescue. Nights had been spent canvassing the entire city of Duluth, filling packs for Caleb and any other prisoners they would rescue, searching for essential items, materials for the Molotov cocktails, and cold weather gear for them all.

It was now October 24th. Well, at least it was when Aaron and Soraya had started their night shift. The more time passed, the harder Aaron found it to remain focused on the mission at hand. The coming winter teased them with nightly frosts, and Aaron's little basement stove had become more appreciated for its warmth than cooking abilities.

One of the most crucial preparations had been impossible until tonight. They *needed* a hidden entry to the compound to make the plan work, which meant they *needed* to cut the fence, which meant they *needed* something to cut it with.

It wasn't until last night that Ty and Leah had finally hit the jackpot. They found a heavy-duty bolt cutters in the rubble of a half-destroyed garage. There was much rejoicing back at the house that new progress could now be made.

Aaron and Soraya's mission tonight would take them closest to the Chinese compound any of them had been yet. The south end, where they would cut the hole, was mainly storage for train cars, most of which were full of coal and other natural resources waiting to be shipped out of the country. Security and, therefore, lighting were both at a minimum.

The riskiest element was the presence of two guard dogs. The train cars were tight to the fence, so being seen wasn't a problem. The dogs' hearing and sense of smell would be trickier to outsmart. Their mission would begin by finding the right location to cut a hole. If all went well, they would cut the opening itself.

Like shadows, they moved silently down through the city. Now, within a mere fifty yards of the fence, crouching at a second story window in an old office building, they watched to make sure everything was still as it should be.

Aaron checked his watch: 1:30 a.m. If their information was correct, they had maybe a half hour before the guard would be relieved. As soon as the replacement was recognized by the dogs, Soraya would use the distraction to scamper down and cut the fence.

But where?

Soraya huffed on her fingers, trying to keep them warm. There was only the slightest bit of moonlight to illuminate the ground along the fence, adding to the difficulty.

"There's some brush over there to the left which might be a good place . . ."

Aaron followed the direction of her nod.

"It's still too open to get there from the cover of buildings." After a minute, he pointed to their right. "Look, those two buildings are only an alley width away from the fence. If there's room between them, it would make a nice access. You wanna check it out?"

"Sure," she agreed and, without a sound, they slipped back out to the street.

Aaron led the way, choosing each step carefully. Even the sound of crunching glass or creaking metal could attract attention on a quiet night like this, well, as quiet as a night along Lake Superior can be anyway. There was almost always the sound of waves rolling in and breaking on the rocks to fill any silence. Gingerly, they navigated around burned-out cars, broken chunks of cement, and a twisted bicycle. Soraya followed close behind, careful not to let the cutters strapped to her back swing around and hit her gun. Truth be told, she loved the exhilaration of these missions with Aaron. She hadn't asked herself yet whether it had more to do with the adrenaline or Aaron. But one thing she did know was she never felt afraid when she was out with him.

"Ok." Aaron turned and whispered close to her ear. "This is the first building. We're almost there."

Soraya nodded and kept following. A minute later, they reached the far corner of the brick building. The color of the structure had long been lost to the soot and dirt covering each brick and now Soraya's hand as she leaned against it to steady her steps. There was a narrow alleyway separating it from a second old warehouse just wide enough for service vehicles.

After Aaron made sure it was clear, he leaned close and whispered, "I like it. It's mostly empty except for an old dumpster which will be a good cover. Let's move closer to the fence. It's almost two o'clock."

Without another word, they slipped around the corner into the alley. Right away, Soraya noticed how empty it was. There were scattered piles of junk along the walls, but it lacked the pervasive rubble seeming to impede their every step in this town. Suddenly, a small form darted across the alley in front of them. They both froze instantly until they recognized the shadowy movements of a stray cat poking around the dumpster. They walked quickly past the silent hunter and the dumpster and approached the end of the alley facing the fence.

Aaron stood at the opening, glued to the dirty wall, and scanned the fence line. A dog suddenly barked from inside the compound, followed by a man shouting to silence it.

"We're out of time," Aaron quietly shot over his shoulder. "They're changing the guards." He pointed to the fence slightly to their right. "See those bushy weeds over there? They'll help mask your silhouette. Stay low and quiet, I'll cover you from here. Go!"

Soraya silently leapt from the shadows and glided across the short open space to the fence, careful not to trip over any fallen bricks on the way. She could hear the two guards greeting each other as the fresh guard headed for the tower. Hopefully, the exchange would keep the dogs distracted long enough. Their plan depended on it. She quietly swept aside some vines that were growing through the cement and climbing up the fence. If she could slightly camouflage the flap, it should never be discovered.

She gently laid down her rifle and pulled the bolt cutters around to the front so she could use them on the fence. Turning, she looked at Aaron one more time. She couldn't see him through the shadows, but she knew he was there, watching, guarding, protecting. With a deep breath, she turned back to the fence and opened the cutters.

The fence was stronger than she had hoped; it took all the strength in her arms to cut the link. With a faint snap, the wire broke. Soraya paused to make sure the tiny sound hadn't carried. All remained quiet, except for the sound of the Chinese guard slowly climbing the metal rungs of the tower. As she placed the cutters around the next link, there was a sharp bark from the other side of the train car hiding Soraya's presence. She jumped at the nearness of the sudden alarm and instantly the second dog's barking joined in. *Crap!* In a single motion, Soraya slung the cutters back over her shoulder, grabbed her rifle, and sprinted for the alley.

At the first bark, the guard's steps had quickened the climb up the tower, and Aaron knew they only had seconds before the search light would be on them. Soraya reached him, her eyes wide with terror. The dogs were now at the fence barking and snarling at them.

"Come on!" Aaron hissed as he grabbed her arm and wheeled into the alley. His foot hit something soft, and the cat spun away with a hiss. Instantly, he dropped Soraya's arm and grabbed the offended feline. Before it had a chance to react, he chucked it out of the alley toward the fence. It landed, spitting and snarling, just as the searchlight found the place Soraya had knelt less than twenty seconds ago. The light froze on the cat as it darted away from the still barking dogs. As the two ran down the alley toward the city, they could hear the guard shouting at the dogs to shut up.

Once they hit the street, their pace became much more difficult as they clambered over all the debris in their way. Aaron knew they had to keep silent if they wanted their little cat trick to work, but everything inside him was telling him to run.

"Hurry up!" he whispered over his shoulder.

"I *am!*" Soraya answered as she clumsily slid down a pile of tires.

They swung around the back of another building and pulled up to catch their breath.

"What happened?" Aaron panted as they stood, backs against the wall.

"Nothing! Nothing happened! I don't know how they found me!"

"We have to get out of here."

She just nodded.

He took off again, Soraya at his heels. It was all uphill back to the house, and his lungs were starting to burn from sucking in the freezing night air. Clearing a busted-up section of roadway, he heard a sharp gasp behind him. Turning, he saw Soraya sitting among the broken-up asphalt holding her ankle. For an instant, he saw agony on her face, but then it was gone. He rushed over to her, but she was already pushing herself back to her feet with determination.

"Are you ok?" he asked.

"I'm fine," she returned, and took a step. With another sharp intake of breath, her ankle gave way, and Aaron reached out to keep her from falling.

"You're not fine."

"Yes, I am. It's only rolled. Let me just walk it off."

Unconvinced, Aaron helped her finish crossing the pile of rubble. On level ground again, Soraya gently took his hand off her arm.

"Thank you, Aaron. I can get it from here."

He started off again but slower this time, taking frequent looks over his shoulder to make sure she was able to keep up. After another ten minutes of zig zagging, they reached the tracks by the house. Soraya was still limping but seemed to keep pace pretty well. He helped her up the steps just as Sara opened the door to meet them.

"Thank you, Jesus! I heard the dogs start barking. What happened?"

"A close call," Aaron answered tersely, then, without looking at Soraya, he marched upstairs.

Walking into the master bedroom, he threw himself down onto a chair and dropped his head into his hands. *What went wrong? What did I miss?* Before his mind could even begin to find answers, he heard Soraya's steps entering the room.

"Where's Mom?" he asked, without looking up.

"She went downstairs to make us some spruce needle tea."

Aaron finally sat up and threw his head back. "Aaaargh!" he groaned in distress, still holding his head. Slowly, he let his hands slide down the sides of his face. "That was too close, Soraya."

"I know, I think next time—"

"Next time?" Aaron practically exploded from his seat. "There won't *be* a next time! You're *not* going back to that fence!"

"But Aaron, we need that hole cut!"

"I know, I know!" He was pacing now. "But you aren't going to do it. It's too dangerous. I'll think of another way . . ."

Soraya also stood up, "We already have a way. It's a good plan, Aaron. We just have to figure out how the dogs sensed us and be smarter."

Aaron stopped pacing and faced her in the dim light, frustration clouding his expression. "Soraya, look at you! Your ankle is sprained—"

"Rolled," she corrected, one finger pointed up to stop him.

Ignoring her, he went on, waving his arms with intensity. "In case you missed it, we almost got caught out there tonight! They would have killed you, Soraya! Do you realize that? You could have died tonight, and for what? For someone who isn't even part of your family. I can't send you out there again. This isn't your fight, Soraya!" He turned around and stared out the glass doors. The weight of responsibility felt like it was crushing him. "I'll figure it out. . . . I don't know, there has to be a way to cut that hole . . ."

As he continued his rant, Soraya slipped closer and moved between him and the night. She lifted her hand and gently touched his face, pulling his gaze down to her. Lifting herself up on her toes, she planted a soft kiss on his mouth. His eyes filled with a mixture of surprise and confusion, but at least he was finally quiet.

"Aaron," she spoke softly but with fire in her eyes, "Don't you get it? Your fight *is* my fight."

He thought his head might explode with all the conflicting thoughts and emotions colliding in his mind. He broke Soraya's searching gaze and went back to his chair with a sigh. She followed him and sat down on the bed close by.

Sitting with his eyes closed, trying to make sense of his own thoughts, he felt Soraya's soft hand close over his as it lay in his lap. Sudden heat flowed up his arm from her touch, and he folded his fingers over hers. He couldn't deny the feelings which were awakening in his heart. He just didn't see room for them in their current predicament and, therefore, couldn't afford to give them a place to stay.

At that moment, his mother entered the room carrying two steaming cups of tea. With a tiny squeeze, Soraya withdrew her hand and turned toward Sara.

As she handed out the cups, Sara rephrased her earlier question, "I take it things didn't go very well. What happened out there?"

Aaron shook his head as he cupped his tea with his cold hands. "It was too close, Mom. It was just too close."

Flags flapped loudly in the stiff breeze blowing off the lake. The ship rocked and strained against the mooring lines as it rose and fell with each wave. The small space under the end of the dock was completely filled by each swell as it came crashing into the shoreline.

There would be no escaping today.

Sam had worked out the details of their escape. Now, they simply needed the right ship on the right day. Unfortunately, the right ship was a rare ship. They needed a smaller vessel with a stern as close as possible to lake level. It had to have life rafts on board, and it needed to be a mess so no one would come looking for them until the end of the day.

The perfect day also seemed to be rare; it had to be sunny, so the sunlight glaring off the lake first thing in the morning would keep the guards from looking east while they made their dismount. It had to be calm enough to ensure they would not drown while they waited for the cover of darkness, and it would be nice if there was some sort of moon to be expected, so they could make their way in the dark once they hit shore.

Everything had to be perfect. They had no way of stashing supplies or putting things in order beforehand. They had to be ready to go. The only things they could prepare were their minds.

Caleb and Sam cleaned the ship that day as they had so many others: one room at a time. Both were eager to try out their plan. Each of them knew that to attempt and fail would most likely mean their death. Sam, for his part, had determined not to die a slave, and Caleb had lost enough people he cared about. Sam was the only family he had left. If they died, they were going to die trying; no Chinese captain was going to choose their fate.

Captain Li was growing ever testier. Perhaps it was the impending winter; maybe it was the added stress of the growing number of Chinese colonists he was forced to assist. As far as either Sam or Caleb could tell, he detested his own people almost as much as the Americans. Maybe it was civilians he hated.

Sam cursed under his breath as a new shipload of Chinese colonists unloaded on the neighboring dock. There were only about twenty of them, but he hated them to the last man.

"What right do they have to come here? They haven't worked this land, defended it, watched it take shape!" Sam fumed. "If I manage to escape from this place, mark my words, I'll make them regret it!"

"How? We don't even have weapons," Caleb asked. He had developed a knack for asking the wrong question at the wrong time.

Sam glared at him. "Are you really going to let those people live in your country after what they have done to your family?"

Caleb just stared at him. He had never considered what he would do to the Chinese if he escaped. His plan was to avoid them at all costs. Apparently, Sam had a different plan.

"You're kind of old to be fighting soldiers, aren't you?"

Now it was Sam's turn to stare in disbelief. "Age is like pain . . . it's mostly in the head," he growled, handing Caleb the mop and storming out of the bridge. At times, he wondered why he even wanted to escape with this kid.

Sam would never admit it, but he had grown to love the irritatingly inquisitive boy as much as he had loved anyone in his life. For the first time since he was young, he found himself praying to whatever power there might be, if there were any way possible the boy could be set free.

There was a pleasant surprise at the end of the day. At least, Caleb thought so. Sam, of course, swept in like a rain cloud and put his fire right out. Captain Li had been so occupied facilitating the new arrivals, he hadn't had time to inspect the ship. A subordinate officer had done the inspection and was satisfied and, for the second time since arriving at the compound, Caleb didn't receive any blows.

"It'll be twice as bad tomorrow," Sam muttered.

When they arrived at their home sweet container, Caleb looked up at the old man and cheerfully said, "Maybe we'll escape tomorrow."

Chapter 19

Rain hammered the wharf, forming large puddles everywhere. Soldiers slogged along the docks, ponchos hanging to their ankles, shivering as the north wind drove rain into their faces. Captain Li had elected to stay indoors and sent a subordinate officer to get the prisoners to work. Sam and Caleb were already soaked to the skin by the time they reached the cover of the ship they would be cleaning. It was the perfect ship for their escape: short and complete with life rafts. But with the way she rocked with the waves, there would be no escaping today.

"Stay positive, kid. It'll work out one of these days," Sam encouraged as they worked together in the galley.

Every day they honed their plan more and more. Now, it included leaving one of Caleb's shoes on the stern, along with a suicide note mentioning everything Captain Li hated about Americans, so it would be believed the old man and boy threw themselves overboard in defiance. Sam hoped this would curb any real search efforts. Captain Li wouldn't waste any energy or time trying to rescue a couple of prisoners. At least, Sam hoped he wouldn't.

While cleaning the small ship, Sam decided it would be a waste not to use the vessel to rehearse their plan. Caleb agreed, and the two of them cautiously made their way to the stern. The ship rocked as wave after wave rolled into the shoreline. Sam checked the position of the mooring line, checked the guards, and looked for a good place to leave the suicide note.

Caleb absently walked over to the starboard side of the ship and looked out. The lake looked like it went on forever. The sky sunk into the gray of the water, so it was impossible to tell where one ended and the other began. Shivering, he hunched his shoulders against a new wave of rain soaking through his clothes. Sounds of commotion pulled his attention to the dock below. A soldier was pointing at the ship and shouting something Caleb couldn't understand. In no time, there was a second soldier beside him yelling as well, followed by a handful of them running toward the vessel.

Sam whirled around to see what was going on and looked over the side. "Kid! They've seen you! Get away from the rail!" he yelled.

Then, it dawned on Caleb. They weren't allowed on the deck of the ship. It was not part of their job, so it was off limits. But it was too late. By the time Sam and Caleb scrambled up the ladder and turned toward the bridge the soldiers had reached them.

"What were you doing out there?" questioned the officer on duty.

Caleb looked at the floor and said nothing.

"The boy was feeling ill," Sam jumped in. "He isn't used to being tossed about. I didn't want him blowing chunks all over the galley, so I brought him out here to get some air."

The officer eyed him suspiciously. It was a bit of a stretch, considering they could have simply stepped out of the bridge to get some air. He looked at Caleb who, at this moment, did look a little green.

"Why take him so far?" he questioned.

"Well, I didn't want him making a mess of the ship, and the wind was right on that side to keep things from getting messy," Sam replied, as matter-of-factly as he could.

The officer frowned at this excuse. Caleb's stomach turned to knots contemplating the punishment awaiting them and, in a moment of weakness, his nerves overcame his stomach, and he hurled all over the deck, barely missing the officer's boots as the man jumped back to clear the spray.

"Clean this up!" the officer demanded in disgust and marched off the ship, his lackeys following close behind.

"I think you just saved us, boy," Sam said, grinning.

Caleb held his stomach as a second wave of nausea overtook him, and he hurled again.

"That's it, let it out, kid," Sam said, patting him on the back, grateful for the rain. If it had been Captain Li, vomit or not, they may have been shot. Only yesterday, a prisoner had been severely injured on one of the other ships. Sam had watched through a window as Captain Li boarded the ship, took one look at the man, and ordered his men to shoot him. The old man couldn't keep himself from wondering if one day the captain might decide he was too old and off him as well. Oh, how Sam hated him.

Progress was at a standstill. In the three days since failing to cut a hole in the fence, the group had deliberated endlessly on how to accomplish the task. Aaron considered every possible way to conduct the plan without cutting through the fence, but not a single one of them carried any chance of success. Soraya recounted the night's events over and over as everyone tried to find the solution.

Finally, Wu suggested it was likely that the dogs had simply smelled her at the fence. They were used to the smell of Chinese soldiers but were trained to hunt Americans. Then, gallantly, he volunteered himself to cut the hole in the fence. In a matter of seconds, he regretted the offer, but it was too late. There was no going back.

It was one in the morning when Aaron, Soraya, and Wu met in the entryway of the house. Sara came down from her post to see them off. Wu stood in the corner meditating on what he was about to do. Soraya rolled her ankle from left to right to get it loose for the mission ahead. It wasn't one hundred percent better, but it was close. Aaron checked his weapon. It was loaded. Taking a deep breath, he closed his eyes.

"Aaron." Sara placed her hand on his shoulder.

Aaron jumped, startled by her touch.

"Nervous?"

"Yes," he said truthfully. "Last time we would've been had if it wasn't for that cat."

"The Lord provides, doesn't he?"

"I guess," Aaron said, wishing he had faith like his mother's.

Sara walked over to Wu, who looked pale.

"Are you alright, Wu?" she asked sympathetically, noticing his trembling hands.

"I've never done anything like this before. If they catch me . . . I'm worse than dead."

"Aaron and Soraya would never let that happen. If it's too dangerous, we'll just have to try again another night."

Aaron cringed. They had already been at this for almost a month. It wasn't a question anymore of *if* they were out of time, they *were*. *If I have to cut the hole myself under a hail of gunfire, we are getting the job done tonight!*

Sara handed Soraya the cloak Aaron had made for her. "This will help keep the rain off."

Wrapping it around herself, Soraya thanked her and the three of them walked out the door and disappeared into the damp night. In thirty minutes, they reached the alley. Drizzling rain turned into waterfalls pouring off the rooftops soaking them to the bone. Luckily, the clouds held enough of the moon's light to cast a faint glow on the soaked environment.

Reaching the far corners of the buildings, Aaron looked toward the guard tower. The lone soldier, visible in the glow of the searchlight, sat hunched over, wrapped in a poncho, facing inside the compound. Aaron cracked a knowing smile as the droplets of rain drummed on the corrugated roof of the guard shack.

"Are you ready, Wu?" Aaron asked, looking into the wide eyes of his comrade. "The rain should mask any sound, and the dogs are going to be hiding from this storm. We might not have needed your stink tonight after all," he grinned, giving the fearful man a nudge.

Soraya handed Wu the bolt cutters and gave him directions to the place in the fence where she had begun the hole.

"You'll be alright; we've got your back. I was scared my first time out, but you get used to it," she encouraged him.

Crawling from the alley all the way to the fence, Wu was nearly sick by the time he reached the spot with the broken link. *I have a dragon's courage,* he kept repeating to himself. Taking one last look up at the guard shack, he carefully lifted the bolt cutters to the fence and placed them on the link under Soraya's. Slowly, he pressed the handles together as firmly as he could with his shaking hands. The link gave way with hardly a sound, no louder than the rain on the tin roof. Heart racing, he moved the cutters down the fence cutting link after link. When he reached the bottom, he took a moment to wipe the rain from his eyes before starting back at the top again. Link after link, he worked his way down the fence again as carefully as he could, grateful that, after tonight, he would never have to come near this fence again.

Finally, the cutters clipped through the last link. He laid them on the ground and pressed against the small door he had created. It swung inward with minimal effort. Looking back toward the alley, he tried to catch the reactions of his companions, but all he saw was darkness. Without further delay, he wedged a few bits of vine into the fence to disguise the cuts and scuttled back to the alley, longing for the safety awaiting him in the shadows.

Rounding the corner into the alley at a hunched over run, he brushed past Aaron and Soraya and kept going toward the other side. He couldn't think of anything but the warm safe basement back at the house. He had done his part. He had faced his fears, and now it was time to feel safe again.

"Wu, where are you going?" Aaron called after him in a loud whisper. "What happened?"

Wu stopped at the end of the alley, not sure which way they had come, giving the others time to catch up.

"Wu?" Aaron whispered again.

"I cut the hole just like you told me."

"Then what's the matter?"

"Nothing, I just want to get back to the house," he said, his heart still racing.

"So . . . everything's good?"

"Yes," he replied, looking up and down the street. "Which way did we come from?"

"This way," Aaron pointed while catching Soraya's eye with an amused grin.

Wu started off again, Aaron and Soraya jogging to keep up.

"I'm glad everything went well. Soraya and I were planning on leaving you if things went south, seeing as how I couldn't find a cat," Aaron jested after a little more distance was between them and the fence.

"Aaron!" Soraya chided.

They reached the house in good time thanks to Wu's quick pace. It took nearly the whole trip to convince Wu that Aaron was only joking about leaving him out there. Wu couldn't remember a time in his life when he was more relieved to get home.

Sara met them at the door and, as their shift was only half over, she was surprised to see them back so soon. Before she could ask how it went, Wu threw his arms around her and hugged her like he would his own mother. Sara's eyes met Soraya's, a look of surprised concern on her face.

"He's fine," Soraya assured her. "Just not much for adventure."

Wu peeled himself off Sara, leaving her damp from his soaking wet clothes.

"I'm sorry," he shivered. "Just so happy to see you again."

Sara laughed, shaking her head, "I'm glad to see you, too."

Later that morning, the seven of them gathered together in the master bedroom for a breakfast of Chinese rations and more spruce needle tea. Aaron pulled out the map of Duluth, which was beginning to look mighty filled in, and laid it on the end of the bed so they could all see it. Then he began the morning's briefing.

"Thanks to Wu's courage last night, we're now ready to throw this plan into action." He pointed to an asterisk in the southwest corner of the compound. "Here's the new hole in the fence the diversionary team will use to penetrate the base and get things kicked off."

"Nice job, Wu!" Leah cheered.

"Just doing my part," Wu said, puffing out his chest just a tad.

"Glad to hear it," said Aaron, "Because your part just got a little bigger."

Wu's head jerked up, eyes wide with concern, but Aaron ignored him and went on.

"In light of last night's success, I'm going to give out everyone's assignments for the rescue. Mom," he began, pointing to a building on the map, "You're going to be stationed here on this school rooftop. You're taking Leah, Wu, and Ty with you. You can see it from the window. It's the big, flat-roofed building over there. We need to make sure we scout it out as soon as possible to make sure the roof is accessible. You guys will be in position by 8:30 p.m. At 8:45, Leah, Ty, and Wu will head for the hole in the fence. As soon as you hear the 9:00 radio check, Leah will shoot the guard and the two dogs with her bow as fast as she possibly can."

Aaron was watching Leah out of the corner of his eye, and she immediately stiffened at this last bit of news. It was no secret she had no desire to shoot and kill anyone, and he knew this might be a battle. Sara was glancing back and forth between him and Leah, looking ready to intervene.

"Please let me finish," Aaron quickly said, before she had a chance to open her mouth. "I didn't make this decision lightly. Every job is crucial to our success." Now he was looking Leah directly in the eye. "And I wouldn't have given you this responsibility if I didn't think you could handle it. Please let me finish sharing this plan and we can discuss options afterward."

After Leah's stiff nod, he took a deep breath and continued. "Once Leah is finished, Wu will infiltrate the compound through the hole in the fence."

Immediately, Wu raised a finger and opened his mouth, but Aaron held up a hand to stop him. "You're the least likely to be stopped in your uniform and the dogs are familiar with your scent."

Wu slumped back down in his chair with a sigh. He couldn't argue with that.

"Your job is to quietly climb the HQ fire escape and wait for the train. As soon as the train has breached the gate, you'll use the bolt cutters to cut the communication cables."

All the color drained from Wu's face.

"When you're finished, you're going to head toward the prisoner containers and meet up with the rescue team there."

Wu's stomach turned to knots and he fought losing his breakfast.

"Mom, once you see the communications are down, you're going to shoot out as many guard tower lights as you can possibly hit. When you're done, you're going to meet up with Leah and Ty in the alley by the fence."

Sara nodded.

"Ty, the moment you hear Mom's rifle go off you have to race through the hole with the Molotov cocktails and set the two coal cars nearest the fence on fire. When you're finished, retreat to the alley with Leah and wait for my mom."

Now it was Ty's turn to nod. By this time, Wu was convinced he was getting the short end of the deal.

Aaron's finger went back to the map. "When you're all together, you're going to head north through town and set up here: two blocks from the gate. From there, you can cover the rescue team if we run into trouble. Only shoot if you must. Once the rescue team has cleared the gate, wait only for a moment to see if we're being pursued. If not, head to the rendezvous point, which has yet to be determined.

"The rescue team will be made up of myself, Seth, Soraya, and Wu when he gets there. The three of us, not including Wu, will jump on board the ten o'clock train as it rolls past the house. When it enters the compound, the diversionary team will spring into action. This will draw the soldiers to the south side of the compound as the smoke from the coal cars heads north. My hope is, with the lights gone and enough smoke, the soldiers will be tied up for some time trying to figure out what any hostiles on the south end of the compound are up to.

When the smoke reaches the train, which will hopefully be stopped dead on the tracks due to the diversion, we'll jump off. Using the cover of the smoke, we'll make our way to the prisoner containers and cut each lock until we find Caleb. Hopefully, Wu will have joined us by this time.

Once we have Caleb, we'll take him and any other liberated prisoners and head out the gate, which should be blocked open by the train. As soon as the diversionary team sees we're clear, they'll take off as well. If everything goes according to plan, we'll meet at the rendezvous point sometime after midnight."

Aaron looked around at the wide-eyed company. "I know this is going to stretch all of us. . . ." Wincing slightly, he asked, "Does anyone have any questions?"

Wu's hand timidly crept up.

"Yes . . ." Aaron acknowledged him.

Wu swallowed hard. "Can I trade with someone else?"

"I'm afraid not. Being Chinese, familiar with the base, and the only one who can fit into your uniform, you stand the best chance at making it to the headquarters building unhindered. If you fail to make it, the whole plan goes up in smoke. We can't have them radioing for help. I'm sorry, Wu, but there just isn't another way."

Wu nodded slowly, the horror of his task still sinking in. He wasn't a soldier, had never wanted to be, and now it was likely he was going to die like one, at the hands of his own countrymen to boot.

"Ummm, I don't think I can shoot someone," Leah's small voice wavered.

Aaron sighed in regret. "Leah, I am so sorry. I never wanted to ask this of you. Here's our predicament; the dogs have to be out of the way, or nobody goes through the fence undetected. If we shoot the dogs but not the guard, he either hears the commotion, sees Wu, or radios for help to put out the fires before we get enough smoke. If a gunshot is heard, the whole base shuts down and no one is getting in or out. Your bow, with your accuracy, is our only hope of pulling this off. I know it won't be easy, but please be willing to try."

Sara put her arm around Leah, attempting to pass on some strength for the job ahead. Leah's arms were wrapped around herself and her head was down as she tried to imagine what she had to do.

"Ok," she said at last, "I'll try."

"Thank you," returned Aaron with considerable relief.

"I had another question, though," Leah piped up again. "If Wu has the bolt cutters on top of the HQ building, then how are you going to be cutting the locks on the prisoner containers before he gets there?"

Aaron's forehead wrinkled as he ran the plan over in his mind, then, blushing, he admitted, "That's a good question, I guess we'll find another pair or something." Gathering himself, he asked optimistically, "Anyone else?"

We are going to die for sure, Wu thought to himself.

Chapter 20

Suddenly, everything felt different. Everything they had been planning and working toward was about to take place. They were ready to rescue Caleb. The anticipation in the house could be felt in the air. There was only one last big job to do, and it was going to take all day to get ready for it.

Stopping to grab packs and running with them after the rescue would be suicide. The alternative was to carry all their supplies to the rendezvous Aaron had mentioned in advance of the rescue. The place needed to be about a half day's walk from Duluth, which meant it would take an entire day to make their deposit. Today would be spent packing; tomorrow they would carry it all away.

As the most experienced packer in the group, Sara took charge. They uncovered a couple windows in the back of the basement for more light.

"Ok, troops," she commanded. "I want to see everything we have to our names spread out here on the floor!"

Rushing to obey, the team gathered and emptied the entire contents of the house onto the basement floor. Besides what they had brought with them, they had scavenged a significant number of useful items from the city. They also had gathered packs and supplies for up to six additional prisoners, since they didn't really know how many they would be leading out of town. Along with their survival gear, the floor was now piled with an assortment of boots, clothing, and coats with various degrees of rodent damage. No one knew what condition Caleb or any of the other prisoners would be in. They may as well be prepared.

Sara worked with Soraya, Leah, Wu, and Ty dividing what they had between the packs as best they could. Aaron was on watch, and Seth had ditched the packing party as soon as he could escape to join him.

"What?! Wu, what is this?" Sara stood, holding up a small porcelain teapot by the handle.

Wu looked up from a pack and blushed. "How do you know that is mine?"

Leah snorted in amusement and the others were smirking at his embarrassment. Sara just raised an eyebrow, teapot still dangling from her finger.

"You said to bring everything we had to our name. I found that last week. It is for making our tea."

"I know what it's for, Wu. We have pans to make our tea in . . . pans that won't break.

Wu huffed in disbelief, marched over, and rescued his precious teapot from Sara's finger. "One cannot *have* tea from a pan . . . *having* tea is an art: one requiring a teapot!" he finished righteously, as he began to carefully wrap it in an extra shirt.

"How are you going to keep it from breaking?" Leah asked.

"With love and care," was his only answer.

"Hey, Wu," came a call from the top of the stairs. "Come up here for a second, would ya?"

With a parting tuck of his fragile package into his pack, Wu headed up.

"What is it?" he asked, seeing both Seth and Aaron by the stairs to the second story.

"We need a Chinese-sized frame," Seth started to explain. "Come on, we'll show you."

He turned and waved his arm to follow as he led the way upstairs. Wu just shrugged and followed. At the landing, Seth took him by the arms and backed him up against the wall opposite the steps they had just climbed.

"Ok, you just stand still right here and Aaron can trace you on the wall," Seth finished.

Confusion furrowed Wu's brow at this strange request as Aaron took a marker and outlined his silhouette on the faded yellow paint. Things got even crazier when Seth trotted back down the stairs, turned, and regarded him from the bottom with tilted head.

"Ok, move over now, Wu," he said, waving his hand to the side.

Seth's face broke into a grin as he took in the outline on the wall and settled his hands to his hips.

"Perfect!"

As Wu looked back at the wall to try to determine what was so perfect, Seth took off for the basement calling Leah's name.

"Am I missing something?" he finally asked Aaron.

"Well, we know Leah will have a hard time doing her part in the rescue. We thought maybe having a target to practice with could help. We just needed a model, and you were about the right size." After his explanation, Aaron returned to his guard post by the balcony.

Turning stiffly, Wu observed the target he had just modeled for, and a mixture of horror and sadness swept over him. Horror that the target's shape was himself, sadness that one of his own people was going to die. *Am I doing the right thing? Why do I have to choose sides?* His questions remained unanswered, and he heard Seth returning with Leah at his heels.

"I guess so," Leah was saying uncertainly.

"Ta da!" Seth pointed to the target triumphantly when they reached the bottom of the stairs.

Leah looked up and, in her horrified expression, Wu saw a glimpse of his own heart reflected on her face. She quickly gulped, closed her eyes, and sank against the wall beside her.

"I don't think I can do this," she whispered.

Wu saw Seth deflate in despair. He looked back at the target for an instant and knew immediately what he had to do; Seth wasn't going to be any help. Wu ran quickly down the steps and placed his hands on Leah's shoulders.

"Leah, look at me."

She opened her eyes and met his intense gaze.

"That target up there is not a man. It is just a target! It is there to help you perfect your shot. You will practice with it. You will get perfect. And when you shoot a figure which looks like that shape on the night of the rescue, you will be perfect. You know why? Because your brother needs you. Caleb needs you. To think about what you are aiming at that night is not your job. Saving your little brother is your job. That is all you think about, ok? Nothing else!"

Leah's eyes had filled with tears during Wu's charge, but she nodded and blinked them back as best as she could. Wu dropped his hands to his sides, and the realization of what he had just done washed over him, leaving him weak and a little confused. He needed air.

"Excuse me," he muttered, then he disappeared out the back door.

Seth and Leah were left looking at one another in silence.

"I'll get my bow," Leah finally spoke. In a minute she was back, bow in hand. She nocked an arrow, and drawing the bow, she took a deep breath and let it fly.

THUD!

Without even looking, she turned away and went back downstairs to help pack. Seth remained where she had left him standing, staring up at the arrow stuck deep in the Sheetrock wall, right between where the target's eyes would have been.

Darkness had finally returned, and with it came the time for the last night mission. All rotation schedules were over now that everything was practically ready, so Sara went with Aaron tonight to scout the school rooftop. It was already October 29th, and it was cold; they guessed around forty degrees, not including the windchill, which was probably significant based on how it was whipping.

It didn't take them long to reach the three-story building. Inside, it was a mess. Garbage littered the hallways; lockers hung at crazy angles. They passed open school rooms filled with broken desks, shattered glass, and chairs scattered everywhere. They needed to find the roof access which meant finding stairs. The flicker of their lighters reflected off something metal.

"There's the elevator," Aaron spoke quietly.

They examined the walls on either side and, sure enough, there was a service stairs entrance.

"Bingo," he whispered triumphantly.

They propped the door open so they wouldn't have to make noise when they opened it again, and then proceeded up the dark stairwell. As they had hoped, the stairs led all the way to a heavy door labeled *Roof Access*. Aaron had carried the bolt cutters along in case there was a lock to break, but it looked like they were not the first people to use the roof since the country had fallen apart. The door swung open freely and, in a moment, they were on the roof. Sara pulled the edges of her cloak around her as the wind tried to take it away.

"Brrrr!" she said, "it's even windier up here!"

The structure had looked solid from the ground, but their first goal was to make sure it was safe. After walking around a few minutes and testing its support, they were convinced they would be in no danger from the building itself. Moving to the east edge of the roof, they turned their focus toward the compound.

"Ok," Aaron began. "It's most important to make sure you can make out Wu's signal on the roof of the HQ building. How does it look?"

Sara took her time scanning with the binoculars. It was obviously harder to make everything out at night. The harsh lights left many dark shadows to play tricks on the eye when it came to recognizing shapes. The top of the HQ building was only slightly illuminated and filled with shadows.

"Yes, I think it'll work. If he comes to the edge, I shouldn't miss his signal."

"Good, how about lights? How many do you think you could take out from here?"

"Let's see, I can take out the entire south half for sure; that's five. The next one up on this side is the main gate light. I'm not sure. It's pretty far."

"Well, all you can do—"

Suddenly, the whirring of helicopter blades came from behind them, and they spun around in alarm. A chopper was cresting the hill and descending toward the compound.

"Down!" commanded Aaron and, dropping immediately to the roof, they tucked themselves as close to the low safety walls as possible. It was pretty dark; hopefully the pilot wouldn't notice two figures on top of a roof in a supposedly abandoned city.

Aaron and Sara looked at each other in the darkness, hearts beating in their ears.

"Drat those helicopters!" Aaron breathed.

"Well," returned Sara with a half-smile. "I think we're done here!"

Once the helicopter had passed them, they quickly made their way back to the stairwell and down to the quiet street below.

When they reached the house, Sara crossed out their mission from the list.

"That's it," she announced to her family with a smile. "All we have left is dropping off our packs tomorrow and we're ready!"

Smiles and a little cheer went up from the group. It was about time, and they were more than ready to put Duluth behind them.

Everyone went to bed early since they would be setting off before dawn. Sara climbed the stairs, her wool blanket pulled tight around her shoulders, to the balcony where she would be taking the first watch. As she entered the room, a faint silhouette at the windows startled her.

"Wu! What are you doing in here? I thought you had already gone to bed."

"I'm sorry, I didn't mean to bother you." He returned his gaze to the window as Sara reached his side. "I was just . . . I don't know, looking."

Sara sensed anxiety in his voice.

"You know," Sara spoke softly, "Without you, we wouldn't have such a good plan and, without you, we wouldn't be able to carry it out."

Wu sighed and his shoulders drooped even further. He looked over at Sara with the eyes of a lost boy.

"That is the problem. I'm Chinese. And yet, here I am, conspiring against my own country. Not that I don't want to," he quickly added. "They have no right to keep your son and you *should* try to get him out. Besides, I kinda made my choice when I ran away. I guess I just never thought I'd have to actually *betray* them." His eyes went back to the well-lit compound, its lights reflecting on the lake. "I am a man without a country."

After a moment of quiet, Sara spoke again. "I wish I could take away all your apprehension about this rescue, but I know I can't. That's something you'll have to settle within your own heart. There's a promise in the Bible which says God will keep in perfect peace the one who keeps his mind stayed on Him because he trusts in Him. I believe our strength and peace is only as deep as the One we trust in."

"I don't have a god or a country. All I have left is you guys."

Wu turned and headed toward the door.

"Wu," Sara softly called after him. "America was created by hearts like yours. Maybe one day you'll let her be your country."

Wu paused in the middle of the room for a moment and considered her words. Then, he turned and bent in a respectful bow. "Thank you," he whispered and disappeared into the dark.

"Is everybody ready?" Aaron spoke into the candle-lit basement. He was answered by a conglomerate of responses to the affirmative. There was still over an hour before dawn. At a consistent pace, they should be more than a mile beyond Duluth by the time the sun rose. It was still windy and misting outside. It had been like that for over a week now, but if they waited for good weather, it would be too late. It was now or never.

"Ok, let's go!" Aaron led the way up the stairs.

There were six of them making the trip. Sara was staying behind to keep tabs on the compound in case anything happened in their absence. They carried their own packs, Sara's pack, and six extra packs for the prisoners they would be rescuing, including Caleb. That meant each person had to shoulder two packs except Ty, who carried a third one. As the troop climbed up the stairs from the basement, Leah let out a little shriek as the weight of her packs started pulling her backward.

"Gotcha." Ty put out his arm from behind her and pushed her upright again.

Seth started snickering, "This is going to be interesting!"

After they all piled outside, Aaron gave his mother a small hug and kissed her on the forehead.

"I love you, Mom," he whispered.

With a wave of his arm, they fell in line and started out leaving Sara, wrapped in her cloak, to watch them fade into the mist.

The first part of the trek was the easiest. They just followed the train tracks northeast until they turned toward the compound. At the curve, they angled straight north. Their plan was to cut through a mixture of tiny Duluth suburbs and bits of wilderness until they reached Arlington Road. Once they found it, they could follow it north out of civilization.

Slowly, they lumbered through the dark, crossing yards, abandoned streets, and patches of woods, trusting Aaron's compass to guide them through the dark.

The sun had risen behind the clouds by the time they came to the edge of an old highway. Stopping in the cover of trees, they took a breather and let Aaron scope it out. Ty piled his packs in a heap and then laid on his back across the top. Stretching out his back into an arch, he groaned. Everyone agreed as they, too, tried to work out the kinks.

Returning from the highway, Aaron reported, "The road is definitely in use but probably not often. I can see good cover on the other side so, if we just cross it quickly, we should be fine."

"Uh huh," offered Seth, sitting on his pack making no move to get up.

"The sooner we find a good spot, the sooner we can drop all this gear." Aaron tried encouraging the exhausted crew.

Soraya was the first to shoulder her packs, and the rest slowly followed suit with only minor grumbling. After listening to make sure the coast was clear, they crossed the highway and moved into the woods on the other side.

"Ouch!" Seth staggered as his foot caught something in the undergrowth. He bent over to pick it up. "Hey, I think this used to be a golf course," he announced. He held in his hand an old hole marker flag. There wasn't much left of the plastic flag part, but its identity was obvious.

Hours passed. Even with the wet, cool temperatures and the steady wind, everyone was sweating from the weight of their cargo. Eventually, it seemed like they had left most of the suburbs behind. Following creek bed after creek bed, they worked ever north. Finally, Aaron stopped and pointed.

"Look at that overhang up there. That's our spot."

Sighs of relief filled the tiny gorge.

"Well, it's about time!" Seth spoke for all of them.

It really was a perfect hiding place. The rocky sides of the miniature gorge rose at least three feet from the creek and then leveled off, leaving a wide ledge which was overhung with more rock and tree roots. More than one person could tuck themselves under there if they tried and never be seen from above.

Aaron took out a tarp and spread it over the rocky ledge. Everyone gratefully set down their packs for the last time. As it was well past noon by the time they arrived, they pulled out some Chinese meals and sat down to eat their fill before starting for home. Seth and Ty stretched out on the ground trying to give their backs a break. The others sat on the rim of the ledge to let their legs dangle as they ate.

"Here's some water," Soraya said, passing around a couple jugs filled from the running stream.

"I've been thinking," started Aaron thoughtfully. "We really don't know what kind of chase to expect from the Chinese or if we'll encounter more of them on our way north. Strategically speaking, it would be advantageous for us to split into two groups after the rescue so the PLA would have to divide forces if they chase us. It's also much easier to care for and evade detection in a smaller group." He stared at the creek as he finished, avoiding the looks he knew were being thrown his way.

He was right. There were plenty of looks. Seth and Ty had both sat up and were exchanging surprised glances. Soraya had frozen in the middle of tearing open a packet of applesauce, her eyes widened in dismay. Wu just looked from person to person in alarm, not knowing if all hope for staying alive had just ended. Leah was the first to find her tongue.

"That's the dumbest idea I have *ever* heard!" she declared unapologetically. "We're all a family. Families don't just split up 'cause it's easier."

Wu sighed with relief; this made much more sense to him.

"Leah," Aaron faced her, "I don't like the idea either. But look at it this way, if we run as a single group and the PLA come after us, they can focus all their efforts on our trail. If they're looking for us with everything they have, it'll only be a matter of time until they catch us. If, however, we divide into two groups, they'll either randomly pick a trail to follow or else divide their resources. If they divide their resources, we have a MUCH greater chance of both groups getting away. I'm just trying to keep everyone safe."

Soraya bit her lip and looked down at the food in her lap. No one could argue with his logic but since when does the heart follow logic?

"So . . ." Ty interjected, "Have you already figured out who would go with who?"

"Well, I figured you would lead one group, Ty, and I would lead the other. The rest of my family would bring us up to five after we get Caleb back. Soraya would go with you, of course, and Wu could be your second guy. That's three. We don't know yet how many prisoners we'll be releasing, but they could be in your group unless we need to split them up for any reason. We also don't know the physical condition of any of them yet and whether they'll slow us down. I guess we'll just have to cross that bridge if we come to it." He looked around at the somber faces all around him. *Whoever says being a leader is easy has no idea what they're talking about . . .*

"You're going to have us meet back up together afterward, right?" Leah challenged, now on her feet with arms crossed.

"I guess I didn't think that far, but yeah, I don't see why not," Aaron admitted, shrugging his shoulders at the idea. "What do

you all think about that?" He was relieved to give the others
something positive to consider.

Soraya glanced up quickly at Leah's suggestion with new hope
in her eyes. "I think that's a good idea."

Aaron looked her way for the first time since introducing the
new plan.

She tried to give him a smile. "I would like that," she said
softly.

"I know I have not been a part of you for long," Wu piped up,
"And perhaps I have no place to speak, but I would like to say I
am definitely in favor of reuniting."

"Sounds good!" Aaron said, hopping down from the rock
ledge feeling lighter already. "Let's get our gear secured here and
head back.

Together, they packed everything tightly together including the
now empty water jugs and extra weapons. During the rescue, only
Sara and Ty would be carrying their rifles. The rest of the guns
would be deadweight and only slow down the escape and,
therefore, they would be left here to get picked up afterward.
Soraya and Seth had already stashed their rifles, but Aaron loathed
to put his down.

He stood by the tarp trying to remind himself why he had
decided this was a good idea. That AK was like his father's face to
him. It had never left his side since the fateful day which seemed
so long ago now. To leave it here almost felt like he was leaving
his dad behind. Aaron shook his head to try to clear it and quickly
laid the gun with the others before he could change his mind. He
gave the stock a parting touch. *I'll be back for you.*

The only thing left to do was to wrap the extra half of the tarp
around their belongings and secure it well with heavy rocks and
branches. By the time they finished, it was well camouflaged.

"Well, I'm guessing we have a good six miles or so to cover to
get home." Aaron said as they surveyed their work. "We've got
plenty of time since we want it dark by the time we get there.

We're all sore; it'll be nice to take it easy. Also, keep a sharp eye on the landmarks we pass so everyone can find their way back here in the dark."

Everyone nodded, and they began the trek back the way they had come. It was fairly simple to retrace their steps. They just had to keep Arlington Avenue on their right and follow it back across the highway. After that, they had the high ridgeline, which was also to the west, to follow all the way back to the train tracks.

The group fell into an easy stride. Only Ty, with his rifle, had anything to carry so, even with the overcast sky and occasional light rain, the journey was much more enjoyable. Aaron let Ty take the lead and soon found himself at the rear of the column with Soraya. She gave him an easy smile as he looked over at her beside him. She made it effortless to relax, and he found himself returning her smile as they walked side by side.

Chapter 21

Sara shook her head in disgust as she sat near the patio doors staring out at the bleak mixture of clouds and drizzle. She had been awakened early that morning by a visitor to her bed; a six-inch-long rat had run right over her. After recovering from the shock, she got up and fixed herself a cup of spruce needle tea. It really did lift the spirits to have something warm to drink on these cold mornings.

It had been raining off and on for almost a week and a half now. Every day she hoped the wind would switch out of the southwest. They had been ready for three days, but the weather didn't seem to agree. *Heavenly Father, please, send us the right wind,* she prayed silently, knowing she was going to have to watch her son slog to work yet again.

It was several hours before the rest were up and moving. Aaron and Soraya were usually the last to get up. They had worked the night missions for so long their bodies no longer operated on a normal schedule. When they had all gathered in the master bedroom for breakfast, Sara reported that Caleb had gone to work like usual.

Aaron sat on the bed brooding over his map. Somehow, he had believed when they got ready to go the weather would just cooperate. He was eager: eager to get Caleb out of there, eager to get this mission over, and eager to get up north.

For days, they had been drilling their roles in the plan, memorizing every detail of their individual parts and of the mission as a whole. Soraya gave Wu a haircut and shave. He woke up every morning with knots in his stomach, dreading the night he would find himself back in the compound. Sara took pains to wash his uniform so it was crisp and clean. Anything to increase their odds.

Leah had put so many arrows in Wu's silhouette, it was more of a hole in the wall than a head. She had been quiet lately, focused. She too just wanted to get the rescue over with. Until her horrible role was finished, she could think of nothing else. Sara's rifle had been completely field stripped and each part cleaned and oiled. The action was as smooth as silk. They were ready.

Aaron motioned Ty over to the bed where he leaned over his worn-out map of Minnesota. "What do you think of this town?"

"Ely," Ty read out loud.

"It's almost straight north of here, one of the last towns before we hit Canada. We can build a camp on the north side right by these two lakes. If we need anything, we can see what's left in town. I don't think the Chinese will be pushing that far for a while."

"Looks like home," he smiled.

"I've been there," Sara said from her seat by the window. "It's a lovely area: trees, lakes, wilderness. It was before I met your father. My family took a vacation to the Boundary Waters, and we stayed in Ely for a couple days. I remember the people there seemed to live slower than people did in the big city. They drove slower, ate slower, talked slower; no one seemed to be in a hurry. I guess it makes sense. Why live amid all that beauty if you're going to be too busy to enjoy it?"

Aaron looked over at Soraya as she spoke. She sat on the floor opposite Seth, playing Go Fish. He watched as she reached up and tucked a wavy lock, which had gotten loose from her ponytail, back behind her ear. He loved it when she did that. He wondered if they would make it. If the rescue worked, would he ever see her again? She must have felt him staring at her and she turned to look his way. Aaron glanced back at the map.

"Ely it is then," he said, louder than necessary.

Ty smiled and slapped him on the back. "All we need now is the right wind, and we'll be off."

Soraya looked over at Aaron. She caught his glance and held it. She smiled and tucked the rebellious strand of hair back in its place once more. She would do whatever it took to make this rescue a success, if only they could meet again when all this was over.

Waves rocked the giant tanker as Caleb mopped a particularly foul head. Oddly enough, there was a slight smile on his face and a fresh zeal to his mopping. Today, the perfect ship had sailed into the harbor.

The two prisoners were busy cleaning the bridge when Sam had chanced a glance out of the rain spattered windows just as the relatively small cargo vessel rounded the jetty. Sam had watched it carefully, not a single visible lifeboat. It had to have rafts. The stern sat low, roughly ten feet from lake level. She was everything Sam could have hoped for. Even as the rain battered the windows and waves had rocked the ship, they were sure this was the one.

"I can't wait to be free again!" Caleb exclaimed. "No more mopping."

"Oh, yeah? What if I want you to mop our humble dwelling when we get out of here?"

Caleb stared at him, appalled.

"Just pulling your leg, kid."

Caleb smiled; Sam was always trying to get his goat lately. He was glad to see the old man so lively. Only the sight of Captain Li could throw water on Sam's fire now, and for good reason;

Captain Li had intensified his injustice toward the prisoners, as
dreary day gave way to dreary day, for over a week. Everything in
the compound was wet, every job was wet, every time a new group
of settlers arrived Captain Li had to get wet: wet and cold and
angry. His own men had learned to avoid him, prisoners braced
for the cane before he even raised his hand.

Yesterday, Sam had made eye contact with the madman during
their inspection, his face still bore the stripe where Captain Li's
cane had rained down without warning. Sam took the stripe with
all the mettle Caleb had learned to expect. The old man was a rock.
The weather didn't leave either prisoner with much hope today
would be any different.

"Does it hurt, Sam?" Caleb asked.

"It'll hurt a lot less tomorrow when we're hidden away under
that dock," Sam answered emphatically.

While they were still busy mopping, the compound siren rang
out a short blast.

"What in the world does that mean?" Sam wondered out loud.

His question was answered by a poncho-draped sergeant.
There was to be a formation.

Caleb looked at Sam in concern, but there was no time to
speculate. They were marched off the ship, across the wharf to
the headquarters building, and placed in formation with the other
prisoners. This formation was somewhat different from the
formation after the prisoner had escaped. The soldiers of the
compound made up one leg and the base of a squared off U-
shape, while the prisoners made up the other leg. The prisoners
faced the soldiers opposite them, and beyond them, the lake.

Soldiers and prisoners alike stood shivering in the cold mist
which was all that remained of a system finally ready to move on.
The wind, which had blown for days out of the northwest, had
dwindled down to a light breeze, no longer strong enough to lift
the saturated flags hanging from the poles.

Captain Li emerged from the headquarters building wearing his best uniform, shadowed by his faithful aid and a soldier with an umbrella to keep the captain dry. He inspected each section of the formation, correcting any irregularities with a sharp word and a quick flick of his cane.

Caleb smirked as a soldier in the formation across from him received a sharp rebuke and a cane to the leg. It was nice to see his enemies get a taste of their own medicine. Once he was finished with the soldiers, Captain Li assigned three guards to keep the prisoners in order. There was no hope of making the wavering rows of haggard prisoners look anywhere near as orderly as the ranks of soldiers, but Captain Li expected it all the same.

No one knew why they were standing there, dripping, waiting. Waiting for what? The captain strutted over to the end of the dock and stood expectantly.

Caleb looked toward the dock, and there he saw it. The ship they had watched round the jetty, their perfect little ship, was gliding into the dock. The ship pulled up until it was parallel with the dock and stopped. Mooring lines were tossed from the bow, stern, and a couple from the center of the starboard side. The lines were fastened to the dock and a short gangway was moved into place.

Caleb held his breath. Was it a general, the Chinese President, or some form of royalty?

A white umbrella appeared on the deck. A small group of people made their way toward the gangway. Caleb was grateful he had been placed in the front row. Had it been any other row, he would have been caned trying to see around a prisoner in front of him. As it was, he had a front row seat.

The entourage made its way down the gangway, and the individuals came into view. There were three of them. Two wore white and walked under the shelter of the white umbrella held by a third figure in black. The clean appearance of the visitors captivated Caleb. It was so unfamiliar and out of place, he almost forgot where he was. A cold trickle dripped off Caleb's hair, hit the base of his neck, and ran down his spine. He shivered involuntarily. He glanced at the nearest sergeant to see if his reaction had been noticed but, thanks to the newcomers, it had not.

As the three figures reached the shore, Captain Li called the company to attention. Like a machine, the entire troop of soldiers thundered into position. The prisoners did their best to mimic the company, but their poor condition made for a sad display.

Out of the corner of his eye, Caleb could now make out the mysterious figures. A woman, dressed in white, took the captain's arm. Holding her hand stood a young girl wearing a matching white dress and coat. Caleb guessed by her appearance she must have been about ten. Lastly, he saw it was a man in a black suit holding the umbrella. Captain Li bent over and gave the little girl a kiss on the cheek before he continued with his presentation of the troops.

Captain Li took the white umbrella from the man in black and led the woman and her daughter past the soldiers. Beaming with pride, he introduced them to each platoon leader as they went. When they reached the American prisoners, Captain Li whispered in the woman's ear with a smug look on his face. She nodded, her face expressionless as they walked along.

Caleb did his best not to shiver where he stood as the captain and his guests approached. He watched out of the corner of his eye as the woman raised her hand to shield her nose from the stench rising out of their ranks. The little girl caught Caleb's gaze. At first, she looked confused, then her expression melted into sympathy. Caleb quickly shifted his gaze to the ground out of shame and embarrassment. He must look like a filthy dog to her.

In the back of his mind something snapped. Caleb's attitude transformed from shame to anger. *Who is she to look at me with pity? She's just a filthy Chinese, a murderer of innocent people, of my father. She doesn't belong here; this is my country. What right does she have to stand there gawking at me in her perfect white dress and coat while I freeze, soaked to the bone, all thanks to the man who kissed her on the cheek?* Into Caleb's heart crept a hatred unlike anything he had ever known. He could take as many canings as the captain could dish out, but he wouldn't suffer their pity. *If I escape, one day I'll make sure they all beg for pity.*

The ceremony concluded with a theatrical display of military drills. The woman and her daughter were escorted out of sight in the direction of the soldier quarters. The formation was dismissed, and the soldiers marched the Americans back to work.

"Who were they?" Caleb grumbled.

"Apparently, they were close to the captain, probably his family," Sam answered. "Doesn't matter, tomorrow we'll escape from the very ship they arrived in." The old man smiled at Caleb, but Caleb didn't return it.

"What's eating you, kid?" Sam asked, putting his rag down on the griddle he was working on.

"I don't know. They looked at us like we were animals. That woman covered her nose! They're the ones who made us this way!" Caleb protested in disgust.

"Now you're beginning to understand the way of it."

"I hate them," Caleb fumed. "That little girl looked at me like I needed her pity, all dressed up, holding her mother's hand. My mother was *ten* times the woman that lady is."

"I'm sure she was, son."

Sam and Caleb worked their way through the ship as quickly as they could. The formation had put them behind schedule, and neither of them wanted to find out how Captain Li would react with his new guests on post.

Finally, they reached the bridge. Scrubbing it to a shine, Caleb looked out the window and froze. The sun was breaking through the clouds and slowly disappearing behind the hillside. The weather had been wet and dreary for so long he had almost forgotten what a sunset looked like. The pink and orange light filtered into the room with a warm glow.

"Sam . . ."

The old man put his hand on Caleb's shoulder. "Tomorrow we'll rid ourselves of this wretched place, one way or another."

"Yeah . . ." Caleb said, a mixture of hope and excitement pounding in his chest as he watched the bright colors streaking across the sky.

A small blessing came at the end of the workday. Captain Li was so busy entertaining the newcomers he didn't bother to conduct the inspection of the ship. The lieutenant who took his place didn't seem to have any idea what he was looking for and, therefore, found nothing wrong with their work. Apparently feeling he should come down on them in some way, he elected to let them off with a stern warning, and then marched uncomfortably off the ship.

On their way to the container, Caleb took a long look at the wharf. He had no idea what lay ahead, or if they would even succeed but, whatever tomorrow brought, it had to be better than here.

Sam lit a candle as soon as the sound of their escort faded.

"Eat hardy, kid, we're going to need every bit of it tomorrow. It may be awhile before we find anything to eat."

Caleb tore open his ration and dug in. He had long ago realized no matter what flavor the food was supposed to be, they all tasted the same. After consuming the main entree, he paused and looked up at the old man. Sam wasn't eating at all; he sat with a blank expression on his face, like he was somewhere else, his dinner hanging from his hand.

"You ok, Sam?"

Blinking, Sam replied, "This is my last night here." The flame of the candle caused Sam's eyes to glow and his breath rolled out in thick clouds of steam. "I've only known this place for so long, all the suffering, all the death. Tomorrow we'll escape or we'll be killed. Either way, we won't be coming back here. I've been a lost man, Caleb, with nothing left to live for, but too afraid to die. I'm not afraid anymore. You've given me hope. I've found a courage in you I couldn't find in myself. Thank you. No matter what happens tomorrow, we're free, and they couldn't break us. We'll leave this place our way."

"We have to make it, Sam. I just know we will. One day, we'll come back here and make Captain Li pay for what he's done, pay for my family."

"That's the spirit!" Sam said, slapping his knee.

Destiny hung in the air of their container: two hearts, young and old, defiantly resolved to live or die like Americans. Late into the night, the boy and the old man dreamed the dreams of freedom. As the new day dawned, and their door swung open, a brilliant blast of sunlight filled the container. Caleb stepped out into the radiant light; a warm gentle breeze washed over him.

Today would be his last day . . .

Chapter 22

"Guys! Wake up! The sun is shining!"

"Soraya . . ." Ty grumbled, pulling his wool blanket over his head.

"Guys, the wind is shifting; this is what we've been waiting for!"

Aaron shot up. "Did you say the wind is changing?"

"Yes, I noticed it while I was out on the balcony. First it was coming from the west, then it started turning toward the south. The storm is over. The sun is shining. It's a glorious morning!"

Aaron followed Soraya into the master bedroom where Sara was already up, holding her customary cup of tea.

"Good morning, Aaron," she said with a smile.

Nodding, Aaron stepped out onto the balcony and turned to face the wind. Soraya was right; it was blowing softly out of the southwest. He took a deep breath, closed his eyes, and let it out. It was a beautiful morning, a worthy last morning, if it were to be his last.

Sara stepped out onto the balcony beside him. "This is it, isn't it?" she said, without looking at him.

"Yes."

"I'll go get the others up."

As she turned to go, Aaron caught her arm. "No," he said soberly. "This day may end quickly, better it starts slowly."

Sara gave him an understanding smile and walked back into the house.

Aaron stayed out on the balcony for a while. Taking in the sights, he thought it sad he had spent so much time planning and preparing for the rescue, he hadn't noticed how beautiful the scenery was. The sunlight glimmered off the lake like a sapphire gem with a million tiny facets. The harbor was ringed with emerald evergreens and the browns and grays of late autumn. Rock formations jutted out here and there protruding from the trees, blanketing the hillsides. So much beauty.

Another sadness washed over him. His plan was as good as he could make it, but there were so many parts. The odds were heavily stacked against them. If everything didn't work out perfectly, some, if not all of them, would probably be killed and Caleb would be lost forever. He looked back out over the harbor where the seagulls seemed to dance with one another in the air. They were the only ones here with nothing to lose, the only ones left unaffected by the task they would perform that night. *God, if there's a way, help us succeed tonight.*

Aaron gathered his thoughts and returned to the master bedroom. Picking up a permanent marker, he drew the entire compound on the bedroom wall from memory. He sketched in the gate, the towers, the headquarters building, the prisoner containers, the coal cars on the southwest side, and the school Sara would be positioned on. Next, he jotted down every detail of the plan next to each relevant structure, giving each person a symbol for easy identification. He put the time each event was supposed to happen neatly in a box next to the location.

Aaron's small band had been committing every aspect of the plan to memory over the past three days, but he knew it would help if they could all see it. Everything had to go off like clockwork. Every step depended on the step before it; the whole plan hung from a single chain. If one link gave way, the entire plan would fall . . . and they would fall with it.

Sara left the room to get the tea brewing for the rest of the group. Soraya playfully bumped into Aaron as he finished writing a detail.

"Looks like a Picasso."

"Ouch!" Aaron dramatically winced. He had come to depend on her joyful nature even when they were facing the worst possible situations.

"Are you sure about going through with this?" Aaron asked, standing back and looking at the wall.

Soraya took his hand in hers, he turned and looked at her. "I'm sure," she said.

Aaron wasn't entirely sure what she was sure of. The look in her eyes and the sound of her voice didn't seem to match his question.

"Looks like you two are having a good morning."

Aaron dropped Soraya's hand like a hot iron and turned around to see Seth standing behind them, smirking.

"Seth! Good morning!" Soraya said joyfully, taking the interruption in stride.

Aaron turned beet red.

"Love your decorating. I kinda felt the room was lacking some artwork."

Aaron glared at him.

"Oh, lighten up, Aaron, your secret is safe with me . . . at least for now." Seth winked.

"What secret?" Sara asked, returning with the tea. Looking over at Aaron and Soraya she said, "Oh, you mean those two? The only person in this group to whom *that's* a secret is Aaron."

Seth looked at her with disgust. "What? How did you know?"

"I'm a mother," she grinned.

Aaron slapped his hand to his face, wishing the floor would open and swallow him. Soraya just grinned sheepishly and thanked Sara as she handed her a mug of tea.

Leah, Ty, and Wu stumbled groggily into the room. "Did we miss something?" Leah asked hesitantly.

"No," Aaron was quick to answer. "We were just about to start reviewing what everyone will be doing tonight."

"Wait, did you say tonight?" Wu asked.

"That's right. Look outside, a southwest wind rolled in last night," Aaron replied.

After letting everyone finish their breakfast, Aaron began his briefing for the day.

"I'm not going to candy-coat this, it wouldn't be the honest and loving thing to do. So, here's the straight truth, as far as I can see. All of you know how dangerous our time here has been. We've put in a lot of hours preparing for tonight. Everyone has risked a lot. The plan is, unfortunately, more complex than I would like, but there's no way around it. Each part depends on the success of the previous part. If we fail at any part along the way, we fail altogether. If we fail, some of us may be killed or captured. I know this is hard to hear, but we have to try and make peace with that or we won't be at our best tonight. Anything less than our best will end in failure, of that I'm sure. We place it all on the line tonight. When you go out there you can't leave anything behind."

Aaron took a deep breath and allowed his words time to sink in. No one said a word. They were all afraid, but beyond their fear was a fire burning inside each one of them, a fire of hope and love.

"We could do everything to the letter and still fail but I think, if everything works out, we have a good chance. They won't be expecting us and, once things get started, we won't be in there for long. We can do this," he paused, eyeing each one of them. "Ty, Soraya, and Wu, we would be lost without you. You guys are our family, and you're appreciated more than you'll ever know. There's no greater gift than the sacrifice you've made for this family. I know Mom, Leah, and Seth would agree. You'll always be a part of us. Thank you, with all my heart, thank you. We're going to spend the rest of the day drilling every part of this plan. We cannot afford hesitations tonight."

Ty raised his hand as Aaron finished his monologue. "Could I say something?"

"Sure," Aaron replied in surprise.

Ty cleared his throat. "I'm not really one for speeches, but I wanted to say . . ." He paused, looking a little lost. "When you guys rescued Soraya and me, I had come to hate everyone. Even after you saved us, I still hated you. Then I got to thinking about what you said about apples and how you guys risked your lives to save people you didn't even know. I've never been loved like that and, eventually, I guess it broke through. What I'm trying to say is, I never dreamed I'd call a light-skinned apple my brother, but I'm saying it now. Aaron, your brother is my brother, and we're getting him out of there tonight. That's all there is to say about that." He stood up and gave Aaron a bear hug.

"Well then, let's get down to business," Aaron said huskily, concluding their meeting.

Tossing a bit of cotton off the balcony, Aaron watched it ride the southwestern breeze out of sight. Everyone knew their role by heart. There was nothing more for them to do but wait. He checked his watch: 7:30, only an hour before blast off. His stomach churned and, apparently, his wasn't the only one. Everyone had passed on dinner. He had come up to the balcony to check the wind, or at least that was his pretense. Really, he just needed air. He didn't mind risking his own life; he had come to peace with that. It was risking everyone else's lives he was struggling with.

Putting his game face on, Aaron returned to the basement. Everyone was busy donning all the dark clothing they had found. All except for Wu, who wore his uniform. Sara's hard work had

paid off, and he looked good. Seth and Ty were playfully arguing
over whether Ty needed to put soot on his face and hands. Sara
had donned her cloak. Her face darkened with soot, she smiled
when she saw Aaron.

"Are we good to go?" she asked.

"Yeah, wind is good," he said quickly.

"Good. I'm all ready, kinda nervous and excited all at the same
time."

"Yeah, me too," he admitted.

Sara put her hand on her son's shoulder. "Aaron, we're going
to be ok. I really believe that."

"You always believe that."

"There are some things you can't work out in that amazing
mind of yours, some things you can only see by faith."

Aaron checked his watch again: 7:46. He moved from person
to person, making sure everyone had everything they needed. Ty
had his Molotov cocktails, made up of every flammable liquid left
in Duluth, and his rifle. Leah had her bow and five arrows, just in
case. Sara was set with her rifle, binoculars, and ammo. Wu had
the bolt cutters and a sixty-foot length of paracord. Aaron, Soraya,
and Seth only had a hunting knife and themselves to worry about.

Eight o'clock. Sara gathered everyone together in the
basement. She lit a candle and placed it on the floor, then they all
formed a circle around it. Everyone wrapped their arms around
the people next to them.

"This little candle is small compared to the darkness around it
but, once lit, it wields a power the darkness, no matter how great,
cannot overcome. We are that candle tonight. Though the
darkness we're about to confront is immense, by the grace of God,
love will overcome," she spoke with determination. "Bow your
heads, please. Father, thank you for the time we have had, for
Caleb, and for everyone here. Protect us as we forsake ourselves
to save one. Give us steady hands and clear minds. Bring us back
together safe and sound. I ask these things in Jesus' name, amen."

Everyone echoed the amen. Then they each said their
goodbyes and any encouragement they could manage. Sara led her
team up the stairs and to the door. Everyone waited, silent,
stomachs churning. Like paratroopers about to jump behind
enemy lines, they waited for Aaron's go. At last, he checked his
watch one final time.

"Keep them safe, Archangel," was all he could manage.

Aaron watched as his mother and sister vanished into the city
below. Emotions, raw and fierce, overtook him. Stumbling out
the door, he managed to make it to the bushes at the edge of the
yard before he vomited up everything left in him. Standing dizzily,
Aaron wiped his mouth on his sleeve. This was a new kind of fear.
He wanted to rush after them and call the whole thing off, but he
knew they had no choice. There was no calling this one off.

Weaving their way down the cluttered streets, Sara's band made
good time. All their night missions had familiarized their eyes with
the darkness, and they had all been on these roads many times.
Every now and again, they would catch a small glimpse of the
compound growing ever nearer as they made their way to the
school. The night air was cool as it entered their lungs. The half-
moon's silver light glinted off broken glass strewn in the streets.
It was the perfect night.

As her team reached the school, Sara paused and checked her
watch. They were five minutes ahead of schedule.

"You guys come up here with me for just a second. We have
time," Sara instructed.

It only took a minute for the team to reach the roof. Sara
walked them over to the corner where she would be set up.

"I want you all to see what I can see."

They each walked to the edge and looked out over the compound lit up from end to end, the headquarters building looming not far from the gate.

"Aaron calls me his archangel and, tonight, that's exactly what I am going to be. I'll watch over you. If any part of this goes south, you make a run for it, and I'll be watching your back."

Sara stood only five feet tall but, with her rifle in hand, her cloak fluttering in the light breeze, her voice fierce, she was a warrior if anyone ever was.

Sara looked in Leah's distant eyes, "Leah, are you—"

"I've got this, Mom. I'm good!" Leah said shortly.

Leah had run the scenario through her mind so many times she had finally come to peace with what she had to do, but it was a thin peace. If she mulled it over, even one more time, she may change her mind, and it had taken her too much to get this far.

"God be with you guys," Sara said as they headed back down the stairs.

Wu hesitated before going through the roof hatch.

"What is it, Wu?" Sara asked.

With a sigh, Wu turned to her. "I am a man without a country, but after tonight I will be a man without a people."

Sara reached up and smoothed a wrinkle out of his uniform. "Wu, you already have a people, and after tonight you'll never doubt it."

Wu didn't reply; he just turned and hurried down the stairs. There was no time to contemplate Sara's words. Maybe, if he survived the night, he would understand. He joined the others and, together, they made their way to the now-familiar alley.

Nine o'clock. Aaron slid his sleeve back down over his watch. *Any minute now.*

Seth and Soraya sat on the bed in the master bedroom, the patio doors wide open. Aaron stood alone out on the balcony, watching the compound. Everyone waited, waited for gunfire, waited for silence. Waited. Without radios there was no way to determine how the other team was fairing.

"Waiting is harder than doing," Seth groaned, one knee unconsciously bouncing.

"That train better be on time," Soraya said nervously.

Seth fidgeted with his hunting knife. He was afraid but too proud to admit it. Afraid for his mother, his sister, afraid they would fail and Caleb would suffer more than he already had. He was afraid the Chinese would win and everything his father had taught him, everything he loved about his country, would be lost from the world forever. Everything he knew hung in the balance on this night and, somewhere down there, his sister stood, bow in hand, her sights set on the face of a man.

The first link of the chain.

Chapter 23

Leah was standing alone just inside a blown out second-story window, not more than twenty yards from the guard obliviously standing watch in the southwest corner of the compound. She had left Ty down in the alley with Wu. This was something she needed to do by herself; an audience would only distract her. Now, only darkness and silence surrounded her as she prepared herself to carry out what she had promised to do.

On the last leg of his shift, the PLA soldier had grown bored and sleepy. She could clearly see him slumped in his chair after taking a careless scan around the fence. The distance between them seemed so small. If it had been daylight, and their eyes had met across that empty space, she would've been able to tell what color they were. She had no idea what all the symbols and insignia on his uniform meant, but she could see every one.

With a trembling breath, she tried to still her beating heart. *I can do this; I can do this.* She would have to be quick; the dogs were a little too far from this vantage point to take care of them from here. She would have to run outside and shoot through the fence itself to reach them before they sent up an alarm.

Carefully removing an arrow from her quiver, she made sure the broadhead was tight. Three razor sharp blades, blades designed to take a life. Tonight, they would fulfill their destiny. *Destiny.* She was here because her brother needed her; they all needed her. That's all. In one smooth motion, Leah knocked the arrow onto the string and clipped her release to the loop. She was ready.

She looked over at the soldier again, his breath in the cold night air slowly floated away in the breeze as he completed the radio check. The breath of life . . . the breath she was about to end. *For Caleb.* Gritting her teeth, she raised her bow and lined up her sights on the left temple of the man across from her. *Jesus, give me strength.* Her own breath came out in a rush. Her aim was solid.

THAWACK!

The sound was unmistakable. Her arrow had found its mark. The body crumpled to the floor of the tower with a soft thud, out of sight behind the low walls.

Before she could run down the stairs for part two of this nightmare, the rattle of chains drew her eyes back outside. The two dogs had gotten up and moved over to the bottom of the tower, apparently expecting the thud meant the guard was coming down. They stood looking up the stairs, then sat disappointed, bathed in the bright light of the tower.

Looking to the sky, Leah let out a relieved, "Thank you." Knocking a second arrow, she drew her bow back. For a moment, she pitied the creature she laid her sights on. It was only an animal; it hadn't chosen to invade her country. In a way, it was more innocent than any of them.

She gently touched her finger to the trigger, and the dog rolled onto its side, the shaft protruding from its head. Its mate rose to his feet in confusion. Leah grabbed the third arrow and knocked it on the string. She only had a moment, but it was all she needed.

Drawing the bow back for the last time, she steadied her sights just in front of its ear. *Last one* . . . She felt the twang of the string as she released the arrow. The concerned dog raised its head to howl just as the arrow reached its mark. Leah watched in horror as the dog writhed on the ground, her shaft had missed its head as it went to howl and slammed through its throat instead. She quickly grabbed a fourth arrow, but the struggle lasted only a moment and the dog lay still. Her arms relaxed. Three arrows, three targets, three lives.

It was done.

Gasping for air, she realized she had been holding her breath. Taking a step back from the window, she finally let the realization of what had happened wash over her. The twisting began deep in her gut and moved fast. Falling to her knees on the torn linoleum, Leah gaged. Then came the tears. Tears for the life she had just ended. Tears for the innocent dogs. Tears for her own lost innocence. Tears for the cruelty of war. The cost was too high. All she wanted was to wake up from this nightmare and be back home in her father's arms again.

Pulling herself out of the tailspin of emotions, she sat back up on her heels. She had to get out of here. The first link of the chain was complete. Wu would be on his way by now. She needed to rejoin her team.

Wiping her face with her sleeve, she stood and reached for her weapon. Seeing it laying there in the dust where she had dropped it, she froze. In her hands that bow had just killed a man. With a tired sigh, she scooped it up and put her extra arrow back in the quiver. Her thoughts would have to wait for another day. The night had only just begun.

Wu's head spun as the last dog expired only a few yards in front of him. Ducking back into the alley, he slunk to the ground. Fear gripped him; it was his turn. Ty knelt next to him, putting his large hand on Wu's trembling shoulder.

"We all have to do our part. I know it isn't easy, but remember what Sara said; you aren't alone out there, she's watching over you. We need you, or Aaron, Seth, and my sister are going to jump on that train, assuming we did our jobs, and they'll all be killed." Ty held out his hand. "Come on, brother. It's do or die time."

Wu took Ty's hand and was lifted to his feet. Ty's words were true; he knew it. If he stayed, they were dead. At this point, the only chance any of them had of surviving the night was to go through with the plan.

"All right!" he said. "I'm ready."

"Good luck!"

Picking up the bolt cutters, Wu crept to the flap he had cut in the fence, Ty watching over him from the alley. Reaching the flap, he took a last glance at the dogs just to make sure they were dead. Then, heart racing, he summoned all his courage and pressed through the opening. Laying the flap gently back in its place, he breathed a sigh of relief. He had fully expected to be killed on contact the moment he set foot back inside the compound. Yet, here he was: back inside safe and sound. *We might actually make it.*

Working his way between the fence and the coal cars, Wu came to the shipping yard which was dimly lit by the residual light from the guard shacks. It was wide and long, filled with crates, machinery, and supplies, all to be loaded onto ships or trains. Aisles for forklifts separated the rows of cargo and made for easy travel. By the time Wu made his way to the other side, he would be more than three quarters of the way to the headquarters building.

Hefting the bolt cutters to his shoulder, he began navigating the maze before him. He had no idea what he would say if a guard stopped him and asked why he was carrying a set of bolt cutters. Maybe that he had locked his personal trunk and lost the key? It sounded reasonable enough. That is, if the guard didn't recognize him as the deserter. His heart sank at the thought. It was likely his picture still hung in a couple of places around the compound.

It took Wu fifteen minutes to make the parade field. Only one hundred and fifty wide open yards stood between him and the HQ building. Crouching next to the last crate, he checked the field and the area surrounding his destination. It was terrifying and exhilarating at the same time to have come so far into the compound. Wu quickly checked his watch; time was everything: 9:27, roughly half an hour until the train would arrive.

Looking over his shoulder in the direction of the school, all he could see was black. Sara was out there; he had no doubt she would be watching over him. He looked back at the headquarters building. The light hanging above the main entrance illuminated the last thirty or so yards of the field. He would have to be quick. The fire escape ladder leading to the roof was on the backside of the building where it would be dark. He would be safe if he could just make the ladder. Without knowing why, he lifted his eyes to the starry sky and said, "God help me."

He had never given God much thought in his life, except to ponder if there even was such a thing. Sara and the others seemed to believe there was. Anyway, it couldn't hurt.

On his trek through the cargo, he noticed his boots made a terrible racket. Setting his jaw, he decided he would have to make this last stretch without them. He took them off, tied the laces, and hung them around his neck. Inhaling bravely, he squared his shoulders and launched into a dead run.

After the first seventy yards, Wu's lungs were on fire. The crisp air burned with each breath. His heart raced to keep up with his body's need for blood; his legs grew numb. Realizing too late he had failed to prepare for the athletic part of this mission, he drove his body on. Reaching the edge of the light, still moving at a good clip, it was too late to worry about running into anybody. There would be no explaining himself out of this one. Wu rounded the back of the building and sunk under the stairs, trying to control his gasps so they wouldn't be heard by those inside.

Sara wiped the sweat from her palm on the edge of her cloak. Wu was safe for the moment at the back of the headquarters building. She had watched his dash through her scope. Like a passionate fan, she held her breath as he took ground with each stride, willing him to win the race.

Reaching for the binoculars, Sara heard a familiar sound. *It couldn't be the train, it's too early.* She checked her watch: 9:36. *It's early.* Sure enough, off in the distance, the familiar flashing of the headlight breaking through the trees was indisputable.

"Crap!"

She focused the binoculars on the roof of the headquarters. She had lost sight of Wu when he rounded the building. *Where was he?*

"Come on, Wu!"

There was a flash of motion on the rooftop, then he came into view hunched next to one of the dishes. Wu gave a thumbs up in her direction, and then slunk back into the shadows.

"Thank you, Lord."

Everyone was in place. Early or not, everything was working out so far. Aaron's team would be boarding the train soon. *Soon . . . it could all be over soon.*

9:38. Aaron whirled into the bedroom.

"The train's almost here! Let's go!"

Before he could finish speaking, Seth and Soraya were already on their way down the stairs. Reaching the front door, Soraya slowly swung it open. The rattle of the train was clear now; it was close. Aaron slid out the door, Soraya and Seth right behind him. Crouching behind the bushes at the edge of the yard, they waited for the train's engine to pass.

"Do you think the others are ready?" Seth whispered.

"Have faith," Aaron replied.

The engine passed without the engineer so much as taking a passing glance at the house, oblivious to the passengers he was about to pick up. Aaron was gratified to discover there were no troop cars, only a few coal cars and flatbeds.

"This one!" Aaron called out as the fifth car passed them.

Without questioning, Soraya and Seth leaped from the bushes and jumped aboard the crate filled flatbed. There was no need to get comfortable; this was going to be a short ride.

Finding Aaron's hand, Soraya grabbed it. She was afraid, but glad she was with him. He had proven himself over the past month and, though it felt a little silly given the country's circumstances, she had allowed herself to fall for him. Maybe it was nothing more than her hope that there would be a better tomorrow someday. If there was, she wanted to spend hers with him.

"Be ready for anything. If this goes south, follow my lead, and we'll do our best to get out of dodge," Aaron whispered as the train made the last turn and headed down the straightaway, slowing as it approached the gate.

"I was about to come looking for you," Ty said in relief as Leah emerged through the darkness of the alley.

"Sorry," she whispered forlornly.

"That was good shooting, Leah. No one could have done that but you. I know that doesn't make it any easier, but you did your job and that's nothing to be ashamed of."

"Yeah. . . . Did Wu make it out alright?"

"Took a little encouragement, but he went. He's been gone for a while and there hasn't been any shooting or hollering, so I guess we have no choice but to assume he made it."

Faith, Leah thought to herself, *this whole thing was built on faith. Believing in each other, in God, in love. . . . There is no way to take the next step without faith in the one before.*

"Then we're all set," she said, attempting a smile.

"Yeah, and it's a good thing since the train's early. Not that I mind, I'm ready to be done with this. My stomach is so tight I feel like I could hurl at any minute."

"Join the club," Leah said, taking a seat next to him.

Wu sat huddled in the darkness next to a rooftop air conditioner unit. The breeze brought a shiver as it passed over his neck. His uniform provided little protection from the cold settling in as the sun sank behind the hill. He wished he could just cut the cables and be done with it, but that would alert those inside of their presence too soon, and the whole plan would fail. *Timing is everything.* The train was almost here anyway, and as soon as he cut the cables he would be running for his life. It was beginning to dawn on him that he had jumped out of the frying pan and into the fire.

The thought no sooner crossed his mind when he heard footsteps coming up the stairs from below the roof hatch. Mind racing, he tucked himself further behind the air conditioner, holding the bolt cutters tightly in both hands.

The steps grew closer, and then stopped. The handle on the hatch began to turn, letting out a shrill squeak. Wu fought down panic; he would be found for sure. Just then, the train's horn blew signaling the gate guard to open the gate.

On the school rooftop, Sara swung the binoculars from the alley to the gate, to the headquarters rooftop, and back again. The train was at the gate now. This was it. She scanned the train cars looking for any sign of Aaron, Seth, or Soraya, but she knew they would have to be hidden in order to pass under the gate tower undetected. Switching to the alley, she squinted as a faint flicker of light flashed on again, off again. Then it dawned on her: it was Ty, probably nervous, flicking his lighter, poised to rush in and set the coal cars alight. The links in the chain were falling into place.

The gate hummed as it began to open. Sara focused her binoculars back on the rooftop to watch for Wu's signal. Just then, the roof hatch of the headquarters building lifted open and out climbed an armed soldier. All the blood drained from her face as the man walked to the edge of the roof and lit up a cigarette.

Chapter 24

With his heartbeat exploding in his ears, Wu knew he was out of time. He had to do something. Rising to his feet, he raised the only weapon he had, the bolt cutters, and held them above his head. In three silent strides he reached the soldier and, using his momentum, swung the bolt cutters into the back of the man's head. The heavy steel glanced off his skull, spinning him around as he fell forward into Wu's arms, unconscious. Quickly, Wu drug him over to the roof hatch and laid him over the door. He didn't want any more surprises. His hands slipped on the handles of the bolt cutters.

Blood.

There was no time to let it sink in. Wu turned from his fallen countryman and set about cutting all the cables on the roof as fast as he could. The task was more difficult than he had expected. The outer shielding of the cables wreaked havoc on the rusty blades, but he managed to sever every line in a couple of minutes. Then, racing to the edge of the roof, he gave Sara the thumbs up.

Sara could hardly believe her eyes when Wu appeared at the edge of the roof giving her the go ahead. She had turned her gaze back on the train for a moment and, by the time she had refocused on the roof, the soldier was gone. She didn't see what had happened and feared the worst.

Dropping the binoculars and shouldering her rifle, she switched off the safety, placing her cheek on the stock. The first light was easy, not more than forty yards away. She breathed out, held it, and pulled the trigger. There was a shower of sparks and the light went dark.

Unmistakable, the crack of Sara's rifle rang out over the compound. Ty exploded from the alley and rolled through the hole in the fence carrying four Molotov cocktails, the fuse rags already alight. Adrenaline coursed through his veins as he scaled the ladder on the nearest train car. Reaching the top, he found it mounded with rich black coal. He hurled the first cocktail into it and watched it flare up. Tossing in a second cocktail, he watched the car turn into an inferno. By the time he turned to light up the next car, thick smoke was already beginning to move across the compound. He tossed the remaining cocktails into the adjacent car and jumped down, his feet already driving toward the fence the moment they touched the ground.

Rifle shots continued to ring out overhead and light after light went dark. Ty reached the hole in the fence just as the compound siren began to blare. The soldiers would be coming soon.

When he reached the alley, he was greeted by Leah who had tracked the smoke's progression across the compound from the moment the fire was lit.

"I think it's working. It's even better now that Mom has taken down so many lights."

Ty nodded to her, gasping for air, his heart racing.

Wu finished tying off the paracord he had used to lower the bolt cutters so Aaron could grab them as soon as he was ready. He was about to climb down the fire escape when he stepped on the soldier's rifle lying where it dropped when Wu had hit him. Deciding it was probably better to be armed at this point, he picked up the weapon and slung it over his shoulder.

Then he proceeded to race down the stairs to join the others.

The train halted with only two thirds of its full length inside the compound. Aaron, Seth, and Soraya hid, poised, among the cargo. Rifle shots, sirens, shouting. The compound was a mess with noise. Soldiers called out to one another, and the sound of boots could be heard all around them. Peeking through a gap in the crate, Aaron watched as a light on one of the east guard towers went dark.

The gate tower light was still active and, by its illumination, Aaron could see confused soldiers running like ants from an invaded nest. Most of them were sprinting toward the south end of the compound. Then he saw it, thick black smoke rolling up the compound, an ominous cloud swallowing the soldiers as they ran about. It would be there soon.

Aaron turned to Seth and Soraya.

"Get ready!"

Only one light left to go. The gate tower was over 800 yards, further than Sara had ever practiced. She raised her rifle just above the light, let her breath out slowly, held it, then pulled the trigger. The rifle jerked against her shoulder, but the light remained. Grimacing, she ejected the shell and rammed another one into the chamber.

"Come on, Sara . . ." she said under her breath.

She squeezed the trigger, letting the rifle surprise her as it went off. Through the scope, she watched the light flicker for a moment and then go dark.

"Thank you," she whispered, laying her head down on her arm in relief.

She had done her part; the lights were out. The compound was teeming with soldiers disoriented by the smoke, convinced they were being overrun. The siren only added to the confusion, and it would be amazing if they didn't end up shooting each other in the chaos. Knowing it was likely someone had observed her muzzle flash on the rooftop, Sara pushed herself to her feet and raced down the stairs. The night was far from over, and she had another role to play yet.

Smoke swallowed the train car as the light above their heads went dark. The compound grew dim; the only lights left were on the headquarters building, the gatehouse, and two guard towers on the north side. Aaron, Soraya, and Seth slipped off the train car and crouched low next to the tracks.

Just as Aaron had predicted, the cool evening air rolling off the hills held the smoke low. The warmer air rising off the lake created a swirling motion, adding to the ominous appearance of the whole scene.

"We don't know how long this smoke is going to last. Stay alert!" Aaron whispered.

Seth rolled his eyes as they headed out, Aaron was always saying useless things. *Who, at this point, isn't alert?*

The prisoner's containers were only a hundred yards from the gate. Under the circumstances, it felt more like a mile. Soldiers still ran about here and there calling to one another in the smoke, others could be heard coughing and hacking. The siren had died down, and now a harsh voice barked orders over the megaphone. Every now and again flashlight beams flashed about the darkness around them. Aaron led his team tight to the containers surrounding the west side of the compound.

"Hold up!" Seth whispered.

Everyone froze, ears straining to hear.

"There," Seth said.

The unmistakable sound of a soldier's boots was steadily approaching.

"Down!" Aaron hissed.

Leah and Ty waited anxiously in the alley for Sara to join them. Soldiers had filtered into the south end of the compound by the dozens and were already organizing themselves to put out the fires. The two of them ducked back into the alley as soldiers climbed the guard tower and discovered their fallen comrade.

"Come on, Mom!" Leah whispered in exasperation. They had been here long enough.

"Here she comes . . . I think," Ty said, swinging his rifle to cover the far end of the alley.

Faint steps approached. In the moonlight, a cloaked figure appeared carrying a long rifle.

"Mom!" Leah burst out, running to meet her.

"Shhh!" Ty warned, following after her.

"What took you so long?" Leah asked, emotions bubbling up.

"That last light gave me trouble. I'm sorry, I came as quick as I could. We have to get out of here, now!"

Trotting by moonlight, Sara's team headed to their position opposite the gate. If everything was still on plan, Aaron's team would be returning to the gate any minute now.

God help them, Sara prayed silently looking down on the compound from a side street. The base was in total pandemonium and Sara knew if her son's team was captured, there would be hell to pay for this night.

Out of the gloom, a soldier appeared swinging his rifle and a flashlight side to side. Aaron's team crouched motionless, hearts racing, as the soldier stepped ever closer. Unable to escape, Aaron saw the beam of light fall on his brother. The soldier wildly swung his rifle to fire.

Before the man could switch off his safety Aaron jumped on him, slamming his head into the corner of a container. The soldier fell limp to the ground.

Seth rose to his feet, knees shaking.

"I thought I was dead," he said, looking down at the soldier. "I owe you one, Aaron."

"This night's not over. I may need to collect on that yet," Aaron said, continuing along the fringe of the compound.

Wu staggered through the smoke in the direction of the prisoner containers, bolt cutters in hand. Aaron was supposed to have been waiting at the bottom of the tower for the bolt cutters when Wu lowered them but, as Wu discovered when he reached the bottom of the stairs, that had not been the case. He pondered the possibility of their capture and considered heading out the gate and taking his chances but, in his heart, he knew with or without them he needed to try and rescue Caleb. Cutting the paracord, he had set off on his own toward the containers, hoping Aaron would be along shortly.

Wanting to avoid the light of the headquarters building, he headed for the western edge of the compound. Out of the haze in front of him, a soldier in a gas mask emerged carrying a large bag.

Wu feared the worst as the man advanced in his direction. His pulse quickened; he couldn't allow himself to be captured. *Not now.* Dropping the bolt cutters, he raised the rifle. The soldier stopped in his tracks, reached into his bag and extended a gas mask to Wu.

"Captain's orders," the soldier barked as Wu took the mask. Then he continued into the smoke.

Wu nearly fainted as the man disappeared. Without hesitating further, he slipped the mask over his face and secured it. *No one will recognize me now.*

As Aaron turned his team toward the headquarters to fetch the bolt cutters, he hoped they hadn't been discovered. The smoke was thick, and they weren't making good time. *Never enough time.*

They had gone no more than fifteen yards from the western wall when a soldier wearing a gas mask emerged from the smoke right in front of them. Without hesitation, Seth dove on the man, knocking him to the ground. Raising himself on the uniformed chest, he prepared to beat him senseless. Frantically, the man peeled the mask off.

"It's me, Wu!" he said, shielding himself from Seth's fury.

Seth stopped short of delivering a blow, panting with rage.

"Wu?"

"Where were you guys? I have been waiting! I have almost been killed. I had to hit a man."

"We don't have time for that," Aaron said, lifting Wu to his feet.

"Sorry," Seth said, dusting him off as they pushed on.

Aaron's team reached the yard in front of the prisoner containers. The smoke was somewhat blocked by stacks of cargo aiding their visibility. The diversion had worked beyond what Aaron had hoped for. There were no guards left on duty. After all, the prisoners were the only ones in the compound the PLA didn't need to worry about. They were locked up.

"Ok, we're assuming Caleb is being held in one of these containers," Aaron said, pointing to the last four containers in the row. "Wu, you cover us from here. We'll start at the far container and work our way back. Seth, Soraya, you guys have to keep whoever we find in there quiet. The moment we find Caleb we're out of here. Everybody good?" Aaron asked hastily.

Aaron cut the lock on the first container and slowly opened the door. The hinges let out a groan, everyone looked around anxiously.

"Caleb? Are you in there?" Seth called into the container.

Two rough looking men appeared at the door, their awestruck expressions obvious even in the dim light.

"Crap," Aaron muttered, moving to the second container, leaving the two prisoners to Seth and Soraya.

Aaron broke the second lock and cracked the door open.

"Caleb? Are you in here? It's Aaron," he whispered.

"Who?" replied a man's voice.

"Is there a boy in there with you? We've come to rescue you."

A lone man appeared at the doorway, trembling. "I'm free?" he asked.

"Not quite yet," Aaron said, handing him off to Seth.

Moving faster now, Aaron cut the lock on the third container. He gently opened the door and called into the container. "Caleb? Are you here?"

There was no reply.

He pulled the door open wide enough to slip inside. "Caleb?" Silence.

Aaron reached into his pocket and pulled out one of the lighters they had used on night missions and lit it. A faint yellow glow danced on the walls of the container. It was empty. There was evidence it had once been occupied, scratches on the wall to mark days, empty ration bags. A small piece of cardboard with a picture of some sort drawn on it. Aaron's pulse quickened. *Where was Caleb?*

Sara's team had made it to their support position behind a barricade of a burned-out car and debris. The fires at the other end of the compound were all but under control, and the smoke was beginning to dissipate. The plan was out of time.

The sound of the train's engine roaring to life sent the entire team into a panic. The wheels screeched on the tracks, and then, ever so slowly, the train began to roll into the compound.

"They'll be trapped!" Leah cried out.

"What are we going to do, Sara? There's no way to open that gate from this side if they get it closed," Ty said.

"I don't know. If we start shooting, we're going to attract every soldier in the compound and they really won't be getting out of there," Sara replied.

"They have the cutters, maybe they can cut their way out," Ty suggested.

The three of them watched helplessly as the train rolled to a stop inside the compound and the gate hummed to a close behind it.

Leah could bear the emotions of the night no more, wrapping her arms around her knees she began to whimper.

Sara frantically swung her scope from the prisoner area to the gate and back again, looking for any sign of her sons in the dim light. Nothing.

Aaron emerged from the third container to find Seth waiting for him.

"Well?" Seth asked.

"There was nobody in this one," he said without making eye contact, afraid his eyes would relay his fears.

"Well, there's still one left, let's go!" Seth encouraged.

Aaron cut the last lock from the container and wrenched the door open.

The bolt cutters fell from his hand. There, only three feet in front of him, stood a moppy-haired boy and a haggard old man.

"Aaron?" the boy asked.

Stepping forward, Aaron threw his arms around him.

"Caleb, we've come for you," he said, his voice cracking with emotion.

Introductions were brief, Aaron gathered everyone together, gave them the plan, and quietly they headed for the gate.

"Wait!" whispered one of the prisoners. "My brother is here."

Aaron cringed at the unspoken request.

"Where?" he asked apprehensively.

"I don't know where they keep him. He works in the medical building."

"I'm sorry, but we don't have the time to go looking for him tonight. We have to get out of here. If you want to stay that's fine, but we're going," Aaron replied.

There was no time for compassion. They still had to make the gate. As they reached Wu's position, Sam nearly pounced on him, and would have, if Seth hadn't called him off.

The smoke was clearing fast. By the time the band reached the last container before the gate, there was hardly a wisp at all. Aaron peered around the corner toward the gate and, in a moment, all the joy of finding Caleb was drowned out by a wave of dread. The gate was closed.

Aaron spun back around breathing heavily, his mind raced to find a solution.

"What is it, Aaron?" Soraya whispered.

"We're trapped!"

"Trapped? What do you mean?" she said, the surprise in his voice beginning to unnerve her.

"They closed the gate!"

"What?!" Seth fumed.

"Just give me a second to think!" Aaron said, holding his head in his hands.

Fear spread across the prisoners' faces. They knew there would be no forgiveness for this night. Captain Li would surely kill them all.

Aaron turned to Wu. "Wu, it's gotta be you. You can get close; you look just like them. When you're real close, let those two soldiers in the gate shack have it. Then you have to run in and switch the gate open. I'm sorry buddy, but it's the only shot we've got. We'll be right behind you. After the guards are dead, we won't have much time, but I think we can make the gate before anyone will be able to react to the shooting."

Wu stood frozen with fear. He had already hit one soldier, probably killing him, now they wanted him to kill more. He fought to find a solution which didn't involve him.

The look in his eyes betrayed him; it was apparent to everyone he was terrified. Then, from the side, someone jerked the rifle from his hands.

"I'll go!" Sam said, dashing around the corner.

"No!" Caleb called after him, but it was too late. Caleb looked around the corner as Sam opened fire.

The old man jogged toward the guard shack firing the rifle from his hip. The soldier standing just outside the shack was hit and fell to the ground. They watched as a round ripped through Sam's back leaving a growing crimson stain on his dusty shirt. Sam jerked as the round passed through him, but it didn't slow him down. Another round blew out the back of his shoulder blade as he made the door of the shack and emptied the last few rounds into the remaining soldier.

"NO!" Caleb shrieked, as the old man fell into the gate shack.

There was no time to lose, Aaron seized Caleb's hand and ran for the gate. Caleb fought to get his hand free.

"No, Sam, No! Let go of me! Sam!" Caleb screamed.

Sara trained her scope on the gate shack. *What is going on?* She scanned to the left and right. She had no idea who was shooting or why. It all happened so fast. She knew someone had rushed the shack and had made it inside, but who? Then she heard him . . . she heard her son . . . screaming something she couldn't quite make out, but it was him.

"There," Ty said, looking through the binoculars. "They're nearly to the gate."

"Who?" Sara asked. "Can you see who?"

"There's a bunch of them. It's so dark I can't make anyone out yet."

"Oh, God. Oh, God. Oh, God," Leah prayed, rocking back and forth.

Sara's pulse raced, she now looked beyond them, determined to knock down anyone converging on her sons.

In the shack, Sam crawled across the body of the fallen soldier toward the control panel. He felt his life fading, his strength giving way to mortality. He had been a fighter all his life, usually on the wrong side of things, but this boy . . . this boy was worth fighting for. Sam reached the bench and forced himself to his knees, the burning pain of his wounds fading into a tingly numbness throughout his body, and finding the green "open" button, he pressed it.

Outside the shack, the gate hummed to life and began to open. Sam looked out the dingy Plexiglas window and watched as the prisoners ran to freedom. Lastly, Aaron and Caleb arrived at the gate, Caleb fighting all the way, still calling his name.

"Go, kid," Sam whispered.

He watched Aaron throw the boy over his shoulder and disappear into the night. A faint smile spread across the old man's face.

Good.

He slumped to the floor, his last breath hanging defiantly in the air. Then, like his spirit, it vanished from the world.

Chapter 25

Finally, the figures sprinting toward Sara's team were recognizable, and she could see her son, her little boy, over Aaron's shoulder almost within her reach. The rest of the plan flew right out of her mind as relief washed over her. She was a mother bear within sight of her stolen cub. The tears couldn't be stopped.

"Caleb!" she cried brokenly as she dropped her rifle and jumped to climb over the barricade. All she knew was her son was now free, and there was agony in his voice. He needed her, and she was coming.

Ty grabbed the back of her cloak and pulled her back down.

"I'm sorry, I'm really sorry," he explained, "But it's not over yet. We have to let him go. We have to make sure they aren't followed."

A helpless, broken sob was her only response as she watched Aaron lead the band out of sight.

"I'm coming, Caleb, I'm coming . . ."

Leah had crumpled back into the shadows after watching them fly by. She was now shaking in the wake of the adrenaline which had risen as she had willed Aaron and Caleb through that gate.

They turned their attention back to the guard shack and the steel gate, which was now wide open. The area, still only lit by the small light above the shack's door, was now crawling with soldiers who had quickly appeared in response to the gunfire. The two dead guards had been discovered, along with the body of whoever had opened the gate. It was still a mystery to them who had sacrificed himself to open the gate and let the other prisoners go free, but Sara knew they owed him everything. The shouting and confusion could be clearly heard by the three crouched behind the rubble. They watched as the man's body was pulled from the shack. Through the windows, they could see a soldier lean over and slap a button. The gate began to slide shut.

"They have no idea what happened!" Ty whispered incredulously.

"Well, let's not wait around for them to figure it out!" Sara returned, scooting back from her position and getting to her feet. "Sooner or later, they're going to check on the prisoner containers, and then we'll be in for it. Come on, maybe we can catch up with the others."

Quickly and silently, they rose like shadows in the night and, turning their backs to the city once and for all, they set off at a jog into the darkness.

Huffing, Aaron stopped near a tree and put Caleb on his feet. Caleb had ceased yelling and fighting and had just hung limp for the last couple hundred yards, his soft sobs barely loud enough to hear over the sound of his brother's panting.

"Caleb, I'm sorry about your friend. He saved us back there. He saved you. I can't keep carrying you, and we can't stop. I need you to carry yourself for a bit. When we get where we're going, maybe we can rest for a while before we head north. I know this whole thing has hit you out of nowhere, but I need you to try," Aaron pleaded, leaning down to look him in the eyes.

Caleb stared blankly at his brother, a mixture of tears and snot had made a mess of his dirty face. His eyes were the only part of him saying anything. They spoke of pain and loss.

"Caleb?" Aaron prodded.

A hand softly touched his shoulder and Soraya said, "I'll look out for him."

Almost instantly, he felt a weight lifted. There was something about her that just brought peace to his frenzied mind, a peace he was apt to forget if she hadn't come to his rescue so many times.

"Alright," Aaron said, casting her a grateful glance.

Soraya took Caleb's hand as they started off at a quick walk.

"I know you have a lot of questions, Caleb," Soraya began as they walked along. "I'll do my best to answer some of them."

She thought for a moment. *Where to start?*

"Ty and I bumped into your family two nights after you were taken, on the outskirts of Duluth. We were intending to head around the city that night, but your family told us what had happened to you and that they were planning to rescue you no matter what the cost. There was no other choice. We were going to stay and help.

"Together, we found a house which gave us a good vantage point on the compound and could serve as a base of operations. Your mom kept tabs on your comings and goings every morning and evening. We conducted nearly a hundred different missions to gather information and supplies for your rescue.

"Your mom and Aaron wanted to charge in everyday and rescue you, but there was no way to make that possible. We've been working around the clock for a month to make sure Aaron's plan had the best shot at success. We even took a prisoner who turned out to be a friend. We would never have been able to pull this off without him," Soraya said, gesturing to Wu. "His name is Wu, and he's given up everything to help us."

Soraya told him of the plan, what each person had done, about the smoke, his mother's shooting, Leah's arrows, Wu's bravery, and his brother's resolve. She concluded her tale with Sam's selfless sacrifice. The other prisoners had changed up their pace in order to hear the daring rescue story.

"I didn't know your friend, Caleb, but he must have loved you. John 15:13 says, 'Greater love hath no man than this, that a man lay down his life for his friends.'"

Looking down at Caleb, she could see tears glistening on his cheeks. He didn't make a sound, didn't move to wipe the tears, he just kept on walking.

Images and thoughts flashed through Caleb's mind as he tried to make heads or tails of what had happened.

He had started the day believing his family was dead, and Sam was his new "father." Now *that* family was dead, and his *real* family was alive. His emotions conflicted with reality. He had let go of this family, had already gone through the pain of burying them in his heart, and now Sam?

All he could see was the red, the spreading red on the back of his shirt. Sam's body jerking, and then red. *Why did he do that? Why didn't he wait for someone else to go? Why did they even need to rescue me? Sam's plan would have worked out eventually.*

But Sam hadn't waited for someone else; he went himself. There was no escaping it. *Sam wanted me to live, to escape, to be free, but why? Why did Sam want me to be free without him?*

Looking away from his little brother, Seth shook his head with the confusion in his own mind. He had thought for sure they would all be heroes if they actually succeeded in pulling off the plan. He had anticipated an excited reunion, rejoicing, and a feeling of noble goodness. The pain on Caleb's face was a far different reality. In its shadow, Seth didn't feel like much of a hero at all. *What did we do wrong?*

Finally, they reached the familiar little creek channel. After a mile or so of trudging through the icy waters, Aaron finally called out, "We're here."

"Thank God!" Soraya said, leading Caleb over to her pack to grab a bottle and get some water.

"Where's Mama?" Caleb asked.

"She's with Ty and Leah. They covered our escape. They'll be here soon," Soraya assured him.

Aaron walked over to his pack and pulled out another water jug, filled it up, and handed it to the other prisoners.

"Thanks," said one of the younger men. "I'm Jason, and this here's Ben."

The last prisoner stepped forward, a monstrous dark-skinned man in his forties. "I'm Tonell Jackson. Thank you for rescuing us. I heard what you did from the girl. I know you didn't have to take us with you. I've never heard of anything that courageous in all my life."

"You're Americans. All we have left is each other," Aaron said humbly. "I wish I could give you guys more of a rest but I'm afraid, as soon as they get their communications up, the PLA are going to call in the cavalry. We need to be long gone by the time they do."

"No, they won't," Wu said matter-of-factly. Everyone looked at him in surprise. "Captain Li only lost a couple of soldiers and some prisoners. He isn't going to risk his career, maybe his life, by reporting his compound was breached on his watch. Oh, he'll be plenty mad, and he does have quite a little army under his command, so I'm not saying we should stay long. I'm just saying there won't be any support, or helicopters for that matter."

"Really? Hmmm," Aaron said, pondering this revelation. "By the way, you were amazing tonight, Wu. We wouldn't have been able to pull this off without you. You definitely have a dragon's courage."

Sara's feet were freezing, but she hardly gave them any thought. They had been walking in the edge of the creek, for what felt like a mile, to mask their scent.

"We're almost there," whispered Ty from the front of the column.

She adjusted her rifle strap on her shoulder and could feel her heartbeat quicken. Well, the truth was, she didn't know if it had ever slowed down since she saw her boy on this side of the gate which had kept him away from her for so long. Suddenly, she heard a low voice float through the darkness.

"I thought I was dead for sure!"

It was Wu!

Pushing past Ty, Sara started running up the creek. She didn't care if her splashing could be overheard. She had to get to her son. Only a few seconds later, she heard the voice which had cried to her in her dreams almost every night since this nightmare began.

"Mama?"

"Caleb!" she cried, running up the bank where he was coming to meet her. The tears swimming in her eyes made it even harder to see him in the faint moonlight. Dropping her gun, she threw her arms around her boy.

"Oh, Caleb, oh, my Caleb," she sobbed into his hair, holding him tight against herself, her hand holding the back of his head tenderly.

"I thought you were dead," Caleb cried into her shoulder, clinging to his mother like he would never let go.

"Oh, baby, I'm sorry. I'm so sorry! I've got you now, Caleb. It's going to be ok. You're safe now."

Sara wasn't sure how long they stood there, crying together but, when she looked up, she could see everyone was respectfully giving them space. Ty and Leah were also there now, Leah unashamedly weeping for her little brother.

"Look," Sara whispered to Caleb as she gently lifted his head. "Here's Leah."

Caleb looked up through his tears and sniffled. Seeing his sister, he gave a half smile and turned toward her just in time for her to run forward and grab him in a bear hug, bawling as she held him.

"Oh, Caleb, I'm so sorry! I missed you so much! I thought I'd never see you again!"

"Me too," he answered quietly, squeezing her tight in return.

Aaron swallowed the lump welling in his throat and blinked back the tears rising in his eyes. Watching Caleb and his mom together made everything worth it. He had never let himself ponder failure at rescuing his brother, but he couldn't deny the slight feeling of surprise that, not only was it finally over, they had actually succeeded.

He wanted nothing more than to be done, to just stay here and enjoy being a family again. But that would be foolish, and he knew it. It would only be a matter of time before Captain Li organized a search and came after them. They weren't far enough away to be safe yet. He looked around at all the people under his care. The three prisoners were a little winded from their run, not surprising given their life for the past however long. Everyone else's emotions from the entire night had exhausted them. They needed a break. Maybe it would be ok to stay until dawn.

"I don't know if anyone can sleep at this point," he spoke up to the group. "But I'm willing to take the first watch so we can try. Tomorrow we'll be heading north. Winter will be here soon, and we have to make the northern forests with enough time to prepare. The pace will be quick, and the terrain is rough. We've collected gear to outfit each of you for the trip. I know this is all really sudden, but we're out of time, and this is the best we can do. You're welcome to strike out on your own if you'd like; no one owes us anything," Aaron concluded, taking up his father's rifle.

Soraya, Ty, and Seth worked together to get the prisoners set up for the remainder of the night. Sara prepared a place for Caleb next to her. She doubted she would ever take her eyes off him again. Wu, still too keyed up from the rescue, wandered over to where Aaron had sat down on a log and joined him.

Somehow, deep inside, Wu felt like a new man.

Sara lay on her back, wide awake, listening to the sound of Caleb breathing next to her. Tears stained her face as the reality of his presence brought waves of emotion crashing over her as the hours passed by. She heard him moan next to her as he struggled to get comfortable. Every time he rolled to his back, he let out an involuntary groan and rolled back onto his side.

Finding the lighter in her pocket, Sara pulled it out and gave it a quick flick. In the soft yellow glow, she could see his back facing her. His rib cage, expanding and contracting with each breath, was obvious through his tattered shirt. Then, something caught her eye near the bottom hem. The shirt had ridden up during his tossing and turning, revealing a maroon stripe.

Reaching over with her free hand, Sara gently slid Caleb's shirt further up his back. Her fingers slid gently over bumps, both rough and smooth. As she moved the lighter closer, she gave a small, strangled gasp. His poor young back was riddled with scars, scabs, and welts!

"That isn't the worst part," Caleb said.

His voice startled her.

"We were going to escape today. Before you got there, we had a plan, a ship all picked out. When we woke up this morning, the ship had left in the night. Sam called it a bad break. He said there would be another someday soon."

He drew a quivering breath.

"He went down fighting . . . for me. I know he did it for me. He wouldn't let Captain Li have me . . ."

Caleb pulled his blanket up over his shoulders and, taking a deep breath, fell quiet.

"I'm so sorry, Caleb," Sara whispered, settling back into her own bed.

Tears filled her eyes as her heart broke. This was injustice, cruelty. Her eleven-year-old boy didn't deserve this, to know the pain of all this. She wished she could take it away, take him away, and heal his broken heart. His sweet innocence was gone. Death, war, and hate had taken it from him, and there was nothing she could do.

There was no going back. But thanks to the love of a man she would never know, they would go forward. Caleb had a future, and perhaps, by the grace of God, he would heal.

The hum of military trucks filtered through the trees. They were a long way off, but close enough to ruin a perfectly peaceful morning. Night was quickly giving way to dawn and Seth, who had taken the last watch, knew it was time to get everyone up.

"Aaron," he said, shaking his older brother.

"I hear them," Aaron said, obviously already awake. "We'd better get moving."

"Yeah," Seth replied, moving to wake his mother who had heard their conversation and was already sitting up.

"Morning, Mom," Seth said with a smile. "Sleep at all?"

"Not really, but the rest was nice anyway."

Soraya, Ty, and Leah got up and started reloading their packs. Caleb and the other prisoners seemed to have gotten the most sleep out of the bunch. Their bodies were exhausted, and freedom, even in the woods, was more peace than they had known in a long time.

After everyone was up, Sara handed out breakfast rations.

"There's no escaping these things," Ben joked.

Sara gave a half laugh. "I wish we were back home; I'd cook you gentlemen a breakfast of omelets and hash browns, whole wheat pancakes, and maple syrup."

"Mom, stop! How am I supposed to eat this crap with you talking about pancakes?" Seth whined.

"I'd give Seth's right arm for a pancake right now," Aaron jested.

Breakfast was finished with bits of conversation here and there. The relief of leaving Duluth had everyone in high spirits, and the laughs came easy.

Sara watched Caleb as they ate; his melancholy mood troubled her. She prayed time would heal her little boy's wounds and that, one day, she could have him back again.

When the rushed breakfast had concluded, everyone finished loading up their packs and the band headed north, slogging their way up the creek. The plan was to follow this creek north as far as they could and then split ways, each group taking a slightly different route to their common destination just north of Ely.

A strange mixture of excitement about being on the road again and sadness for the upcoming separation filled every heart in the group. Soraya had to will her feet forward through the shallow water, her heart unconsciously trying to delay what it dreaded. She had grown used to working by Aaron's side. And she liked it. She felt more alive in his presence. She couldn't think of anywhere else she would rather be. And she was about to say goodbye: maybe forever. Ely was a long way away. There were many miles and unknown dangers to be crossed by both teams. She might never get there, or if she did, she could end up waiting for a man who might never be able to come. *Why is he so stubborn?* She kicked at a rock in her frustration and ended up sending a spray of water up Ty's back.

"Hey!" he exclaimed, looking around in surprise.

"Sorry!" she returned sheepishly, as she trudged on. Every time they rounded a curve she braced for the signal to split ways. Each time it didn't come, she sighed in relief. *This is silly! It's not like we're talking or even walking next to each other!* But it was no use. There was no fighting it, just knowing he was there made all the difference.

Then the signal came.

"I think this is a good spot." Aaron pulled out his map and called Ty over. "Ok, I'm guessing we've come about this far," he traced their route with his finger. "You stay on this main creek for a while, and then head to the highway we talked about before. We'll follow this little stream which joins just up ahead and stay to the east."

"Sounds good," Ty answered, comparing notes on his own scavenged map.

"Well," Aaron tucked his map away and faced the others. "I guess we just need to say our goodbyes then."

Most of the sappy stuff had been said before they had launched the rescue, so there wasn't much left to say. The three new members of the group expressed, again, their heart-felt appreciation to the Reddings. Sara and Leah exchanged long hugs with Soraya. Seth surprised everybody by giving Wu a bear hug and commissioning him to watch over the others.

Soraya lost sight of Aaron in the chaos of hugs and well wishes and started looking for him. As she turned around, she almost jumped in surprise. He was right there, facing her. Their eyes met. *Maybe . . .*

Aaron awkwardly stuck out his hand, "Well, good luck out there and Godspeed. We couldn't have done this without you. Hopefully, we'll see you in a couple of weeks."

In complete shock and disappointment, she woodenly let him shake her hand. Desperately, she searched his eyes, willing him to say something else, to give any indication that everything they had gone through together meant something, but all she saw there was firm resolve.

Ty called his team to move out, and she turned to follow her brother further up the creek. After a few steps, she turned to see Aaron one last time and saw him slowly trudging to the front of his family. *I guess that's it then.* With a sigh, she squared her shoulders and slogged after Ty.

As Aaron moved to the head of his own team, Sara stopped him.

"Are you just going to let her walk away like that? Aaron?!"

He froze and looked down at her with a mixture of helplessness and frustration. Without a word, he continued to the front of the line and began to head up the tiny stream, expecting his family to follow.

"Let's go."

What could he have done? There was no way to ensure either one of them would make it to Ely and even less of a chance both of them would. They had spent almost two months just trying to get this far and, by the grace of God, had only lost his father and Caleb's friend. How could he risk causing the kind of pain Caleb was feeling, the kind of pain his mother felt, on anyone else, or himself for that matter. This wasn't a world to fall in love in, or to get close. As far as he could tell, that road only led to pain. Perhaps in another life, a safe life, they may have had a chance.

He wished he could dismiss his feelings for her, but his logic seemed to have no effect on his heart. He tried to chase the memories away but, as the miles wore on, his mind kept drifting back to her smile, her touch, her voice. *Why is love so foolish?*

Chapter 26

"Aaron? I wanted to apologize for being so forward with you when we left Ty, Soraya, and the others. I wasn't trying to embarrass you. I just . . . I guess I was trying to keep you from making a mistake—that's all," Sara confided, walking far enough ahead of the rest of the family to afford some privacy.

It had been two days since they left the others, and Aaron had hardly said a word to any of them. He had never been one to bare his feelings without some prodding, and Sara had grown to respect his space, but it wasn't like him to shut her out.

At first, Aaron just kept right on walking, and Sara began to wonder if he had heard her at all. Finally, he spoke.

"How can you be so sure I was making a mistake? What if the mistake is to allow someone to care for you to a point where losing you leaves them heartbroken and alone forever?" he asked, clearly uptight.

"What do you mean?" she asked, brows furrowed.

"Like you and Dad. He's gone, and I've watched you sneak away to cry out your pain or return from your alone times with red eyes. Look at Caleb. He got close to that man, and now I'm not even sure he wanted to be rescued," he said, throwing up his hands. "Life is so dangerous now; we have no idea if we'll even make it through the day most of the time. We have no hospitals, no medicine, no doctors. Our weapons are almost out of ammo, little food, no shelter, a handful of iodine tablets. . . . What could I possibly offer her other than pain, hunger, and probably death!"

"Love! Aaron! You could offer her love."

Aaron threw up his hands again. "You can't eat love, Mom!"

"Listen to me, Aaron. Love can do a whole lot more than just feed you. Love just saved my boy. Against impossible odds, love overcame. Fear could not hold it, odds could not beat it, and darkness could not hide it. Love drove that man to give his life for Caleb, and Caleb stands with us today. Love for your family, for your father, has guided your every step since we set out on this crazy adventure, Aaron! It has brought us food, shelter, water, but more importantly, hope."

Her words clashed with the logic in his mind.

"You're right about me, though. I do feel alone at times without your father, but that's only because the time we had together was so good. I would rather live with the pain of his absence than to never have known his presence. I only feel alone at times because I have been loved, and his love will carry me to my dying day. You see, love isn't safe. You could say it was made for a time such as this. Love is why we live, son. Without love, we don't live. I've never seen anyone so unafraid to die, and yet so afraid to live. That girl loves you. I see it every time she looks at you. Please don't let fear keep you from loving her back."

Sara slowed her pace to give her son some room to think. She could see the battle in his mind written on the features of his face. They had been through a lot, and she didn't want him to believe she was disappointed in him. The truth was quite the opposite. His planning and leadership had saved Caleb. He had brought them this far, and she couldn't be prouder of him.

Days of hiking turned into a week. Aaron led his family day in and day out with a fierce resolve. Frost taunted him every morning, and the barren trees rattled in the cold wind. He had purposely given Ty the easier route to their rendezvous point. Aaron was the better woodsman, and Ty had the prisoners, so it only made sense. If they were keeping a good pace, Aaron figured Ty should reach Ely a day or two before them. That's if they managed to avoid any trouble.

Sara's words from the other day lay siege on Aaron's mind as he contemplated their arrival at the rendezvous point. *Am I really afraid to live? Isn't this living?* He tried to imagine life after their arrival. *What will I live for?* Up until this point, he had simply lived to keep them alive, but once they arrived and everything was set up, it would just be a daily grind. *Isn't it enough to stay alive?* His heart answered the question before his mind could; the image of Soraya grabbing him in the midst of mental panic and rocking his world with her kiss flashed in his memory. Her tone had been firm, "your fight is my fight," she had said. The memory burst into his mind unapologetically, and he felt his heart ache. For the first time, in his heart, he felt alone.

The Reddings emerged from the woods into a clearing forming the southern bank of a large lake. Aaron gave the word and everyone dropped their packs to rest. Sara noticed the puzzlement on Aaron's face and walked over to where he was standing, already holding his map.

"What is it?"

"I think I made a navigational error," Aaron said with a hit of frustration.

He pointed to a moderately large lake on the map, near a smaller lake. Pointing out over the water before them, he said, "See that bend over there and the point just beyond it?"

Sara nodded.

"Well, I believe they're here on this lake," he said, tracing the outline of the lake on the map.

"I was hoping to hit this bit of land between these two lakes and shoot right up the middle, but it appears I led us right into the center of this lower lake." He let out a sigh, "I think it's going to add an extra day to our trip."

"I wouldn't care if it added ten days, Aaron. We're alive, together, and almost there. You've done a tremendous job." She put her arm around his shoulder and gave him a squeeze. "Now let it go and come sit down for lunch."

Sara thanked God for their many blessings, for her family, for the warm breeze, and the sunshine. When she finished, they all echoed the amen. Lunch was rations again, but no one complained. It was better than being hungry. Sara watched her children laugh and joke, tell stories, and dream of what lay ahead.

"I am so blessed," she said quietly.

Seth sat on a large boulder carving on a piece of wood as they relaxed in the sun. Aaron leaned over his map as usual, looking up every now and again to react to a comment or throw in his own teasing. Leah leaned back against Seth's boulder, idly weaving cattail leaves together, while Caleb skipped a few stones on the lake.

"I think we're making pretty good time and, even with this little set back, we should be about a week out," Aaron commented.

"I vow never to move again when this is over," Leah sighed.

When they were finally ready to hit the trail again, Seth hopped off the rock.

"Finished!"

He walked over to Caleb and showed him his work.

"For your friend," he said.

It was a wooden cross with the name Samuel on one arm and the date on the other.

"I didn't know his birth date so I kinda left that part blank," Seth said, putting his arm on his little brother's shoulder. "This is a beautiful place to remember him."

"Thanks," Caleb said in genuine appreciation, biting his lip to keep the tears at bay.

Seth took the cross over near the bolder and beat it into the ground with a rock. When he finished, he stepped back and took off his winter cap. "Thanks for giving me my brother back."

Everyone took a reverent moment to remember Sam's sacrifice, and then it was time to strike out once more.

The Reddings had walked for another week since planting Sam's marker, through forests, bogs, up hills and down hills, and now they stood on the edge of an immense boggy clearing. Dead trees, cattails, and thick grasses covered the landscape for almost a half mile. Their journey was almost over; Aaron could taste it, but something just didn't add up. His tattered map was of little use, but it didn't matter, he had nearly memorized the whole thing anyway. Checking his compass, he stared out over the clearing. *Where's Ely?* The thick trees all around the clearing made it impossible to see beyond them. He turned to Sara and the others.

"We're close. Ely is out there somewhere, or it's possible we missed it. If we did, it's not by much. We're out of food, it's getting cold, and we only have a few hours of daylight left. We could stay here tonight and keep going in the morning, or we can push through those trees up ahead and Ely could be right there."

A stiff northerly breeze blew through the group as they huddled in a circle. Each of them was wearing their wool blanket with a hole cut into the middle like a poncho to help block out the cold.

"How sure are you that we're close?" Sara asked through chattering teeth.

"I'm sure I just don't know if we skirted it somehow, or if it's right in front of us. I should have just stuck to the roads," Aaron replied.

"What do you think is more likely?"

"We haven't come across any roads in a while, so I'd say we're not directly below it but maybe kitty corner. That's my best guess anyway."

"I don't want to spend another day on the trail. My vote is to press on," Seth said, holding his blanket close.

"Me too," added Leah.

Caleb was silent, but that was normal since leaving Duluth.

"Alright, let's press on a little more," Sara said.

Aaron nodded his head in agreement and they stepped out into the bog.

Like all the bogs before, the going was slow; the thin, frozen crust gave way beneath their feet and left them soaked in mud midway up the calf. Every now and again one of them would stumble in the mud, driving their hands and knees into the quagmire, forcing them to stop and help one another out of the muck. Each of them shivered as they went, tired and rank but resolute.

Aaron stumbled at the head of the column. Rising to his knees, he flung mud from his hands letting out a frustrated shout.

"Maybe we should have gone around," Sara suggested, walking up to help him.

"Too late now!" Aaron snapped, rising to his feet still shaking mud from his hands. "We're almost halfway."

Large snowflakes began to fall from ominous clouds forming overhead. The wind whipped the snow into a fury, like a million frozen hornets stinging the Reddings' exposed cheeks and hands.

Sara prayed for mercy as they slogged on. Then, suddenly, there was a cry from the back of the column. Everyone turned to see Seth waving his left arm frantically, his right leg completely absorbed by the bog.

Everyone raced to his aid. Aaron grabbed hold of his arm, careful to avoid the sinkhole, and pulled with all his might. Seth hardly budged. The suction of the wet mud wasn't going to give up its victim easily. Sara reached into the mud and grabbed him by the belt, while Leah and Aaron lifted him by his arm.

"One, two, three!" Aaron counted.

With a mighty pull, they were able to get Seth halfway out of the hole and, with another, he was free. Everyone stood for a moment gasping for air. The Reddings hadn't eaten in a day, and the bog was quickly draining all the energy they had left. There was no denying it; they were in trouble.

"We have to keep going," Aaron shouted into the wind. "It's the same distance either way at this point."

He wished now they had decided to camp for another night, but that was foolish thinking. The only thing they could do now was make the far side, find a little shelter, and wait out the storm. He was tired, dog tired, and so was everyone else. It was no longer about finding Ely; it was about staying alive.

"You good, Seth?" he asked.

"Yeah, I'm wearing so many layers it didn't soak through, just scared me is all," Seth said, wet past his waist but relieved to be out of the hole.

What would have taken them fifteen minutes on dry land had already lasted an hour, and they still had half the distance to go. It would be night in another couple of hours, and already the temperature was dropping. Aaron slogged back to the front of the column and continued, one difficult step at a time.

The wind tore at them like some ancient demon standing guard over the forest. The snow fell hard, nearly blinding them to the woods ahead. Seth began to tremble, his soaked clothes exposing him to the icy elements. Sara watched as he began to stagger back and forth in front of her. Something was wrong.

"Seth!" Aaron heard his mother yell from behind him.

"Aaron! Something's wrong with Seth!" she called.

Aaron turned back in time to watch Seth stumble out of line three steps and then collapse into the muck. Sara slogged to his side as fast as she could move. Rolling him over, she could feel him trembling uncontrollably.

"I'm fine," Seth mumbled through chattering teeth. "Just help me up."

Aaron arrived and helped Sara get Seth to his feet. Still trembling, Seth continued forward.

"We're almost there, buddy, another hundred yards, and we'll be there," Aaron said with a stiff nod.

Heading back to the front of the column, Aaron knew Seth wasn't ok. If they could just make the woods, he could start a fire and—

"Seth!" shrieked Sara.

Seth had fallen again, and this time he couldn't push himself back up. Sara beat Aaron to him and rolled him up on her knees to keep him out of the mud. Aaron knelt beside her, and Caleb and Leah huddled close to block the wind.

Seth tried to speak but his words were all a mixed-up mumble. Sara wiped the mud from his cheeks with her hand and felt for his pulse.

"His heart is racing, Aaron. We have to get him out of his cold!" she said, her voice frantic.

Get him out of the cold? What does she think I've been doing all this time?! Aaron looked all around them. Nothing, nothing but bog, and the woods a hundred miserable yards off. Nothing to make a shelter out of, nothing to dry his clothes with, nothing but snow, and wind, and mud. What was he supposed to do? He didn't know how to fix this. There was no plan, nothing to work with, nothing!

His mind froze. Time stood still, the snowflakes moving in slow motion around them. This scene was familiar: the mud, his family, the fear, the tears, horrible, and familiar. *Not again. God, not again.* In that moment of time, of a breath, all hope seemed lost. Aaron looked ahead to the woods, so close, he had led them so close. "Keep them safe," he heard his father's voice say. So close. This entire journey had been walked out in the light of his father's words, his father's hope, his father's fire. It wasn't enough. It could carry them no further. In his heart, Aaron let go of his father's hope, and the flame was snuffed out.

As he looked back at his family, he realized he had believed they could do anything, survive anything. That, somehow, the strength his father had taught them would carry them through. Seeing them now, in his heart he knew. He didn't even want to think it, but he knew they weren't going to make it. And he let go of faith.

As he stared helplessly at his brother, quivering in the mud, his eyes met Seth's and he saw him mouth the words, "I'm sorry."

Aaron's heart sank. "It's not your fault, Seth. It's not your fault," he said, taking Seth's hand in his own.

Closing his eyes, Aaron felt the tears burning against his lids.

"I'm sorry, Dad," he whispered.

He had done everything he could to keep his family safe, to follow his father's plan the way he knew his father would. If only his dad was there, he would have done it right, would have kept them safe, but he wasn't. He wasn't there because of Aaron, because his gun had jammed, and he had frozen, and the soldier was going to kill him. The soldier had shot at Aaron and hit his father instead. *Why?!*

Tears began to cut trails through the mud on his cheeks. Why had his father jumped in front of that gun? If he had just let Aaron die, his family would be safe. Why did he do that? "Love is why we live," his mother had said. Was love enough? To live and die for love, was his father's reason that simple? Had his dad taken the bullet meant for him simply because he was his son, and he loved him, and that was enough?

Aaron's mind ached. John Redding had died for love, but they were just dying, dying for nothing. Dying in mud, and snow, and wind . . . for nothing.

A fire began to grow in Aaron's belly. His father hadn't saved him to keep them safe, he had saved him because he was his son, because of love.

"Love never fails," he murmured, as a fire in him stirred his strength anew.

Aaron realized, in that moment, that he had made this entire journey on his father's words alone, living in the glow of his father's fire. But now, he understood who his father was, who he was. *This journey isn't about getting up north to survive at all. It's about family, about love. No matter where we end up, or how we end up, if it's for love, then it's worthwhile.*

We're not dying here for nothing! The flames of love had been kindled in Aaron until his fire could have matched his father's blaze for blaze. For the first time in his life, Aaron had his own reason to live.

"No!" Aaron growled, rising to his feet. He took one look at John's rifle and dropped it into the mud. He shook off his pack, letting it fall away. Sara and the others looked on as Aaron tore his gear off like a madman.

A gust of wind washed over them, and Aaron turned and faced his foe, his face brazen with a new fury.

"No!" he yelled into the snow.

Dropping back to his knees, he pulled out his hunting knife and went to work on the straps of Seth's pack, ripping it from his shoulders. Sara had to duck as he tossed it to the side.

"Help me!" he commanded as he lifted Seth to his knees by the chest of his jacket.

"You listen to me, and you listen good, Seth Redding, you are *not* dying on me! Not today!"

With a mighty jerk, Aaron hefted Seth over his shoulders, holding him in a fireman's carry. Staggering, he rose to his feet.

From over Aaron's shoulder, Seth caught his gaze and the look in his brother's eyes told him all he needed to know. He had always known Aaron loved him the way brothers do, but that wasn't the look he saw. This look was different, was deep and clear. Aaron was going to die for him.

Aaron trudged forward and, as he did, Sara reached for his pack where it lay in the mud.

"Leave it," he said, and she did.

It was twenty paces before Aaron stumbled for the first time, dropping to one knee. He steadied himself under the load and lifted himself back to his feet, Sara beside him to steady Seth. Then, out of nowhere, a voice called out over the wind.

"Helloooooo!"

Chapter 27

Aaron's heart almost stopped. *Could that be Ty? Had they actually made it?* The sloppy sound of heavy feet hurrying through the muck came closer, and the figure of a man finally became visible through the snow.

"Aaron? Sara? Is that you?"

Aaron, partly bent over with Seth's weight across his back, stared blankly at the newcomer.

"It's me! Tom! The Lord be praised! We thought we had missed you. What happened?!" he exclaimed as he moved toward Seth and Aaron.

Recognition finally dawned. Tom and Kathy! The first people they had saved from the Chinese all those weeks ago when this journey had begun.

"Tom!" Sara cried out, almost sobbing in relief. "Seth needs help. He's getting hypothermia!"

Tom immediately rushed over, threw his own gun over his shoulder, and reached for Seth. "We have shelter not far from here."

"No," Aaron pulled away, "I've got him."

"I know you do," Tom answered matter-of-factly. "Just let me help you. Give me an arm and we can lift his legs above the water."

Aaron nodded and let him take Seth's right arm and pull it around his own neck. Then, together, they each picked up a leg with their inside arms and lifted Seth to a sitting position. Slowly, they moved forward. Each step was a battle: a battle to stay on their feet, a battle to not drop their precious burden. Seth's head bobbed with every jolt. His eyes were closed, his lips blue. Tiny puffs of breath, quickly snatched by the wind, were the only sign of life he had the strength to offer.

After what felt like forever, they entered the cover of the trees and left the swamp, with its mud and agony, behind. The wind was less vicious here. The trees quickly grew thick. Fallen logs and partly exposed rocks and boulders made their steps still dangerous, but at least they were sure of firm ground. Darkness was falling with relentless speed and, in the shade of the forest, they were losing light faster than what seemed fair.

There was a little crash and a squeal from behind them. Without slowing down, Aaron called back, "Are you ok?"

"I'm good!" came Leah's answer through chattering teeth.

"We're almost there," Tom grunted as they hefted Seth over yet another ancient pine laying across their path. "Maybe a hundred more yards."

"Seth?" Sara called from behind her son. "Do you hear that, Seth? We're almost there. Hang on, son. You're gonna be ok, you hear me? You just keep hanging on, Seth. You're gonna make it!"

Through parched and frozen lips came an answer so faint it only reached the ears of those who carried him. "I'm . . . trying."

Aaron wanted to scream. His brother didn't deserve this! Through gritted teeth and burning eyes he whispered back to his brother.

"You're the best fighter I know, Seth. I know you won't give up."

Just then, Tom gave a shout, "Jake! I found them! Go tell Kathy we need a bed in the big house!"

A figure of a man stepped out of the shadows.

"Holy crap! I can't believe it!" he said in wonder, and then took off at a run, disappearing in front of them.

In another five minutes, the smell of smoke met their noses, and then the soft glow of several small fires came into view.

"Oh, thank you, Jesus!" came floating toward them, followed by a woman running to meet them. Kathy. There was no mistaking her voice and care as she immediately began to mother them all.

"Hurry up. I've got a spot all ready for you. Oh, you poor thing! Get him inside quick."

They were nearing the low, shadowy form of a long structure, and Kathy was motioning them to enter. She held a heavy flap aside, and Tom and Aaron had to turn sideways to fit themselves through the doorway with Seth. Sara followed with Leah and Caleb in tow. There was a bright fire burning in the middle of the long, wide-open room, and there were several benches, stacks of supplies, and even a few raised beds against the walls.

"Now, put him right over here," Kathy bustled around grabbing blankets and motioning to one of the beds.

"I'll take good care of him; don't you worry about a thing! We'll just get these wet clothes off and get him all warmed up in a jiffy! Tom, get these poor folks to bed. They look ready to die on their feet."

Despite their protests, she shooed them out the door and there was really nothing left to do but obey orders. Seth was in good hands, and they were too tired to put one straight thought in front of the other.

"Come on over here," Tom put a hand on Sara's shoulder and pointed through the dancing firelight. We've got a place you can spend the night right over there. Don't worry. We'll call you if Seth needs you."

He led the family to a little igloo-looking hut and motioned them inside. The floor was thick with pine needles and a fire was burning in the center. Piles of blankets beckoned the weary travelers and, after a refreshing drink of water, a quick wash, and change into dry clothes, the Reddings curled up under the blankets and slept like the dead.

When Aaron next opened his eyes, it took a moment to remember where he was. Soft morning light was gently shining through a hole in the center of the ceiling. Seeing by the soft rays, he looked around him. The little hut was shaped by bent over branches with mud and moss chinking. The fire, which had been burning brightly in the middle of the hut the night before, was barely smoldering. He noticed a little pile of wood next to the wall so he stirred up some flames and threw a few pieces on. A thin wisp of smoke lazily floated up and escaped through the hole above. His mother, Leah, and Caleb still slumbered peacefully on the soft floor.

Peace. It was a feeling he couldn't remember feeling in a really long time. The knowledge of being safe had given him the ability to sleep uninterrupted, and he felt genuinely rested. Who would've thought Tom and Kathy would head to the very area they were! He knew his mother wouldn't call it a coincidence. He honestly didn't know what would've happened with Seth if Tom hadn't shown up. Seth. He needed to get to Seth. He needed to make sure he was ok. Making as little noise as possible, Aaron made his way through the low entry tunnel and lifted the flap, which appeared to be an old rug, hanging over the doorway.

Then it hit him: Soraya! Were they here, too? Standing up straight in the early light of dawn, he quickly searched the area with his eyes. He saw a huge clearing cut out as high as a man could reach under ancient pine and cedar trees. Above his head, the branches closed together leaving the smoke from several fires to thread its way up through the boughs and disappear and the sunlight to softly filter down to warm the earth below. Scattered throughout the clearing were about a dozen little hovels, almost identical to the one they had spent the night in. A short distance away from where he stood, in the middle of the camp, was the long building they had brought Seth into. Tom had called it the "big house." It was built the same as the rest except it was taller and at least five times the size of all the others.

Aaron mentally kicked himself for being disappointed. What did he expect? To step out of the hut and find Soraya waiting for him? After the way he had treated her when they said goodbye, he didn't deserve anything from her, much less a warm welcome. Besides, what difference did it make? His mother could say what she wanted; he couldn't offer what Soraya deserved. *Maybe it's better this way.*

He started toward the big house to find Seth. As he neared the door, he paused as a new sound reached his ears. Humming, deep and soft, floating in the stillness of the morning. It felt no more out of place then the fallen pinecones at his feet. His pulse quickened. He knew that voice! Could it really be?

Swiping the flap aside, he ducked into the large room. The humming stopped as he straightened and waited for his eyes to adjust to the dimness. Then he saw with his eyes what his heart already knew. She was here. On a stool next to a bed, she sat with her big, dark eyes fixed on him. One look told him her feelings hadn't changed.

He felt his heart would explode. No more logic, no more fear, no more excuses. He allowed himself to see her from his heart for the first time. If real love was living, then he would give this girl the best life anyone had ever lived!

"Soraya," he breathed.

In less time than seemed possible, he covered the distance between them and in the second it took Soraya to rise to her feet, Aaron was already there. He wrapped her close against him, her arms around his neck. He felt her face against his own. Lifting his hand, he combed his fingers into her hair and held her against his cheek. *How could I have been so stupid?*

"I'm so sorry, Soraya," he whispered into her hair.

"I know," she answered with such gentleness it took his breath away.

Fears had given way to love. Life was fragile, dangerous even, but empty without love. He was different, stronger perhaps, more sure of himself. One thing she knew for sure, in his arms, she felt like she was home. Home, a feeling Soraya hadn't known since the day her parents were killed. She doubted she would ever let him go.

With a hand on each side of her face, his fingers almost touching behind her long neck, he pushed her back enough to look her in the eyes. Her deep eyes, shimmering with unshed tears, gazed unwaveringly back into his. Eyes which had never given up on him. Eyes, which even now, only expressed love and trust.

"I love you, Soraya."

As he moved his lips to hers, tears of joy rolled down her cheeks. She had dreamed of this day, longed for it, her love had been denied, disappointed, but never broken. And now, he was hers and she was his.

How much time passed before they emerged from the big house was anyone's guess. There was nowhere to be, no missions, no enemy. They laughed, cried, held one another, and laughed and cried again. Aaron couldn't remember ever being so happy, so satisfied. They had nothing to call their own except for each other.

Enough, Aaron thought, *more than enough.*

"So, how's Seth this morning?" Sara asked, meeting them as they emerged.

"Seth . . ." Aaron blushed, slapping his palm to his face.

Spinning on his heels, he rushed back into the big house dragging Soraya behind him.

"I'm fine," Seth called out as they reentered. "Thanks for asking."

"You've been awake?!" Aaron said, his hands now holding his head.

"Yeah, I was wondering when you were gonna come up for air."

"I have a good set of lungs," Soraya shot back with a grin.

Sara could hold it in no longer, she burst out laughing. Aaron's mortified expression was just too priceless. In a moment, Seth and Soraya were laughing as well. The sound was so joyful and free, even Aaron eventually joined in.

A little while later, Tom found them all at the little hovel they had spent the night in.

"I imagine you guys are mighty hungry. Kathy's got some grub cooked up for you in the big house, if you wouldn't mind stepping over."

"Wouldn't mind?" Seth blurted out, "I'd be willing to wrestle a bear if it meant getting some grub!"

Everyone filed out of the hut and followed Tom to the large building.

"Tom? How did you guys end up here?" Sara asked as they walked across the clearing.

"Well, when you told us to go north, the only place I could think of was Ely. I grew up here. My father was a forester, and I know the area."

"And all these people?" Aaron asked.

"These folks are just Americans like us, trying to stay alive. We number over thirty including you guys. We have a work schedule, guard duties, meetings, even working on our own miniature government," he said with pride.

"Wow! That's amazing, Tom," Sara marveled.

"We'll let you guys have today, and tomorrow I'll give you the rundown on work duties and fit you into the schedule."

They were now at the door of the big house.

"I'll leave you here, just go on in. Kathy's waiting for you."

As their eyes adjusted to the dim light inside, two figures stood up from a bench and walked toward them.

"Hey! It's Ty and Wu!" Seth declared when they recognized them, and the room immediately filled with hugs and exclamations: "You made it!" "It's so good to see you again!" "What took you so long?"

This was finally interrupted by Kathy bringing a tray of smoked fish from the fire over to a table.

"Ok now, there's plenty of time for catching up later. Come sit yourselves down and get some food in your bellies. Lord knows you need it!"

Everyone laughed and did as they were told. After a few minutes of eating, Aaron noticed Caleb stop chewing and close his eyes. Sara must have seen it too, because she softly asked him if he was ok.

Without opening his eyes, he slowly answered from around the fish in his mouth, "This is really good."

"Well, eat all you want," Kathy reassured him, "there's more where that came from."

About the time the last bit of fish was scraped off the last plate, there was a commotion outside and Tom entered the big house again.

"There's a few folks out here who are mighty anxious to say hi to you guys," Tom explained with a grin on his face.

Everyone wore puzzled expressions.

"Who?" Aaron asked for them all.

"People who wouldn't be here if it weren't for you. We met up with a few prisoners you had set free from some small outpost on our way up here. Then we ran into a couple and their daughter who claimed to have been rescued by a woman referred to as the Archangel, and we knew it could only be you. Hang on, you can just see for yourself." Moving back to the door, he stuck his head out and called, "Come on in, folks!"

The Reddings rose to their feet in surprise as seven or eight people now crowded in behind Tom.

"Introductions!" sang Kathy, pushing her way to the middle of the impromptu gathering. "We need introductions!" Waving with her hand, she started pointing out people.

"This is Mark and his wife, Sue, and little Abbie, of course. And over here is Jake, Darrian, Andy, and Heidi. Where's Antonio?" She stood on her tiptoes and leaned around to see. "Oh, there he is. And Antonio! Now, for those who don't know the Reddings, this is Aaron, Caleb, Leah, and Seth."

Then, with a dramatic flourish, she moved over next to Sara, putting an arm around her shoulder. "And, of course, our very own Archangel!"

At that, all the guests began clapping and cheering. Sara just blushed and shook her head.

"We aren't heroes," she tried to explain. "We just did what we thought was right."

She held out her hand toward the rest of her family and, looking Aaron right in the eyes, she smiled, "We make a good team."

Aaron smiled back. They did make a good team. He proudly gazed at his sister and brothers who were smiling and looking generally uncomfortable with the praise. Except for Caleb. Caleb's expression was far away. His face was filled with sadness more than anything. *If only we could've saved Sam.*

"Come on outside," Tom broke in, his eyes twinkling, "We all have something to show you." He led them all to the edge of the little clearing to another hovel one and a half times the size of the one they had stayed in.

"This one's yours. We just finished it this morning. We started on it the day Soraya and Ty showed up here and shared your wild tale with us all."

"Are you serious?!" Sara asked in amazement. "Thank you, everybody, so much!" Then she moved to give each one a heartfelt hug.

"Really, Tom," Aaron echoed, "You didn't have to do this."

"Yes, we did. Family takes care of family. It was just our turn." Tom shrugged his shoulders matter-of-factly and then continued before Aaron could get in another word.

"Now I'm afraid I must be off. My guard shift begins soon, and Kathy will want me to fetch some water before I head out."

Everyone thanked Tom again and watched him head out across the clearing. The others also scattered, leaving the Reddings with only Ty, Soraya, and Wu.

"Look," Wu piped up, "We are all neighbors! I share this hut next to yours with the other guys from Duluth, and Ty and Soraya's is the next one."

"This is wild," Aaron admitted, shaking his head as he tried to wrap his mind around what was happening. "I've been unable to think about anything but the work we were going to have to do once we got here to prepare for winter, and look, by God's grace, it's all been done for us. This is beyond anything I could've imagined."

Without a word, Sara gave him a tight hug, and then briefly placed her hand on the side of his face before she turned and ducked into their new home. She hadn't had to say anything; Aaron knew exactly what she was thinking. *I told you He was watching out for us.*

———

The Reddings were thrilled to find all their gear had been recovered from the night before and was waiting for them inside the hut. Aaron and Soraya decided to take a walk and fill the water jugs while Seth got firewood. Sara and Caleb unpacked the family's belongings and organized the hovel. After an hour or so, there was a knock at the door. Sara poked her head out of the flap to see two of the prisoners from the outpost with five cot-sized beds made of woven cattails and cedar branches.

"Why . . .? What's all this for?" she stammered in confusion.

"How does one thank someone for giving them their freedom?" asked the woman named Heidi. "Everything we had wouldn't be enough. Let us bless you with what we do have."

Before Sara could think of what to say, several more people approached. One by one, they laid various supplies by her door. Overwhelmed, she just watched, tears running down her face. *Jesus, you are so good!*

Chapter 28

Christmas Eve. A little over a month had passed since the Reddings had staggered into camp. Excitement filled the air as the residents of the little community, dubbed Elysium, which means a place of happiness, prepared for Christmas. They had collected wild winterberry branches to add a touch of holly to every hovel. In the big house stood a Christmas tree covered in handmade ornaments. Kathy put together a choir, and their sweet carols could be heard all across Elysium as they practiced.

Most of the Redding family were out at the lake with some of the others trying their hands at ice fishing. Inside their hovel, Aaron and Sara worked together on a pair of snowshoes: a gift for Caleb. Their door was sealed against the frozen breeze, leaving the small hole in the ceiling and the flames of their fire to provide the only light to work by.

"Mom? How did you and Dad get together?" Aaron asked, tying another cord to the frame.

"You've heard the story. We were best friends in high school and—"

"No, I know that part. I mean, like how did you guys . . . you know, get married?"

"I'm not sure I understand what you're asking," she said, putting down the snowshoe.

Aaron dug his heel into the floor searching for the right words.

"I guess I'm asking . . ." He took a deep breath. "How did Dad ask you to marry him?"

Sara's eyes widened. "Oh, I think I know where you're going with this now," she said with a smile.

She spent the next ten minutes walking Aaron through the do's and don'ts of a good proposal. When she finished, she slipped her engagement ring off her finger and held it out to him.

"You can't go asking that girl to marry you empty handed." Her eyes twinkled as she placed the ring into his open hand.

"Mom, I can't. Dad gave this to you," he said, trying to give it back to her.

"What your father gave me doesn't reside in gold and stones. Its home is here," she said, placing her hand over her heart. "I want you to have it, Aaron."

He closed his hand over the ring and held it tightly in his fist.

"I have no idea what I'm doing," he choked out.

"You'll be fine, just speak your heart," she said. "So, when are you planning on asking her?"

"Tomorrow, before the party," he smiled.

"Ahhh, Christmas Day, easy to remember."

"Something like that," Aaron said, finishing the webbing on his snowshoe. "I'm not even sure what a wedding up here would look like . . ." he continued. "If she says yes, of course. We don't have a minister or a church. Who on earth would perform the ceremony?"

"There you go worrying about all the details again, Aaron. Has God failed to meet your needs yet?" she paused to let her question sink in, then continued.

"You just worry about your part. Let Him handle the rest. You're a good man, Aaron. I have no doubt you'll make a fine husband." She gave him a gentle shove.

Sara had been his rock ever since his father died. Aaron wished more than anything his dad could be there now. All these people. Soraya. All of it was because of the man his father had been and the family he had raised. In Aaron's heart, Elysium was a monument to his father's spirit, and everywhere he looked he could see him.

That night, Aaron couldn't sleep. He went over the proposal again and again in his mind, and each time he sounded more foolish than the time before. Soraya deserved so much better. . . .

He tried again to sleep. Nothing. He tried to think of something else but, as he was quite smitten, his mind refused to acknowledge anything or anyone else existed on the entire planet. *This whole proposal thing would be a whole lot easier if Soraya was the one doing it,* he thought. She didn't mind looking foolish; she even found ways to make her foolishness look like it wasn't. He, on the other hand, had a knack for looking foolish no matter what he did.

"Just sleep!" Aaron whispered, squeezing his head.

At last, the dawn's light filtered in through the hole in the roof. Aaron could bear the sleepless battle no longer. Donning his wool blanket poncho, he snuck out the door. He didn't know where he was going exactly but, eventually, he ended up at the lake. Closing his eyes, he stopped and took a deep breath.

"You've got this," he said.

Then the nausea hit him, and he vomited. *Some hero,* he thought. He had braved enemy camps, liberated prisoners . . .

There was a snap of a twig behind him, and he spun around expecting to see Soraya, fearing he'd have to talk to her and would make a mess of the whole day, but it wasn't. Leah had come to the lake to get in some early morning ice fishing.

"Are you sick?" she asked, wrinkling her nose.

"No," he said, moving quickly back up the trail, leaving Leah to herself.

"Merry Christmas to you too!" she called after him.

"ARGH!" he wailed. "Why is this so hard?"

Now he didn't even want to talk to the girl he was hoping to propose to.

"Rough night?" Sara said as he arrived back at the hovel.

"I'm so nervous I'm sick to my stomach," he admitted without reservation.

"Good. It means more that way," she said. "Now, come help me decorate the big house. It'll take your mind off it."

Aaron had avoided Soraya all day. He felt bad, but the sight of her made him want to throw up. It wasn't that he was afraid she would say no. The stress of only having one shot in forever at this "magical moment" overwhelmed him—but only when he thought about it.

As evening drew near, he knew his moment had come and, for better or worse, he set off to find Soraya. Elysium was small and, even if he had wanted to drag out the hunt, it wouldn't have taken him long to find her. She was working with Ty on some sort of toboggan near their hut.

"Hi, guys," he said as he approached.

"Hey, Aaron," Soraya replied. "You've been hard to find today."

He blushed. "Yeah, I've been pretty busy helping Mom."

There was a moment of awkward silence, then he cleared his throat.

"Ty would it be alright if I borrowed Soraya for a moment?" he asked, trying his best to mask his nerves.

"Sure," Ty said cheerfully. "I was about to quit and get ready for the festivities anyway."

Soraya got up and brushed herself off, then, taking Aaron's hand, they headed off down the trail leading to the lake.

"Is everything ok?" she asked as they walked silently along.

"Soraya," he began, butterflies and all. "When I first saw you at the outpost, you were asking me to please help your brother. I remember turning to see who was talking, and when I saw you I—I couldn't breathe. You were standing there, jeans and a hoodie, covered in wet sand and mud, your hair a mess, your dark eyes, even then, ablaze with life. My heart burned in my chest at the sight of you."

"Yeah, I was a mess," she said, blushing.

"No, I'm being serious," he stopped at the edge of the lake and turned her toward him, taking her other hand.

"Soraya, I've been in love with you since that moment. You have invaded my heart, soul, and mind. I can be a complete wreck and a thought of you brings me peace. I was so foolish when we were in Duluth, so occupied with the mission I didn't even give you the time of day."

"Aaron, you were—"

"Please don't stop me, or I may not finish," he said, almost trembling. He swallowed hard. *Why is my throat so dry?*

"I don't want to be anywhere else than where you are, Soraya. Your laugh, your smile, your heart, I—I don't want to live my life without knowing your heart. I was so afraid of love, and now I can't live without it. I have absolutely nothing to offer you. I have nothing but myself."

He dropped down on one knee as she raised her hands to cover her mouth, the reality of what he was saying setting in.

"Soraya, if you would have me, I offer you all I am, for as long as I live, I will love you. Would you marry me? Will you be my wife?" He held out his mother's ring in his trembling hand.

Now it was Soraya's turn to tremble. Tears flowed freely down her cheeks. Nodding her head, she whispered the word "yes," and he slid the ring onto her finger. When he finished, she collapsed into his arms, burying her head in his shoulder sobbing tears of joy.

"I'll love you forever, Aaron," she whispered.

When Aaron and Soraya arrived at the big house, everyone was already sitting in a large oval around the fire. They must have missed the opening prayer because everyone was already busy eating a meal of wild rice, venison, duck, and a few items Aaron couldn't identify. Sara had saved them a couple of seats near her and waved them over.

"Welcome to the family," Sara said, giving Soraya a knowing hug.

Soraya's joy was impossible to hide, and Sara couldn't stand to let the thing remain a secret.

"Everyone!" she called out. "I would like to announce the engagement of my son, Aaron, to his bride-to-be, Soraya!"

The room erupted in applause and congratulations. Everyone took turns shaking hands with them and giving bits of encouragement or advice. Kathy couldn't contain her excitement and began discussing plans for a wedding with Sara immediately.

Amid the fanfare someone called out, "When's the wedding?"

Surprising himself, Aaron blurted, "Next month!"

"Next month?!" Soraya choked. "It'll take you longer than that to build me a proper house." To which everyone, including Aaron, burst out laughing.

When the night settled down, they took time to remember what Christmas is all about and talk about the new year. They were all grateful to be alive and safe, but that was only for now.

As they looked to the future, Mark leaned back and asked, "What will we do now? America is lost."

With firelight glowing in his eyes, Aaron slowly rose to his feet and placed his hand on his mother's shoulder.

"If America is lost, then let's go find her."

What did you think?

I'd love to help other readers enjoy this book as much as you have. If you'd just take a minute and let them know your favorite scene, how the story impacted you, or what book or author you'd compare it to, it will help other readers find it. It's your best way to show your support for us and we greatly appreciate it!

Just scan this QR code to get to the Amazon review page and leave your review!

(Even if you purchased or received this copy from somewhere else, you're still eligible to leave a review on Amazon if you have an active account.)

Sneak Peek of Book 2!

For You, My Dove

She had never wanted to kill anything or anyone. Before the wars, before the world had gone mad, before evil had forced itself upon them, Leah wouldn't have even given the idea a passing thought. But the wars did come, her dad was killed, and her world set on fire. Even so, she refused to succumb to the madness. If she must kill to live, so be it, but that didn't mean she had to like it.

Stepping cautiously on the wet leaves, Leah crept down a deer path paralleling the river. The October morning was cool, a fine mist collected and dripped from the trees above. The sun would rise soon, its rays were already coloring the sky. She stared through the understory as far as her eyes could carry her. Nothing stirred. A few more steps and she stopped, scanning again. Nothing.

She repeated the processes several more times until she came to a small oval clearing, the remnants of a dried-up bog.

Crouching behind a deadfall, she waited again, scanning the clearing. After a short while she got up, intending to press on, when her eyes caught movement on the far side. She froze, allowing her eyes to focus through the tall grasses. There, a flick of a tail, a twitching of ears, the shape came into focus.

A mature whitetail doe ate cautiously only forty yards away. Dropping back behind the deadfall, she waited, watching. Her pulse drummed in her ears, and her body trembled slightly. Step by painful step the doe inched down the narrow trail towards her, pausing every now and again to sniff the air. Leah held her bow out towards the trail, connecting the release to the string. The doe browsed ever closer. *Only five more steps, four, three . . .*

As the deer dropped her head for a bite, Leah drew her bow, her pulse racing. Another step, and another. Setting her sights just behind the doe's shoulder, she touched her finger to her release. The bow jumped in her hand, and she watched the arrow's fletching disappear into the deer's hide. The doe sprang into the air before bolting back through the clearing, disappearing into the woods beyond.

Watching until the doe was out of sight, Leah sat down on the fallen log. She took a moment to catch her breath before taking out her radio. Switching it on, she spoke, "Mom, this is Leah."

"Go ahead, Leah."

"Mom, I just shot a deer. Could you please send one of the boys to help me with it? I'm about 400 yards up the deer trail that follows the river to the south, if they stay on that, they can't miss me."

"Good job, Leah! Your brothers are fishing for breakfast upstream, but Ty is here, I'll send him."

"Thank you," Leah said, setting down the radio.

She looked back across the meadow; the doe wouldn't have gone far. She'd lost count of the deer she'd harvested and knew her shot was a double lung hit. She shuddered as the adrenalin subsided. Studying her bow laying in the leaves beside her, she remembered how excited she'd been when she'd seen it strapped to Ty's pack almost five years ago. Its turquoise strings were no longer bright, and the limbs and riser bore the scars of their hardships, but it still shot true.

"400 yards?" gasped Ty, trotting up to the log. "Try half a mile, I was about to call you on the radio."

"Sorry," winced Leah. "I'm not the best with distances."

"Heard you stuck us some dinner; which way?"

"She went that way," Leah pointed. "Through the clearing."

"Want me to carry your bow?"

"No thanks, I've got it," Leah said, tucking her hair behind her ear.

Ty, who'd been with them since before Duluth, was built like a linebacker. He could move mountains and was brutal in a fight, but he was always gentle with her. She followed as he pushed his way through the tall grass following the trail of blood left by the doe. He was always careful to hold back anything that might be a danger or obstacle to her.

"You know, you shouldn't be going out so far on your own," Ty chided. "They may be in retreat but that doesn't mean they couldn't leave a few behind or set traps for us as they go."

He held out his hand as they reached a narrow stream at the far side of the clearing. She placed her hand on his palm and his dark fingers closed over hers.

"Ready?" he asked.

She nodded.

"One, two, three . . ."

She jumped as he swung her across. Once she had regained her balance, he followed, leaping over the stream in a single stride.

"Thank you," she said.

"Nothing to it, little Dove."

They'd only walked a few yards into the woods on the far side of the meadow when Ty spotted the doe where she'd fallen. A quick poke with a stick confirmed that her journey was over. Kneeling beside the creature, Leah stroked its neck.

"I'm sorry, girl."

"It'd probably be easier if they were ugly," Ty offered.

"No," she said. "It isn't what she looks like, it's her life. Life is beautiful. The innocence. When it's gone there's an emptiness. Death is always empty," she said, standing.

"Yeah. I try not to think about it, but you're right," he said. "I know you don't like the gutting part; you can stand behind those trees if you'd like, I'll take care of her."

"Thank you," she said, taking him up on his offer.

Leaning back against a thick oak trunk, she closed her eyes. The cool damp air refreshed her as she took it in. She was glad for Ty. Times were tough and everyone needed to do their part, but adding the ugliness of gutting the deer to the ugliness of taking its life was a lot. Ty wouldn't mind the mess of it, boys seemed to lack the ability to decern the disgusting. Well, most boys anyway.

Ty had changed since she'd met him. He'd been beaten to a pulp and barely clinging to life when her family had rescued him and his sister back in Minnesota. He was quieter now, slower to anger, often gentle. He was helpful and caring, quick to volunteer. Since her bother Aaron had married his sister, Ty had kept a watchful eye over Leah.

When she was younger, the four years between them had made a friendship seem awkward, but now that she was twenty, it didn't seem odd at all. Though she wouldn't admit to anyone else, he was her most intimate friend.

"All set," Ty said, dragging the doe to the trees. "I found your arrow, still intact, I'll rinse it in the stream when we get there."

"That's a relief," Leah smiled. "Those things are hard to come by."

"Lead the way," Ty said.

Together they pushed and pulled their way back to the stream where Ty paused to wash the arrow and his hands, drying them on his pant leg.

"You ready?" he asked, holding out his hand.

She took his hand, and he swung her across. Then he picked up the doe by the front and back legs and tossed her across, before jumping across himself.

"Why do you take such good care of me?" Leah asked.

"I have to, I still haven't recovered from that berating you gave me back in Duluth. 'I may be a Redding, but I am *not* my brothers . . .'" Ty said in his best impression of her.

She shoved him, laughing. "I don't sound like that, and I'm glad it made such an impact, don't you forget it!"

As they made their way into camp it was obvious something was up. Her brothers and a few of the other guys were huddled around a map, deep in strategy.

"Ty, I'm glad you're back. We've got a situation," Aaron said, waving him over.

Ty looked to Leah, "Sorry, looks like I've got to go, I'll get her strung up after this is over."

Leah nodded. "Thanks for taking care of her for me."

"Leah!" Wu said, trotting up. "Thank you for finding us something to eat, nothing like Chinese rations to make you appreciate the real thing."

"Yeah," she said. "Do you know what that's about?" she gestured to the huddle of men looking over the map.

"We found a prisoner compound like nothing we have ever seen before. Our scouts say it is a coal mining camp, about fifteen miles south of here, near Freelandville, Indiana. They said the number of American prisoners was beyond counting. Aaron fears the PLA will either ship them further south by the trainload, or kill them as we continue our push," Wu said.

"I guess we won't be getting that rest they promised us," Leah sighed.

"The war is complicated, Aaron has to work with what he is given," Wu said.

"I know," Leah sighed again.

"I think we are going to need everyone on this one," Wu said apologetically. "Everyone."

Find *For You, My Dove* and learn more at JERibbey.com

About the Author

J.E. Ribbey, a husband & wife team, deploys a compelling writing style, combining a fast-paced action thriller with deep character immersion, giving readers an edge-of-your-seat adventure they will feel in the morning. A combat veteran, outdoorsman, and survival enthusiast, Joel enjoys mingling his unique experiences and expertise with his passion for homesteading and the self-sufficient lifestyle in his writing. A homeschooling mom, homesteader, and digital designer, Esther brings the technical, editorial, and design skills to the author team. Together with their four kids they manage a small farmstead in Minnesota, where, besides taking care of the animals and gardens, they also run an event venue and small campground. If you'd like to know more, you can find the Ribbeys on Instagram @j.e.ribbey or at their website JERibbey.com.

Made in the USA
Columbia, SC
21 December 2024